The Black Book of Hessig-Lorthglol

or
An Allegorical Tale
In Three Parts

By
Prof. Bentwick Pestbog

The Black Book of Hessig-Lorthglol

Hand Pig Publishing

"The meaningless absurdity of life is the only incontestable knowledge accessible to man."

- Leo Tolstoy

Foreword to the Second Edition

The present work is a result of automatic writing, transmitted to this intermediary by an intelligence from the very fringes of your solar system, dwelling on a world so recently a planet but yet demoted to a status less than planetary by academic propeller heads who can't seem to look down long enough to prevent sudden descents into open manholes or five gallon buckets. You know: astronomers.

Not more than a paragraph in and I've already digressed.

This intelligence, The Hand Pig of Yuggoth (so named because, if asked, it would probably jump into your hand and frolic diminutively in its warmth, hailing, as he does, from a very cold world), sent unto me, in the year 2012, being his emissary on your planet, a strange and awesome tale that was, in turn, delivered to him by very different means, regarding events toward the end of a different universe from your own, and events immediately following its rehabilitation. A very curious time, to be sure, detailing the final moments of the Great Sucking to the odd tale during – and just after – the Great Wiggle.

You might be wondering what happened to the first edition and why, so many years later, a second and revised edition has decided to make an appearance. Good question. The Hand Pig is quite a furtive and mysterious creature. Perhaps he thought the time was not yet right, in 2012, to reveal this tale to the mostly-hairless bipeds that inhabit our blue-green orb. Perhaps he was being lazy. Perhaps he forgot. Perhaps current events presented the appropriate circumstances for its reception. Whatever the reason, this story was finally given the green light for publication and, along with a few minor amendments, it is here at last, made available for the edification of you, the reader, to make of it what you will.

- Prof. Bentwick Pestbog
Moreau Island
2025

Editor's Note

This is a True and Unabridged Account, written in the Third Person for the Benefit of Posterity and Any and All Who May Inquire, of Certain Happenings that Transpired concerning Something about Some Nameless Crisis that Somewhat Annoyed a Minor and Not Very Influential Part of the Demographic Sector of a Not Very Important Part of a World that Itself Seems to be of Little Interest to Anyone Else.

Be it Known, Henceforth, that the Subsequent Allegorical Tale, Fraught with Intrusions by Horribly Mangled Metaphor and Uninvited Simile, has been Acknowledged to be True, Correct, and Otherwise Related without Deception of Any Kind by the Very Same Individuals Who Set to Print this Testimony, Assuring Posterity of an Utter Lack of Bias or Conflicts of Interest or Any Other Fancy Things that Peculiar and Eccentric Types like to Insert into Conversation to make it seem like they are Listening and are Always Right.

This Notice, having been Properly Stated At the Beginning of this Great Work, as it Should Be, the Tale as it Shall Be Told,
 Shall Be Told.

Thusly,

and So…

And so it is so spoken and so spoken I have so said it is. I set forth my Seal of Ultimate Veracity upon this Nonsense and I don't want to hear any Arguments!

> -Rob Pharisee Goldpinch III, Editor-in-Chief of Hand Pig Publishing, an Imprint of Mammon Publishing, LLC, Pseudoscience and New Age Chicanery Division, itself a subsidiary of Big Bucks International [*R.P. Goldpinch III is also the author of* **How to Get Rich Selling Pipe Dreams, False Hope, and Hysteria to the Uninformed Public, the Bereaved, and the Frightened – A Primer**. *Available now wherever books are sold! Get your copy right now!*]

Part One
An Agony in Twenty-Four Fits

"I speak now of a quorum of idiots, exceptional morons, an elite cabal of stupefied dolts who've mastered stupidity with remarkable distinction."

- The Rumpled Rodent of Runkshire

Prologue

A red and ulcerous sun sank below the boggy horizon, its image wavering through layers of undulating miasma as it's scorching light was suddenly extinguished like a fever. It disappeared from sight just as the moon, gangrenous and fungal, rose like a lidless, sepulchral eye, peeking through ragged shreds of noxious clouds to look out over its hideous domain of sweltering, foetid, swampland; an endless tract stretching in all directions as far as line-of-sight would permit, broken only by an immense and crumbling stone manor off in the distance.

This lumbering edifice sent five crooked towers skyward like a rotting hand jutting from cthonian hells, the tallest and most central of all capped by a dead fingernail to silently scrape and blaspheme a careless heaven. Even now the night was being illuminated by dull stars that provoked nausea, not twinkling but slowly pulsating, like the wriggling of dying maggots. Even their color suggested decay.

Amid these lovely sights a crow alighted upon the charred branch of a lightning-blasted tree, very much annoyed. It cocked its head here and there, espying the surrounding territory with an impatient disgust not common for a crow. A few of his brethren passed by overhead and he cawed at them angrily, his disgust turning instantly to malignant disdain. This was no ordinary crow.

"Fuck," he grumbled, and sat on the charred, sooty branch, hunched and sullen. He closed his eyes and ruminated on his long existence. Far, far overlong for a crow, certainly. Opening one eye he glared with preternatural malice at the overhanging moon, a drooping rictus carved permanently on its never-changing face, reminding him not only of this life but of the great multitude of others he'd already lived, each as pointless and interminably dull as the last. And as if that wasn't enough, he was cursed with the greatest of misfortunes: remembering every one of them, forever reborn into one form or another. The only break was a momentary sensation of darkness at death and then...the choking agony of screaming life was visited upon him once more - and the full sentience to appreciate every stupid moment of it. "Shit," he croaked.

He sensed the air around him. There was a tingle of electricity, as of a storm that had come through this way but not yet fully passed. He sighed and flapped his wings. Leaving the dead tree alone in the swamp he flew toward the manor. Maybe there would be some crumbs to eat, or a disgusting, but juicy, grub. "Ech," he muttered.

He was nearly to the central tower when a bolt of lightning struck him out of the sky, a tiny rain of downy feathers being all that remained of his physical existence. He hadn't even the time to cry out a condemnation of his Fate and the uncaring universe before he expired.

The feathers, meanwhile, slowly fluttered their way to an open window in the side of the tower. A warm and lazy breeze gently ushered them inside where they fell lightly upon the steps of a staircase slowly winding up the tower to its terminus.

If the feathers had been still part of a crow that was alive it would have heard the sound of footsteps slowly approaching from below. This would be soon accompanied by the sound of labored breathing. And a few moments after there would materialize, out of the gloom, a panting and sweating face attached to an immaculately-dressed and well-perfumed, though slightly decrepit gentleman who did not look at all pleased at his exertions.

Mopping sweat from his brow with a kerchief he stepped down heavily near the feathers which promptly scattered and puffed up into the air near his face. He violently swatted them away, though some insisted on sticking firmly to his cheeks and nose, which tickled and made him sneeze. This caused him to sway backward on that steep stairwell and he nearly lost his balance, which would have been decidedly inconvenient for he was about halfway up, and a long tumble to the bottom would have followed had he not suddenly remembered more youthful times and grabbed at the mouldering wall with surprising speed and agility, arresting his surely fatal descent.

Panting and shaking, shot through with adrenalin, the immaculately-dressed and well-perfumed, though slightly decrepit gentleman took a moment to catch his breath, mop his forehead yet again, and allow himself to calm down before resuming his climb to the tower's apex.

Being Chamberlain, in service to the Baron of Slugborn Manor, obviously afforded him certain perquisites. The quick way to the top of the highest tower in the manor was not one of them. Lord Smirch did not like anyone, let alone his menials, to have easy access to his personal chambers. And the Chamberlain, being chief among such menials, had occasion to visit those quarters often, much to his everlasting regret.

Usually he was impatient with this ritual, having need to reach the top in haste. Today, however, was different. The news he was to bring was not particularly good news and the long ascent gave him time for some cogitation before presenting himself to his master.

All of his consternation could have been avoided had the Chamberlain's spies intercepted those of the Proconsul's before they'd time to report their findings to him. It seems they had uncovered the mounting controversy surrounding the swiftly approaching Apocalypse (and the subsequent panicky effect on his subjects) sooner than expected. However, the Chamberlain could not, himself, imagine any way in which the people of this esteemed province of Lothwit Feeng could not have been *more* noisy about the whole thing and what he could have done to keep it quiet. Lord Smirch's orders to him had been clear. The Proconsul was to have knowledge of this impending threat *delayed* until Smirch's plans could be finalized and move forward. Alas, the Chamberlain's spies were too late and Vug found out. And though Vug, the Eminent Proconsul of Lothwit Feeng, was as dumb as a handful of topsoil, he was quick to react if he felt even slightly threatened by anything he didn't fully understand – which was nearly everything.

The Chamberlain sighed as he climbed higher. Now Vug was on the alert...and *meddling*. Since the trouble with his subjects dealt with an Apocalypse, the Proconsul decided to send for Three Wise Men of the Realm to investigate. Apparently, according to the Chamberlain's spy network, these so-called Wise Men were part of some obscure religious sect that held to some even more obscure prophetic ravings about the Apocalypse. Since their religion had the word "Apocalypse" in it Vug, of course, assumed they would have some sort of expertise in the matter and sent for them to appear before his Most Esteemed High Office for the purpose of deputizing their investigation as official Provincial business and to find answers post haste. As far as Lord Smirch's plans were concerned, any such investigation was anathema.

To make matters worse, the Chamberlain had just received word that Vug was now commanding Lord Smirch to provide experienced assistants to help the Three Wise Men in their mission! What a bad stroke of luck! To be forced to have to help an investigation into your own secret plan! What would Lord Smirch do? More importantly, what would Lord Smirch do to *him* once he got to the top of those stairs and passed this little tidbit along? He easily imagined being thrown from the tower to his death, with plenty of time to think about it as he fell.

The Chamberlain could only ruminate upon these tidings and their effect on his own corporeality. How it would affect Smirch's plan he couldn't say since the Baron had been keeping the details of said plan secret from everyone for years. The Chamberlain only knew it *existed*.

At last, the final step had been surmounted. Before him stood the grand double doors to Lord Smirch's chambers. They were dark, heavy affairs, intricately carved with images of some weird and twisted hellscape. The Chamberlain's morale did not lighten.

He brought up his hand, clenched in a fist, knuckles facing the door. He hesitated. More sweat poured out of him now than during his whole climb. Then, after a bit of futile self-reflection, he rapped on the wood three times.

It sounded like a coffin.

The doors swung open slowly and silently and on their own. The Chamberlain lowered his eyes and cleared his throat.

"The three have been sent for, my lord," he intoned from the doorway.

Lord Smirch of Slugborn Manor lay on his bed, swathed in a robe of soft, purple silk that in no way concealed his rolls of fat. In fact, if anything, it accentuated them. Heavy jowls framed either side of his pudgy lips like engorged, pink cherubs. His piggy eyes squinted evilly underneath bushy, frowning brows that grew together in the middle over his nose. He had no beard to cover his six chins and his skull was denuded of hair. His fingers looked like links of summer sausages as they sensuously massaged man tits large enough to fire off streams of milk like *The Miraculous Lactation of Saint Bernard*. To add insult to imagery his robe was partly open and when the Chamberlain raised his eyes from the floor he quickly looked down again, forever after unable to burn from his mind a vision of a plucked turkey neck juggling raw meat balls.

Lord Smirch rolled his immense girth onto a bulbous side so as to see his chief menial the better. "So, news of the End of the World has reached even the ears of our dense Proconsul, eh? And he has sent for the Three to investigate?"

"It would seem so, my lord," said the Chamberlain stiffly. A hint of apprehension momentarily betrayed his reply.

There was silence at this juncture. A silence that oppressed the air itself as the Baron's eyes stared unblinkingly at his servant.

The Chamberlain, uncomfortably revolving inside his skin at a high rate of speed, cleared his throat yet again and continued in a wavering voice. "In addition...my lord, the-the Proconsul requests your assistance in this matter. He wishes you to supply e-e-experienced servants to help the Three in their mission."

Lord Smirch rolled his rotundity once more onto his back and smiled quietly for a moment as various machinations paraded themselves through the darkness of his infinitely wicked brain. The

Chamberlain tried to shift his growing discomfort from one foot to the other in the silence that followed. At last, Lord Smirch spoke again.

"Yes. Provide the Proconsul with whatever he requires."

"You intend to help him?" the chancellor cried, aghast. "But all your years of planning –"

"Never fear, Chamberlain. The servants I provide will be of my choosing. In addition, put my chief assassin on the job as well as my head of public relations. Promise them rich rewards on successful completion of their task. They will handle this personally if necessary."

"Rich rewards? Gold? Power? A fiefdom?"

"Better!" Lord Smirch cackled maliciously. "Much better! My plans have never been more secure! The Three are no more than a temporary impediment to my steady progress!"

The Chamberlain, realizing he wasn't going to be thrown from the tower, became emboldened enough to attempt satisfying some of his curiosity. "What progress, my lord?" he ventured.

From out of the dimly-lit room came another bout of raucous cackling. "You will soon see, dear Chamberlain, you will soon see. Now leave me to dwell on pure evil for a bit – and get me a plate of those tasty sausages."

"Yes, m'lord."

"And some of that roast duck."

"Yes, m'lord."

"And four racks of lamb."

"Uh, yes, m'lord."

"A keg of the finest wine from the cellar -"

"Yes, m-"

"Don't interrupt! Eight boxes of Krappy Kreme donuts slathered with ketchup, a forty-ounce cut of filet mignon – freshly slaughtered, a side of giraffe meat, seventy hamburgers drenched with high fructose corn syrup, a hundred-and-eighty-two pounds of chicken dumplings, a bucket of lard and...

"...a salt lick."

Lord Smirch fell silent. The Chamberlain turned slightly, unsure as to whether he could leave or not. Timidly, he asked in a quavering voice, "Is that all m-"

"NO!" Lord Smirch roared. "I want ninety-nine legs of mutton, five-hundred gallons of blood pudding, seven hundred boiled lobsters smothered with peanut butter and whipped cream, a sack of raw potatoes, a herd of cattle brought here alive so I can drink all the milk I want straight from the source, six hundred deviled eggs, a hundred pound bag of candy, and a small Caesar salad. I want it all brought here by thirty-seven castrated midget jugglers who will entertain me while I gorge myself. And send up a serving wench, covered in chocolate, with some of those multi-colored sugar sprinkles. That is all! Now, begone!"

The Chamberlain ran from the room, down the stairwell, down to the kitchen, wondering all the while where the hell he was going to get a serving wench that hadn't already escaped from Slugborn Manor.

Lord Smirch, grunting and sweating with the effort it took to heave his massive frame to a sitting position, pressed a button on his nightstand. A holoprojector turned itself on and cast a three-dimensional image in the air before him. A robed figure "stood" in Smirch's room, the hood covering the head and casting its face in shadow. All that could be made out was a cigar moving back and forth, between clenched teeth, from one side of its mouth to the other.

"Whaddayou want?" said the figure.

Lord Smirch, as evil as he was, still found himself trembling slightly in the presence of this hooded creature.

"My Lord," began Smirch, fighting hard to keep the nervousness out of his voice, "Lord Vug has-"

"Yeah, I know. Don't worry about it. Just keep doing what you're doing. I'll send a couple of my minions. Between the both of us we should be able to keep a lid on this shit. Now, fuck off and stop calling me all the time! You're worse than my ex-girlfriend!"

The figure reached out a stained, white kid glove and flipped a switch out of view. His image disappeared.

Lord Smirch exhaled a tremulous breath and eased himself back down on the bed, doing his utmost to keep his mind occupied on the upcoming feast.

I never imagined, he thought, *that I would ever encounter a greater monster than myself. One day I'll outmaneuver that snake and I'll never have to deal with him again.*

The door to his chamber suddenly opened and a terrified girl, covered in chocolate and sugary sprinkles, was pushed toward him by a horde of diminutive jugglers wearing jester costumes complete with merrily tinkling bells. Carts laden with food followed immediately after.

Lord Smirch licked the drool from his lips and cackled.

But...for now...first things first.

Fit the First

Fennelgurg the Semi-Proximate, whom we may call Felix, and Burthdrool the Endearingly Foliate, whom we may call Bill, were standing in Felix's backyard, having recently nursed hangovers earlier that morning due to excessive tippling the previous night. The purpose of the celebration was ostensibly a house-warming for Felix who had purchased the property in which he and Bill were now standing as well as the associated ruin which somehow managed to remain perpendicular to it. It is said that, in some languages, such a structure could be loosely referred to as a 'house' or 'domicile' of sorts. To use *Bill's* words, however, would require an altogether different and more colorful language which would be uncouth to repeat.

As mentioned, Felix and Bill were standing in Felix's recently purchased backyard next to three broken lounge chairs and a pile of empty beer cans between them, staring with a mixture of growing disbelief at the fence bordering one edge of the property, on the other side of which were some decrepit-looking trees that grew in the neighbor's yard. The object of their rapt attention was a small, grey squirrel making quite a lot of noise and throwing nuts at them. It scrambled from one tree to another, chattering and shrieking hideously. Apparently deciding that this wasn't sufficient it donned a hard hat and tool bag and scampered down to the ground, out of sight. Rather than ceasing its obnoxious racket the terrible ruckus was augmented by the sound of something being quite professionally demolished.

"What in bloody heavens is it doing I wonder?" Felix asked the air.

From the neighbor's yard came the sound of scraping and wood knocking together. After a few minutes of this Felix made a tentative step toward the fence as if to take a peek over it when suddenly a great mass of lumber flew up in the air and fell in a jumbled heap into Felix's yard.

"I think that squirrel just tossed a pile of broken lumber over my fence," said Felix, speaking again to breathable molecules of gas. The squirrel climbed over the fence after the lumber and approached it with an air of serious intent, towing a thick electrical cable and some power tools.

"I wonder where Carter's got off to?" Bill asked, speaking, not to the air, but to the anonymous narrator who reports events in the third person.

In answer to this query, while they continued to goggle in quiet bewilderment at the squirrel's chaotic but seemingly purposeful antics, the pile of beer cans spoke in a rather slurred rumble of plaintive muttering. Bill looked over at it briefly, turned back to the squirrel who had since built a small wooden henge out of the broken lumber, goggled a bit more, then returned his gaze to the pile of beer cans from which issued a drink-enfeebled claw.

"Ah, Carter! Welcome back," said Bill. He kicked at the cans until Carter, also known as Crumwax the Quasi-Intelligible, was revealed. He sat up, rose unsteadily to his feet, said "Worfklj," and fell again to the ground.

"Yes," said Bill, looking down at Carter's prone form sympathetically, "I agree. It *is* uncanny, isn't it? Especially that part you were saying about the fish follicles in the champagne."

"Slofglugw!"

"Indeed! Now be a good chap and make us some coffee, would you?"

Carter slowly made his second attempt at verticality and shambled to the 'house,' but not before falling in that short distance exactly sixteen more times. A few minutes after disappearing into the wretched hole that in some languages is laughingly called a 'back door' there came a clatter of breaking dishes and a loud thump of something heavy and soft landing on the floor, a muffled "Drpkljuff," and then silence.

When Bill returned his attention to the squirrel he observed a massive, fortress-like tower rising ominously from the center of the henge, topped with a massive cannon-looking thing that the squirrel was busily rotating on its axes, apparently testing its mechanical functionality and doing some calculations with a slide rule, viciously writing figures down in a notebook.

"That can't be good, can it," said Felix blandly.

"He seems rather angry about something."

"Yes…yes…rather…"

"I wonder what he means by it?"

Bill looked round then to ask how the coffee might be coming along when a small boy came out of the house. His eyes were abnormally large and half-lidded, a string of drool issued from thick lips. He waved a stubby-fingered hand in their general vicinity and walked toward the squirrel's fortress with an unsteady gait, jerking along by them and saying things with carefully selected monosyllables to no one in particular.

"Who's that?" asked Bill.

Felix glanced only briefly at the child. "Oh, it's just the retarded kid who lives across the street."

"What's his name?"

"Um – Puzzle, I think," said Felix distractedly. The squirrel was now running conduit throughout the structure, pulling high-voltage wiring through them and hooking up power, checking everything with a little meter.

"What a cruel thing to name a child," Bill remarked, following Puzzle's painfully awkward movement toward the squirrel's project. The squirrel looked down with what could almost be called something between amusement and alarm as the boy crawled over the henge and began to climb the tower.

"Ho there!"

Felix and Bill both turned at the salutation and a Royal Messenger – fancy stockings, powdered wig, and all – stepped from the 'back door' into the yard.

"You must have left the front door open," said Bill.

"As you noted yesterday it's hard to close a door that isn't there." Then, to the Messenger, Felix hailed, "Hello yourself, sir! And what brings you to my humble abode?"

The messenger looked behind him at the teetering debris to which Felix referred. He snorted sharply, but only once, keeping whatever snide remark he had in mind unvoiced. Aloud, however, he spoke his message.

"You have been summoned by Sir Vug, the Elder Statesman of Lothwit Feeng and Proconsul of our Most Esteemed Province. You are to come with me immediately and speak to His Eminence concerning a matter of Gravest Importance and Utmost Gravity."

"It's about that tax shelter you've got in the Caymans isn't it," Bill whispered.

Felix jabbed him in the kidney and said, "My good man, could you perhaps enlighten us as to the nature of this matter?"

The messenger, maintaining his haughty posture, rolled his eyes a bit but deigned to respond. "I am merely a Humble Messenger, sent by the Proconsul. The nature of the emergency is not known to me. You are simply to ride with me in my carriage this instant or be shot and beaten and flayed alive, in that order."

"I say!" exclaimed Felix. In high dudgeon he responded, "You *dare* speak in such a manner to the Three Wise Men representing the Triune Deities Whose names we bear, Who Observe and Take Due Note of the One Hundred and Forty-Seven Thousand and Twelve Apocalyptic Signs as Revealed by Zanzer Gackspin, Their Prophet on

Earth, Under the Heavens and Over the Shadowed Underworld of Gnath and Sideways to the Leftward Realm of Argn-"

"I have never heard of you and do not care now that I have. I am a Humble Royal Messenger of the Realm and may lord over you the Power of Life and Death at my slightest Whim. Therefore, as the Basest of Servants, I demand, with the greatest Humility, that you obey me in All Things and come with me this Instant as you have been commanded or face Certain Death."

All of this was stated as though from a script. The tone was one of boredom. It was apparent this messenger had been doing his job for quite a long time and would not be balked or convinced to do anything contrary to the will of the eminent proconsul. There was obviously no choice but to go.

"Good Messenger, we shall go with you," Felix declared.

The Messenger made a face that said, *That's obvious, idiot.* He turned stiffly about and made for the 'house'. Felix looked over his shoulder toward the top of the tower and saw the squirrel showing the drooling Puzzle how to operate a recently constructed gun turret.

"Oh, well," he said, "It's about time we were going anyway."

They trudged through the house, Bill rousting Carter off the floor on the way, and stepped out into the street. A gleaming Sarthe Silver Aston Martin DB9 LM - with Magnum Silver finishes on the meshes and rear crossbar, red brake calipers, black leather interior, Tertre Rouge facia trim, and diamond turned alloy wheels - was parked in the driveway.

Bill cooed and aahed over it, doing his best not to drip saliva on the paint job. "Felix," he whispered, "look at it! An Aston Martin DB9..."

"Yes, yes. I know what it is. Since when did you become interested in cars?"

"Five-point-nine liter V12 under the hood..."

Felix rolled his eyes.

"Four-hundred-and-sixty-nine horse at six grand, four-hundred-and-forty-three foot-pounds of torque at five, one-hundred-eighty-six miles per hour top speed, zero to sixty in four-point-six seconds..."

"Oh," said the Messenger snootily, "read that right off the Wikipedia page, did you?"

"That's enough, Bill," Felix said impatiently, "your eyes are turning into spiraling pinwheels."

The Messenger held the door open for them but made all three stuff themselves into the back where plastic had been laid down- especially Bill, whom he didn't want drooling all over the leather on the passenger seat. Then he got in himself, sliding behind the wheel, and they sped off.

Just thirty-three seconds later a beam of radioactive death made a smoking hole in the ground where Felix's 'house' had once been. Atop the tower, Puzzle cheered incoherently while the squirrel hopped and raised its forepaws, squeaking with victory. Puzzle picked up his new-found friend and hugged it with all the unreserved love that only a special child can give, squeezing it until its eyes popped and its guts ran out of every orifice, dribbling wetly and sloppily to the ground below.

Fit the Second

The Messenger stood at the entrance to the Proconsul's chambers while the Three Wise Men huddled in the center of a lush carpet, surrounded by tapestries and library shelves, a great globe in one corner, and a massive mahogany desk before them, behind which sat the Proconsul in a leather chair, scratching away in a massive book with a giant, four-foot-long quill. He dipped this obscenely large feather into an inkpot for what was probably the hundredth time and continued his scribblings.

They had been waiting for more than an hour like this. Felix stared at a spot above the Proconsul's head while Bill gnawed absentmindedly at his nails. Carter swayed as was his usual wont, pulling off a piece of surgical tubing from his arm. He dropped the empty syringe, the contents of which were now floating around in his cardiovascular system quickly bringing chemical Samadhi to every one of his other systems. "Gaa," he burbled.

Without looking up or breaking step with his scratching the Proconsul finally spoke. "Who are these people Chauncey?"

"These are the men you sent for Your Eminence," the Messenger stated from the doorway.

"And what are their names I wonder?" said the Proconsul.

Felix snapped himself out of his reverie and, pulling a scroll from a pocket of his robe, read from it in a stentorian voice.

"We are the Three Wise Men, Fennelgurg the Semi-Proximate, Crumwax the Quasi-Intelligible and Burthdrool the Endearingly Foliate. We bear the names of the Triune Deities that Observe and take Due Note of the One Hundred and Forty-Seven Thousand and Twelve Apocalyptic Signs as Revealed by Zanzer Gackspin, Their Prophet on Earth, Under the Heavens and Over the Shadowed Underworld of Gnath and Sideways to the Leftward Realm of Argnweirwoldheimschlistcrockenpit, but Rightward of the Land that is only Slightly more to the Right of the Leftward Land by a Tiny Smidge, which is certainly more than a Scotche, but Less than a Hair clipped from the Scrotum of a Serious-Minded Bacteriophage Swimming about in the Argyle Mud of Glacklon Hroog which floats about a Misty White Star One Hundred Trillion Furlongs distant, but of which some has been Collected by Crumwax the Quasi-Intelligible, wherein he keeps it in his Bathroom Medicine Chest so that He may Look Upon It in Odd Moments.

"I am Fennelgurg the Semi-Proximate, but you may call me Felix."

"And I am Burthdrool the Endearingly Foliate, but you may call me Bill," said Bill.

Felix glanced over at Carter who was still swaying, eyes closed, with a half-smile on his lips. He stamped hard on Carter's foot causing the latter's eyes to snap open for a fraction of a second. He drew a deep breath and said, in one exhalation, "Amblzxkl snarfhejw qwerty uiop."

Felix sighed and shook his head. "And he is Crumwax the Quasi-Intelligible, but you may call him Carter," he said, adding in a low voice, "the Entirely *Un*intelligible."

Felix put the scroll away and they waited. The Proconsul still did not look up or cease his scribbling. Several minutes more passed before he finally said, "Yes, very stentorian – in a simian sort of way. Sign here."

He pushed a thick pile of papers across the desk at them with his free and non-scribbling hand. Felix stepped forward to examine this tragic waste of a perfectly good tree. Each page was extraordinarily thin, almost transparent, and completely covered on both sides with the most miniscule typeface imaginable.

"What is this?" Felix asked. The Messenger called out from the doorway, "*That* is your contract. Please turn to the bottom of the final page - a task which you may facilitate by simply turning over the entire stack. There you will find three lines upon which you will each sign your names. Fingerprints, toe prints, palm prints, photographs, retina scans, voice prints, blood samples, urine samples, semen samples, rectal probings, throat swabbings, hair and fingernail clippings, X-rays, sonograms, dental casts, DNA profilings, and copies of all birth certificates, licenses, national identification documents, and all other background data will be requested and provided after your meeting with His Eminence."

"A contract for what? I can't even read it the print's so small. There must be thousands of pages here! We have to thoroughly look this over in the presence of legal counsel before we can do anything as absurd as *signing* it!"

"You will observe," replied the Messenger forcefully, "that the Law, as clearly and unambiguously stated in the Provincial Penal Code, Volume 5063, Article 8997, Part AA978, Subpart JXZHG143, Page 11,699, Paragraph 384, Sub-paragraph 432, Sub-sub-paragraph 1100, References one to Provincial Civil Code, Volume 1,221,800, Article 12, Part X789, Subpart XCV2089, Page 478, Paragraph 897, Sub-paragraph 349,948, sub-sub-paragraph 2,345, sub-sub-sub-paragraph 2, verse 19, element 84, under the 90th nuance as elaborated by the Great Proconsul Gulg in the Year 466, that upon entering the environs of the Proconsul, all who do so waive the right to legal counsel, life, liberty, happiness and/or its pursuit, as well as a last meal and cigarette prior to immediate and painful execution if the Proconsul chooses to exercise that option at his whimsy. In addition, any and all contracts offered by the Proconsul must be signed before knowledge of what the contract concerns may be divulged. Nor may you leave the environs of the Proconsul until an offered contract has been signed and any and all signing said contract are bound, body and soul, to it."

Aghast, Felix swooned and asked weakly, "And what are the bloody environs of the Proconsul?"

"The environs include the Proconsul's domicile and all lands surrounding it, up to and including the borders of the known universe. Now sign now or die upon the rack!"

"Who's the Proconsul here, anyway," Bill muttered.

Sighing, Felix picked up a quill, not quite as large as the Proconsul's, and, dipping it into a pot filled with ink the color of blood, signed the first line of the contract. He handed the pen to Bill who did the same and then passed it to the bleary-eyed Carter who promptly dropped it twice, then spilled the inkpot onto the floor. This, surprisingly, aroused no response from the Messenger or the Proconsul, who went right on scribbling. Carter finally got down on his hands and knees, taking the last page of the contract with him, and dipped the quill into the red pool seeping into the carpet. He succeeded at last in placing total gibberish onto the paper nowhere near the line it was supposed to be.

Felix picked up the soiled sheet between thumb and forefinger, tossed it onto the stack, his shoulders hung with defeat.

"Chauncey," the Proconsul said abruptly, "bring me the next volume, would you please? There's a good chap."

The Messenger left the room briefly and returned with an even more massive tome than the one in which the Proconsul was writing. Felix unobtrusively peeked at the Proconsul's volume and noticed that each page consisted of long lists of names in the leftmost column, dates in the next, a 'judgement rendered' column which were all marked "yea" beside each name, and a final 'judgement ratified by' column. It was this column in which the Proconsul had been busily signing *his* name for each and every name in the list. He was just signing the last one when Chauncey approached the desk, extending the new volume. The Proconsul slammed his own shut with a loud crack that made two of the Wise Men jump and traded it with Chauncey for the new one. On each cover was one word in bold, golden print: **EXECUTIONS**.

Without ever looking at any of them, the Proconsul opened the new book and, turning to the first page, began signing his name again and again down the columns.

"Now then," he said without stopping, "the four of you have been charged with-"

"Three, Your Eminence," said Chauncy.

"What?"

"There are only three of them."

The Proconsul had not stopped what he was doing, but vexation shadowed his countenance. He reached into a drawer with his free hand and consulted a file of papers. "I think not, Chauncey, my figures say four and figures never lie. Yet we have three men here, you say. I don't like that. I don't like that at all. Where is the fourth man?"

"I do not know, Your Eminence."

"Hmm," said the Proconsul, putting the file away. "I don't like things that aren't known either. Don't like it at all. After this meeting is over I want you to raise up our secret army of undead and search for this missing fourth man. I want him thumped on the head and brought here at once so that I may grind justice into the back of his skull with the heel of my boot. Then I want him shot and sent to the Master Interrogator for questioning. I want to know just what he means by this affront to my arithmetical acumen. I won't have doing my sums made a chore by being mocked and insulted by some invisible fourth man who, in all probability, is another one of those smelly peasants tasking my administrative duties. Everyone must be accounted for, no matter their olfactory condition."

Meanwhile, Felix and Bill were feeling nothing but rising panic, and looking around for quick means of egress. Before Chauncey had interrupted, sending the Proconsul into a verbal tizzy, the Elder Statesman of Lothwit Feeng had said the words "charged with" which immediately sent chills down their rapidly yellowing spines. Charged with what? And they sincerely hoped that the Proconsul would fucking get on with it before they both died of terror or did something rashly irreversible.

When it seemed the Proconsul had no more to say on the matter, Chauncey said, "Yes, Your Eminence," and returned to his position at the door.

"Now then, as I was saying, you - who are currently three but will, perhaps, one day be briefly four until the fourth one is executed - have been charged with -"

The Proconsul dropped his giant quill; it fell to the floor with a frightening "whump." His eyes never leaving the book, the Proconsul calmly folded his hands upon it.

"Oh, Chauncey. Get that for me, would you?"

As Chauncey sprang from the door to retrieve the enormous feather, Felix and Bill tensed for action, ready to kill everyone in the room and jump through the plate glass window to their left. In addition to cutting themselves to pieces they could expect a healthy bruise or two since they were standing on the third floor.

Chauncey fussed about, experiencing some difficulty getting the business end of the quill into the Proconsul's hand.

"You have been charged with-"

The quill fell to the floor again. Could they fight their way out downstairs? Every means of escape seemed suicidal. Bill was starting to tremble and Felix was slowly edging toward the window.

Chauncey managed to get the quill into the Proconsul's hand again, securing it with a roll of tape.

"You have been charged with – Chauncey, more ink please."

Bill collapsed to his knees, resigned to whatever doom should befall them.

Chauncey filled the inkpots on the desk. The Proconsul dipped the quill and resumed writing.

"You have been charged with – Chauncey, a glass of water."

Bill groveled on the floor and began to sob. Felix managed to position himself before one of the window panes but jumped back when he encountered the visage of a snarling, winged raccoon wearing rubber gloves and holding a syringe filled with gods-knew-what merely because the anonymous narrator who reports events in the third person couldn't figure out something better to impede Felix's planned suicide. Carter turned himself about in a slow, shuffling circle, making nonsensical signs in the air with his thumb and forefinger.

Chauncey quickly returned with the requested refreshment and set it on the Proconsul's desk.

"You have been charged with-" The Proconsul's unseemly quill knocked over the glass, spilling water everywhere. "Chauncey! Mop!"

Chauncey ran hurriedly from the room, coming back with a mop and a peculiar bucket which oddly seemed to be screaming obscenities at no one in particular, complaining of this abuse to its person while Chauncey used the mop to collect the fallen beverage from the floor, the desk and the Proconsul's sleeve. At no point did the Proconsul look up or cease signing his name. When Chauncey was finished, standing at attention with the mop, the Proconsul cleared his throat to speak. The bucket continued its remonstrance, carefully enumerating a list of grievances until, without looking, Chauncey kicked it into silence.

"You have been charged with-"

A telephone began to ring stridently from somewhere inside the Proconsul's desk. "Chauncey, get that, would you?"

Chauncey scrambled about the desk, opening and closing drawers (which must have numbered in the several hundreds) in search of the elusive telephone, twice knocking the quill from the Proconsul's hand which had to be then reaffixed with greater quantities of tape. Felix stared out the window, debating with himself as to his ability to take on a flying raccoon brandishing inauspicious medical implements while Bill took to gnawing at his toes between wracking sobs. Carter batted at invisible flies.

When the as-yet-undiscovered phone stopped ringing Chauncey resumed his former posture with the mop, taking the sound and preemptive precaution of kicking the bucket before it got the idea of talking again.

"You have been charged with – Chauncey, a nip of that hideous cough syrup that grandfather used to brew in the basement before I had him properly beheaded please."

Chauncey once again sped from the room, intentionally banging the disgruntled and murmuring bucket against every nearby object on the way out. Felix, having apprehended an appropriate plan, seized Carter and pushed him toward the window, intent upon tossing him through it so as to shield him from the raccoon first, with the added benefit that Felix would have something soft and pulpy to land on when he followed suit. Bill attempted throttling himself while Carter, a quill still in hand, but without ink, began writing invisible and quite meaningless hieroglyphs on his robe, made all that less meaningful by Felix's jostling.

Chauncey returned with a goblet of bubbling, smoking brew. The Proconsul took two sips and cleared his throat once more.

"You have been charged with-" He opened another of the many drawers in the desk as if to confer with some oracular piece of paper. Felix tensed himself to throw Carter through the window. Bill was turning blue. Carter stared transfixed at something fascinating in the seventh dimension.

"You have been charged with...

"...a task."

Felix turned his head toward the Proconsul and heaved an audible sigh of relief. If he could have gotten away with it he would have strangled the Proconsul on the spot. Bill looked up from his prone and semi-asphyxiated position, smiling blearily at the Proconsul while wiping snot and spittle from his tear-streaked face. He slowly rose on bloody feet to resume his previous stance. Carter giggled and, crawling about on all fours, counted threads in the carpet.

"This task is an official Quest on behalf of the Realm. Being beneficent in my manner and heedful of the needs of my people I have detected some slight unrest in the behavior of a few of these sickening peasants that may infect the rest of the herd with their twaddle. I speak, of course, of nothing less than the End of the World. Perhaps you've heard of it? Good. I want you to find out what it is and where it comes from and how I might grind my Boot of Compassionate Justice into the back of its skull. Apparently it has something to do with an ancient calendar and some awful planet filled with slavering gods that can't wait to steer it right into us and make a frightful mess of my bookkeeping. I have heard additional rumors that the sun is going to boil us up like lobsters, that the planets will align and cause earthquakes and temperamental weather, that there will be a massive gravity imbalance in the entire galaxy, that some sort of Galactic Beam will bathe the Earth in a rather unpleasant radiation which will also somehow be simultaneously shielded from its beneficial rays when the sun comes between us and it, or some other interminable rot. It's really far too complicated to keep my interest. As you can see I am a busy man. It all sounds like the usual peasant complaints if you ask me. Chickens won't give milk, cows won't lay eggs, women turn sour, parents don't obey their children, everyone is writing a book, ad infinauseum. I think they're just trying to get out of an honest day's work to avoid paying their ruinous taxes. But, they can't fool me. I will not be thwarted. Justice will be meted out in the end, won't it Chauncey?"

"By Your Compassionate Boot it will! Yes, Your Eminence!"

"There, you see? Now then-"

"Floop bykderfty cbn," Carter mumbled from the floor.

For the first time Vug, the Eminent Statesman of Lothwit Feeng and Proconsul of this Most Esteemed Province, sat erect in his chair and gazed upon the Three Wise Men with earnest, lawful eyes. His writing hand was still.

"I think not," he said calmly. Felix and Bill glanced nervously at Carter and took two sideways steps away from him.

"The answer to both of your questions is 'no.' Addressing the first I must say quite truthfully that my wife would never engage in the sort of act which you suggest. Not with me anyway. Maybe when she goes slumming around town with those ruffians she likes to dally with. But, I can assure you that you're not her type. You're just not peasanty enough and you really don't look as though you could stoop to the level of degradation she seems to be comfortable with. Addressing the second, you three will be heading this Quest and will be ultimately responsible for the results, so you will not be going alone. I have arranged for several experienced adventurers to accompany you. They have been assembled at the estates of Lord Smirch of Slugborn Manor and await your direction. There you will also meet a John of Evergrool who knows more about this whole End of the World nonsense. Chauncey will escort you to your vehicle which you will use to go where needed on your Quest. Good day and may I never lay eyes on you again."

The Proconsul immediately bent back to his work of consigning thousands of people to their deaths and did not look up or speak to them again.

Bill collected Carter from the floor and Chauncey took them all to their conveyance.

"Maybe we'll at least get to drive the Aston Martin," Bill said hopefully.

Fit the Third

"Well, this just blows doesn't it?" said Bill through clenched teeth.

The Three Wise Men violently bobbed up and down upon the back of Hangnail, the Six-Limbed Riding Monkey - undeniably the worst form of transportation ever conceived.

The giant monkey tended to use only its four legs when walking or trotting, but assisted itself with its arms when breaking into a full run. However, not only was it an excruciatingly dizzy and jarring ride, it frequently got side-tracked and was impossible to control. They got lost more than once and often had to wait when the monkey found something that took its fancy. Another unfortunate problem was that it was in a perpetual state of heightened libido and would stop anywhere from six to twenty times a day to anxiously hammer away at its enormous genitalia, making a disgusting mess in the process. Thus, anywhere from six to twenty times a day, Felix and Bill would find themselves hurling their lunch into the shrubs, not counting the loss of stomach content that occurred during the ride. The only one who seemed to be enjoying himself was Carter.

Slugborn Manor was not close either. In fact it was a few hundred miles out of the way, on the other side of three mountain ranges, a malarial swamp, tar pits, quicksand and a dense jungle filled with giant snakes and predatory, cross-eyed reptiles that ran about on powerful hind legs, with forelimbs that looked like gas-powered hedge clippers had been grafted onto them.

The journey was long and grueling, but the countryside was quite beautiful in its harsh, climatological extremity. In fact, the history of the region is quite intriguing, really, and a rather elaborate dissertation concerning this topic has been prepared which shall now be related for the edification of the reader.

"Oh, Great Anonymous Narrator," said Felix between bouts of retching, "Would you be so kind as to skip on a bit, thank you."

But this dissertation took months to carefully research and –

"It would *really* be *most* decent of you, Oh Anonymous Narrator, if you could just scratch all that and get us to where we're going, if you *please*!"

But –

"IF – YOU - *PLEASE*!"

Fine.

Asshole.

Fit the Fourth

Starved, emaciated, sick and nearly dead from the rigors of travel and being repeatedly raped by Hangnail, the Six-Limbed Riding Monkey, the Three Wise Men were unceremoniously dumped at their destination, beaten up a little bit, and smeared with feces. Hangnail then lustily skipped off after a giant basketball, and was soon out of sight, beyond the reach of any possible vengeance by the Three Wise Men who suddenly had at their disposal a loaded .357 Smith & Wesson with three rounds. Since there were no multi-appendaged monkeys to shoot at, it was possible they might simply end their miserable lives now and save us all the trouble.

Felix felt the weight of it and, slowly coming to the inevitable conclusion, clicked back the hammer and raised it to his temple. His friends looked on in horror as he –

"Oh shut up and just get on with the story!" yelled Felix at the slightly miffed anonymous narrator.

"Slightly!" exclaimed Bill. "You're trying to kill us!"

Anyway, Felix put the gun in his pocket, deciding that getting a sandwich would be more productive at the moment. But he still left suicide on the table as an alternative to insulting the anonymous narrator.

Maybe later.

Perhaps after he ate his sandwich.

"Oh, knock it off!"

"So, where do we get sandwiches?" asked Bill.

Bill turned his head just a little more to the left…and then a wee bit more…and finally stopped being stupid long enough to see the tavern that was right next to him.

"Ah, yes I see now," Bill grumbled.

"Great," said Felix with dreary sarcasm, "the *Crumb & Toad*. An *excellent* establishment."

And through the blood-stained oaken door they went.

It had already been getting dark outside, and inside was darker still with but a single window and just two torches, one at each end of the room. All of the tables they could see were presently empty. No one sat at the bar except the tavern keeper who, on observing their entrance, skittered around to his place behind it. He thrust his hands out onto its stained surface and beamed idiotically at them.

They started making their way toward a table near the window as Felix called out to the tavern keeper. "A round of ales and some mutton if you don't mind."

"Ales and mutton!" cried the tavern keeper with delight. "Right!" He looked under the counter and, nodding to himself in a satisfied sort of way said, "Nope, sorry."

The Three Wise Men stumbled to a halt. Felix raised an eyebrow and responded, "'Nope, sorry' what."

"No ale," the tavern keeper said, smiling still, "or mutton," he added.

"Well, then we'll take a round of wine and some fowl, thank you," and they moved again toward the table, but stopped a second time when the tavern keeper cheerfully responded, "Nope. Haven't got any 'o that either."

"Look man," Felix said irritably, "what *have* you got?"

The tavern keeper scooped up three menus and waddled his rotund form toward the table they'd been trying to get to. "Fair amount of nothing really. Please, be seated. Make yourselves comfortable and I'll take your orders in a moment."

They all sat down and looked briefly at the menus, each page filled with line after line of precisely nothing as the tavern keeper had said.

When he returned with a little pad of paper, Felix cleared his throat and peevishly asked if there was some water at least.

"Nope, sorry. No water."

"Well, where's everything gone off to then?"

Grinning, the tavern keeper pointed to a table set in the darkest corner of the room. "*He* ate it."

Sitting at the indicated spot, a food-spattered bib still tied to its front and an empty pile of dishes before it, utensils still clenched between slimy fists, was the most enormous, ugliest, wartiest toad they'd ever laid eyes on. A tarnished and battered crown sat on its head, cocked at an extraordinary angle between its protruding eyes which stared, unmoving and unfocused at nothing in particular. A gooey, wet tongue snipped out of its mouth and caught a few of the flies that buzzed around the remains of its last meal.

Felix looked away in disgust. Just then Bill caught his attention who was staring at Carter with an incredulous frown and a slack jaw. Apparently Carter had ordered nothing off the menu and was busy chewing happily while cutting another small piece of nothing off of a larger piece of nothing with his fork and knife, making squeaky noises on the empty plate that had been set before him. He seemed to be relishing every bite, eyes closed, sighing with contentment, even going so far as to wipe invisible dribbles from his chin now and then with his napkin.

Felix narrowed his eyes. "You *are* a moron, aren't you?"

Carter merely nodded, belched, and set to with renewed gusto.

"I am the one you seek," intoned a voice from the corner. It sounded as though someone were walking through wet gravel inside a deep well.

Felix and Bill turned back to the toad, leaving Carter to enjoy nothing for a while longer.

"Um," said Felix. "Did you, um, say something Sir...Toad?"

"Yes," it said. It flicked a few more flies out of the air and went on in its ponderous speech. "I am the one you seek. You are the Three Wise Men. You require companions for your quest. I will provide these companions."

"Well, um, thank you very much. Uh, you wouldn't, um, you wouldn't by any chance be a Lord, uh, a Lord...Smirch, would you?"

The toad's hands sprung open and its utensils clattered to the floor. It rocked dangerously for a moment on its stool and its eyes closed and opened once.

"Say not that name again. That filth of a pig profanes the very air!" The creature paused a moment to regain its composure. "Now," it said, "you must take up your forks and knives and eat me alive."

Bill gasped and turned away. Felix cupped his hand to his mouth, fighting back the rising gorge. Carter opened his eyes and looked at the toad for the first time with actual interest.

"You must do this," continued the repulsive creature. "You must do this and then take my bones behind the tavern and cast them upon the ground. From them will spring your companions, for it is these bones into which the Fiend of Slugborn Manor has changed them in his wickedness. It is his way."

"Uuuuhhh," said Felix behind his hand.

The toad rose and walked toward their table, webbed feet slapping against the hard floor. Carter attentively appraised its amphibious features, licking his chops hungrily.

The toad arrived and lay down, face up, onto their table. Its crown clattered to the floor boards. "Commence," is all it said.

Felix and Bill stood up and backed away. But, Carter sprang forward - fork and knife in hand - and stabbed the frog in its gut, cutting away great greasy slabs of meat. The toad groaned and bellowed pitifully, but Carter would not be deterred. Bill fainted and Felix ran outside in a fit of dry heaves. The tavern keeper simply smiled and sat down at the bar. He stared out the window, perhaps remembering more prosperous times - or at least times that actually made sense.

Carter had never felt more famished and did not stop until every last bit of flesh had been consumed, including all the nasty bits. He had been careful to scrape the skin and handed it to the tavern keeper to toast a bit in the oven. Then he sat down, truly satisfied at last, licking his fingers until the tavern keeper returned with the crispy toad skin. Carter gently rolled it all up, lit a match, and set one end alight while puffing on the other.

Felix returned a while later and grimaced at the gore on the table with a newfound distaste for Carter and the pleasure he had taken in creating it. Then he gagged at the fetid smoke and dry heaved all over again.

Bill eventually regained consciousness and crawled outside for some air.

It took a bit for Felix to pluck up sufficient resolve in order to gather the bones. He took one look at Carter's stoned and contented expression, shook his head, and went out with the carcass, tossing the remains onto the ground as instructed.

Several people immediately sprang up from the earth where the bones had been, holding their heads or their stomachs, moaning plaintively at their sudden retransformation.

"Right," said Felix. "I guess we'll do introductions later."

Fit the Fifth

Bill was standing outside the *Pox and Buzzard*, a more agreeable watering hole – its food not having all been consumed by a giant toad. He was about to head back inside, having just sent for some transportation, when he was accosted by an elderly gentleman who asked if he'd be willing to sell his hat.

"My hat? Well, it's starting to get a bit chilly and I kind of need it right now."

"I'll give you five-hundred bucks for it," rasped the old man.

"Five-hundred! It's yours!" The exchange was made and Bill went back into the tavern, chuckling to himself at this turn of luck. He sidled up to the busy bar and ordered an ale from the barkeep.

"That'll be five-hundred," the barkeep said with an up-turned palm.

"Five-hundred! What do you mean?"

"Exactly what I said. Five hundred."

"But that's expensive!"

"No, *that's* inflation."

"But, I just sold my hat for this money!"

"You got ripped off. Look, do you want this ale or not?"

Bill drooped and handed over the bucks. The barman took the money and held out his hand again.

"What!"

"Tip."

"Oh, for heaven's sake." Bill pulled out a couple more bucks and put them in the barkeep's palm who looked at the crumpled leaves with disdain.

"Cheapskate!" he sneered and shoved the ale at Bill, spilling half of it on the bar. Bill grabbed what was left before anything else happened to it and slumped off to the table where Felix and Carter were talking over the Quest with their new companions. Alright, *Felix* was talking over the Quest with their new companions. *Carter* was doing something naughty with his belly button lint.

When he arrived, Felix looked up at him and then at the mug. "Oh, you didn't just get the ale, did you?"

"Yeah, why?"

"It's awful. You should definitely go with the *mead* in *this* place."

"This ale cost me five-hundred bucks!"

"You got ripped off."

"What!"

"Sit down. We've got problems." As Bill pulled up a chair, slamming his worthless half-pint of ale on the table, Felix explained.

"We've discovered some underhandedness after all the introductions were completed. It would seem Lord Smirch is something of an asshole. He certainly gave us our companions as ordered by the Proconsul, but threw in a few extras to boot. There were *four* unanticipated additions in all: three low-brow types handing out literature, spreading something called 'the Word,' and this traveling salesman bugger selling these little eye-Pud or sly-Phone gizmachees. They've got all sorts of colorful gimmicks and blinking lights and such. In addition, they apparently also 'twitter' and 'tweet' among other assorted hoojibbery, allowing you to transmit and receive idiotic messages with total strangers and – "

"Is that those things with the wormy, half-eaten apple logos pasted on them?"

"Yes."

"Well. Where are the other three?"

"Oh, I've already taken care of them. I had this shiny, new Smith & Wesson and I took them out back and gave them a round a piece."

"Serves 'em right. You can never make heads or tails of that 'Word' gibberish."

"Anyway, *they* were easy. It's *this* twit I can't seem to get rid of."

Said twit swiveled his head around, speaking directly to Bill. "Hey there, fella! How about a slick new communication device to increase productivity and make you an all around better human being? This thing will get you laid and bring world peace. And just this once, I can make this special offer. I can *give it to you* for just $499.99 and let me tell you - *that* - is a steal, brother!"

"Dammit!" exclaimed Bill, "I could've bought one!"

Felix grabbed Bill's shoulder in alarm. "Er – I don't think you want one of those things, Bill."

"Why not?"

"They're terribly expensive and the productivity he claims is entirely unspecified. I mean, productive at what exactly? It's rather dubious, don't you think, claiming efficiency and productivity by using a device that allows dunderheaded conversation with all sorts of strange people at all hours of the day and night? What do I care about someone in China informing me – for no conceivable reason - that he just took a nice, long dump? Or that someone in New York is getting ready to enjoy a terribly good 'knuckle sandwich' – whatever that is? I've heard people going on about similar twaddle in things called flogs and macebook – or something like that - regurgitating the most banal facets of their daily lives to the entire world. Even worse yet are the people who have nothing better to do than respond to such garbage with equally trite nonsense! Where's the productivity in that? *'Efficient connectedness for busy people'* they eulogize, but all I ever see is an utterly dull waste of time. It's bad, Bill, bad. It's one of the Hundred and Forty-Seven Thousand and Twelve Apocalyptic Signs as Revealed by Zanzer Gackspin. Another distraction taking valuable and finite time away from the *really* important things."

"Hmmm," said Bill. "Got any more rounds in your Smith & Wesson?"

"Sadly, no. I only had three and I used those."

Bill looked hard at the salesman who was then jabbering at one of the adventurers, phallicly stroking a scintillating pud-Phone while extolling its benefits.

"See, guy?" the salesman smarmed, "That's all you gotta do to get one of these babies started. Same as the ignition on a Prius. Just make like you're the most awesome person in the world jacking himself off and *gackff*– "

Bill grabbed him by his necktie and jerked him out of the chair. There were some hearty cheers from the others at the table.

"I'll take care of this, Felix. You go on with the others and fill me in on the details later." Bill looked narrowly at the blue-faced salesman. "This might take a while. I don't like being taken for a sucker."

He dragged the salesman out the rear exit and was gone. Felix watched them go, shrugged, and engaged the remaining party members.

"At last, fellow companions, we can plan our Quest in earnest. John, I was told that you possessed some crucial details that you would, perhaps, like to share with the class."

John of Evergrool looked up, still a bit dazed from the salesman's pitch.

"Um, yes. That's correct. In order to put a stop to the End-of-the-World Threat, we need to seek out two prophets, one of whom knows the whereabouts of the other."

"Mmm. We're going to be doing a lot of shuffling about, looking under rocks and things, aren't we?"

"'Fraid so, yes sir."

"Oh, well. Carry on."

"Anyway, the first of the two prophets was last seen in or around the Temple of the Heckling Pigeon – "

"The Temple of the What?"

"Uh, no. The, uh, Temple of the Heckling Pigeon."

"Heckling Pigeon," Felix said, stroking his chin. "Now why does that sound familiar?"

John blushed, embarrassed. "Er, well...it should, sir, as you were – as you were once – a *monk* there."

"Ah, yes, yes, how time and recollection flies," Felix said, having no recollection at all.

"Uh, yes. As you say sir. Anyway, Crasspot the Dwarf, the Venerable Resident of the Temple Proper, knows the whereabouts of this prophet."

"Crasspot...Crasspot...yes, why does that name sound familiar as well?"

Embarassed yet again, John of Evergrool looked around the table and back to Felix.

"Well, as I'm certain you must recall, Crasspot has been a monk at the Temple for some five centuries and was the one who bestowed upon you your monkhood and certified you as a teacher of the prophecies as told by Zanzer Gackspin, even naming you after the chief of the Triune Deities that Observe and take Due Note of the One Hundred and Forty-Seven Thousand – "

"Yes, yes. I know the rest. Thank you, John, that will be all," said Felix perfunctorily, having not the slightest clue what the fuck John was talking about.

At that moment, Bill burst in through the door of the tavern, covered head-to-toe with blood, picking bits of meat and gristle from his robe.

"Ah," he said, "quite therapeutic."

"Um, yes. Right," Felix replied. He looked over the table at all the besotted additions to their party, their eyes glazed with the partial brain damage they'd acquired from the salesman's incessant drivel. He stood up, knocking his chair to the floor and banged his hands on the table, rattling cups and dishes. "Let's do some adventuring!" he cried.

A few feeble cheers "erupted" from the table and they were off.

Fit the Sixth

Since we haven't done so yet, let us take a moment to introduce the new traveling companions.

MEET THE CREW:

John of Evergrool you've already met, so we'll leave him to googling incorrect directions for their trip and reading maps upside down.

Moving on we have Felchenham the Quintessentially Brilliant and Albiblquim the Preternaturally Not Nice. Two very sharp instructors from the Lycaeum of Dunderwit & Pizzle. Say hello, fellas!

"Howdy!"

"Fuck you."

Next, we have Unctuous Frogfart the Unspeakably Well-Mannered, a high-society pretty-boy who is currently cutting his teeth at a lower standard of living so he can see how the "other half" lives. He will probably be the first to die.

"The pleasure really is *all mine.*"

Then we have Splendicorn the Ultra Fastidious Ranger of the Woody Dales and Feelington the Empathic, Melancholy and Slightly Gay Elf Who Likes to Touch You.

"Hail and well met, traveler! I see your boots are a bit dirty and your cloak is torn. Let me get my kit and I'll take care of that for you. Now, stop touching me there Elf! How many times do I have to tell you I'm not gay!"

"Oh, everything's so dreary today, isn't it? Don't you feel it? The grayness? The utter futility of everything? It makes me sad. Don't you feel the sadness, too? I can feel it. I can feel its hard, fleshy protrusion between my-"

Uh, and over here we see Balfert the Salutory who irritatingly says "Hello!" to everyone and is even more annoyingly happy and friendly.

"Hello! Glad to make your acquaintance! I am at your service! Just ask and I shall – "

Yeah, whatever.

Jerk.

Next up is Dabblenard the Deft. What he's deft at is not yet determined, but he suspiciously hangs around the Elf a lot.

"Hi, there!"

And here we have Pamperlorn the Vituperatively Smug –

"Smugly Vituperative! Get it right, dipshit! What are you, retarded?"

- and Tenebrous the Cryptically Trite.

"Yesterday there were two crows on Farmer Dale's roof. Now there is only one."

Oookaaaay. Great.

And over here, farting silently and blaming it on the barmaid he's unsuccessfully trying to get it on with, is Batwick the Astonishingly Uncool.

"It's Pulcrust. I changed it last week."

Pulcrust. Hardly shocking that it isn't any improvement over Batwick, is it? Let me tell you something about Pulcrust. His ex-girlfriend once wrote forty songs, each one about an ex-lover who had wronged her and made her life miserable in some unique and heart-breaking way. Seeking catharsis through the sharing of her music, she decided to make an album which Pulcrust (being a music producer) published for her. Naturally, being in control of marketing and design, he couldn't resist removing her heart-rending title and substituting it with his own just before it went to press. She broke up with him the very next week, but not before burning his mansion down by making a bonfire in his living room with one-thousand copies of *Forty Licks for Forty Dicks*. Astonishingly Uncool? You bet. He also somehow managed to give his guinea pig carpal tunnel.

Moving on.

Next, we introduce Bunglich the Absurdly Obtuse –

"Huh?"

- and his brother Hochphlegm the Equally Absurdly Obtuse.

"Where are you?"

And then we have Pelkinghorn Sunbeam of the Gnashing Teeth, who doesn't speak or eat as he is constantly gnashing his teeth.

Over here by himself is Thuribis Dumpsterspunk the Flagitious who, for easily imaginable reasons, no one likes, and over there is Grogsnot the Inane who worships Quagmool the Insipid (a god of some kind) and likes to recite unsolicited and very horrible poetry.

Then we have Slog the Intransitively Verbose. Watch it. Don't get too close or he'll talk to you. Next is Crod the Functionless, a sort of lumpy blob with four vestigial appendages, a thin and wide line marking a mouth that doesn't appear to have been open for a long time, if at all, and two wholly unremarkable eyes that stare off, unblinking, at – whatever. It seems to be the chief job of Bunglich and Hochphlegm to carry this thing about on a litter.

And finally, we come to the last two members of this merry band, Scraggins the Chiefly Preoccupied with his Smelly Navel Lint and Part-Time Bootblack, and...Pederastro...the Magician, a strange foreigner with a complicated last name that translates literally as "Who Smiles Meaningfully at Small Children for Some Reason."

And there we are: twenty additional companions to add to this Great Fellowship on their Great Quest, twenty redoubtable champions, twenty intrepid explorers...twenty additional mouths to feed, causing logistical nightmares for both the Three Wise Men and the anonymous narrator who reports events in the third person.

"Yes," said Felix, "I was meaning to have a word with you about that. I'm wondering if we couldn't just – eh – arrange to lighten things up a bit. You know, since it's in both of our interests."

The anonymous narrator considered this possibility while they all set off to the Temple of the Heckling Pigeon in an enormous, dung-smelling hay wain drawn by eight horses.

"Dung smelling!" Felix cried. "Come on! Have a heart!"

It was looking like all twenty adventurers were going to survive the trip. In fact, there was a rumor that more might be joining later.

"Right," said Felix. "Smells better already. Kind of like it actually."

Fit the Seventh

The arduous journey of our stalwart swashbucklers came to an end at the granite door of the Temple of the Heckling Pigeon. The great portal swung silently open and monks, just as silently, greeted them.

Their travels had not been without tribulation, having lost a few of their number. Pelkinghorn Sunbeam of the Gnashing Teeth, who did not speak or eat, slowly withered away for want of food and was buried with honors in a ditch on the side of the road. Slog the Intransitively Verbose had been hog-tied and gagged. Alas, also for want of food, he had withered away and was buried with honors in a ditch on the side of the road. No one ever admitted who had tied him up and gagged him, so naturally it was concluded that he'd tied and gagged himself. Unctuous Frogfart the Unspeakably Well-Mannered was found with his head in a toilet after they'd stopped for a rest at an inn. It seemed the toilet seat had accidentally slammed into the back of his head a hundred and seventy-two times while he was getting a drink. Or so Felix claimed. But, no one was going to argue with one of the Wise Men. At the same inn, Dabblenard was spotted doing something Deft with one of Feelington's Melancholy testicles and both were set on by an ignorant mob of peasants who had discovered them and "didn't take kindly to that sorta thing" in those parts. So, they were left to hang from a gibbet in the town square. Sadly, there was nothing the Wise Men could do.

When they passed through the big city, they lost two more. Pederastro, seeking gainful employment to make a bit of money for the band, set himself up doing magic tricks at a local elementary school at Felix's prompting. However, he could never quite convince the parents and faculty that his name didn't really mean what they thought it did and they ended the poor magician's life by stoning him to death. Thuribis Dumpsterspunk the Flagitious committed suicide by stabbing himself in the back with a chainsaw.

Later on, as the hay wain climbed up into the mountains, Splendicorn, the Ultra Fastidious Ranger of the Woody Dales, suffered a series of misfortunes involving mysterious, reappearing stains on his tunic along with malfunctioning cleaning products. In a few days he went completely insane, ending it all by drinking a bottle of lemon-fresh liquid detergent with Color-Safe Plus.

At another inn, Pamperlorn the Smugly Vituperative and Albiblquim the Preternaturally Not Nice were accidentally locked in a room together. They traded insults all night long and, neither one being able to best the other, died of shame before dawn.

"Okay," Felix muttered, checking names off of a list. "That leaves us with…let's see – ten companions. Are you sure that's all we can do?"

Somebody suddenly remembered that Scraggins hadn't been seen on the whole trip. Apparently he'd been so engrossed with his malodorous belly button fluff that he'd not gone with them. He was probably still at the *Pox and Buzzard*, rooting around in his navel.

"Uh, since he's still about, acting on his own volition, well, that might mean he could show up later in the story, don't you think?" Felix pointed out.

Scraggins was, at that very moment, plummeting to earth in a burning passenger jet.

"Thanks. So, that leaves nine. I suppose we can make do with that. There'll be opportunity to get rid of them later I should think."

The monks ushered the greatly reduced party into the Temple, provided them with much needed nourishment, and showed them to their rooms. It would have all been very relaxing if there had not been so much noise. A single gray pigeon flitted from one rafter to another above their heads, hurling all manner of verbal abuse.

"Hey idiots," it shouted, "when're you gonna give up this bunk religious horseshit? There *are* no gods, fuckheads! There *'aint* no hereafter! Morons!"

It flew in a tight circle over Crod the Functionless and shat a nice stream of grayish-white, semi-liquid feces on his head. It laughed uproariously and repeated. As usual, Crod just sat motionless, did nothing, and stared at nothing.

"Look at this lump a shit," exclaimed the pigeon. "The most intelligent one in the bunch. Now *there* is a fucking genius if I ever saw one! Ha!"

When the monks had gone, Felix accosted John of Evergrool.

"A few things, if you don't mind. What's with this bloody pigeon? And why don't the monks speak? Some sort of vow of silence or something? And when are we going to meet this Crasspot fellow?"

John, trying his best to hide a look of dismay said, "As *you* well know, sir, the monks do not speak because they can't hear."

"Why ever not?"

"Sir, the Heckling Pigeon has been screaming obscenities at pilgrims and the twenty monks that live here at any given time for over a thousand years. It is Immortal and quite impossible to kill. The monks tried for centuries but finally called it quits and poked holes in their own eardrums instead. It is said Crasspot the Dwarf started this practice and all monks who come to serve here have been doing so ever since."

"But, that was centuries ago! Crasspot's still alive?"

"He's extremely long-lived, sir."

"I see. And deaf as a stump I imagine. So, where is he?"

"We'll be meeting him tomorrow morning, after we've rested."

"Rested! How can we bloody rest with that ghastly bird insulting us!"

"Hey, fuckface!" the pigeon heckled from on high, "Yeah, you! What's your fuckin' problem, dipshit? Wanna go to sleep but can't 'cause a superintelligent talking bird is screaming at you? Fuckin' tough shit! Look at you! You're pathetic! Do you want your bottle you big baby? Did you lose your binky? I'll give you somethin' to suck on, shit-for-brains! Ha! You're just speechless in the face of superior intelligence, aren't you? What? Did you say something? Wanna piece a me? I didn't think so, you fucking turd bucket!"

The pigeon shat another stream of fecal matter at Felix, narrowly missing by inches. Felix seized the momentary break in the pigeon's relentless assault while backing up toward one of the many metal trash receptacles in the hallway.

"What on earth is *your* bloody problem? Do you bother to make any kind of sense or do you just choose insults at random, like a parrot?"

"Parrot! Why the last guy who called me a parrot-"

"Did what? Feed you a cracker and call you 'Polly'?"

"You son-of-a-bitch," the pigeon screamed, apoplectic and shuddering with rage, "I'll shit down your throat and peck your junk off!"

"Oooh, does Polly want a cracker? Does he? Yes, he does."

"That's it! You're dead, you useless fucking cock stain!"

The pigeon flew up to the roof of the temple and then arced down, wings back, beak targeted at Felix's skull, in a killing dive.

Felix, meanwhile, had surreptitiously pulled the metal lid off the trash receptacle, concealing it behind his back. When the pigeon was within feet of dealing death from the skies, Felix merely held the lid over his head. The pigeon, having no time to stop, slammed right into it and the metal lid clanged horribly. Stunned, its limp body slid from it to the flagstones. Felix simply picked it up by one wing between thumb and forefinger, went into his room, found the lavatory, and flushed the Heckling Pigeon down the toilet. Dusting his hands off with a sense of a job well done, he returned to observe John gaping at him.

"But - that was the Heckling Pigeon! It's Immortal! This Temple has become famous because of it! You just can't *do* that!"

"As you can see I just did, so let's just get on with this, shall we? I'm not going to wait a night and a day for this Crasspot chap and I feel sufficiently rested. The Quest is afoot and I'd like to move it along."

John of Evergrool, still in a state of open-mouthed shock at the sudden loss of the Temple's mascot, shook his head and said, "What? The what is afoot?"

"The Quest! Let's get on with it!"

"Actually, sir, the Quest is not officially begun."

"What?"

"Well, as I mentioned before, we must seek out two prophets. Crasspot knows the whereabouts of the first prophet, Stodgehrump the Back-Handed. And Stodgehrump knows the whereabouts of the second prophet. It is only after we've received instructions from the second prophet that our Quest really begins."

Aghast, Felix collected his wits and said, "Look. Joe."

"John."

"John. What Fit is this?"

"The Seventh, sir."

"The Seventh. Seven bloody Fits and you're telling me that the bloody Quest hasn't even bloody started yet?"

"That's about it, sir."

"I see. And what, pray tell, have we been doing thus far? Playing with ourselves?"

"It would seem so, sir."

Felix cuffed John on the back of the head.

"Now, look here. I've had just about enough of this. I want to see this Crasspot fellow immediately."

John, scowling and rubbing the back of his skull, went to rouse one of the monks. He returned a minute or two later, a burlap-shrouded mute in tow. The monk indicated the proper direction with a gesture. John and Felix followed.

The chambers of Crasspot the Dwarf were dank and poorly lit by some kind of phosphorescent moss that clung from the ceiling. A trickle of water leaked from a hole somewhere up on the wall, feeding a little stream that tinkled past a stone chair in the middle of the room. On this chair sat Crasspot. Or what was left of him. A grey-bearded head lolled about on top of a limbless torso.

No. "Torso" isn't really a proper description. More like a few exposed organs, some vertebrae, and a couple of ribs.

"The Venerable Crasspot suffers from autophagia," John whispered, "and has been gently nibbling himself down to his spinal cord for the last five-hundred years."

"Why are you whispering? Everybody here is deaf."

John frowned. "I'm trying to be properly respectful."

"Respectful! Of what? A deaf lump that's been chewing on itself for five centuries?"

"I've had about enough of your irreverence, sir! If it weren't for me we wouldn't be here."

"Listen, you tit. *I* wouldn't be here at *all* if I hadn't been coerced into this by the Proconsul! So far, this whole business sounds like it was dreamed up by a bunch of lunatics. I'd much rather be at home, or at least in my backyard, drinking beer and shooting squirrels."

"Heh? What's all this?"

A grey and raspy voice squeezed itself from the lolling head. John was immediately all obsequiousness.

"He has licked out one of his eyes, so he's essentially half blind, and you should make a point of approaching him on his right side so as not to frighten him."

"His right side, eh? Say there, old boy! How about telling us where this Stodgehrump fellow is?"

"There's no need to shout. He can't hear you."

"If you can whisper, I can shout. It makes me feel better. But, if he can't understand me, how are we going to communicate?"

"I'll interpret for you. I know sign language."

"Whatever, just get on with it."

John approached Crasspot with a seemingly endless procedure of genuflection and gesticulation that was getting Felix sick.

"Look, man. I haven't got all bloody year!"

John finally finished his silly acrobatics and stood before the Dwarf, its one good eye returning a baleful stare.

"What? What's all this? Heh?"

John then made a series of hand movements and finger wrigglings that Felix was quite sure meant absolutely nothing.

"What?" Crasspot shouted hoarsely, eye rolling wildly in its socket. "What are you doing with your hands, you fool! Get away! Assassin!"

Felix took out a notebook and pen, scrawled his question and, pushing John aside, shoved the notebook under the Dwarf's nose.

"Eh? Stodgehrump? The Back-Handed? Never heard of him."

Felix felt like back-handing this rotting torso. He looked hard at John who shrank visibly as though expecting another blow on the head.

"What does he mean he doesn't know who Stodgehrump is? Do you actually know anything about this Quest?"

John frowned silently at the trickling stream, stole a glance toward Felix who was still staring, and quickly averted his eyes again to the floor which was apparently more interesting.

Felix then wrote a new message, "WILL PULL TEETH SO YOU CAN'T NIBBLE YOURSELF ANYMORE IF YOU DON'T ANSWER QUESTION!" and held it in front of the dwarf's eye socket that still had something in it. Crasspot looked at the paper, looked at Felix, then gave an ever-so-slight chuckle.

"Oh, *that* Stodgehrump. Yeah, he lives under a bridge in Philadelphia. Scalps tickets and exposes himself to unwary passers-by. Loony."

"Relative to you he sounds bloody normal."

Crasspot's brow furrowed. "No, wait a minute. That's Rupert Dumpdirt. Stodgehrump died two years ago. Some drippy pecker disease or something. Whatever. Now, get out and don't come back or I'll-"

And Crasspot died.

John, shocked for the second time in under an hour, opened and closed his mouth in soundless horror and clutched at his hair, having no idea what to do with this sudden demise of his Venerable Object of Worship. The monk who'd shown them in simply picked up the expired bundle and carried it away...hopefully to be buried and not to become part of some weird feast. You never know with these wacky cults.

Felix turned to John who was gibbering and making ridiculous signs with his hands at the empty throne. Felix slapped him to get his attention.

"Oh, calm down you moron. Who was the second prophet we were supposed to find?"

"Old – old Arthwaite D-d-dufferscum, the crotchety hermit who lives in the Dolorous Downs."

"Who *lives* in the *Dolorous Downs?*" Felix yelled, yanking John's face close to his own by way of John's collar. "I *know* where the Dolorous Downs are, you imbecile! Back almost to where we started! The Downs are just a few miles from the *Pox and Buzzard!*"

Fit the Eighth

"Where's John?" asked Felchenham the Quintessentially Brilliant as they all piled back into the hay wain.

"Uh, he decided he wanted to remain here and become a monk at this fine temple," Felix smilingly responded. "Anyway, we're heading off to the Dolorous Downs."

"But, the Dolorous Downs are back where we came from."

"Yes, I know. But, that's just the way these things are sometimes, eh?" he said jocularly, nudging Felchenham playfully in the ribs.

"Yeah. I guess," Felchenham said with frowning doubt, rubbing his side.

"Say, be a sport and fetch us some lunch from the care package the monks sent along with us."

Felchenham rummaged around in the back of the cart as Felix whipped the horses into motion. He returned in a bit with a basket filled with sandwiches and started chewing on one of them.

"Hmm. Kind of gristly."

Felix turned green. "Ugh. Maybe we shouldn't eat those after all. There's a tavern a few miles up the road. We'll stock up our provisions there."

"You know," said Felchenham thoughtfully, ignoring the admonition against eating the sandwiches, "we sure have lost a lot of party members just traveling to and fro in a cart. I wonder what the odds are of so many people dying or vanishing in such a short amount of time simply moving about in probably the safest conveyance one can possibly imagine."

"Uh, pretty good, I'd say. I believe I remember reading somewhere that deaths associated with riding in hay wains are at an all-time high throughout the Realm. Leading cause of death, doctors are saying, trumping even heart disease. Never would have thought it. Fascinating stuff, medicine."

"Really? I've read no such thing. Where did you find that?"

"Can't quite remember. Say, I noticed a newspaper over in the temple. Did you happen to catch the results of the game?"

Felchenham was looking out over the mountain slopes, brow wrinkled in thought, munching absently on another sandwich and its questionable meat.

"No, I didn't. But, now that I think about it, how did Slog ever get hog-tied in the first place? If memory serves it was *you* who suggested he hog-tied himself. But, that doesn't make sense. How could a man tie his own wrists and feet together for starters, and then lie there for days in the bottom of a smelly cart until he dies? That's silly! Plain absurd!

"And then there's that Frogfart fellow…"

There was more like this, every case dredged up and examined in turn. With each having cast on it the shadow of doubt, Felix became glummer, unable to dissuade Felchenham from the topic. He could only say things like "Yes, very interesting," and "How observant you are."

By the time they arrived at the tavern, Felchenham was eyeing Felix with a suspicious squint. But, as things sometimes turn out, the party left an hour later quintessentially fewer. No one who remained saw fit to question Felchenham's absence.

Fit the Ninth

"Dude," said Pulcrust the Astonishingly Uncool, "there's a grey hair in my sandwich. Fucking monks!"

He threw the sandwich away and rummaged for another one. They had just arrived in the Dolorous Downs and had paused for a bit of lunch, except for Felix, who wanted nothing to do with the debatable sandwiches.

With their repast finished, they set off once more down the road, admiring the gentle, green hills and flowering fields, wondering why anyone would call this place dolorous.

Grogsnot the Inane took the opportunity to break into verse.

> "Perhaps it was slain by a wandering Gnu?
> "Not by the hair of my guinea pig shoe!
> "The answer spake you,
> "And thusly it's true,
> "Though aardvarks are aardvarks
> "I ask thou art who?"

"Yes, yes," said Felix, yawning, "That will be all. Let's just enjoy the quiet, shall we?"

For some time there was nothing but the incessant creaking of the cart, the steady clomping of the horses' hooves on the dusty path, the buzzing of an occasional fly, and Carter's spasmodic giggling (which was often preceded by the glugging of an upturned bottle containing some obnoxious result of the fermentation process).

About an hour or two later, the stinking wain schlepped over a rise and the eyes of all within collectively fell upon a stubby tree that grew near the road's edge. An old man sat, cross-legged and ragged, at its base. A dead, thorny branch lay on the ground before him. His eyes were at half mast, looking across the road and out at some distant point, far away over the downs. He did not move or make any visible indication that he was aware of them.

Felix drew rein and the cart stopped.

"I say there, good man. We are looking for a prophet, an Arthwaite Dufferscum by name. He's apparently a hermit who lives in these parts, reputed to have a most disagreeable comportment, but knows certain information relating to the so-called End of the World Threat. Have you seen such a one as this?"

All that Felix got in response was a slight breeze rustling the grass and the buzzing of some hidden katydids. The old man neither moved nor spoke.

"Yes, well. It would be most helpful if you could tell us anything. Anything at all, actually. For instance, 'Hello,' would be a good start. Maybe a 'how do you do,' that sort of thing."

"Hello!" Balfert shouted. "At your service! You need but ask and I-"

Felix reached over and slapped Balfert across the face. "Shut up, you jerk! Always going on with your 'Hello' and 'At your service!' and 'Can I get you anything?' and all of your preposterous kindness! Grow up!"

"It swallows the fish with pride. The doctor plays the fiddle," said Tenebrous the Cryptically Trite.

"Oh, not you too," cried Felix. "That's it, off we go!" He cracked the whip and the horses plodded on. Carter, giggling, threw his bottle at the old man. It bounced off his grey, balding head and landed at his feet without so much as causing him to blink.

The cart rumbled away and was gone.

In the hermit's notion of time, maybe an hour passed, maybe a day, maybe it was a year. Who knows? But, eventually, he slowly bowed his head and looked upon the gift that the gods had seen fit to bestow. It was a bottle. Inside the bottle was some sort of liquid. Outside the bottle was a label. The hermit dredged up faint memories of reading and slowly deciphered the script.

It was a bottle of 200-proof *Mendasi Brain Thinner*. **Guaranteed Satisfaction**, it informed pleasantly. Though it claimed to be a perfect all-in-one solution for the destruction of slugs, snails, ants, locusts, pandas, unicorns and other garden pests, it was pretty much capable of wiping out entire phyla from taxonomic charts. It was also an excellent solvent for removing aircraft paint, softening road base and general synaptic disintegration. At the bottom was the usual Surgeon General's admonishment against imbibing this substance at any time for any reason and a coroner's phone number for the benefit of the foolhardy.

The hermit had subsisted on nothing more than occasional rainwater and that nasty-looking, thorny stick for eleven years. So, when he finally shrugged and took a swig off this wondrous gift, the words "gastronomic surprise" that emblazoned themselves in neon red letters upon his inner eye, naturally came as something of an understatement.

He was at first flushed, a bit tingly, and then a bit out of sorts. His eyes widened, there was a twitch to his upper lip, a loud grinding of what teeth he still loosely possessed. Not much activity on the outside.

But, *inside* was a much different picture. "Mental chaos" doesn't quite grab the nuance of it. His brain was a broken instrument panel hurtling through the Bermuda triangle, lit up like a casino, gyroscopes and gauges spinning crazily; all the metaphorical indications of molecular insanity going about its insane business. Floating chemical globs that had never been seen before were waging a fanatical pogrom against other floating chemical globs that had been burbling around, wholly unconcerned for over a decade, completely unprepared for the slaughter that was befalling them. The zealous chemical berserkers gleefully slashed and hacked their way through the cardiovascular system, relentlessly and mercilessly onward to the citadel they sought.

Deep in the frowzy recesses of the hermit's frontal lobe was the fortress of Sound Judgment which was presently finishing brunch and just thinking of trundling off for a nice snooze when it chanced a glimpse out the window, eye twitching at the terrible sight beyond the ramparts.

Squeaking with dismay, Sound Judgment tended to the impotent task of defense. But, the marauders were far too numerous, and the epic failure of Sound Judgment was the result.

The hermit's face danced with remarkable contortions as though a wet hamster were trying to force its way into both nostrils at once. But, suddenly, he relaxed. There was a brief pause and then the hermit did two things which he had not done in eleven years.

The first thing he did was speak. Not one word. Not two. Not a carefully crafted, articulate sentence expounding some esoteric profundity. Rather, a sudden and unending barrage of stream-of-consciousness diarrhea that would have made Ginsberg retch into a hat.

As he spoke, the hermit turned his gaze to the nasty and thorny stick that served as his daily victual. A large, black beetle crawled upon the moist, chewy end doing whatever it is beetles do when crawling upon moist, chewy things. The hermit, having no other audience to benefit from his divine inspiration, picked up the stick, held it close to his face, and spoke to the beetle.

The beetle, on the other side of things, did not take the torrent of verbosity directed at it with much enthusiasm. It stared at the wet and chewy stick in consternation, morosely assessing its new situation. At last, having come to some sort of sad conclusion, the beetle crawled to a thorn and impaled itself, leaking its vital fluids upon the stick, uttering an unheard cry of condemnation at its Fate and the uncaring Universe as it expired.

The hermit threw down the stick and its poorly-treated - but decidedly better off - deceased audience and did the second of his two things.

He woozily erected his torso upon the twin withered vines that passed for legs. Wobbling perilously, bottle clutched in one dirty claw, the hermit walked – or, rather, lurched – down the road.

Fit the Tenth

"I must say, too bad about Balfert and Tenebrous," said Felix.

Bill and Carter nodded agreement as Hochphlegm and Bunglich were filling in the graves for the two noble adventurers who had recently died of something which it would be nice to know about so that the anonymous narrator may report it faithfully in the third person.

"Hay wain accident," said Felix.

Ah. Right. The cart must have struck a rock and tipped over, crushing them instantly.

"Er, actually the wain caught fire and poor Balfert and Tenebrous weren't fast enough to escape the flames."

Even though the narrator's explanation is more credible than that two grown men couldn't jump from an open cart that mysteriously burst into flames, we'll just run with Felix's story for the record and move on.

Belying his title, Crod was currently serving the function of chair for Pulcrust who was sitting on his head, picking his nose (his own, not Crod's) while the funeral ceremony was wrapped up.

Grogsnot had opened a little book and was giving some kind of sermon.

"I greet thee in the name of Quagmool the Insipid!

"Hallowed be the name of His Vastly-Encompassing Vacuity!

"Let us pray:

"Oh ye of little fate
"Thy destiny is small.
"Though thou dost walk through the valley
"Of insignificance,
"So shalt thee go unnoticed.
"The mites that burrow in pig dung
"Are greater than thee.
"Yea, verily, mighty are the ticks
"And fleas in comparison to thy
"Stature.
"Indeed thou art a mere nothing
"Under the Great Eye of the Universal

"Something-Or-Other,
"That which sees all the minutiae of creation
"Except thee.
"Thy stride is shuffling,
"Thy shoulders bent.
"Hunchbacks hath
"Better posture than thee.
"The smell of crust-laden undergarments
"Is a veritable bouquet relative
"To thy hideous stink.
"Thou shalt not receive
"Judgement
"That will mark the
"Final moments of
"The Awfully Rotten Time.
"Thou wilt walk the earth forever,
"Annoying the unwary until thou
"Art bitten in thy left ear by a
"Most unnoteworthy Blue-spangled,
"Red-and-green-striped, Star-headed,
"French Warbler bearing upon its crown
"A solid gold emblem
"Resembling the sovereign seal of Pablo Geryc,
"Worshipped in some unnoteworthy countries
"That export rare minerals by equally
"Insignificant people who are
"Unusually tall and move about suspiciously
"Across the land carrying important
"Magical texts under their extraordinarily
"Beautiful cloaks made of dragon scales
"And mumbling words of profound wisdom
"Under their breath --
"Or some other silly thing no one
"Notices or cares about as they are completely
"Unimportant and not very noteworthy in
"The least bit.
"Thou that art beneath even the
"Slightest sideways glance of
"The gods shalt receive the fullest
"Weight of their Apocalyptic Doom
"Of Grand Scale. A great waste
"Of cosmic resources shalt be heaped
"Upon thy unnoticeable, nonspecific,

"Utterly uninteresting soul.
"I spit upon thee."

He spat.

"Amen."

"Amen," the others chorused.

"Abl," said Carter.

"All right then," said Felix. There's a rather good-sized town about a mile from here. Let us make haste and get some decent food, shall we?"

Fit the Eleventh

"I've been doing a bit of research, Felix."

Bill sat down at the café table and ordered a skim-milk, decaf latte with light foam, heated to precisely 122.64 degrees, with cinnamon and chocolate sprinkles and a dry, tasteless scone. The gentleman taking the order politely told Bill that this would be no problem since *all* of the scones were dry and tasteless.

Bill placed a giant volume on the table and began leafing through the pages, searching for something. Felix noticed the cover which sported five-pointed stars, heart-shapes and smiling suns.

"What on earth are you reading?" he asked, taking up his mocha which he had ordered special. It was made with thirty shots of espresso, steamed rhinoceros milk, a tincture of spotted owl gizzard, gorilla paws, and diesel fuel sprinkled with essence of tiger testicles. He choked before it even touched his lips and upended the elephant ivory cup onto the patio where it burned a hole through the cement and set fire to a baby seal napping under the table. He angrily tossed the cup over his shoulder, knocking a dolphin senseless to the ground that had been minding its own business, munching on a tuna sandwich and reading the paper. It wasn't dead but would eventually awake with a severe migraine and permanent brain damage resulting in incurable depression and its own eventual suicide months later when it would drive a truck laden with amphetamines into a killer whale tank at the city zoo – but that's another story.

"*Feverish Fred's Fantastic Fates Foretold!*" said Bill, holding the book up so Felix could see the spine.

"Astrology! Bill, that's another one of the Hundred and Forty Seven Thousand and Twelve Apocalyptic Signs as Revealed by Zanzer Gackspin! It's ignorant nonsense, all of it. I thought you knew better."

"I'm not looking in this for my horoscope, Felix. There's an advertisement in back for an astronomer who's presenting a paper next Throg'sbuttday which he claims debunks this whole End of the World business. We might want to go see him. He says that the planet that's supposed to crash into us doesn't exist and everyone's theories about it are all unfounded. Could it be that our Quest is nothing but garbage?"

"What Quest?" Felix snorted. "As far as John of Evergrool was concerned we haven't even begun that lunacy until Old Dufferscum tells us what to do."

"Maybe we should go see this astronomer fellow. Professor Bentwick Pestbog, it says here. Out at Land's End."

"Yes, maybe, but don't forget," replied Felix, seeming to have forgotten his utter denial of a Quest just a moment before, "we still have a Quest to fulfill on pain of death by our fearless Proconsul."

Bill observed Felix curiously, then shrugged after a while with a muttered, "Indeed," sipping his latte and breaking off crumbs from his scone for the birds that were meandering brazenly around the tables. Knowing better than humans, the birds refused to touch them.

Some minutes passed while his gaze wandered. Some more minutes passed until his mind caught up with his gaze before it took off in a taxi and, reunited, compared notes and realized that his gaze was gazing *at* something.

"Say," he said suddenly. "Look over there!"

"What is it?"

"Look, in the square. Isn't that the old codger we passed on the way here?"

Felix craned his neck and squinted. "You know, I think you're right!"

They left the café without paying and sauntered casually over to the old man who was standing in the middle of the square bellowing, at the top of his lungs, the divinely inspired, endless tract that had been delivered to him in liquid form by the gods.

Naturally, no one paid him any attention and just walked around like they would a piece of particularly revolting furniture. He waved his arms and preached, undaunted, if he was even aware that he was being ignored.

"Excuse me, my good sir," Felix called out. "Who in blazes are you? You wouldn't by any chance be Old Arthwaite Dufferscum of the Dolorous Downs would you?"

Like a faucet turning off the old man stopped screaming at the sky and peered at them. He squinted and cackled evilly. His voice was rough, sort of high-pitched, and very deranged. He was also very dirty and smelled like an unflushed toilet.

"You are the Seekers of the Way!"

"Uh, yes, I suppose so."

"Now, you shall know what you must do!"

"Yes, that would be very nice. You're too kind."

The old man drew in a deep breath and let loose.

"You must find the 192 Rune Stones of Snulg…"

"The what?" asked Bill.

The old man continued. "Each is highly radioactive and glows with Cerenkov light. They're six billion tons apiece and the size of Providence, Rhode Island. Each is guarded within dungeons full of ingenious and deadly traps buried under Great Mountains rising out of Plains of Fire and Acid Mists at the North End of the World. The North End of the World can only be reached through a multidimensional portal named Hemrin who can only be invoked by chanting the hopelessly obscure and unpronounceable incantations from the Black Book of Hessig-Lorthglol."

"This is ridiculous," said Felix, shaking his head.

Bill looked around at the people walking by, obviously embarrassed, but the pedestrians utterly rejected any awareness of their existence.

"These unpronounceable incantations can only be voiced by the Giant, Bespectacled and Mute Owl of Abusardis who can only be made to speak by the wiles of the Fairy Princess of Rottenlog which lieth under Magical Oaks in the Forest of Krakhor which can only be gotten to via the Unicorn of Infinite Gratitude that is Locked in the Stable of Woe on the Isle of Grapht by a hideously deformed Imp by the name of Steve who gave the Key to the Stable to a Giant of the Clan of Kartslewidge who has recently died in the Frozen Southern Canyons of Nyargyl, the location of his Tomb of Eternally Raining Gumdrops being only known by Salient the Rude who has also recently died but wrote the information down on the back of a theater ticket which has fallen down into the Sewer of Ultimate Futility and was swallowed by the Very Fat but Painfully Wise Rat of Raynardo Heights which is close by the Sewer of Ultimate Futility and wherein lives a man who has invented a Special Dish that consists chiefly of the Very Fat but Painfully Wise Rat of Raynardo Heights of which he would like someone to fetch for him so that he may complete his Culinary Masterpiece for the Enjoyment of the Mayor of Raynardo Heights who owns a Gun of Amazing Accuracy and a Bullet that Never Misses and that also Slays the Very Fat but Painfully Wise Rat of Raynardo Heights and would be most willing to part with these Objects of Veneration in exchange for 87 vigintillion Enchanted Dumplings that can only be produced by the Dark Elf of Sumpy Swamp with his Magic Bake Set that I have borrowed last Groog'sday and will give you now for Seven Pence and a Stick of Gum."

"What? This is retarded! Come on!" said Felix

"Wait a minute," Bill interjected, "You haven't even told us what we're supposed to do with these bloody runes!"

The old man cackled and said, "The 192 Rune Stones of Snulg must be Arranged with Care upon the Tablet of Mockery and Pompous Self-Importance by the Light of a Trine Moon filtered through the Glass of Vitupegrak, then Drilled through their Centers with the Awl of

Doom, forged from the Volcanic Smithy of Mason Gree, the Greatly Expanded Harpy of the Lowlands, and into these Holes must be placed Enchanted Rods of Adamant, carved by the Lapidaries of Spaulent Nimrot whose Secret Names must be known prior to requesting their Services. Then the Rune Stones of Snulg must be spun simultaneously about their Axes until a Great Whirring is heard which Waketh the Demon Lord of Fung from his resting place in the Abysmal Abode. Once the Demon Lord of Fung has been Slain and his Foetid Corpse Buried Under the 79 Altars of Obsessive Upholstery Cleaning, the End of the World shall be Averted and One Week of Peace shall Reign before being plunged Once Again and Forever into Darkness and Ignominy."

"Well, that's not very likely to happen, is it?" said Felix.

"All that for one bloody week of peace? That's not even worth it!" Bill cried out. "Not to mention," he said, "that everything we're supposed to accomplish is utterly impossible!"

"Well, except that bit with the seven pence and the gum," said Felix, having some second thoughts about leaving.

"What do you want to do then? Start off the most insane and pointless Quest I've ever heard of?"

"Well, Bill," Felix sighed wearily, "we do have the issue with the Proconsul at the moment."

"But, Felix-"

"I said *for the moment*. For the sake of being thorough I want to hear what this idiot has to say if we give him what he wants. Do you have any gum?"

Bill sighed testily and searched his pockets. He soon came up with half a dirty, green, lint-covered stick and handed it to Felix. Felix meanwhile dug into his pockets and counted out seven pence. Then he gave the money and the gum to the old man who grabbed it all, popped the gum into his mouth, and chewed with gustatory relish followed by another bursting round of horrid cackling.

Several minutes passed.

"Well?" asked Bill.

"Before I may remit to you the Magic Bake Set I require the Hedgeclippers of Sog which can only be-"

"Oh, for fuck's sake!" cried Felix.

"-found under the Vorpal Rock of Rabbly Grove which is protected by the Voorish Undead of Glume, Ruled by the Unlikable Liche of Lichee Nut Lane who waves unnecessarily a cardboard placard proclaiming the Ventriloquist of Snathwrill will only listen to those who wax Phantasmagoric on Every Third Leap Century counted from the Establishment of the City of Unter Bockwroth which has-"

Profoundly irritated, Felix and Bill left the old man to his rambling and cackling and departed the square to round up their fellows.

When they were all assembled, Felix told them they were all going to journey to Land's End and speak with a professor there about the subject of their Quest – and hopefully get some straight answers at last.

The remainder of the day was spent gathering provisions and appropriate transportation, everyone getting a bit sick of smelly carts and tired nags. Carter spent some time at the apothecary's to down a few bottles of whatever without even looking at the labels while Bill took in some local culture by way of the town's red light district. Felix was looking to upgrade his .357 Smith & Wesson for something more "youthful and edgy." The unsmiling, heavily-muscled Russian arms dealer he encountered at the "novelty" shop was quick to oblige him.

"We have here only novelty paperweight, sold for entertainment purpose only. This is paperweight," he said, handing over a Glock nine-millimeter. "Look and function like real thing. For entertainment purpose only."

Felix duly entertained himself at the firing range in back, obliterating a wooden target that looked like it might once have been a carven image of Trotsky.

"Indeed, good fellow, it certainly does seem like the real thing. Fooled *me*! I'll take it."

Satisfied with their purchases, the Three Wise Men scampered out of town.

Fit the Twelfth

They had been riding in a taxi for more than an hour to Land's End when the driver suddenly lost control of the vehicle following a very loud report and crashed into a telephone pole. Pulcrust and Bunglich flew through the windshield and were killed instantly.

"Well, at least *I* didn't have anything to do with it this time," muttered Felix, dragging Bill and Carter away from the wreckage. Hochphlegm enlisted the aid of Grogsnot to extract Crod. The decapitated driver was left where he was.

"Did you hear that noise before we crashed, Felix?" said Bill, panting heavily.

"Yes, sounded rather like a gunshot."

Trees lay thick on both sides of the road making it quite impossible to see anything beyond. Grogsnot and Hochphlegm succeeded in setting Crod upright, who performed his usual schedule of nothing. When the bullet went through his head he didn't move, blink or gasp. Grogsnot dived flat to the ground and Hochphlegm screamed. Another rifle shot struck Hochphlegm between the eyes and he was down.

The shots seemed to be coming from the right side of the road, so the Three Wise Men ran for the cover of the left.

"Are you sure you had nothing to do with this?" Bill whispered after they had concealed themselves behind a large redwood.

"I'd love to take credit, Bill, but I'm afraid not."

Silently, across the road, three debatable figures emerged from the trees. Two identical, rough-looking villains (one of whom was carrying the rifle) and a loping creature with long arms, greenish-gray skin and mangy hair, approached their hiding place.

They stopped just a couple yards from their tree. The one with the rifle called out to them. "Come out from behind there! If you don't come out on the count 'o three we'll 'unt you down and blast you full 'o 'oles! One...two..."

The Three Wise Men stood and came out, arms raised, before the lethal numeral was reached.

"Search 'em!"

The ugly creature with green skin loped over, efficiently stripping their pockets of all their belongings, stuffing them into a bag it carried for the purpose. Its yellow eyes never left them as it searched and it grinned a nasty grin with teeth of the same color. Its breath brought on a delirious nausea and it smelled like it had only just recently bathed in sewage. When it was finished it stepped back, leering.

"Now then," said the ruffian with the artillery, "you three are to come with us. The other one stays."

By 'other one' he meant Grogsnot. By 'stay' he meant the troll tearing Grogsnot's skull from his shoulders.

"Well, I guess that's all of them," said Felix. "At least *some* good's come of this."

"Shut up," said the rifleman. "You just need to know three things. My name's Tweedle, his is just Dum, and that one over there is Stump the Hydrant Troll. We're all gonna walk through these 'ere woods to our secret hideout located at the house of the Limping Leprechaun of Lamehaven on 209 Filbert Lane. Got that?"

"209 Filbert Lane, got it. But, that was four things, not three," said Felix, giving Bill a surreptitious nudge. Bill felt around in a hidden pocket and pressed a button.

"Whaddayou mean?" said Tweedle gruffly.

"Well, you gave the names of yourself and your two friends – that's three – and then the location of your secret hideout – four."

"Ha! You're tryin' to trick me into givin' away the location of the secret hideout! You can't fool me you creep!"

"Let's beat 'em to death," said Dum, producing a cudgel.

"Don't be dumb."

Dum frowned and scratched his head. "But, I *am* Dum."

"The Leprechaun paid us to bring these three to 'im alive so he can talk to 'em about the End of the World which is nigh. *Then* we can kill 'em."

"Now," Tweedle said to the Three Wise Men, "let's get movin'!"

"Let's eats them," said Stump.

"No, you idiot. We're not goin' to eat 'em! I just told you that we gots to take 'em to the Leprechaun and we can't take 'em to the Leprechaun if they's ate! Now, let's get movin'!"

Stump suddenly noticed something on the ground and picked it up. "Oh, look, Tweedle! A starburst!"

"I wouldn't open that if I was you, Stump," said Dum.

"Why not? I's hungry I am."

"Just opening the wrapper on one of those'll teleport you straight to Wisconsin. The Grey Ones from Zeta Reticuli told me that," said Tweedle, proudly, at this rare display of knowledge (and somewhat shocked at himself as well).

"Heh heh," said Stump. "Right. Wisconsin. You're all daft."

Apparently the seriousness of the matter was lost on Stump. One moment he was there, scoffing, and in the next he was gone.

"Hope he likes cold weather and cheese," said Dum, sadly shaking his head.

"Oh, it'll be all right. It's summer there about now."

"Eh, how do you two know so much about Wisconsin?" asked Bill.

"'Cause," said Tweedle, "we's fictional characters in a nonsensical tale of fiction. We can know whatever we please, if'n you don't mind."

"Actually, we do mind," said Felix.

"Now don't go bein' unpleasant!" yelled Dum.

"Or rude!" exclaimed Tweedle.

"Or skeptical," said Dum.

"Yeah, we don't like being questioned by know-it-all creeps like you. How do we know you isn't some kind of disinformation agent for the Great Conspiracy?"

"Yeah! Let's beat 'em up and search 'em roughly for identification papers!"

"Yeah, are your papers in order, creep?"

"Papers?" Felix asked. "Em, you just searched us and emptied our pockets of everything we had. And I'm afraid we're not agents for anything."

"So says *you*, creep! Look how groveling and sniveling and creepy you are, skulkin' about like that!"

"Uh, no, 'fraid we're not skulking either, sorry."

"Oh, yeah?" yelled Tweedle. "Prove you isn't – creep!!"

"Do you know any other defamatory epithets besides 'creep'?"

"Ah, see? There you go again with all them suspicious questions!" said Dum. "I gotta mind to pummel you to smithereens!"

"What? Who talks like that?"

"I gots a cudgel with your name on it, creep! How would you like a cudgel sandwich? You'd like that wouldn't you! Well, you 'aint gettin' any! Now buzz off before I do something *really* weird!"

"Oh, all right," said Felix, "we'll just be off then."

The Three Wise Men started walking back into the woods and were almost out of sight when Tweedle smacked his forehead and fired a shot at them.

"Oh, you're a tricksy sort, 'aint you! Almost had us there!"

Tweedle and Dum caught up to them, rifle aimed and cudgel ready.

"Now," said Tweedle, "you're gonna go with us to the Leprechaun's house, 'aint you?"

"Oh, are you asking us? We thought we'd rather just take a little stroll through the woods and enjoy some fresh air, maybe head back in a bit and wait for a lift."

"I 'aint askin'! You're goin' to follow us right now!"

"Well, if you insist," Felix responded. He sighed, resigned. "Lead the way!"

And so they were scuttled off deeper into the woods, with Tweedle making meaningful gestures with the rifle that he'd already let on couldn't be used until he got paid.

Several hours later they came to a cheery, thatched-roof, little cottage with smoke rising from a chimney. Tweedle knocked on the door with the butt of the rifle and a moment later it opened. In the doorway stood a disgustingly cute and fuzzy teddy bear thing with wide, moist eyes and a happy smile.

"Gooba!" it said with delight. It giggled like a child and skipped out of the way, letting the Three Wise Men and their chaperones inside.

The room they found themselves in was brightly illuminated with windows and a crackling fire in the hearth over which boiled a pot of some pleasant-smelling stew. Seated around a large oak table was a collection of woodland animals that muttered among themselves, deliberating over a map of the woods and the valley beyond. Sitting near the fire in a big, comfortably-cushioned chair was a Leprechaun wearing a green tunic, a wide-brimmed hat and shiny black shoes with smart, brass buckles on them. In one hand he held an over-sized briar pipe and in the other was a mug of something surely alcoholic. When the Three Wise Men came in he hopped off the chair and walked over to them, dragging his left leg along. Not only was it obviously unserviceable as a leg, it was also six inches too short.

"I am the Limping Leprechaun of Lamehaven," he said, giving a little bow. This set him off balance and he nearly tumbled forward. One of the animals at the table snickered.

"Silence!" he roared. Steadying himself, he turned to his captives.

"So, you are the Three Wise Men I've heard so much about."

"Just how did you find out about us, Mr. Leprechaun, sir?" asked Bill.

The Leprechaun narrowed his eyes and drew himself up, not that it helped.

"We are shrewd and crafty woodfolk, O Wise Man, and we have our ways. You must also be shrewd and crafty or you would not be Wise Men. Therefore we have something in common, and more. We also seem to have a common problem. This whole End of the World matter. It has caused me endless consternation and I want it stopped."

"You want us to stop the End of the World?" asked Felix.

"No, I want you to stop all the noise that's been going on about it. There is a professor not far from these woods. He lives beyond the valley north of here and is about to give a lecture, presenting a paper of his, at the Lyceum in Swatswich. He intends to debunk the small matter of a planet crashing into us."

"Well, that's what you want, isn't it?" Bill asked.

"Under normal circumstances that would be fine. We wouldn't even care. But, he advertised that he would be doing so and there has already been such a frightful blather about the arrival of this planet that people have been camping out in front of his house, protesting and making such a racket that it's disturbing the tranquility of the happy residents of these woods. We want you to break up this protesting nonsense by whatever means are necessary."

"But," queried Felix, "if the professor is going to clear everything up with his paper, why is everyone protesting?"

"Because most of the people are believers in the coming of this planet and think the professor is trying to censor it. The other protesters are protesting the former protesters claiming that the whole idea of this planet smashing into the earth is horseshit and *want* it to be censored by the Royal Space Administration. Thus, the former protesters are now also protesting against the latter protesters claiming them to be agents of the Great Conspiracy. And then there are a certain number of the latter protesters who are protesting the professor's impending lecture because they believe that, even though its purpose is to debunk the matter, it just adds fuel to the believers. They feel that the government should paternalistically step in and censor all information pertaining to the hoax to save the people from themselves. Naturally, there are others protesting *that* and a whole host of further schismatic groups with agendas of their own. It's a fucking mess."

"Sounds like it," said Bill. "What do you want *us* to do about it?"

"As I've said, we want you to stop the protests. Don't even bother attempting to reason with them. They must all be killed. Failing that, you must assassinate the professor. If he is dead and does not deliver his lecture the protesters will find someone else to harass –

hopefully far away. We will send three of our best agents to assist you: the Mindlessly Insane Weasel of Ipton Sklar, the Vomiting Parrot of Flogburton, Pookins the Interminably Cute Wonder Cuddly-" nodding his head toward the snow-furred teddy bear thing gurgling to itself by the door, playing with a rainbow – "and Pigdog the Confused Half-Pig-Half-Dog of Dumpy Delve."

"Jesus, what's with all the fucked up titles," muttered Bill.

"That's *four* of your best agents," said Felix, "not three."

"Uh, yes," said the Leprechaun. He would have shuffled his feet if it didn't involve losing his balance again. He cast a furtive eye over at Pookins who was blowing bubbles and catching moonbeams. "He's, eh, not so good."

"I see. *Then* what? I imagine there are an endless number of hideously-complicated hoops we're to jump through."

"Well, you must all go to visit the Sulking Beaver of Ulger Deep who will cast a magic spell that will allow you to breathe underwater. You must consult the Even Sulkier Trout of Ulger Deep, who will give you profiles of all the chief troublemakers within each protesting group and the floor plan of the professor's house as well as the plan of the Lyceum if things come to that."

"Come to what?"

"You know, if it comes to you having to dramatically assassinate him in front of thousands of onlookers while he's giving his lecture, sacrificing your lives for the greater good when you're captured and beaten to death by the unthinking mob."

"Yes, well, let's try to avoid that. Then?"

"That's it. I must now send for the Vomiting Parrot of Flogburton."

"What, he's not here? How long is this going to take?"

"Not long. He's just getting an ulcer looked after. Tweedle!"

"Yes, m'lud!"

"Fetch the Vomiting Parrot of Flogburton!"

"Right! Where is 'ee?" said Tweedle, brandishing his gun.

"No, I don't want him killed. You do understand 'fetch' don't you?"

"Right, right. Fetch. Like a stick or a ball. So, where is the bird?"

"He is with Bumblefret the Lemming Doctor of Vool."

"Ee's with who?"

"Bumblefret the Lemming Doctor of Vool."

"What's a Bumblefret?"

"He's not a Bumblefret, that's his name. He is a doctor."

"Oh, 'ee repairs lemmings then?"

"No, he *is* a lemming."

"*Thinks* 'ee's a lemming."

"*Is* a lemming!"

"I see. 'Ee fixes doctors then?"

"No. You are, in fact, an idiot. Dum!"

"Yes, m'lud!"

"Go fetch the Vomiting Parrot of Flogburton!"

"The Bumbling Flogot of Lemmiburton! Right!"

"No, the Vomiting Parrot of Flogburton. He is *with* Bumblefret the Lemming Doctor of Vool."

"Right! The Fretful Doctor is Flogging the Lemming Who Vomits Parrots!"

"You idiot! That's not right! Where is Stump!"

"Stump's gone to Wisconsin, sir," said Dum.

"He opened a starburst?"

"Aye, 'ee did, though we told him not to."

"I see. Pookins!"

"Gooba!" said Pookins with sickening joy. He pranced up to the Leprechaun, sprinkling fairy dust and little pink kisses on everybody.

"Pookins," ordered the Leprechaun, "show these two louts to the house of Bumblefret the Lemming Doctor of Vool."

"Gooba!" said Pookins, and whisked away in a tinkling cloud of tiny unicorns and pee.

The Leprechaun sighed. "It seems you will be leaving *without* the Vomiting Parrot of Flogburton."

"That's okay with us," said Bill.

"Then it is time to-"

"Eh, just a second, Mr. Leprechaun," said Felix. "There *is* the small matter of our companions that you've brutally slain not a few hours ago."

"We're sorry about that but-"

"No, no! Don't apologize! They were quite useless, always getting underfoot, and ate a lot. I actually just wanted to thank you."

"Oh, I'm glad you feel that way. As I was going to say, it was something that had to be done. We are aware of this Quest set upon you by Proconsul Vug, but he is quite irrelevant. It is Lord Smirch who provided those companions, and I must inform you that their sole purpose was to hinder you and sabotage your efforts for he definitely does not desire these protests to end. Even now, as the Even Sulkier Trout of Ulger Deep will tell you, his agents have penetrated all of the protesting groups and are orchestrating them to even headier heights of controversy and hysteria. The last thing Lord Smirch wants is for you to succeed in your Quest, because you would inevitably discover the truth and uncover his real plan."

"Which is?" Felix prompted.

"Which is to-"

Just at that moment, a squad of Space Marines from the planet Zog Beta 12, out of the Bortvar Battle Station, burst into the cottage and shot up the place, killing everything except the Three Wise Men.

A gruff, beady-eyed sergeant with a jaw that looked like it could break cinder blocks in half, stepped smartly forward out of the smoke and saluted. The Three Wise Men sheepishly saluted back.

"Sir! Mission accomplished, sir!"

"Yes, thank you, sergeant," said Bill with a small groan as he looked at the carnage.

"Sir! Are there further orders, sir!" His eyes glistened at the idea of more killing and destruction.

"Uh, no, sergeant, that will be all."

"Sir, yes, sir! Returning to base, sir! Fall out!"

The Space Marines stamped out the door and were gone.

A few hours before, at the time of their capture, when Felix had nudged Bill and Bill had pushed the secret button, a steady and certain chain of events had been set into action. The panic button sent a constant signal of distress, along with their tracked coordinates, to a top secret communications satellite hovering in geostationary orbit above the planet. This satellite amplified that signal and sent it to another top secret relay station behind the moon which then transferred the signal at superluminal speed toward the Antares military communications interchange and then on to the Grock Sector commlink and the Dreck 4 hyperjunction where it finally beamed the call to the Zog Beta 12 Bortvar Space Marine Battle Station which immediately scrambled a squad into a Fast Attack Personnel Carrier. Within hours the signal's source was tracked to its most recent location and the Space Marines unloaded to do their destructive work.

Of course, the Three Wise Men had forgotten about this chain of events after the button had been pushed and their situation had changed.

Now the Three Wise Men stood in a heap of decimated animal parts and one shredded Leprechaun, wishing very much to be somewhere else.

"Oops," was all Bill managed to say.

"I think we'd better leave," said Felix.

"Gwulfer worblish," said Carter.

"Oh, you're still with us? I always seem to lose track of you."

As they stepped out into the pine-fresh air of the woods Felix said, "I wonder how we get to Ulger Deep?"

"We knows 'ow to get to Ulger Deep," said an unfortunately familiar voice. Like a drunk-driving incident where the innocent victims always seem to get maimed or killed while the drunkard who caused it walks away unscathed, Tweedle and Dum emerged from the bushes.

"Oh, for the love of God," Felix moaned.

"We was standin' just on either side of the doorway, so when them creeps come bargin' in on us, we just dives out the door and into these 'ere shrubs we did. So, you don't have to worry about us no longer."

"Worrying wasn't exactly what we were doing."

"You need to get to Ulger Deep. We knows the way. We'll take you there," said Tweedle.

"If'n you gots money," said Dum.

"No," Felix said, "sorry. Don't need any guides, thank you."

"Well, you'll need protection at least," Tweedle suggested.

"No, we can take care of ourselves, thanks."

"We don't have any money," Bill added.

"'Oy, wait! They's already paid, Tweedle! When we's emptied them pockets back on the road!"

"That's right, Dum! We're gonna 'elp you fellas anyways, seein' 'ow you already paid and such."

"But," Felix reasoned, "Stump was holding the bag when he was teleported to Wisconsin, and that's where the money is."

"Ah, no. We wouldn't trust that slimey creep 'oldin' our spoils, would we Dum?"

"That's right, Tweedle. You see, we gots this other bag. When stuff is put into the first bag, it disappears from *that* bag and reappears in *this* one. Tricksy, eh? So, we can send the troll to *grab* the loot, 'ee thinks 'ee's 'oldin' the loot, but we actually *gets* the loot."

"Yes, very clever. You can keep the money; just give us our stuff back."

"All right, but no tricksy tricks!"

Dum passed them back their belongings, including Felix's Glock, which is what he really wanted.

"Now, we goes to Ulger Deep," said Tweedle.

"Yeah, follow us!"

And they marched off into the forest. The Three Wise Men, seeing they had no other choice, hung low their heads and trudged after.

"I wish people would stop helping us," grumbled Bill.

Fit the Thirteenth

"Well," said Felix, "now that we have a better idea of what's going on and that Lord Smirch is up to something illicit, we can actually begin our Quest in earnest and find out what the hell is going on."

"You mean," Bill said, "the Quest we could've been done with already if we hadn't called in the bloody Marines. The Leprechaun was on the verge of telling us what this nonsense was all about."

"Let's not ruminate too hard on that. Water under the bridge, eh?"

"Eh."

"Flibblkj," said Carter.

"Look, nobody was talking to *you*. Go eat some mushrooms or something." Carter wandered off, unnoticed.

"However," said Bill, "we're not really fulfilling *Vug's* wishes by finding out what Lord Smirch is up to, are we?"

"I was thinking about that. All the Proconsul tasked us to do was find out what this End of the World business is about and how he might set about punishing it properly. And his last words to us were an expressed desire to never see us again, a wish I will carefully adhere to. Our job is merely to report, which I plan to do in a letter, rather than in person, not to worry. We're fine on that score. As for *what* to report, well that's what we're doing now: reconnaissance. And here is where we will hopefully get the intelligence for that reconnaissance."

Before them was an expansive lake, the water deep, green and placid. Running roughly around the edge was a massive dam made of sticks, twigs and tree trunks, in the middle of which was a log stump with a furry thing sitting on it, hunched and sullen. Its frown could be seen even from where they were standing. A dark little cloud hovered above its head letting fall a gushing downpour, tiny bolts of lightning flashing within. They had arrived at Ulger Deep, and yonder was the Sulking Beaver who sulked on it.

"We'll just wait 'ere while you goes and talks to it," said Tweedle.

"Yeah," continued Dum, "we's a bits tired of talking animals of late. They just gets shot at and don't pay."

Felix and Bill took a few tentative steps onto the dam, found it sturdy, and walked with greater confidence down its length to greet the Beaver.

"Hail, O Sulking Beaver of Ulger Deep!" said Felix.

"Hail yourself, fuckwad," replied the Beaver crossly.

"How rude," said Bill, taken aback.

"Don't like it? Turn around and head back the way you came, jerkoff."

"Oh, Puissant and Sulking Beaver of Ulger Deep," said Felix, bowing. "It is with the greatest humbleness we ask your permission to speak with the Even Sulkier Trout who lives in said same Deep."

The Beaver just sat and sulked, saying nothing.

"Oh, Supreme, Sulking Master, it is with utmost meekness that we ask of you your blessing upon our onerous task and allow us to enter the cool and refreshing waters of the Deep so that we might speak with-"

"Go ahead," growled the Beaver, "it's a fucking cesspool. Knock yourselves out."

Felix and Bill gazed into the water for a moment, which looked to them like the cleanest lake they'd ever seen in their lives.

"Oh, Great Beaver, Mighty and Brooding, it is with the greatest hesitance that I say unto you – for great is your wisdom - that we are but lowly dwellers of the land and cannot breathe the sweet, aqueous medium that is your magnificent kingdom."

"Well," said the Beaver, "I guess you're fucked then."

"Oh, Magnificent and Pouting Beaver, it is said that you possess immense thaumaturgical skill and that you would provide for us a means to access the depths of the Deep so that we might speak with-"

"You wanna see a magic trick?" the Beaver asked.

Felix and Bill looked at each other and then back, nodding enthusiastically.

The Beaver produced a slide whistle and began playing it. From somewhere deep in the lake, bubbles began to surface and pop. After awhile a trout thrust upward from the bubbles, bloated and bursting with a serious case of bends. It floated toward the dam and the Beaver waddled over, plucked it from the water and tossed the carcass at Bill's feet.

"That the fucker you wanted to talk to?" asked the Beaver.

"Well, not anymore it seems," said Bill dismally.

The Beaver waddled back to his stump and plumped down audibly with a little grunt. "Well, that's all you get. Now beat it. Let a Beaver pout in peace."

Felix, grimacing, prodded the trout with his foot and noticed it had disgorged some contents from its exploded innards.

"I say! Look, Bill. Parchment! Two floor plans and a list of names. Just like the Leprechaun said!"

"You know the Leprechaun?" asked the Beaver menacingly.

"Well, yes. He's the one who told us to come here."

"Goddammit! You should've said so, you morons, instead of puking up all that flowery bullcrap! Dumb assholes."

Bill bent and retrieved the odious, dripping documents. "Well, this is what we came for, so I guess we'll be off now. Thank you very much for your help."

"Go fuck yourself," said the Beaver and lapsed into a Sulkier Sulk than he'd ever Sulked before.

When they arrived back to shore they found Carter playing draughts with Tweedle and Dum. Apparently many games had already been played and the two idiot mercenaries had lost a considerable amount of money.

"We have what we came for," said Felix, so let's be off."

"Zdfrigu," said Carter.

"Why do we keep bringing him along?" asked Bill.

Fit the Fourteenth

They were seated at the bar of *The Broken Strumpet* tossing back mug after mug of grog, listening to a shitty local band cover the hits of famous bands that, at one point in their careers, actually had *real* talent. The barmaids were buxom, the clientele boorish, but it was busy. Land's End was just a couple miles up the road and the protesters numbered in the thousands, bringing lots of business to this and other watering holes in the region.

The Three Wise Men were going over the documents thoroughly and formulating their plan of attack – a dull task that's always easier to do in a noisy bar with lots of scantily-clad barmaids serving enormous quantities of alcohol.

"Shut up, Carter," said Felix. "Even if you had the best plan in the Universe, I wouldn't ask, because I can't understand a fucking thing you say. Bill? What do you think?"

"I think we should-"

"Right! That settles it! We go directly to the professor's house and find out what his paper is all about. Then we assassinate him if necessary. If the protesters don't leave, we insinuate ourselves among them and sabotage them from the inside."

"You won't get past the professor's guard at the door."

"What's that Bill?"

"I didn't say anything."

Felix looked over at Carter. "I know *you* didn't say it, because it made sense. Who said that?"

"I did."

Felix looked suspiciously around the bar. There was no one else besides Carter and Bill. Tweedle and Dum were off dancing with some protesters, the *Proletariat Princesses of Peace*, or something stupid.

"For the last time, who said that?"

"I did," said the voice, and this time it came from somewhere underneath the table.

"Where are you?"

"You're sitting on me."

"Eh?" said Felix, jumping up suddenly.

"'Tis I."

"I who?"

"I am Howie the Wretched Barstool. Glad to make your acquaintance. Not often a Wise Man sits on me."

"Why wretched?"

"Well, look at me. I'm a sentient barstool. How good can things be?'

"How did you come to this condition?"

"He's a prince!" exclaimed another voice near the bar, behind him. "And so am I!"

"And who said *that*?"

"Look behind you, to your right."

Felix peered over his shoulder and saw a bucket awkwardly smiling up at him from the floor. The reason for a bucket being positioned so near them next to the bar he didn't want to know, though he suspected it had something to do with Carter's green visage and his swaying manner.

"I am Sput the Dread Bucket. My friend over there is Howie the Wretched Barstool, and we are Princes!"

"How utterly dreadful."

"Yes, isn't it?" said Sput.

"If you're Princes, why are you shaped like a bucket and stool?"

"It's magic," said Howie wretchedly. "A wicked religious fanatic changed us. We're on a Quest to save Dogbiscuit the Extraordinarily Ugly Princess from the Priests of Ma'alox."

"Dogbiscuit?"

"Well, her real name is Everphesia of Svelte, but everyone just calls her Dogbiscuit."

"I see. And what has your Quest to do with the professor?"

"He can change us back to Princes!" said Sput.

"But," said Howie despairingly, "the guard at the door of the professor's house is a mean old bastard. Won't let anyone pass, least of all a barstool and a bucket."

"But you're Wise Men," shouted Sput gleefully. "You can help us."

"I see another impossible list of tasks coming on," Bill said.

"Never fear, Bill. Something's just wrong with the narration."

Oh, really?

"Yes, these barroom utilities were supposed to help *us*, not the other way round."

They were?

"Yes."

Oh. Let me check my notes.

*　*　*　*　*

"We," said Howie forcefully, wobbling a bit to give a nod toward Sput, "will help you gain entrance to the professor's quarters. You can have faith in us. We were there before the Priests of Ma'alox changed us. Isn't that right, Sput?"

"Right you are, Howie!"

"Oh," said Felix to the anonymous narrator, "not even a word eh? Not a 'You were so right, Felix!' or a 'My mistake!' Just give a few asterisks to suggest a pause and then on with the story, is that it?"

What do you want from me?

"A fucking apology would do nicely. You're supposed to be narrating and we seem to know more about what's going on than *you* do?"

Oh? Like the murder of Balfert the Salutory and Tenebrous the Cryptically Trite? I swallowed your version of events for the benefit of the reader but I know the truth! You killed those two men in cold blood and set that cart on fire to hide the evidence of your foul deed! Didn't you! Didn't you!!!

"Foul deed?! You helped me eliminate more than half the party you hypocrite!"

"Gentlemen!" said Bill, interceding, "Gentlemen! Let bygones be bygones. The tale is near conclusion. Don't ruin it just before we finish!"

"All right, all right!" said Felix angrily, all ego-bruised and butt-hurt.

"Shut up, you!" said Felix to the perfectly innocent anonymous narrator.

"Innocent! I *really* wouldn't be here if it weren't for *you*!"

"Gentlemen!" exclaimed Bill, yet again. "The stool and bucket want to go with us. They can guarantee entry to the professor's residence, but we must go now because the Priests of Ma'alox are going to be here soon for their evening meal."

"When will we get there if we take another cab?" asked Felix.

"In half an hour," said Howie.

"Half an hour! To go a couple of miles?"

"The cab drivers are notoriously dishonest in these parts."

"I'll bet," Felix grumped, "Let's get going then."

Fit the Fifteenth

The taxi ride through the valley was uneventful, the roads smooth, the sights scenic, the beers that Carter had bought cold and refreshing.

"Too bad," said Felix, "about Tweedle and Dum, eh Bill?"

Bill, frowned. "I think you're getting a little too comfortable with this killing thing," he said.

"Well, as long as you still make up excuses and continue to be an accessory, you've got nothing to worry about, do you Bill?"

"What do you mean by that?"

"Oh, nothing. Say, look, a refugee camp."

"That's the protesters, Felix."

"Ah, what a bunch of lousy good-for-nothings. Look, that chap thinks he's actually making a point by smearing his own feces on the courthouse door. And those blokes over there bogging down commuter traffic, preventing people from getting to their places of employment. Nonsense. Another one of the Apocalyptic Signs, Bill. Just another one of the signs."

"You're drunk."

"Blame Carter; he bought the beer. And it *is* quite delicious, I must say."

"We're almost there," Howie said from the front passenger seat.

"Worblfrugmvig."

"What's that, Carter?

"That was the Dread Bucket," said Bill. "He's in the trunk."

"Oh. Well, what did he say?"

"I haven't a clue."

"He said," said Howie, "that we might want to stop and have a look around. Get a sense of what these protesters are about."

Howie had the taxi driver pull off near an open field where some tents had been set up. Camera crews from local and national TV stations were milling around. As the Wise Men got closer to the nearest news reporter they began to hear what all the tumult was about.

"...and controversy abounds at this remote field just a mile away from Land's End. Arseburn, a local sheep farmer, discovered mysterious circles in his field this morning and reported them to the authorities. The investigation, led by Land's End Police Chief Albert K. Hall, could find no clues as to the source of these mystifying formations. Baffled, the police turned to Crop Circle expert Doctor

Richard Chowder of Pompous Asshole University out of Codswollop, Ar-Kansas, who is here today, examining what he believes are not proper Crop Circles at all, but more mundane Crap Circles caused by lopsided sheep. Apparently one whole side of these poor animals is paralyzed, caused by a stroke, which makes the sheep graze in circles. Knowing this makes for boring news, we called in another expert, Great Zak, the prophet, who maintains that the Crap Circles are still mysterious and are messages from the gods that live on the approaching planet. The fact that the cause of the strokes the sheep have suffered are still unexplained gives him, he says, the right to invoke *supernatural* causes without providing even the slightest bit of supporting evidence, a method we journalists certainly agree with. This is Crock Blather of *Gee Fuckin' Whiz News,* reporting live from Land's End. Back to you Wacky Wallace…"

They moved through the mass of journalists, avoiding the vortex of rancid cologne and oil-slicked hairdos, to get a better look at the Crap Circles in question. Out in the field were more journalists snapping pictures and police gathering samples of ordure.

The Three Wise Men, the Bucket and the Barstool turned their attention to another gentleman who was sitting cross-legged, off a ways, on top of a pile of dung in the center of another spiraling Crap Circle.

"That's Great Zak," said Bill to Felix.

"You know him?"

"No. I've read a few of his books, though. He's the chief proponent of the idea that there are ancient astronauts, described as gods in age-old myths, living on the planet that's supposed to smash into the earth. Apparently he's got the hots for one of the goddesses and fervently hopes to finally meet her."

"He's lusting after an ancient goddess?"

"As I said: apparently. She can't look too good by now. At least not by modern standards. But, I suppose if that happens he'll at least be saved an instant later when the planets collide and blow to pieces."

"Some back-up plan. That won't work out too well if she turns out to be absolutely ravishing after all."

"Yes. I don't really think he thought that through too carefully," Bill mused. "But, given some of his bizarre theories, I think he's probably *used* to not thinking things through."

"Oh Inanna," Great Zak called out to the sky, arms upraised, "come to me! I await thee! For your slightest favor I beseech thee!"

And then Great Zak lowered his arms and exploded with insane laughter.

"Krikey!" Felix shouted, "He's gone clear off his rocker!"

"A few tools short of a shop," Bill remarked.

"And now," said Great Zak with mad glee and to the horror of onlookers, "I shall pee into my mouth!"

That was enough for the Three Wise Men. They turned heel and fled the scene, not slowing their pace until they were back among the tents where Crop Circle hucksters of every stripe were selling books, DVDs, lecture tapes and T-shirts.

"We're only a mile away from Land's End proper," said Bill. "Why don't we just walk from here on in?"

"Good idea, Bill."

So, taking a circuitous route through the tents so they could avoid paying the still-waiting taxi driver, they crossed a few empty fields and didn't come back out onto the road until they were safely hidden from view behind a line of trees.

Fit the Sixteenth

The town of Land's End was a shambles. The protesters had so completely overrun the place that the townspeople had taken up signs and shouted slogans, protesting the protesters. The normal functioning of the town had been utterly turned on its head. Electricity, gas and water had been shut off in most places. The majority of businesses, except a few pubs, had closed their doors. The town hall now served as sleeping quarters for indigent hippies who had been drawn to the manic carnival like flies.

Drugged-out weirdos talked to themselves or to inanimate objects in the streets. People, numbering in the hundreds, were mugged and beaten daily. Emergency services had been effectively cut off, the police station now being used as headquarters for the dominant crime family. Fire trucks and police cars lay on their sides or were set aflame. Hospitals and churches were burnt to the ground.

None of this stopped various sleazy corporations from making a buck. Hiring mercenaries to protect their ventures, several bazaars had been established in the central town park selling all manner of snake oil and disaster-preparedness malarkey, not to mention the usual New Age staples: crystals, tarot decks, astrology texts, incense and the myriad knick-knacks from Eastern and Western traditions that always seem to proliferate in such venues. Traditions, it should be added, that would be horrified at this ignorant larceny of their philosophical notions if they weren't making so much money off of it themselves.

Since there was no waste removal, the portable shitters that had been set up began to pile high with feces and soon there was crap everywhere. Between the wandering nut-cakes, hippies, and unwashed religious whack jobs, the lack of appropriate sanitation, and the unremitting sales of New Age crud, the air around town smelled constantly of sickening incense, rancid body odor, shit, and patchouli. After mingling in the nose for a while, one began to wonder if there was really any difference between them.

The mass of people had only thickened since the Three Wise Men left the Crap Circles and would have had to abandon the taxi at any rate. They pushed their way through the baying herds, passing stall after stall of shiny trinkets and protesters handing out leaflets.

"What are *they* doing here?" Felix asked, pointing to a gaggle of sign-wavers.

"What everyone else is doing, Felix - protesting."

"But, what have *they* got to do with all this?"

The crowd in question was a group of religious fundamentalists shouting that everyone should "Teach the Controversy!" at the top of their lungs.

"What do they mean, *teach* the controversy? And to what *controversy* are they referring?" asked Howie.

"They mean," answered Sput cheerfully, "to teach both evolution and special creation in public schools. As far as they're concerned, one theory is as good as another, so both should be taught rather than just evolution as is currently the practice."

"Well, that sounds fair," said Howie.

"However, the two concepts are not equal. One relies on assertion in the form of faith, the other on evidence, and there is much more evidence pointing to evolution as opposed to the notion of special creation which we *only* know about because someone said so. Further, it is a fundamental precept that we, as a people, maintain the separation of church and state. Inviting the teaching of religious scripture into publicly-funded schools obviously presents certain problems. And, though it sounds fair on its face, the fundamentalists really don't have any interest in equity. This is just another ploy by extremist wingnuts to get religion and the fear of God force-fed into the brain of every child on earth."

Bill looked at Sput with a dumb-founded expression. Sput looked around as if he'd just come out of a trance and reflected Bill's slack jaw.

"Did I just say all that?"

"But," said Felix impatiently, "what I want to know is what *they* are doing *here*? There's no religion-evolution debate going on that *I* can make out."

"They're probably just taking advantage of the fact that there are so many people here in an environment with, to put it mildly, intellectually lax standards," said Sput, again out of character. He immediately clamped his mouth shut and said no more.

Meanwhile, Carter was amusing himself at a nearby kiosk. A hip, rock star-looking dude was hawking his wares. His blond hair was done up in corn rows and he was wearing semi-transparent orange shades, a black t-shirt, pre-torn and faded jeans and those silly sandals with big holes in them. The words "Grow and Think Rich" were silk-screened on his shirt above a giant pot leaf, under which, in smaller print, was some corporate logo that couldn't be made out clearly. Among the garbage he was selling, next to a series of children's books elucidating - in disgusting detail - the benefits of our bodily functions, were more T-shirts. Some of them were like the one he was wearing.

Others essentially proffered the opposite message, in no uncertain terms, that mind-altering drugs of any kind should not ever be ingested for any reason whatsoever or a parent or deity might get angry. Interestingly, the same corporate logo could be found on these as well.

Carter appeared to be fascinated by the children's books - no surprise - and was guffawing raucously at two of the last ones in the series, *Everybody Bleeds* and *Everybody Dies*. Under one of his arms was another book which he'd already grabbed up. A grotesque cartoon character in the form of a sponge or, perhaps, a Swiss cheese danced wantonly on the front cover. A cartoon bubble suggesting speech emanated from its mouth containing the book's title, *Huffing Glue for Things To Do!* Apparently Carter found this horrible volume worth purchasing and, wiping away tears of mirth, did so.

The Wise Men, the Dread Bucket, and the Wretched Stool, shoved onward through the ocean of stinking humans.

Scene 42

"Where the hell are we?" shouted Bill.

"In a forest," said Felix.

"A what?"

"What do you mean, 'A what?' Look around you! You're in a bloody forest!"

"Why, in the name of the Triune Deities are we in a bloody forest? We were almost there! The professor's house was within sight! Why?"

"Why, indeed," moaned Felix. "Oh, Anonymous Narrator," he said resignedly, "why have you done this bullshit to us yet again?"

It is with most sincere regret I inform you that the Editor-in-Chief of Mammon Publishing, LLC, has seen fit to remind me that, according to His charts and graphs, the general public does not have the patience or attention span - Rowling and Eco novels notwithstanding - for lengthy prose.

"You call *this* prose?" muttered Bill.

I heard that.

"You *wrote* that," said Felix.

Therefore, I have had to cut eighty-two chapters from this work that were deemed unnecessary.

"Thank God," Bill quietly whimpered.

Having shortened the span of the story, I have had to do all sorts of juggling about and have decided that important plot developments need to be addressed from Scene 42 which was actually supposed to take place *before* your arrival at Land's End. That being said, enjoy this nice scene taking place in this idyllic forest and when the scene is finished you will be returned to Land's End to meet the professor. Thank you.

"What a bunch of crap," said Bill.

Felix looked accusingly at the anonymous narrator, waggling a finger. "Look, you! I think you just forgot to have us do something relevant to the plot before arriving at Land's End!"

Eh? What makes you say that?

"We were just in the sixteenth fit, having already arrived in Land's End, and now we're in some 42nd scene that was supposed to take place some time earlier?"

Yes.

"I don't believe you! That makes no sense at all!"

And yet that's just how it is.

"What do you mean, 'that's just how it is'? You're writing this! Why don't you properly edit your work instead of being lazy and just shuffling papers around? Or, better yet, just excise the scene entirely and think of something else?"

I'm not going to have an argument with a fictional character. Do as I say!

"No!"

As you so sensibly pointed out, *I'm* fucking writing this! Not *you*! Goldpinch of Mammon Publishing has seen fit to –

"Rob Pharisee Goldpinch the Third doesn't exist! Are you trying to tell me that you answer to fictional characters?"

There was one of those eerie silences with some crickets.

"No there isn't! You just wrote that!"

So I did. Now you just make nice and play along.

"No! I'm taking control of plot development from now on."

You're insane.

"Actually, no. You're arguing with characters in a story that don't exist. *You're* insane."

I'll violently write you out of this idiotic tale! You know I can.

"I'd be quite happy if you did."

I'm warning you, Feelington –

"Felix."

- Felix - that I can cook up some far more painful ways for you to linger in this story as a maimed cripple, constantly tortured and harassed by the Thrice-Accursed Demons of Literary Banality. A fate, I assure you, far worse than striking you repeatedly with the Key of Deletion!

Felix's eyes were wide with fear. "The Thrice-Accursed? You wouldn't dare!"

Out over the far horizon the sky dimmed and morosely bubbled as something slow-witted and thick oozed from the very earth, spewing its terrible inanity into the atmosphere. Writhing distortions, like heat waves, undulated there, shocking all who saw it with awful visions of dull story structure, trite witticisms, mangled grammar and confused metaphors. The specter of horrific spelling, cliché aphorisms, and purposeless paragraph indentation hovered over all like a vicious parasite, mindlessly draining those who witnessed it of any possible interest in subject matter.

It was a dark and stormy night –

"No! No!" two of the three wise men cried together. "Make it stop! Make it stop!"

"Grrblik! Choflx!" cried Carter, averting his tear-streaked face from the terror that slowly burbled toward them from out the tulgey vapors.

"Whatever you want!" Felix screamed. "Whatever you want! We'll cooperate! Just make it go away!"

As suddenly as that grotesque mockery of the written word had appeared, the sky once again returned to a normal color of blue. Birds twittered in the sky. The squalid gloom of awful story-telling was gone.

We cool?

"Yes, we're cool," said Felix faintly between panicked breaths.

I'll give you three a moment to compose yourselves and get back into character. Have a beer.

Three beers appeared in the wise men's hands. They drank them slowly as they gradually recovered their wits. A bubbling brook appeared next to them to help soothe their nerves while a bard plucked a lyre atop a mossy rock on the other side. The music and the sound of the water wafted about them as butterflies flew angelically above their heads. One landed on Carter's beer can and he giggled. Bill and Felix slowly felt the terror they'd just experienced ebb away. They drank their beers as they drank in the sweet odor of pines and oaks, soaking in the sounds of breeze-rustled leaves and the happy chirping of birds as they collected small twigs for their spring nests. The bard's strumming filled them with a sense of almost meditative peace they hadn't felt for some time.

How you feeling?

"Um, better," said Felix.

Good. Ready to get back to it?

"Yes. I think so."

You sure?

The Three Wise Men nodded. "Yeah," Felix said, "yeah. I think we're ready."

Good.

Hidden somewhere in the forest a Gatling gun sputtered, frightening the birds away. The bard fell forward into the brook and expired, face down, coloring the tinkling water a deep red. The lyre crashed against the rock, twanging off-key as it fell.

A drab hovel appeared out of thin air before the wise men's eyes. The door hung uninvitingly open revealing a dark portal from which issued a nasty miasma tinged with the odor of dead fish and unwashed socks. The anonymous narrator shoved the Three Wise Men, the Bucket and the Stool through the doorway and slammed it shut behind them so as to get this scene moving along.

90

Inside was a repellent bundle of rags, hunched over the source of the ghastly pall: a bubbling cauldron filled with a repulsive, noisome stew. The grey creature shuffled about and they could see within the tattered remains of linen a wizened face peeking out at them. Its eyes were two pools of milky white, its nose a carrion bird's beak, its mouth hidden behind soiled and matted hair that may or may not have been a beard. Its sex was indeterminate, and its voice could nowise help in clearing up that ambiguity. It rasped, clucked, cackled and made other disagreeable noises. Its movements were even more disconcerting. One moment it was stirring the pot, in the next it was by a low table cluttered with trash, and then it was standing before them, grunting and hissing.

The party screamed in unison and fell back.

"Heh heh heh, yes, yes. Now we shall know that which we must yet find out, heh heh heh. 'Twixt perhaps and maybe little difference we see, let the question go round and the answer is found, heh heh heh."

"What's he blathering about," said Felix, cupping his hand over his nose and mouth from the stench.

"Yes, yes. Heh heh heh. Three Wise Men and Two Princes, 'tis the Wise Men we want, yes. Heh heh heh. Three Wise Men? Nay, but two, for the third is dead, heh heh heh."

"What do you mean 'dead'?" asked Felix. "No one here is dead! What *is* this nonsense?"

"But, heh heh heh, one of you *is* dead. But, we shall find out, won't we, heh heh heh, if he passes from the Valley of the Heretic King in the ghoulish land of Krans Jabwock. Heh heh heh. There you must go and seek Thartible the Thrice-Crowned if you wish to see the end of your Quest. And *if* you find him then all is well and the two are yet three. Yes, heh heh heh. You must seek him with thimbles, you must seek him with care. Heh heh, you must pursue him with forks and hope. You must threaten his life with a railway-share, yes, heh heh heh. You must charm him with smiles and soap."

"What on earth is this loony on about?"

"Something about time-shares and hygiene, I think," said Bill.

"But!" the creature enjoined them, "if it should not be Thartible the Thrice-Crowned and is instead his twin brother Scragmoth the Ravenous, then you are doomed. For if he should lay his claws upon you then you shall – heh heh heh – softly and suddenly vanish away and never be met with again! Heh heh heh! Heh heh heh!"

"Um, yes, that's all very well," said Felix, "but I think we should be getting on now and thank you very much for your - er – hospitality."

The ragged bundle frightened them again as it vanished and reappeared by the table of trash. It rummaged through the deep piles of junk until it found two boxes. Then it winked out once more, materialized before them and produced another gasp of astonishment.

"Please stop doing that!" Bill reproached.

"You will take these, yes, heh heh heh."

Since no one was being very quick to receive their great gifts, the anonymous narrator thrust the boxes into Felix's reluctant hands and pushed them all outside, turning off the hovel and the forest once they were out.

Standing in the town of Land's End they examined their prizes.

"Thimbles and forks in this one," said Felix disdainfully. "And a railway-share and some soap in the other. The old duffer's joking, right?"

"Let's just get on before something else keeps us from ending this awful story, Felix."

Right. And on they went. Of course, Bill, being the clumsy oaf that he is, tripped over some air and broke his nose.

"Damn you!"

Twice.

Chapter XVIII

"Only one guard!" said Bill in amazement. "All these protesters stamping around and only one guard at the door? That's all he has keeping them from invading his grounds? I don't believe it."

"Believe it," said the guard. He was an older, working-class man, rough about the edges, slightly bent in posture, but with a keen eye for bullshit. His manner said clearly he would have none of it. A clean-cut head of gray hair bristled under a jaunty cap. He wore a stained, long-sleeved shirt of light blue under a stained black vest; heavy, stained workman's dungarees and heavier, stained workman's boots. Oh, and he wore a button on his collar that read, "**NUKES ARE FOR SISSIES**," in bright neon purple.

Many had tried to argue with him, all failed. His response to such quarreling usually involved a measure of terse fustigation with a length of steel pipe he always carried that was itself stained and bent as though weary from many years of use. One end of it was currently in the guard's hand, leaning casually against his shoulder.

"Just you and that pipe? How do you manage it?"

"Come closer and I'll show you," he said. The barest of smirks touched his lips briefly and was gone.

"Well, we need to see the professor," said Felix. "If you'll just let as poke our heads in and give a little 'hello' I'm sure he'll let us see him. We've come a terribly long way and we have orders from Vug, the Proconsul of-"

"No one sees the professor. Now leave off."

"But-"

"One last chance or it gets the pipe."

"Howie! Sput!" said Felix, "Now would be a good time to do whatever it is you're going to do."

The Wretched Barstool and the Dread Bucket came out from behind Carter where they had been cowering.

"*You* two!" exclaimed the guard. "I thought I already beat proper sense into you. Want some more, eh?" The pipe left his shoulder and swung down in deadly fashion. A most convincing display of menace. It was hard to take the very real possibility that they might, after all, need to just turn around and go back because of this one man. Mere *inches* behind him was the door to the professor's home. It was already dusk as well, and they didn't relish the idea of picking their way through this nightmare town in the dark.

"All right," said Howie, "this is it, Sput! It's now or never, our last chance at freedom and our mission! Charge!"

Howie and Sput rushed the guard. In two whacks with the pipe, the stool was reduced to broken splinters and the bucket was crushed beyond recognition. The guard kicked them into a pile and resumed his former pose.

"I was needin' some firewood."

"That's it?" cried Felix. "*That* was their great plan to get into the professor's house? Rush the guard like morons? Bloody hell!"

Just then, from stage right, Pookins the Interminably Cute Wonder Cuddly skipped gaily toward the guard. Little bluebirds of happiness and twinkling fairies of joy circled about its head. It farted bliss and belched elation, gently liberating playful bubbles of cuteness that tingled like little golden bells when they popped, releasing a pleasant odor of honey-drenched love and unconditional kindness.

Nauseating.

The guard kept a chary eye on it, fingering his steel pipe, as it came to a stop before him. It raised its fuzzy arms and hopped from one fuzzy leg to the other like it had to piss, or wanted to be picked up, or some other stupid thing.

"Gooba!" it said gleefully.

As has been said before, the guard was nobody's fool. Being the eminently practical and unimaginative fellow he was, he simply swung the pipe down hard in a graceful arc, giving Pookins a proper whack, braining it where it stood. Pookins collapsed, twitched twice, and that was it.

"Bloody simulacra," he muttered. Then he gave it a good punt into a crowd of horrified protesters. He didn't even smile when he did it. Just another task; all in a day's work.

Before the Three Wise Men even had time to react, the door was flung open and a thin, smartly clad gentleman stepped halfway out of it. A mop of salt-and-pepper hair, a long moustache, a monocle, a single-breasted, black frock coat and grey waistcoat, Cashmere striped trousers, and button boots.

"What's all this?" asked the man who was obviously none other than Professor Bentwick Pestbog.

"Cretins," said the guard, "trying to get in."

"Who are they?"

"We are Three Wise Men," Felix interceded, "Fennelgurg the Semi-Pro-"

"Why didn't you let them in? I gave you strict instructions to let in anyone identifying themselves as the Three Wise Men."

"They didn't identify themselves."

"Did you ask them?"

"Well, no, but-"

"And what is that?" the professor asked, pointing at the pile of refuse that was once Howie and Sput.

"That blighted stool and bucket canard."

"Again? Who in blazes keeps sending those things?"

"I don't know m'lord."

"Well, throw them away with the others." The guard bent to pick up the detritus and the professor waved at the Wise Men to step forward.

"You three, come inside this instant before those dullards out there realize this door is open."

They walked in and were met by a dour old butler who took their cloaks.

"If you should require anything – coffee, tea, the like – just ask Laphroaig and he'll get it for you. Now, I'm very busy, so if you don't mind you'll have to follow me about if you wish to talk."

With that the professor turned on his heel and walked purposefully through the impeccable manor out the back way. The grounds were just as immaculate, the topiary neatly trimmed, and a high, wrought-iron fence kept out the riffraff. The professor lit a kerosene lamp and carried on down a quaint path of crushed white stone, past a reflecting pool and out beyond a row of hedges where they were met with the unmistakable salty tang of the sea. Soon they could hear the dull roar of waves battering against rock and the barking of sea lions.

"Excuse me, good professor," Felix called out, "but how did you know that we would be coming?"

"Not an hour before I opened the door I had been phoned by that oaf, Vug."

"I see, yes. Well, how did *he* know we'd be coming here?"

"It would seem," answered the professor without breaking step or looking back, "that he was not receiving regular reports from that other scoundrel, Lord Smirch, so he had his menial, Chauncey, go scout the neighborhood and see what was up. Evidently he discovered your destination and sent word to Vug who subsequently telephoned me. He's quite displeased that you've not thought to give him a ring and let him know what's what."

"Christ," muttered Bill, "if we could've just had that Aston Martin we could've done all this in an afternoon."

"What's all this about telephoning and giving a ring?"

"A telephone is a modern invention that people use to transmit and receive audible communication across great distances. Perhaps you've heard of it. If you're still a little fuzzy you can examine mine in the foyer."

"Uh, I know what a phone is. I was simply under the impression that I was to give a report of my findings when something had actually been found to report."

"Oh, yes," the professor chuckled humorlessly, "the End of the World, you mean?"

"Yes, you know something about this I take it."

"Yes."

"Then why didn't *you* tell him?"

"I tried to actually. But, as you must already know, the Proconsul is incalculably dim. He just wouldn't listen. Kept saying he had to hear it from proper channels and all that rot. So, I told him to bugger off and hung up."

"You told him to what!"

"Bugger off, I said to him."

"But, aren't you concerned that he'll come here in the middle of the night and arrest you and throw you into some dank pit under his manor?"

"Hardly," and this time the professor was really laughing. "Afraid of that vacuous sod? The Proconsul of Lackwit Feeng? Being the Astronomer Royal to the King himself gives me certain perks, I can assure you, not the least of which is being able to mouth off to his henchmen and hang up on them when I feel like it. Vug would think more than twice before entering my home uninvited, and for him thinking once is work enough. We're almost there now, so watch your step."

The hiss and growl of the ocean had grown steadily in volume as they strode through the night. The evening was moonless and it was black as pitch beyond the cone of lamp light that encircled them. When the machine appeared, it distressed them at first because it was suddenly standing right in front of them as it came within range of the lamp's short radius of illumination.

The Three Wise Men could only gaze in silent awe at the massive, superbly-crafted telescope. Professor Pestbog patted it, beaming with pride.

"Beautiful, isn't it? Twenty-four inch Clark refracting telescope on an equatorial mount, 386 inch focal length and an objective lens worked with glass tools."

"Are we at the edge of a cliff?" asked Bill.

"Yes. As I mentioned, watch your step. Just a few feet away is Land's End and then the endless ocean. Poetic, isn't it? A hand-crafted icon of my life's work out here at Land's End? Someday I'll get around to putting up a handrail. I don't usually entertain guests. But, for now I enjoy the open feeling of limitless space while I make my observations. Now, tell me what this is all about. I know Vug has sent you on an errand to find out about the End of the World. I'm assuming he didn't mean *this* End of the World," he said, gesturing at the precipice. "So, just tell me what events brought you to *me*, specifically, and begin at the beginning."

And Felix did just that, relating the whole of events as they occurred, from the day they stood in Felix's backyard to this very evening they stood in the professor's. Naturally, he glossed over some of the less important details such as the ultimate cause for the demise of several traveling companions, but these things happen. Bill only interjected a few times during Felix's telling of the tale, to clarify a salient point here, a neglected particular there. Carter, meanwhile, had gotten an entire bunch of bananas from somewhere and was doing a smashing job of wolfing them down and tossing the peels carelessly on the ground. Bill told him quietly several times to knock it off, but like an errant child, Carter paid no heed.

"I see," said the professor at length as he twirled dials, took notes and peered through the telescope. "And who did you say you represented?"

"Er, the Triune Deities, Fenn-"

"Deities!" Pestbog snorted openly with derision. "Pah! You're in a house of science, man. No deities need apply *here*."

"Ah," said Felix, "not too keen on deities are we?"

"You chaps claim to want to know the truth concerning these so-called End Times and yet you mumble about serving deities and watching for signs of the Apocalypse, paying heed to the slobberings of drunken prophets."

The professor looked up a moment from his notes with an air of stern rebuke about him, but then his expression shifted to a grudging acceptance, almost pity.

"Oh well. I suppose, in your own ham-fisted way, you believe you're doing the world a service – at least in part. Getting off one's posterior to go find something out is certainly laudable. But, just look a moment at the manner in which you've conducted yourselves throughout your so-called investigation. You've tramped all over the back of beyond, doing strange and unreasonable things with exceptionally odd people – and for what? I imagine if the issues at stake were important enough, exerting all that energy might prove itself to be worthwhile. But, for this? Gentlemen, *you didn't even need to leave your homes*! A simple phone call or two would have sufficed. And I'm not even oversimplifying for argument's sake. That is quite frankly all that needed doing; which ought to give you an idea as to the real magnitude of the threat.

"To your credit you were at least willing to come to my home and hear an opposing viewpoint, but it really wasn't necessary to journey so far. Not on account of *this* blithering poppycock."

"I *knew* we were wasting our time," murmured Bill.

"Well, if you knew it you should've said something a bit earlier back, don't you think?" said Felix crossly. To the professor he asked, "Look, Professor, if the issue is as unimportant as you say, why all the people outside your estate frothing at the mouth? Some of them feel that the Royal Space Administration ought to just censor the whole matter for the sake of public safety. Yet it hasn't. Why not? Looking at what's happened to the town of Land's End it really doesn't sound like such a bad idea."

The corners of Professor Pestbog's mouth turned down and his brow creased in restrained exasperation. Then he seemed to calm himself, breathing deeply. He was a man far too reserved and of gentlemanly demeanor to allow the outburst he struggled valiantly to retain. Raising a didactic finger and with carefully modulated delivery, the professor gave his rejoinder as though in a court of law.

"Listen to yourself. It isn't the RSA's job to censor information. Should the Royal Space Administration spend money and time exhaustively searching out the proponents of every crackpot theory on earth? Should they, perhaps, establish a department fraught with seedy-looking types with black bags that go abroad and silence self-proclaimed whistle-blowers? Should they do all this just to keep what amounts to a small demographic margin from panicking and doing *themselves* harm?"

"Small margin!" Felix cried. "How can you say small? Have you been outside?"

"Look. Ask the typical man – or woman – on the street whether they're worried about the End of the World; and if they even know what you're talking about, look at them carefully to see whether or not they're truly concerned. A human being should be judged not by what he says but by what he does. A person truly alarmed at such a catastrophic event would have long since abandoned all hope of a long and prosperous life or would be, at that moment, seeking some means of survival. If he says he believes in the coming end but is still walking to work, what does that tell you about the magnitude of his belief? However, you will find that the vast majority of people in the world couldn't care a whit about the ramblings of a few loonies on a ridiculous television program. Only a few people have actually been affected by the irresponsible reporting of various dispensers of news: the ignorant and, more tragically, children too young to know the proper questions to ask. One young woman that I know of actually committed suicide. But, does that mean we need to resort to censorship? Why not education? And I don't mean merely educating people concerning this singular topic, or propagandizing about *what* to think. I mean teaching people *how* to think, about *any* issue!

"We're speaking of a tiny fraction of the population. Some are concerned that the world is ending, and for most of them I argue that their degree of heartfelt belief is dubious. Others claim disbelief but suggest that we turn to a large institution, whether the RSA or some other, to take on the task of preventing bad information from getting to the public. That cuts both ways, doesn't it? Who decides what is bad information as opposed to what is good? If we allow some agency the power to make that decision without checking with us first, what power of our own have we given away? Yet, there are some who are always willing to give it away for the sake of a little safety; people much too eager to let someone else do all their thinking for them.

"And *that's* the key to this whole affair. If this same handful of people were to simply find things out for themselves they would have discovered early on that there was nothing to get worked up about in the first place. There would be nothing to censor. They would give up some freedom for the sake of safety, and the thing they were afraid of didn't even exist! What kind of message do you think that sends to powerful people with moral compasses that don't point true? De-emphasize education. Let critical thinking go away. Create a greater pool of the gullible. Then what? You can take away their power by manufacturing nonexistent threats and all you have to do is say so. Certainly less costly than creating wars for people to fight and no one need worry that it might get out of hand. It's like owning two newspapers and pitting them against each other to generate controversial news. There's never any danger of things getting out of hand because you control both sides of the reporting. In the end, however, who will be left to disbelieve anything they're told. How's that for a *real* conspiracy theory? And you don't even have to have anyone at the helm running it. It just happens on its own. It's already been happening. You can always count on the factors of human greed, ambition and carelessness to come together and create just the sorts of environments that incubate and give birth to totalitarian systems. No mad conspiracy needed. Just humans doing the self-interested things they always do without a single thought given to others."

"I say, Professor, you're the first person we've met who actually makes sense," Bill said quietly. He gave Felix a sidelong glance as if to say they should not do what they came here to do. Felix caught the look and nodded in understanding. To the professor he said, "Indeed, Bill's right. You ought to tell all that to the Proconsul – or, really, his subjects. There'd be an insurrection!"

Professor Pestbog lightened up a bit and gave a little smile and nod. "Yes, it would be nice, wouldn't it? But, the Vugs of the world are becoming fewer. Power no longer rests with those who can exert brute force, executing undesirables. Most of the world has become too sophisticated for that sort of thing. No, power lies with those who control *thinking*. Those who, in their short-sightedness, teach the next generation *what* is important, which is too often what only a few influential people think is important, and not *how* that next generation may discover what is important for themselves. We give too much reverence to the old guard, to those who came before us. Yes, it is instructive to know how the present came to be and to give due credit to those who have truly worked for the betterment of those that come after them. However, the fact remains: the reason we have our present problems is due principally to that very same old guard we have been taught to revere. It has been to our collective detriment that history in public schools is so poorly taught. Imagine what it will be like when it isn't taught at all."

Felix, apparently, was still stuck on a particular point of dispute. "Yes, that's very well and good, Professor," and he gesticulated wildly behind him, toward the town, "but all those people! You're trying to tell me that every single one of them is an ignoramus?"

The professor thought a moment before answering. "Maybe not every one down to the last man. But, then, of the remaining few that claim they are not I would have to ask, 'Why are you here with a sign in your hand?'"

"Are you trying to tell me that there is absolutely nothing at all to this business? Even a kernel of truth? Not a drop of good reason for a single person out there to behave the way they are?"

The professor had returned to fussing with the telescope while Felix spoke. Turning more knobs and peering through the eyepiece he said, "They really don't even know what *this business* is about any more than - as seems obvious - *you* do. Listen to them. Some are saying that harmful radiation from the galactic center will exert itself upon us, causing untold destruction and mayhem on the appointed day of doom. Others are claiming the exact opposite: that the rays, whatever the rays are – details are sketchy on that point – are beneficial. Further, others claim that we are constantly receiving these beneficial rays but, on the appointed day, the sun - or some other object - will come between us and these life-giving radiations and untold mayhem and destruction will result.

"Now, the selection of the end date under discussion is not random and has something to do with the Great Calendar of Uffish Thwit that somehow predicts the end of civilization. Some, as this date approaches, are already hedging their bets and claiming that nothing adverse will happen; if anything, humanity will blossom in a new era of spiritual peace and cosmic understanding. A few are even saying that we won't realize this great change has occurred until many years after the end date, and at some nebulous time in the future when we're all holding hands singing hymns we will point to that date and rapturously proclaim that this was when it all started to happen. Rather convenient. At least it gives them plenty of time to sell more books when nothing noticeable occurs. Still others are asserting hosts of entirely dissimilar scenarios that are almost always mutually exclusive with one another.

"Like homeopathic remedies that cure all possible ills, apocalyptic hysterias produce all possible ends. This is not a sign of good science my friends. It *is*, however, evidence of the mental garbage that has plagued humankind for centuries, and plagues us still, even in this so-called enlightened epoch.

"Do you realize how many times in the past the world was prophesied to end? You probably wouldn't believe me if I told you. Yet each time we came to a proclaimed date, and each time we woke up to the following morning. Here we are *still* and none the worse for wear. This hysteria will pass, and when it does I venture my own prediction. It will be replaced by yet another hysteria, to take place at some other future date. Great Zak himself claimed that his beloved planet, Nibbledeeloo, was going to arrive just a few years ago, but when he heard about the end of the Great Calendar he hopped on this popular bandwagon and simply changed the arrival date to correspond with it! I am truly sorry, but planets just don't whirl about, changing their orbits at the drop of a hat – and certainly not at the whim of crazy prophets!"

"Well," Felix ventured, "what about those saying that the RSA is censoring information about Nibbledeeloo and suppressing the full extent of the peril?"

"Think man! How do you censor the existence of an entire planet? The RSA isn't the only institution with a telescope. If this thing is supposed to crash into us in just a couple of years it would already be visible to the naked eye and thousands of astronomers, both professional and amateur, would have to be in on the cover-up."

"But," Bill asked, "what about the idea that it's hiding behind the sun?"

Professor Pestbog stopped fiddling with the telescope and chortled stridently. "My good man, hiding behind the sun you say? Lying in wait? And at the allotted moment, I suppose, it shall suddenly leap out at us! Ha!"

When he realized that the Wise Men remained stone-faced and uncomprehending he became serious and explained. "What *do* they teach in schools these days? The earth, as you may or may not recall, *also* goes round the sun."

"It does?" said Bill, shocked. Felix glared at him.

"If," continued the professor, "the planet were behind the sun it would not be hidden for long. To remain invisible to observers on earth it would have to follow such an absurdly spiral path and travel at such absurd speeds we would be talking now of a thing which no astronomer in history has ever observed. Not to mention this totally ignores the fact that others claim to have identified the planet in photographs taken from earth, which, by the way, also suggests that the almighty RSA conspiracy hasn't been doing a very good job keeping the planet's existence quiet."

The Wise Men were silent for a time while the professor puttered with the telescope. He didn't seem to have anything more to say.

"So," Bill hazarded, "no Nibbledeeloo then."

"Definitely not," the professor said curtly.

They were silent for another time while the professor still puttered with the telescope.

Felix opened his mouth as if to say something, closed it, made as if to say something again, did not. Several more minutes of awkward silence followed them like a particularly aggressive panhandler. Bill began to pace in a vain attempt to avoid it.

"So, um," Felix began, "so, what about the end date on this Great Calendar thing?"

"What about it?" asked the professor, slightly annoyed at the question. "Humbug I should think. It's very ancient and purported to be more precise than our modern time-keeping methods – presumably more precise than our atomic clocks. In addition it apparently doesn't require adjustment using leap days, accurately predicts future events and I would imagine doesn't need rewinding and will take out the trash if you ask it nicely. I repeat: humbug."

"Why humbug?" asked Felix.

"With all due respect, but do I have to do all of your thinking for you? Go see Abercrombie of Tarkington and you can find out for yourselves."

"Abercrombie of Tarkington, right."

Then Bill stopped pacing and spoke up. "Professor, if all this end of the world stuff is such utter nonsense, what's really in it for the people who are going out of their way to promote it?"

The good doctor sighed, took off his monocle, polished it a bit on a shirt sleeve, replaced it over his eye, and turned to Bill.

"What do *you* think? All the books, DVDs, TV programs and lecture circuits aren't enough to tip you off as to where all this is going? All of the disagreement over what is supposed to happen, all of the protesting, the media-driven hysterics? It all serves one purpose: to fuel controversy. And as long as there's controversy there's money to be made."

"So, it's all just about making money?"

"Don't be stupid, Bill," said Felix, "it's always about money."

"So, that's what Lord Smirch must be up to, organizing all the protests to fuel controversy!"

"Yes," said the professor gravely, "Lord Smirch is the worst of all. Some of these apocalypse theorists are, though still culpable in my book, sorry cases of one believing one's own bullshit, if you'll forgive the vulgarity – Smirch *does* bring out the worst in me. He is consciously stoking the flames, building up the frenzy *purely* for the intention of making a profit. He doesn't believe the world is going to end any more than I do, but that isn't going to stop him from preying on people's weaknesses: their fears and ignorance. His is of the utmost callousness and though I have little respect for the believers, I have absolutely none at all for him, perhaps less if such is possible."

"Well, what's he planning to do exactly? Publish a book? Give lectures?"

"Oh, no. Far worse than that. He plans to-"

The professor's answer was interrupted due to a most unfortunate circumstance in which he suddenly found himself. He had moved round the telescope to make some sort of adjustment on the side closest to the precipice when he slipped on several of Carter's banana peels, bringing him teetering to the very edge. Indeed, he was overcome by the sudden urge to do a bit of accounting, heroically attempting to adjust the ledger of his center of gravity by flapping his arms rather comically on the credit side to counteract the debit column which manifested itself as the aforementioned precipitous drop of many hundreds of feet.

The Three Wise Men stared, bug-eyed, in alarm at this tragic exhibition of bookkeeping. Alarm was traded up for horror as the professor's rapidly accrued liability depleted his capital account and over the edge he went, his corporate viability decreasing with each passing second of acceleration until all of his energy was finally transferred to a mildly surprised sea lion and his velocity and viability balanced out to zero.

"Fuck!" Bill screamed.

Felix whirled about and stalked right up to Carter. "You nimrod! You've killed the professor!"

"Wrbl?" wrbled Carter.

"Fuck!" screamed Bill.

"God damn it!" yelled Felix. He tore at his hair and stamped about in little circles. "I've got to think! I've got to think!"

"Fuck!"

"Shut the fuck up, Bill! I'm trying to think!"

Bill gibbered and gasped. "Th-that was not a bloody nice thing to do. Felix! No one else is about, right? No one saw?"

Felix stopped stamping and stared at the fateful rim of the cliff. "No. No one saw. Look, here's what we're going to do. I'm sure the professor usually spends all night out here. Laphroaig might check on him later, but we'll be long gone before then and, in any event, the evidence is way the fuck down *there*. We'll say a nice goodbye, tell the guard he's doing a great job, and then potter off down the road like nothing's amiss and never look back. Got it?" Felix grabbed Bill and shook him. "Bill! Do you understand? We just act normal and walk out!"

"Y-yeah, sure Felix…"

They spent a few more minutes gathering their wits, Felix talked them through it once more, and they marched back down the path. Laphroaig was just coming out of the kitchen with a tray of tea and biscuits when they sauntered through the manor.

"Oh," said Felix abruptly, "ah, Laphroaig. Say, we're leaving now. Thank you for your hospitality and all that."

"Yes," said Laphroaig "very good. I will see you out."

"Right. And, uh, Professor Pestbog said to tell you he wouldn't be needing any tea or biscuits tonight."

"Master said this? But, Master never takes tea and biscuits when he's working."

"Oh, uh, well he-"

"These are for our Fomorian guest, Monsieur Balor."

"Fomorian?"

"Yes, he's a giant with a single eye that kills anything he looks at. He claims that he can see everything that happens to the ends of the earth and can even see in the dark as if it were day. He is currently applying for a position here as grounds keeper and chief of security for the estate but Master has not yet interviewed him."

A giant with an all-seeing eye that kills. Fucking great, thought Felix. "Um, where is he now?"

"Oh he is out near the gazebo getting some air."

"MURDERERS!" boomed a voice.

Laphroaig looked calmly toward the back door as heavy footsteps approached.

"MURDERERS!" the voice repeated, more closely now.

"Well, we must be running along. We'll let ourselves out," said Felix hurriedly, dragging Bill and Carter along after him.

"THE PROFESSOR IS DEAD! STOP THEM! MURDERERS!"

But, the Three Wise Men were already out the door.

Fit the Nineteenth

Out in town things had become quite a fracas. The mob was now in a state of dizzying pandemonium. Factions were fighting each other with whatever weapons were at hand. More than half the buildings down the avenue were burning and townspeople were finally evacuating in droves.

A pack of snarling activists, their t-shirts identifying themselves as the infamous *League of Totally Uninteresting Gentlemen* were throwing Molotov cocktails and ninja stars at the guard who was doing an admirable job of batting the projectiles away from him. But, he was quickly losing ground as the *League* gradually moved in. It appeared the old guard had met his match. Several cocktails struck him at once and he caught alight, going up like a torch. Yelling an ancient battle cry he ran straight for the rabble, grabbing whomever he could, spreading the fire among them until he expired moments later.

Suddenly there was a mighty roar and the giant, Balor, stepped over the iron fence from the professor's property into the street. The dancing flames cast him in hellish radiance as he reached for the iron ring that, by its weight, held closed his lidded eye.

"Run!" Felix yelled. The Three Wise Men bolted into the crowd, dodging fists and rocks and gunfire. Anything but to be seen by the open eye of Balor and be struck dead.

"Felix," said Bill breathlessly, pointing, "there's a bus over there with people in it!"

Felix looked in the indicated direction and, indeed, saw a tie-dyed bus chugging slowly through the crowd. A torn sign on the side of it announced that one should be concerned about the fate of the left-handed bole weevil, a singularly unimportant insect that could actually be safely ejected from the ecosystem without anyone noticing.

The Three Wise Men ran for it and pried open the accordion door which the driver was – quite sensibly – refusing to open for them. They clambered inside and were met with angry shouts of dismay from the people filling the bus.

"Oh, but we're with you! Save the bole weevil!" Felix shouted.

"We're not *those* idiots," the driver snarled, "we kicked them out hours ago! We're the ones demanding that everyone speak in iambic pentameter! Now get the fuck off our bus!"

"But, *you're* not speaking in iambic pentameter!" Bill shouted.

Felix chambered his Glock. "Well *I* speak in imminent nine millimeter!" He shoved the business end to the driver's cranium and said, "Now drive, fucker! Step on it!"

"But, I'll run over all those people!"

Felix fired a round into the window to the driver's left. The driver's foot suddenly became leaden and there were sick-sounding thumps as the wheels ran over objects we may as well not mention. You get the idea. Putting personal safety above all and shoving morality up the ass of principle had saved the day once again. The horrified passengers simply stared mutely at Felix and the gun he had pressed against the driver's skull, trying hard not to apprehend anything that was going on *outside* the bus.

After several hours of unmitigated awfulness they were finally out of town. Felix made the driver stop only after they had gone a significant distance away from the dreadful Land's End, depositing them at a moderately-sized village near dawn. The bus wasted no time speeding off, obvious relief painted on the face of every occupant.

The Three Wise Men found a diner and ordered up a hearty breakfast. Felix and Carter wolfed down their chow with abandon while Bill barely touched his own.

"How can you eat at a time like this?"

"One must tend to the needs of the body if one is to survive the rigors of this hardhearted world, dear Bill," Felix said between mouthfuls. "Are you going to eat that biscuit?"

"We killed the professor, Felix."

"Shhh!" Felix scowled and looked around. There were only two other people in the diner and they were at the far end of the room, completely disinterested in their dialogue.

"First off, *we* didn't do anything. Blame Carter, if you want to point fingers. Secondly, and more to the point, it was simply an unfortunate accident. He slipped and fell, Bill. That's all. Nothing we could do. Are you going to finish that bacon?"

"I suppose," Bill said mournfully.

"You suppose you're going to eat that bacon?"

"No, I suppose you're right. It just seems so utterly pointless. We came all the way here to find out about the end of the world only to find that it's all hogwash. If we'd never come at all, the professor would still be alive. He died for nothing, Felix."

"Maybe, maybe not. You saw how things were going. The mob finally broke the guard. All they had to do was open the door, dispatch the butler, and waylay Professor Pestbog. Until, of course, Balor, the as-yet-unhired watchdog winked at them. Are you going to finish those eggs?" Felix helped himself to Bill's plate while Bill went on.

"But still, Felix, our whole mission is balderdash! All those people you killed, and for what?"

"God damn it, Bill!" Felix hissed between clenched teeth. "Would you mind not talking about stuff like that in a fucking diner?"

"Sorry Felix."

"Anyway, I wouldn't worry about it. They're just simulacra. And there's still this Great Calendar we ought to look into just in case there's really something to it."

"You think there might be?

"I don't know. But, in the interests of thoroughness, we might as well. Tarkington's not far from here and we can be there in a couple of hours if we take the train. Are you going to finish that sausage?"

"It's just that our meeting with the professor made me think about us – you know, what *we're* all about. He came within a hair's breadth of flat out calling us fools. Here we are investigating signs of the Apocalypse when we preach the signs of the Apocalypse as revealed by Zanzer Gackspin."

"Yes, but that's a different thing altogether, Bill. Have you forgotten your training? Those other people are crudding up the airwaves, yakking about signs which *predict* the end of the world. Our Hundred and Forty-Seven Thousand and Twelve Apocalyptic Signs are the signs of the Apocalypse that's already occurred. As far as Zanzer Gackspin was concerned, the Apocalypse has already happened and we're just living in the aftermath. I mean, look at what the signs are: products that don't increase efficiency, incredible wastes of time and energy, increasing distractions, lunatic cults and desperate religious nuttery of every stripe, deteriorating education, the demolition of the family unit, runaway corporate greed, ineffective politicians, uncontrolled consumption of natural resources, the ever-widening gulf between rich and poor, weak-willed bureaucrats fattening themselves on the backs of the working class, unrestrained media advertising, and on and on and on. If this isn't what it's like to live in a post-Apocalyptic world, I don't know what would be. All the catastrophe scenarios that wipe out humanity just seem a little too easy-going. My vision of an Apocalypse is something more like what we have now. Insensate people trying to eke out some futile semblance of a living in a totally absurd world that has never - and *will* never - make sense. Are you going to eat those pancakes?"

"I hear what you're saying, Felix, but I've been thinking about that. I mean, every living creature has to expend energy to live. It constantly has to scrounge for food and make every effort to adjust to, or modify, its surroundings. It has to engage itself in endless upkeep. That's order. Order needs input energy from somewhere else, ultimately from the sun, to maintain continued order. And what are we struggling against? Entropy: the natural tendency for every system to collapse to a lower, more stable, energy state. Every civilization in history has complained about nearly the same things that we do in one form or another. The trappings change, but the fundamentals remain the same. At any point in the past you could argue that we are living in the end times or are living in the hell after the end has come and gone. You can always argue this because no system is perfect. Every higher energy system of order is constantly battling entropy, the signs of which are always around us, little chinks in our well-regulated organization offering glimpses of the chaos that will eventually consume us when the sun finally runs out of nuclear fuel. Visible signs of disorder are always waiting in the wings, ready to catch us the moment we cease to be vigilant. The center does not hold and falls apart. Disorder is always present, so we can always point to it as evidence and say, 'See? Civilization is collapsing.' 'See? The world is going to end.' 'See? There goes the neighborhood.' But, that's already happened a million times. These are the little Apocalypses. The little ends of the world, all the way down to the tiny terminations that each human being faces when his body can no longer sustain the energy needed to fight its own entropy and finally expires. These, though, are just the deaths of the actors. The *real* end of the world is still billions of years off, when the whole stage goes. But, I guess *that* Apocalypse is too far away to frighten anybody into giving up their money."

Felix sat back in his chair, sucking food from between his teeth. He looked at Bill rather blankly for a full minute and a half.

"You know, Bill, sometimes I can't tell whether you're a total moron or an unintelligible genius." Felix paused a moment and squinted. "Or maybe you're a high-functioning idiot savant. You know the ones I'm talking about. Those shuffling hard luck cases that fool you into thinking they're normal because they've got the parts in the right place: eyes aren't where their nose should be, feet are on right way round and such – yet they have the brain of a fish stick, that sort of thing. I don't know. In any case you think too much."

Felix gargled the last bit of his coffee, eructated vociferously, strained a little toot from his hind quarters, then stood, stretched and yawned.

"Best get going. We can sleep on the train."

Fit the Twentieth

"Yes, well I like to work on clocks sometimes, except when I sometimes hear the master tell me sometimes to knock it off and do something constructive sometimes. And then other times I sometimes make little whirly things that go whoooooo! and then go read a book sometimes. Otherwise it's very dull here sometimes. But, I digress sometimes. I do believe you asked me a question."

"What the hell is wrong with him," Felix mumbled.

The home of Abercrombie of Tarkington was indeed filled with clocks and little whirly things that presumably went "whoooooo!" It was also filled with incomprehensible charts and graphs and cartographic gibberish stuck to every vertical surface like wallpaper. Diverse globes, animal skeletons, human skulls and the expected jars of unidentifiable remains among other curiosa littered the residence in no discernable order. This was certainly one of those places where entropy had gained the upper hand. Notably absent was the "master" of which Abercrombie spoke and it was never entirely clear whether he meant a corporeal entity or a product of his own *mental* entropy.

"Erm – yes, well, perhaps you could explain something to us about this Great Calendar of Uffish Thwit. Apparently it ends on a certain date in the not-so-distant future and some are concerned that it predicts the end of the world at that time. Could you shed any light on this?"

"Oh, sometimes, yes. I like, sometimes, to sit and ponder the Great Calendar…sometimes. It is quite a grand thing to see it all at once…sometimes, which so few may do."

"I'm sorry," said Felix, "but I'm afraid I can't avoid asking you what the 'sometimes' business is about. It's a bit distracting."

"Oh, yes, of course. I understand…sometimes. I suffer from *Sometimes* disease…sometimes. If you just hit me smartly on the skull sometimes with that truncheon over there in the corner sometimes, I can be thus induced sometimes to speak for a short time without saying sometimes…sometimes."

"You want us to strike you on the head with a truncheon? Have you gone starkey?"

"I don't think we ought to do it, Felix. I still feel bad enough about the professor and all those people we ran over in the bus. What if we hit him too hard and his brains ooze out all – what are you doing Carter?"

Carter had ambled over to the truncheon, picked it up, felt its heft and then moseyed on over to Abercrombie who just smiled in a dim sort of way. He lifted it high and whacked Abercrombie such a blow that Felix and Bill thought he really *had* killed him as he slumped in his chair, out cold.

Speechless, Bill ran to Carter and pulled the truncheon out of his hand which had raised itself again for another strike.

"Carter! What's got into you? You're no killer!" Bill exclaimed. "Well, except for that toad…and maybe the professor."

But, Abercrombie stirred. He mumbled. He shook his head.

"Ah, yes, that's much better," he said coherently at last. "Now then, what is it you gentlemen want?"

"We're um, needing to know more about that Great Calendar," Felix explained. "It is said that it is more accurate than modern calendars, that it requires no adjustment, and that it makes predictions of future events. Does that sound right so far or am I just getting ahead of myself?"

"Oh, indeed you are correct. It is also very old. It is thought to have been invented by the Throck tribe of Upper Nantucket."

"The who?"

"The Throck tribe. Of course, that's all thoroughgoing trumpery. Everybody knows it was invented by the Mayans who descend from alien astronauts from prehistoric times. In fact, the Mayans were a space-faring race who frequently explored other star systems at the height of their empire. It was during that time they discovered chocolate, which comes from Sirius, home of the Oannes – the fish people who visited the Sumerians, bringing with them the fruits of civilization."

"What in blazes are you talking about? Look, just tell us about the calendar!"

"Oh, of course, of course. I would show you the real thing, but it's 30,557 hectares. But, I have made small scale models of critical parts of it. Here, look," he said, holding up a miniature. It looked like someone had crashed the space shuttle into a modern art museum and then forced a bunch of blind chimpanzees to reassemble what was left. No matter which way you turned the thing it looked exactly like incomprehensible shit.

"You see," he said, pointing to a peculiar cog-looking thing that looked to be roughly in the center of a bunch of other cog-looking things, "this is the crux of it. If you look closely, you can see glyphs around the perimeter representing different days, like 4 Goat Bugger, 19 Tractor Beam, 13 Squirrel, 8 Dog Balls, 28 Aha, 7 Gotcha, and so on. When it turns, the others turn in relation to it. Let me demonstrate."

He began fussing with the small cog and a horrid grinding sound was heard by all. They waited to see the thing work as he turned it, but as far as they could tell it just looked like he was breaking it.

"Now this part of the calendar goes round and round, see? It follows the menstrual cycles of the Venusian swamp duck. This other part of the calendar goes round and round the first part in the other direction and-"

"You mean backwards?" Bill asked, puzzled.

"Oh, by all means, yes. It couldn't be any other way. You see, it follows the path taken by Edward III of Hulphingshire when he commanded his troops to retreat from the Holy Swamp of Yizz. They took him quite literally and retreated, step-by-step, backwards, all the way to Hulfphingshire, never letting the enemy out of their sights."

"Walked backwards! For three thousand miles! Are you stupid?"

The sage ignored this and continued. "These next three cogs consist of 94 weeks of 1 day each and are carefully calibrated against the twitching eye of a cormorant every time a stick is waved in its face. These other 186 wheels follow the meandering route of the drunken prophet of Wadmoor, and this *great* wheel over here, graduated into seven billion, five-hundred and sixty-seven million, eight-hundred and ninety-two thousand, nine-hundred and forty-one days oscillates at random based upon the throw of a 71-sided die and the final position of three and a half metric tons of kangaroo entrails dumped from a bucket at a height of 86 feet. Just beautiful, I must say. The mathematical genius of these ancients knew no bounds! It's no wonder this calendar is more accurate than ours. No wonder at all.

"So, as you can see from this, it logically follows that this calendar will only be off by 152 years every four days! No intercalation nonsense needed! A miracle of ancient wisdom if I do say so myself."

"152 years? Every four days!" Felix slapped his forehead with an open palm and wiped it down over his face. He walked off, muttering.

"Well, what can you predict with that?" Bill asked.

"Oh, that's the beauty of it! It will precisely predict when a particular shadow will fall across a particular rock on the surface of Mars, plus or minus 10,273 days! Splendid, isn't it?"

"What!"

"I said-"

"I *heard* what you said! That's bloody useless! What's the significance of a bloody shadow on a bloody rock on a bloody other planet?"

"Ah, yes, I see what you mean," the sage said, leaning back in his chair sullenly, "sometimes."

Bill stared, incredulous. He had not really known what to expect - not for certain. In the back of his mind he kind of thought the Great Calendar might be a little far out, but as usual, he had not expected *this* sort of insanity. This was the other shoe and it dropped on his skull, filled with cement. This whole journey, this whole doomsday affair, had been nothing but wasted time. People had died, literally for nothing. There was no justification any longer. He'd even had to come to terms with the fact that his own religion, if it could be called that, was a mockery of lucid thought. Pointless. No purpose. No meaning.

He handed the truncheon to Carter and walked out.

Felix was standing by a cottonwood tree looking quite forlorn and out of sorts.

"I'm sorry we got mixed up in all this, Bill. Even though I didn't really have any interest in this stupid job initially, after a while I thought it would come to something that would validate all the ridiculous crap we've gone through. I'm sorry."

Bill sighed. "It seems there's only one thing left for us to do."

"Yeah, I know."

From inside the house came the sound of, not one, but several muffled cracks as if a large melon was being broken open.

Fit the Twenty-First

"Good idea, Bill," said Felix downing his forty-second cup of mead. "Getting sauced out of our skulls is just the thing after all that rubbish. We'd have been better off staying at home, huffing gasoline until we died. When we get back there I might do that anyway, after I write our report to Vug, of course. And I might at least brush up on the Apocalyptic Signs. It seems I've missed something."

"I don't think you've missed anything, Felix. I think the Signs led us astray. We thought we knew what to look for, placing our faith in the Triune Deities and Zanzer Gackspin to lead the way. But, we didn't know what we were looking for at all. Our Signs didn't even relate to the Signs we were supposed to be seeking. We had it all wrong, Felix."

"Oh, bosh and bilgewater!" cried Felix bibulously. He slammed his cup down on the table, scattering the burnt out candle ends that littered it, and got himself another draught from the keg that had been wheeled to their table. "We didn't get anything wrong, Bill. Stop being such a bloody doomsayer. There's nothing wrong with the Hundred and Forty-Seven Thousand and Twelve Apocalyptic Signs. They didn't have anything to do with what we were looking for because, as it turns out, there was nothing to look for. You heard the professor - may he rest in peace - and you heard that dribbling Abercrombie nutcase. Not to mention, most of the reason we didn't know what to look for is because we were led astray by Lord Smirch and not given the proper information we needed to start with! No, Bill, *Our* Faith is Unassailable. Ha! No one has dared argue with Gackspin! Oh, no!"

"That's because no one *cares* about Zanzer Gackspin *or* his Signs," said Bill peevishly. "The only other people who know about them are twenty or so deaf monks living in the Temple of the No-Longer-Heckling Pigeon. We're irrelevant, Felix. We don't matter."

"Ah! Fiddle faddle! Tommyrot! Enough! I will not have you profane the work of our entire lives! Say there, barmaid! Toasted cheese sandwich please! "

"What do you mean? Our lives are *hardly* over! We're in our thirties. Let's do something else. Something meaningful."

"I thought we were taking care of that bit right now," said Felix as his head hit the table. He emitted a loud snore and that was that.

Bill sighed and filled his own cup with ambition-curing mead. He ordered a flame-broiled gnome burger with fairy wing fries but the serving wench returned with a three-tiered wedding cake instead. When he tried to explain to her that it was not what he ordered, the wench became quite offended. Bill's pathetic attempt to convince her that he was not making a personal attack against her or her abilities as a serving wench only made matters worse and she became enraged. Their conversation ended with the cake being dumped on Bills head.

Meanwhile, Carter was fiddling with a tuning fork, humming a matching note, seemingly oblivious to everything that had just happened.

However, the barmaid was apparently not satisfied with unloading baked goods on Bill's head. She had gone out a moment and then returned with three heavyweights shaped like bricks, each missing the essential part that links the head with the shoulders. They glared from beady eyes and clenched fists that looked more like ham hocks.

Not a word was said. One grabbed Carter who simply went on twanging the tuning fork as though nothing were amiss. The second lifted Felix out of his chair like a sack of melted marshmallows. The third just walked over to the cake-encrusted Bill and bonked him on the head with a ham hock.

We will now draw the curtain on this horrid scene.

Fit the Twenty-Second

And fade in to an entirely new one.

The quarter-deck of the good ship *Albatross*. The sun, high overhead, beats unmercifully down upon our Three Wise Men. Felix is already up and about, vomiting over the railing, one hand clasping the rigging. Carter is humming to himself. He is examining a brass telescope on a tripod. They're not alone. There are other people milling about, in similarly deplorable condition. Except one. He is wearing informal business attire and expensive shoes. His shirt is silk, his cuff links gold. His hair is neatly trimmed, his nails carefully manicured. He turns and smiles at Bill. His teeth are unnaturally perfect. He approaches, wiping what appears to be vomit from his jacket with a silk handkerchief.

"You must be Bill," he says, putting away the handkerchief and extending his hand. "Name's Danforth, glad to meet you. I'm a lawyer for Pilfer, Purloin & Plunder. I was just talking to your buddy, Felix. Seems we've all got the same story. Sitting in a bar, enjoying a nice drink, then getting clobbered and waking up here. I've been trying to get ahold of the Coast Guard or some kind of authority on my cell for the past three days but I can't seem to get a signal out here."

"Three days?" Bill croaks. "I've been out for three days?"

"Oh, no!" Danforth laughs lightly, "I understand your puzzlement. No, these *other* people and *myself* have been here for three days. *You* arrived last night."

"Arrived? Well, at port you must have been able to call somebody."

"Ah, no. We didn't land at any port. You and your two friends just appeared."

"Just appeared? How?"

"Got me there, buddy. You're guess is as good as mine."

"Who are all those people?"

"Oh, let's see, that shady fellow smoking the pipe is Willard Marker. He claims to be a pool shark. That guy over there wearing the funny hat is Elsworth Sneed, a hat maker or something. The other gentleman wearing the less humorous headgear and smoking a pipe like the pool shark - but not as shady-looking – is Erasmus Hengels, some kind of broker. The guy with the weird face, sharpening knives and acting all psycho, calls himself Danby, the Butcher of Holden Field. And that fuzzy thing sitting on the bowsprit glaring at you is – "

"The Sulking Beaver of Ulger Deep," Bill says. "What in the name of all things great and small is *he* doing here?"

"I was just about to ask you the same thing, fucker," grumbles the beaver.

"Yeah, before you two reacquaint yourselves," says the lawyer, "has anyone seen that wheel thingy that steers the boat? No? Just wondering if anyone's piloting this tub. And it kinda looks like we're going backwards, too. Maybe it's just me, I'm no sailor, but that doesn't seem quite right."

Bill looks out over the water and –

"Could you knock it off with the present tense?" Bill asks.

"Please," he begs.

"Okay, pretty please? With sugary sprinkles? A cherry? Chocolate syrup?"

Bill looked out over the water and noticed something out on the horizon. It was just a speck, just barely there at all, but it was something. He stood up, aching, bits of dry cake and icing falling from his person. He stood near the railing, ignoring Felix's retching. The speck gradually became larger, eventually revealing the unmistakable shape of a seagoing vessel like their own.

"A ship!" he cried. "It's a ship! Help has arrived!"

All of the people except the beaver ran to the railing and began shouting and waving their arms like fools. This went on for quite a while until they realized that the ship did not come closer, having apparently changed course to parallel them. It was much too far away to hear their cries, and was not even close enough to see them properly without a glass.

"A glass. The telescope!"

Bill ran to the brass telescope standing on the deck and swung it around to look at the puzzling ship. He looked for a bit and then began muttering to himself until the muttering formed itself into three audible words signifying profound mystification.

"What the fuck?"

It was a very good telescope. He could clearly see the other vessel which looked normal enough. What didn't look normal was what was happening on it. A man (or a woman - the telescope wasn't *that* good), wearing a Phrygian cap, was herding two bears from below decks with a spade toward the bow, a large bear and a smaller one. The person behaved as though he or she was giving them orders and the bears began using some instruments, perhaps nautical devices for navigation. The person then climbed the mast and looked out across the watery wastes, but never, it seemed, at them.

"How weird," Bill muttered.

"What is it?" Danforth asked. "Mind if I have a look?"

"Sure. Go ahead." Bill stepped back from the telescope and let Danforth look. Of course, everyone had to take a gander after that, including Carter who just giggled and somehow got saliva on the eyepiece. The beaver was the only one who abstained.

"Want to have a look?" Bill asked him.

"Fuck off. I can see it from here. I'm on the wrong god damn boat. That one's got a captain that knows his way around. But, no. I'm on *this* floating turd with a bunch of fuckheads that don't know their cocks from starboard. Fuck my life."

"Where's your magic now?" Bill grumped.

"In your ass if you don't shut the hell up!"

"I've got an idea. Why don't you go swim over to the other boat if you don't like it here."

"I'm a freshwater animal, not salt. But, you'd know that if you hadn't failed kindergarten."

Bill groaned. "Why am I arguing with a beaver?"

"Because you're an idiot."

"I've had about enough of you!"

"Same here, pal."

"Fuck you."

"Eat shit."

Bill sat down on the deck and sulked. The beaver sulked sulkier.

No one else seemed to notice the altercation.

This pretty well summed up their activities for the next thirty days. They would observe the ship pacing them, mill about and barely say two words to each other with the exception of the beaver and Bill who would engage in vitriolic dialogue, coming dangerously close to violence, Bill threatening to make the beaver into a throw rug more than once.

Fortunately the hold below contained plenty of fresh water, citrus fruit, salted meats and more casks of rum than they could all drink in a lifetime. Predictably, the rum was the first thing they ran out of. This was particularly devastating to Carter, but his sorrow did not last. He soon discovered everything on board ship he required to ferment the citrus fruit and distill a potent beverage that placed everyone in a coma for nearly another week, at the close of which the beaver excitedly jumped up on the bowsprit and pointed.

"Land ho, fuckers!"

Fit the Twenty-Third

The island was strewn with rocks and was mostly barren of life. Stony outcrops thrust upward from the land and dreary valleys fell away at their feet. What little life they could find was scrabbly. Some blades of grass fit enough to survive brought little cheer to the landscape. The underbrush was sparse and brown. The stunted and dead-looking trees, random sprinklings of sickly leaves on their naked branches, were few and far between.

They had landed easily enough. The good ship *Albatross* simply ran aground. The other vessel had kept on, disappearing around a bend in the shoreline. Perhaps it landed. Perhaps it didn't. The captain of that ship certainly didn't *seem* to want anything to do with them, and after a month of traveling within sight of each other the mysterious mariner must have surely been aware of them.

Felix and Bill took stock of the ship's hold to see if they could salvage any food. They gasped at the sight of it. Barrels, open and empty, rolled about under the influence of the gently creaking wreck. Smashed crates lay strewn, haphazardly, like a disturbed charnel house. Felix and Bill shook their heads in dismay upon finding the wretched corpse of Danforth, the lawyer, feet sticking out of one of the barrels. When they pulled him out it appeared he'd been dead for many days, his stomach bloated and stretched beyond capacity, the last morsel of food still in his mouth. Danforth had been in the hold the entire month everyone else had been stinking drunk. There wasn't a scrap of edible food left. He'd even consumed all of the sacks of raw flour – including the sacks.

"What a fucking pig!" exclaimed Bill, utterly disgusted.

The shabby crew piled out of the *Albatross* in desultory fashion and then walked aimlessly around the beach until, in some random way, they all began to walk together in a certain direction. Their path took them over rocky hills and skirted around giant boulders, cracked asunder as if having been purposely dropped from a great height. They walked by lone crags and a forest of hexagonal basalt pillars that appeared to have been extruded from the earth. The air was still, the sky overcast with a continuous sheet of cloud cover. No birds frolicked in it. It had been merely cool at the beach. They were discovering now that they were *cold*, and getting *colder* as they moved inland.

They entered a dark and ghoulish valley then. Eerie and silent, walled in by vertically fissured cliffs that towered threateningly over them, the only sound was of their own footsteps –

- and an espresso machine.

Straight ahead they saw a lonely booth. Behind the counter a middle-aged chap wearing casual black attire and a green apron was working an espresso machine, burping and hissing steam. His spiked hair was dyed black. Squatting miserably on the bridge of his nose was a pair of horn-rimmed glasses. He looked like he'd rather be sucking back cans of Coke, shoveling cold pizza into his mouth hole and writing code in C; or reading Noam Chomsky books and railing to his peers about the establishment; or attending a Vegan Earth Day feast, annoying humanity with his unskilled plucking of a zither or guitar, warbling dull hymns to the Goddess while he watched his penis shrink.

As the dazed party approached they noticed the logo: an ambiguously-sexed merperson wearing some kind of burkha centered in a green circle.

"Hi, welcome to Morebuck's. Can I get a blended coffee beverage started for you? We also have pastries there to your right."

"Didn't there used to be a less conservatively clothed mermaid in your logo?" Felix asked.

"Oh, yeah. We tried getting a little more risqué but too many right wing oppressors thought it looked too much like a prostitute holding her legs apart so we had to change it."

"Well, why didn't you just change it back?"

"They wouldn't let us. We had to put it in a burkha or get sued by the governments of fourteen countries till our balls fell off. I like my balls. Would you like something?"

"I'll, uh, take a double mocha."

"What size cup?"

"A, uh, the one between the biggest one you've got and the smallest."

"You mean *'grande'*?" he said in an irritated tone.

"Yes."

"Then why didn't you just say it?"

"Look, we just shipwrecked on this island and we'd kind of like to know where we are."

"You're embarrassed to say 'grande', aren't you? I bet you're one of those assholes that'll walk into a place of business and use their products while talking shit about them at the same time, huh? You realize that I have the right to refuse service to anyone, don't you? So, don't come walking in here stamping all over my rights and oppressing me. Got it?"

"Uh, yes, terribly sorry-"

"You think I'm gay!"

"Actually, no – look, could you just tell us where we are and I promise I'll purchase every ounce of coffee in this booth."

"Stop treating me like a child! A gay child! That's the only way you oppressors can view others, isn't it? Little gay children that you can lord over and dominate! Well you won't get by with that line here, you tyrant! This is where the buck stops! I'll fight and resist! I'll wrestle you and-"

"Oh, is that the paper? I'll just take that, thanks."

"- we'll squirm around on the ground and bite and slap each other a lot, but I won't go that easy! You'll have to tie me down and whip me with a cat-o-nine-tails and turn me over harshly, pull down my pants and spank me. But, I won't give in to your imperialist dogma! No I won't! I'll still fight even if I'm forced to go down..."

The insane barista's voice died away as they walked on down the valley.

"This paper is the Krans Jabwock Evening Post. Krans Jabwock... Does that ring any bells?"

"Yeah," said Bill, "remember Scene 42?"

"Oh, right, right. Well, not much news here. 'ROCK FALLS ON TOP OF OTHER ROCK', and that's the *headline*. Oh, wait, here's something: 'Thartible the Thrice-Crowned spotted lurking around island's West End.' Isn't that the gentleman we're supposed to look for?"

"Yes, but why bother? We're done with our Quest and this is just one more thing that's got nothing to do with it."

"We're shipwrecked on an island. Did you have something more important you wanted to scamper off to?"

"Oh, all right. Where are we? Does anyone have a compass? No? Well, how are we going to get our bearings then?"

"Oh, I'm sure we'll get some direction soon. It's no accident that we're here."

"People don't plan shipwrecks."

"Well, most of the time they don't, but doesn't it seem more than a little odd that all this started simply by pointing out that your order was wrong? And then, on that flimsy pretext alone - just like that - you're walloped on the brain bucket, shanghaied, materialize onto a boat with no captain or visible means of navigation, and then shipwreck on the very island we were told to find way back in Scene 42. Maybe it's just me going off my trolley, but that certainly seems to be an unlikely series of events."

"Well, who engineered this hijacking?"

"I can think of someone immediately – a certain anonymous narrator."

I resent the accusation. I had nothing to do with it.

"Oh, knock it off. You're writing this thing."

I have a multiple personality disorder. Sometimes I black out and wake up later covered with dirt and blood and find that twenty pages have been written while I was out. It's my alter ego. Don't point fingers at me!

"All right, we'll play along. Then what do you suggest we do for the moment?"

Go find Thartible the Thrice-Crowned, naturally.

"And which way would that be?"

Just follow the path you're taking to the West End of the valley.

"Fine, then. Oh, do any of you still have those boxes of junk that kooky person gave us in scene 42?"

"You were the last one to have them," said Bill.

Felix searched his pockets until he found one, then searched again and brought forth the other.

"Yes, here are the thimbles and forks. Bill, if you wouldn't mind passing these out. Oh, and here's the soap. I'll just hang onto this railway-share. All right, let's put on our most charming smiles and get on with it."

Fit the Twenty-Fourth

"Where did the beaver go?" Felix asked, looking around them.

They had been walking for three days and still hadn't gotten to the end of the valley. Everyone was hungry and, most importantly, thirsty. Not once had they walked by a stream or lake or bubbling spring.

As for Thartible, the Thrice-Crowned, they had seen no evidence. Of course, they didn't know what he looked like but that hardly mattered here. If they saw *anyone* they'd pounce on him instantly and question him until they knew with whom they were dealing.

"He went with Danby, the Butcher of Holden Field," said Bill. "They mentioned they wanted to strike off on their own. The beaver said specifically that he wasn't going to stick around and die like all of *us* are apparently going to do. It seems Danby agreed."

"Ha! Now that's rich. The beaver took off with *that* bloke? Do you know what he used to do for a living? He told me yesterday. Used to trap beavers in Canada for their pelts. He's murdered them by the thousands. All I see on the horizon is a sulky beaver getting turned into a pair of mittens."

"Of course you do, because that's the way you *always* see things: cynically."

"Well, if by cynical you mean seeing the world and accepting it for the harsh reality it is, then I'm a cynic. Nevertheless, whatever you say I am, I have my faith to sustain me in these times of woe."

"Your faith! You know, I really don't think that you actually believe any of that stuff anymore. I think you just use it to make people think you're actually doing something constructive with your life. You lord those Signs over others, admonishing them for their participation in the Apocalypse when you've been doing it yourself. One of the Signs involves the evils of murdering people because they're inconvenient! You are a-"

"Yes, yes, we're all tired and thirsty and a bit peckish as well. The sooner we find this Thartible the better. I think we should fan out and spread our area of search. What do you think, Bill? I thought you'd agree. All right, let's do it."

Paying no attention to Bill's protests the party spread out far and wide while still remaining in line of sight with one other. Bill finally huffed off toward a distant hill.

They sought him with thimbles, they sought him with care. They pursued him with forks and hope. They threatened his life with a railway-share. They charmed him with smiles and soap.

For the whole rest of the day they searched, under rocks, on top of rocks, around the backs of boulders, atop crags. They searched in the brown underbrush and poked empty holes in trees. But, as time wore on the hopelessness of their task was at last sinking into everyone's minds. They were not merely weary, they were utterly exhausted. But even in their fatigue and hunger, none of them dared turn back to the ship. It was simply too far away and even if they were to return what would be the point? There was no food on board and there was no hope at all of making it seaworthy. The coffee bar was totally out of the question since it was closed on the weekends and would only be manned by the crazy barista in any case. They could only trudge onward. To go back meant doom. To stop meant doom.

And then, from far off on top of a low hill, Bill was waving excitedly at them with both arms, yelling. Though the air of the island was so still and quiet, even from this distance Felix could barely make out what he was saying. Bill was looking at something on the other side of the hill, turning back to them, waving, and then turning again to look at whatever it was. He stepped lower down the hillside until all they could see were his head and hands.

"It's Thartible! I found him! It's Thartible!"

There was a ragged cheer and some much-needed laughter. They started trotting toward the hill in high spirits. An end to the misery at last, they hoped; at least an end to searching around all over for this Thartible fellow who, with any luck, had some food and water on hand.

They were converging together as they jogged and were not yet halfway there when Bill said something that chilled all who heard it.

"No, wait," he said, "Stop! It's Scrag-"

There was a long silence and everyone huddled together, waiting for Bill to just poke his head above the summit of the hill. But, he never did.

"What was it he said?" asked the pool shark. "Scrag?"

"Scragmoth," said Felix wretchedly. "I've killed him. I've killed my friend. If I hadn't split us up we could have fought the beast! I'm sure of it!"

"No," said the hat-maker. "I didn't hear 'moth'. It was something else."

"Nonsense, it was very definitely 'moth'," said the broker.

"I couldn't tell what it was," said the pool shark. "Too far away, and his head was behind the hill when he said whatever it was. Can't get too carried away with *that*."

They marched solemnly up the hill, not knowing what they would find. Felix hoped beyond all hope that everyone was mistaken, that Bill had just slipped and fallen down the hillside, that all would be well.

But, when they arrived at the summit…there was nothing. And they could see the entire side of the hill which sloped down to a rocky plain as far as they eye could see, straight out to the ocean. Carter wept. Even the others respectfully hung their heads. Poor Bill, Burthdrool the Endearingly Foliate, had vanished, softly and suddenly, not to be met with again.

"Ah well," Felix sighed, "I guess that's all over now."

There were five of them standing on that hill, staring off into emptiness and death. Five of them, including Felix. He counted them again to be sure as he produced his Glock. *Yes*, he said to himself, *I have plenty of ammo.*

Epilogue

Felix finally went mad.

But, he didn't go mad at first.

First, he raised his hands to the heavens and said, "Let there be fire!"

And lo, after three days laboring, gathering firewood from the stubby trees and tinder from the underbrush, then another full day with the rubbing-two-sticks-together trick, he caught a spark and had fire.

Then, Felix raised his hands to the heavens and said, "Let there be food!"

And lo, he fumbled about with various rocks and taught himself the delicate art of flint knapping. A week later, and with these trusty tools, he undertook the odious task of skinning four corpses that were beginning to stink. He was sloppy and inefficient with the first but got better with the next until he had mastered the butcher's skill by the last, his dear friend Carter. He chopped them into smaller sections and roasted them until he thought them well done, and lo, there was food.

And yet, he did not go mad.

The food lasted him for a couple of weeks, but at last the final morsel was consumed. He survived for a few more days before he realized that he would starve if he did not get more.

He raised his hands to the heavens and said, "Let there be more food!"

And lo, he skulked down into the ghoulish valley to the coffee bar and there slew the malcontent barista within. With his new found skills, starting a fire and butchering this fresh meat was a snap. Plus there was the bonus of all the nice scones and hot coffee. He survived for a couple more weeks until all the food was gone. And then the rumble in his belly cried out for attention once again.

And yet, he did not go mad.

He raised his hands to the heavens and said, "Let there be, again, more food!"

And he roamed the terrible countryside searching for the only two storehouses of protein he knew to be left, if they had not yet themselves been taken by Scragmoth the Ravenous. He searched high and low for his quarry, and one day, he found them.

They were walking up from the rocky plain in sight of the sea to a parking lot full of cars next to a 9-11. Beyond the 9-11 were houses on either side of a broad avenue, an avenue he recognized.

He followed them calmly into the convenience store, ragged, stinking, covered with old blood, and carrying his Glock in one hand. A woman, walking out from an aisle toward the register, glanced over at him and screamed, dropping her merchandise. Danby and the Sulking Beaver spun around.

"What the fuck do *you* want?" asked the one-time Sulking Beaver of Ulger Deep. Danby, with a calculating eye, simply watched and waited. Butchering in cold blood was his business.

But there is a difference between butchering someone and firing a projectile at them from a distance and Felix fired two very well-placed shots, landing slugs between two pairs of eyes.

And yet, still, he did not go mad.

He raised his hands to the heavens and said, "Now, let there be vengeance."

And lo, he walked out of the 9-11 and down the street, took a left he knew well, and then a right he knew better. When he finally stopped he stared for a long time at the crater where his house once stood. On the other side of it were his backyard and the tower with the ray gun on top. Krans Jabwock had been no mysterious island. It had been merely the stretch of rocky coast not five miles from his home.

And yet, he did not go mad.

He searched and searched, looking high and low for his quarry. He climbed down into the pit and up into his backyard. He searched every corner and then the tower. It was here, what he sought. The object of his revenge lay at his feet. Tiny, crushed white bones, wearing a little hard hat and a tool belt; a little eyeless skull staring up at him, mockingly.

Felix walked away, head hung low. He slid down the crater that was once his home. He climbed back up to the street and stood there. For a long time he stood, just staring off into the distance. A car drove by. The driver glanced up, saw him, and careened into a hedge in front of his neighbor's house across the street. The driver, somewhat dazed, opened the door and looked across the street. He saw Felix for a second time and ran away, patent leather shoes tapping away at the asphalt until he was out of sight around a corner. Felix watched this entire act play out with no feeling, no emotion. He just stood and contemplated.

It was too much. He was a freak now. Too much had happened for which he was accountable. There was no possibility of regaining his old life. There was no turning back. He was the last one left and soon there would be those coming to take him away, to mete out justice, to reabsorb him into the horribly dull expectations the world had uncaringly heaped upon him. Too much. Too much. The squirrel was dead – a collection of bones and incongruous attire. His irrational thoughts of revenge denied, Felix put the Glock to his own head and pulled the trigger.

Nothing happened. A mere click. Out of ammo.

And yet, he did not go mad.

At what point then *did* he go mad?

I will tell you.

Standing there, covered in blood, dressed in filthy rags, matted hair and beard, stinking body, clutching in one hand a satchel he had made out of human skin to hold his stone implements, and an empty Glock nine-millimeter in the other, the flesh of five human beings having passed through his gut and the deaths of countless others on his hands and conscience, Felix stared wide-eyed at the terrible scene that unfolded before him.

Six giant helicopters appeared over the horizon carrying a glorious mansion that they lowered over the pit. The massive cables detached and the helicopters flew away. Behind him TV news crews zoomed up and screeched to a halt, jumping out and instantly taking pictures, asking questions, jamming microphones into his face.

The double doors of the mansion swung open and out poured a procession of everyone he had encountered on his bizarre journey: Puzzle (the retarded kid, who was now not behaving as Felix remembered, giving a little smile and a wave), the insane squirrel, Chauncey the Messenger, Vug the Proconsul, Hangnail the Six-Limbed Riding Monkey, the tavern keeper from the *Crumb & Toad*, the Toad itself (quite whole and uneaten), all of the companions supplied by Lord Smirch, the Heckling Pigeon, Crasspot the Dwarf (being pushed out in a wheelchair, beaming at Felix with his good eye), all the crazy prophets, the woodland creatures and the Leprechaun, Tweedle and Dum, even Stump the Hydrant Troll, the Space Marines, the Sulking Beaver of Ulger Deep, the Even Sulkier Trout (being rolled around in a giant fish tank), Howie the Wretched Barstool and Sput the Dread Bucket, the guard at the professor's door as well as Professor Pestbog himself, Laphroaig the butler, Balor the Fomorian, all of the protesters from Land's End, Great Zak, Abercrombie of Tarkington, their fellow travelers on the ship to Krans Jabwock, absolutely everybody. They came up to him in groups of four or five, shaking his hand, giving him friendly punches on the arms. At the end of this circus came Carter and Bill, smiling and waving. They both hugged him, Carter giving him a quick kiss on each cheek like weirdos from certain European countries do when they want to upset their foreign guests.

You see, it's like this: it was all an elaborate hoax. Carter had won hundreds of billions of dollars from several state lotteries and rather than use that money to establish schools or hospitals or fund scientific research laboratories to find cures for untreatable diseases or help restore ruined economies where people and children are starving to death due to the careless ineptitude of corrupt governments, he decided to spend *all* that money on Felix, creating a complex life lesson for him to live through in order to teach him to stop being an asshole and killing people all the time, kind of like that movie with Michael Douglas and Sean Penn. And seeing how it worked out so well they decided that *this* was the opportune moment to spring the catch on their trick and reveal all.

Or was it?

You see, this isn't the movies. Perhaps it was really like this:

Felix's face twitched and convulsed, his mind trying desperately to make sense of these monstrous twists on reality. He began to hyperventilate, his eyes were wild. He looked like a hunted animal that had been cornered at last. No escape. Then, a grotesquely fat man dressed in royal finery and smelling of old chicken grease waddled up to him from out of the crowd. Felix stared, instinctively backing away from this terrible creature. No one else seemed to notice him. In fact, it seemed to Felix that this massive frame was actually walking *through* Carter and Bill. What was real, what was illusion? The fat man winked a piggy eye, the corners of his ugly and moist lips turned up in an evil grimace. In one hand he clutched a piece of paper and somehow Felix knew that he didn't want to see it, for that piece of paper would reveal to him Lord Smirch's diabolical plan. *The* plan. Was it still real? Was this merely a hoax compounded onto another hoax? Lord Smirch, with fingers thick as sausages, grabbed Felix's throat so he could not escape or turn away. He held up the paper, chuckling nastily. Felix tried to shut his eyes, but Lord Smirch only squeezed tighter, relaxing his grip only when Felix opened them again. He could do nothing but look at that infernal document which filled his vision.

It was an advertisement. Felix read it. "Institute for Human Cont..." His voice trailed off as he read the rest. His face twitched and convulsed again. That was all there was to it? That's what all of this had been about? All the suffering and brain-twisting nonsense? That was it? My God! My God! All of this simply so that Lord Smirch could -

Felix went mad.

He screamed until his throat was raw and bleeding. He tore out his hair in thick handfuls. He beat his face with his fists. Lord Smirch melted away; his demonic laugh lingered a moment and then faded to follow the vanished image.

Dropping to his knees, Felix tore at his skin and eyes, rocking back and forth, screaming, always screaming. He did not stop. Ever.

The faces around him lost their smiles and jocundity. Slowly they filed away, heads hung low at what they'd done. Bill and Carter thanked them all for doing their best and it wasn't their fault and other polite phrases. The police arrived shortly and took Felix away, admitting him that very day to Arkham Sanitarium in Gotham City where he would spend the rest of his days. Or so it was thought.

When everyone had gone and the streets were quiet, Carter and Bill removed their masks, revealing them to be not Carter and Bill at all, but someone in a Phrygian cap who looked like a ship's captain (and was Lord Smirch's hired gun) and Old Man Witherspoon (who was Lord Smirch's chief public relations guy). They stared at the mansion for a long time, satisfied grins drawn on their faces as they gazed at their prize.

The man in the Phrygian cap looked sidelong at his associate and grinned wider, knowing that as soon as they were inside, two bears waited to tear Old Man Witherspoon to pieces, and then it would be all his. But, for now, he let Witherspoon have his five minutes of victory while they continued to admire their mansion: a more obscene and out-of-place disaster of architecture the world had probably never witnessed. This gaudy mass of timber modeled – after a twisted fashion – on that of a Tuscan villa was built in such a way that it looked tawdry, not to mention it completely ignored, and bore no relation, to its locale.

But, what should one expect, as a bonus, from Lord Smirch? Good taste? It would be good enough - for now - thought the man in the Phrygian cap.

Meanwhile Old Man Witherspoon was having thoughts of his own, knowing full well that the bears were dead and the most ruthless Sicilian hit man he could buy waited behind that door to take out the sea captain, and then the mansion would be all his.

Meanwhile, the sea captain was thinking that, by now, his bears might be dead and a ruthless Sicilian hit man was waiting to take him out. However, what Witherspoon didn't know is that the sea captain had anticipated this and had, as backup, a small dragon waiting in the closet that was most likely at this moment having himself a Sicilian barbecue.

However, what the sea captain didn't know was that Witherspoon had recently rolled a saving throw against magic and the dragon, being a magical beast, failed to exist inside the closet, allowing the Sicilian hit man to wait behind the door undisturbed.

But, what neither of them knew was that Lord Smirch had filled the house with explosives that were timed to go off in seven minutes.

What Lord Smirch didn't know was that the sea captain had carefully placed a thermal detonator underneath his throne that was timed to go off in eight minutes.

What none of them knew was that a young woman in Brighton suddenly sat up in her chair and realized the philosophical truth that no one really knew anything and happiness would continue to elude humankind forever (or at least for the next few quadrillionths of a second), regardless of all those little green pieces of paper and nifty digital watches.

Even so, Witherspoon and the sea captain realized they needed to keep up appearances until one or the other opened the doors to the mansion. They turned and looked at each other in apparently shared triumph, jumped, and performed a ridiculous high-five worthy of late 1970s sitcoms.

Epilogue to the Epilogue

Meanwhile, cruising out beyond the ponderous orbit of Pluto was Military Research Station *Illudium Q-36*, the purpose of which was to activate and monitor the largest cyclotron ever built. It completely circumscribed the entire solar system and had the singular function of smashing two particles together at such insane velocities that it would reproduce the energies that existed just *before* the very moment of the Big Bang. No mean feat.

Naturally there were the typical doomsayers that whined about further research being needed before turning the fucker on, claiming that it could cause serious damage to the solar system, alter the orbits of the planets, affect the energy output of the sun, create dense gravitational collapses sufficiently large to suck up planets, create disturbances in the force, cause toast to land jelly-side up, and a whole host of other vexing issues.

Just as predictably, the fellows who had Nobel Prizes waiting for them on their kitchen tables when they got home weren't too excited about all this childish blubbering and countered with logical, point-by-point arguments of their own: that the doomsayers were being too nitpicky, making quite a fuss about nothing, creating mountains out of mole hills, being nervous Nancies, acting like little girls, were chicken littles, yeller, and so on.

The fact was nobody really knew *what* would happen. Like homeopathic remedies that cure all ills, the frontiers of scientific inquiry were fraught with all possible claims as to what might or might not occur when the switch was finally thrown.

In the end, the soon-to-be Nobel Prize recipients brow-beat their way to victory and here they were at last, about to unleash the most powerful and terrifying energies in the whole Universe – under controlled laboratory conditions of course.

In the command center sat Dervis Allthumbs, Chief Switch Flipper. He was an unfortunate case. Thin to the point of emaciation and burdened with a long nose that was not cleaned as regularly as it should be, it oft dripped foul ichor from its innermost recesses. He wore giant glasses at least three inches thick. His yellowish-brown teeth protruded from the upper jaw that never, ever, got brushed. His breath smelled like his teeth looked and hairy ears projected perpendicular from his head oozing orange wax. A lank head of hair that seemed to have been last washed when he was born lay uncomfortably on top of his skull like a sick animal. His body odor suggested gas station toilets. Et cetera. His laugh began with a loud snort, had a jackass guffaw in the middle, and ended with a high-pitched squeal with a slight off-key gargle trailing off at the end. As if all that wasn't bad enough, he had the most shocking case of acne ever seen by mortal eyes. His whole face was a constantly shifting volcanic landscape of exploding sores and scabs. You might be surprised if I told you he had a girlfriend – if it were true.

He was at that moment speaking, in a most annoying nasal fashion, to a colleague, Updike Twitchenfist, Second Mate to the Third Lieutenant to the Fourth Chief Scientist in charge of Pushing the Button. His appearance was much the same as Dervis's, subtracting the acne, so I'll just move on.

Updike was here today because all of the Chief Scientists, all the Lieutenants and even the First Mates to the Lieutenants had suddenly stepped out and – surprisingly - all for the very same reason: a gangrenous, ingrown toenail on the left big toe.

Probability is so amazingly counterintuitive, isn't it?

The real reason is that someone had done some calculations that didn't shuck and jive with some other calculations and told somebody else who couldn't get *his* squigglies to shuck and jive either. Well, shit goes downhill. Apparently so does nerve. They made up their excuses and made sure they all got the story the same, because that's what you do when you're trying to get away with underhanded shit. If the enemy catches two of you and puts you each in separate rooms like they do in cop dramas, you both better have your stories in agreement or they'll toss the key at you, lock you up and throw away the book - or something like that. Right? So, that's how they all ended up calling with the same ailment. The Honchos, Jefes and Cheeses all knew it was bullshit but they let them steal a ship and get far enough out of view before remotely detonating the explosive on board. Who knew where they thought they were going? This was Super MK ULTRA TIPPY TOPPY CANOE SECRET, which meant NO leaks. Period.

"Oh," said Updike, spitting gobs of saliva with each word, "and do you remember the time when that vial of SuperFlu got kicked out the airlock, failed to burn up in the atmosphere and almost wiped out every living thing in Africa?"

(*Snort-guffaw-squeal-gargle*) Dervis laughed, "Yeah, that was a good one!"

Just then the door to the command center slid open exactly like the ones in the original *Star Trek* TV series. Into the lab stepped the Supreme Overseer of Projects. He wore a perfectly white lab coat, buttoned all the way to the Adam's apple. Stalwart, brave, piercing eyes, chiseled features, his gray hair in a neat crew cut, as serious as a snapping neck, he was the epitome of the glorious Space Age and he commanded respect. Nothing got by him and no one slouched in his presence. He demanded that everyone salute him, having served in every single war and police action since Waterloo, and five hundred and fifteen secret military operations since the successful two-pronged invasion of China and Estonia last August.

He was actually the first man on the moon since, in his words, he felt it was his duty as a God-Fearing, Red-White-and-Blue-Balled, American Patriot to make sure the "waters" were safe for Neil. He was the real inventor of the nuclear bomb, the laser, the microwave, and pre-sliced cheese. He was the genius behind hot dogs and baseball and a version of his original recipe for apple pie was made in every household in the country. Fascists turned to pillars of salt under his steely gaze. Vietnam would have been won if only they hadn't pulled him out to deal with the grey alien invasion of Patagonia. He was immaculately conceived by the recovered DNA of every President of the United States in the genetically reconstructed womb of the Virgin Mary. It is said God even visited him once just to say, "Thanks, man, you're really neat." His name was John Wayne Bronson-Norris-Eastwood-Connery-McQueen-Bond and this god damn experiment was going to run as smooth as tank treads greased in Commie blood.

Dervis and Updike stood at attention and saluted so hard you could hear their skulls crack.

He glanced over in Dervis's direction.

"Ah," he said, "someone ordered pizza."

He glanced again and frowned.

"Oh, it's just you."

"Sorry, sir," said Dervis.

"All right," he growled, "this is how this is going to go down. I've inspected every last molecule of dust in this entire outfit for final check except this room. I will now proceed with inspection. If everything checks we will move ahead with countdown procedures, is that clear?"

"Sir, yes, sir!" Dervis and Updike cried together.

"Good. At ease. Dervis, take this clipboard and you check off what I call out."

"Sir, yes, sir!"

"Updike!" John shouted next to his ear.

Updike crawled back into his body and answered, "Sir, yes, sir!"

134

"Go make me a coffee. Black. Boiling. Thick. Acid. In precisely one hour I want to be shitting napalm! Got that?"

"Sir, yes, sir!" Updike would have run through the wall if it were possible. Unfortunately it took a whole microsecond for the door to open and he nearly died from the wait. Subjective eons passed by before it slid aside and Updike dashed out leaving Dervis quailing by his chair, doing his best not to weep.

At last, the Supreme Overseer of Projects began marching sternly about the room, opening panels, taking readings, even putting a thread gauge to screws in the panels to make sure they were all proper mil-spec and not any of that un-American metric crap...how he would love to nuke France once and for all! His teeth grated and his eyes narrowed at the thought. When he was done with this mamby-pamby, egghead research garbage he would go home, walk right into the president's office, tell the chippie of the day to put her clothes back on and shove off, and ask the president nicely if he could borrow a nuke – or two. The president would surely comply and – he smiled at this – "Your ass will be mine, France!"

Taking a great deal of pleasure in this new turn of thought he almost took it easy for a bit and continued the final check leisurely (which for him meant not stamping dents into the floor with his boots).

But then he stopped. What in the Name of God's Balls was *this*???

"DERVIS!" he shouted.

Dervis simultaneously shot urine down his leg, crapped his pants and vomited out his nose

"GET OVER HERE!"

Dervis got - and observed the Supreme Overseer of Projects extending a meaty, quivering digit as though every muscle in it wanted to break free of its skin and utterly humiliate and destroy the offending object it was pointing at: a tiny switch on the control board.

John's other hand closed like a vice on Dervis's lapels. The pointing finger jabbed at the control board enunciating each syllable of what he said next.

"WHAT – IS – THAT!"

"A-a-a-a-s-s-s-sw-sw-swi-swi-tch?"

"I KNOW IT'S A FUCKING SWITCH! WHAT IN THE NAME OF GOD'S ASSHOLE IS IT DOING THERE?!?!"

"I-I-I-I-I-I-I-I-I-"

"Get me the schematics!"

"I can call them up on the co-com-computer, sir."

"NO! I don't trust fucking computers, Dervis! Do you know why? Cause you can't grab 'em by their lapels, Dervis! You can't do *this* to 'em!" he yelled, shaking Dervis so violently that blood squirted out of his ears. "You can't make 'em *scared*, Dervis! You can't strike *Fear of the Almighty* into their soulless lumps of metal and plastic! And without *fear*, Dervis, where would we be now? Living in *caves*, Dervis! Living in *fucking caves*! Bring me real schematics drawn by a real person that I can frighten unholy hell out of!"

Dervis's shirt was allowed to go free. Somehow he managed not to collapse into a puddle of slime on the spot. Each step - a miracle of its own – finally got him out the door.

Lying in the hallway was Updike. It seemed he'd spilled a drop of the coffee on his foot and died before the cup hit the floor, the contents of which were slowly eating their way to C Deck.

Dervis had his own problems. How to produce schematics drawn by a human being that didn't exist? All of the schematics, and even the design of the whole station, as well as the cyclotron, had been done by a computer. There were probably, maybe, ten people who knew how the entire system worked. On Earth. And the SOP wanted a live human to throttle as well as complicated diagrams numbering in the thousands of pages printed on wall-size sheets of paper.

Fuck. Dervis picked up the coffee cup. A drop still remained. He let it touch his tongue and collapsed to join his colleague.

Meanwhile, the absurdity of life being what it is, Dervis's decision was all for naught since the SOP wasn't going to wait for anyone to dawdle in their own time, obtaining for him information he could find out immediately and on his own.

Fuck it, he thought to himself. It's not supposed to be there. It's probably not hooked up to anything anyway. His finger hovered over the switch. Why am I stopping? Me? Afraid? Of a little god damn piece of plastic? Never! I'm John Wayne Bronson-Norris-Eastwood-Connery-McQueen-Bond! God Himself came down from On High and shook my hand! I'll show those eggheads!

He flipped the switch.

Just 42 quadrillionths of a second later after the precise moment the switch was flipped and a little metal contact made contact with another little metal contact (which, by sheer coincidence, was precisely the moment Old Man Witherspoon and the sea captain were high-fiving one another), the cyclotron produced a supermassive black hole that immediately sucked the entire Universe into it and then winked out of existence.

Contrary to the theory held by an ancient philosopher, whose most recent incarnation was busily cursing Fate and the uncaring Universe in the seas of Santraginus V before the black hole sucked it into oblivion, the universe was *not* replaced by something more bizarre and inexplicable.

Nor was it replaced by something more prosaic and easily understood.

Apparently the whole idea of a universe has been finally seen for the ridiculous notion it always was and has been properly shelved.

Thanks for playing.

Who Really Is the Sea Captain
in the Phrygian Cap?

What is Lord Smirch
Really Up To?

The Universe has been
Destroyed, so Does It Really
Matter?

Find Out In the Exciting Sequel!

Part Two
The Wisdom of the Hand Pig
from Yuggoth

Part Three
In the Shadow of the Kreeblevox

*"Nature has left this tincture in the blood,
that all men would be tyrants if they could."*

- Daniel Defoe

"Everyone is as God made him, and often a great deal worse."

- Cervantes, *Don Quixote*

Prologue

In the beginning the void was void and the dark emptiness was dark and empty. Nothing was going about its business doing nothing and other nonexistent entities were accomplishing their daily nonexistence with considerable aplomb. Not a whole lot was happening at that moment and there really isn't much to say about it except that it was really, really quiet. So quiet you could hear a pin drop - if there had been a pin and something for it to fall on. I could go on, but I trust that anyone reading this already has an intimate working knowledge of nothing and can skip on to the next paragraph.

Out of the firmament there collided two lumps of nothing and, with much writhing of quantum fluctuation a Great Wiggle could be seen (if there had been anyone around to see it). The Great Wiggle wiggled and formed itself into a dim, yellow light bulb. From the top of the bulb, upon which rested a great accumulation of dust, extended a dirty and frayed cord that appeared to be in gross violation of several electrical codes. From the opposite end of this cord spanned a ceiling to which some walls were then affixed. At the base of these walls a floor appeared, thus completing the ensemble we can now describe as a filthy room. On one of the walls, high up, a barred window letting in some light manifested itself. The walls and floor, incidentally, were all padded. A door appeared on another wall. The door had a smaller door set within it, about head height, which one could open from the outside in order to look into the room.

For some time the room remained empty. How long no one could say. Hours? Centuries? Millennia? Who knew? There was no one around yet to do any wondering. But, one day perhaps, someone did materialize in the room, wrapped in a straitjacket, apparently dozing in some afternoon light in the corner. He shifted a little in his sleep and began to snore. Deep in the caverns of his subconscious a dream struggled and fussed about. Since we are reading this in the third person we can obviously go and take a look.

In the man's dream he saw the universe. Not just a tiny slice like you or I would see looking up at the night sky, but all of it – the whole thing. It was very dark and big, lit only in one corner by a dim light bulb. However, as he dreamed, he noticed that other little light bulbs were turning on. Some dim like the first, others shining like flood lamps. Around these lights grew rooms, buildings, backyards, streets, neighborhoods, countries, entire planets. Stars lit up for the planets to revolve around, galaxies took shape, then clusters of galaxies, on and on to the edges of the universe.

On all of these worlds whole histories came into being, civilizations rose and fell, intergalactic battles were fought, lives were lived, deaths were deathed, philosophies were ventured, believed, and then forgotten. The universe had been rewound and set ticking.

And in that universe, on one little dust mote of a planet (a small, green world, orbiting a star of pinkish hue), a great ocean lapped at the craggy shores of a barren landmass. At this tidal junction there evolved a precarious ecological niche, crawling with lively inhabitants, doing their lively business of eating each other and producing copies of themselves. One such creature, which looked remarkably like a hermit crab, was sitting alone at the edge of a tide pool, refraining from joining the others in their endless round of killing each other to survive.

It poked an eye out from under its shell and testily observed the antics of the others. Sighing wearily, it cursed Fate and the uncaring Universe it had so unwillingly been thrust into yet again. Of all the major and minor intelligences of the cosmos, it was one of a tiny handful that could remember all of its previous incarnations in addition to being amazingly long-lived – to its infinite dismay.

The hermit crab withdrew its eye stalk into its shell and sulked for several days. Toward the end of this philosophical musing, however, it realized that it was hungry and would soon be forced to engage the others of its kind in the sordid details of living out its shitty little life on this insipid little planet. Wracked with unmitigated boredom, the hermit crab once again extended its eye stalk, staring at the senseless stupidity before it with profound irritation.

"Fuck," it grumbled. With that it crawled, very much annoyed, into the tide pool in search of opiates.

Chapter 1

The man in the straitjacket suddenly awoke, blinking and sniffling. He smacked his lips and tried to adjust his blurred vision to take in his surroundings. He was uncertain how long he'd been in this predicament and tried to remember how he'd gotten there. No memories were forthcoming so he tried to stand and move about. Fortunately for his face the floor was padded. With a grunt he managed to get his knees underneath himself and raise his torso off the floor. With a swaying effort he got one leg up, firmly planting a foot into the padding. Then he managed to raise himself and plant the other foot next to the first one.

The next step was to vomit all over his firmly planted feet. The fact that he had anything to heave from his stomach in the first place showed that he had eaten something recently even though he had no memory of it. Eyes still bulging from the exertion and lips moist with sour spittle, the man groaned a bit and then stiffly walked over to the door. He called out for someone – anyone – to come and open it but no one came. At last, having no hands available for knocking, he pounded on the door with his head. Still no one came. He pressed his ear to the door and listened intently, but there was not a sound from the other side. Finally, exhausted from the effort, he went back to his corner, leaned back against the wall and slid down to a sitting position. He was soon asleep.

When he woke up again the afternoon sunlight was no longer illuminating the gently floating dust in the room. It was quite dark outside and the room was lit only by the sickly light bulb suspended from its decaying cord. Time appeared to be passing. With this information he fell asleep once again.

When he woke once more a different sort of light could be seen from the window. A grayish light reminiscent of dawn. A chill hung in the air and the man found himself shivering. A knot in his stomach informed him that food was required and he repeated his attempt to gain attention to his plight from beyond the door. No one came. He returned to his corner and slept.

This schedule was repeated for several days until the man's pleas were replaced with shouted obscenities. Yet no one ever came and not a peep was heard beyond the implacable door.

One day arrived, however, when a sound awakened him from a rather lengthy stupor. Startled, he looked about for its source. He looked at every corner of the room, the door, the window, and was startled again to discover that the source of the odd noise was his own screaming. With some effort he clamped his mouth shut to stop it. He struggled and writhed then and would have torn at his eyes and skin had not the straitjacket frustrated his efforts. He dimly wondered how many perfectly sane people had been driven to madness simply by taking them against their will, having their arms bound to their sides, and being held in solitary confinement indefinitely without food or water.

Wild-eyed, panting forcefully, he let himself fall to his side and rolled himself to the Implacable Door, kicking it forcefully until his bare feet bled. After exhausting himself in this fashion he rolled onto his back and stared at the dim yellow bulb, gently swaying in a chill morning breeze from the barred window. If only he could get up there and look out, he thought, he might deduce where he was and how he had arrived in this condition. But, as much as he jumped and engaged himself in uselessly silly acrobatics, leaving a pattern of bloody footprints on the floor, he could not obtain sufficient height to catch even a glimpse of what lay beyond his four-walled prison.

More days passed and he was far too reduced by hunger to distract himself any longer with physical acts of wishful thinking. He lay, supine, on the floor of the padded room, staring straight up into the dingy bulb and its feeble illumination.

Insanity sat, leaning back against the wall near the door, smoking a cigarette. Insanity was saying something to him but he wouldn't listen. He stared hard at the light bulb hoping Insanity would just go away, but it didn't. It just went on mouthing silent sentences at him, as if they were engaged in an amiable conversation but with the volume turned all the way off.

By the following day he was sufficiently worn down that he reached over and turned the volume up.

"...so as you can see," Insanity intoned reasonably, "you need but wait a little longer and you'll be thin enough to simply slip from your straitjacket unimpeded."

"And what then? I have not strength enough to bend or break bars from the window or hurl myself against the door with any hope of bursting through it."

"Just wait until you're even thinner and you can just slip under the door."

"Your logic is sound. I will wait."

And so he waited. Insanity waited with him.

"Who am I?"

Insanity took a long drag on his cigarette. "You don't need *me* to find that out, do you?"

"What do you mean?"

"You know. You just don't want to remember."

"I don't understand. Why am I here?"

"You know that too."

"You're not very helpful."

"*I* know *that*. I'm *Insanity*. *Helpful* is on another job."

"Just tell me what to do so I can get out of here."

"You don't need me for that."

"What the hell *do* I need you for?"

"To stay in *here*."

"Why on earth would I want to stay in here?"

"So you don't have to deal with what's out there?"

"What's out there?"

"*You* know."

Vexed by this non-answer the man in the straitjacket changed the subject to other fascinating topics and found Insanity quick to oblige him. They spoke at length of many things: of shoes and ships and sealing wax. The man in the straitjacket talked for many days on the life cycle of cabbages and Insanity waxed philosophic with regard to kings. They collaborated for another week, each adding to a rather long but engaging dissertation as to the nature of the sea and why it is boiling hot. Insanity then followed up with a very learned monologue on the ancient question as to whether or not pigs have wings. When Insanity had finished with his concluding remarks the man in the straitjacket would have applauded had he been able to do so.

As each day came to a close, however, the man would always ask Insanity who he was and what he was doing in this lonely room. And each time the response was always the same.

"*You* know."

"What's so awful outside that I should remain here?"

"*You* know."

And so it went on, for days and days. They would embroil themselves in heated dispute concerning the beach and how long it would take to sweep all the sand into the sea or how the sun might shine at night. But, at the end of the day, the man would always ask his futile questions and, at the end of every day, receive his useless answers.

One day, however, the man had finally had enough. He wriggled in his straitjacket and cursed at his inability to extricate himself even though, by now, he should have grown suitably emaciated to do so easily. Sweat dripped into his eyes and fell from his nose onto a spot just in front of his crossed legs. He pondered this for awhile and ceased his writhing.

"Who am I?" he asked, knowing the answer.

"*You* know."

"What day is it?"

"You know that too," Insanity replied with a shrug. He took another long drag off his endless cigarette and looked hard at the man in the straitjacket.

"What are you doing?" Insanity asked.

"Thinking."

"Why? That'll only bring trouble."

"I haven't gotten any thinner and we've been chatting in this room for at least a month. I'm sweating and haven't had a drop of water for as long. How many days have really passed?"

"Don't go there my friend. Hiding from your own knowledge isn't always a bad thing."

"How long have I been here?" the man yelled.

Insanity puffed on his cigarette, smiled briefly, and very calmly said, "*You* know."

The man quelled the rising fury at this expected response and counted to ten backwards. He thought, he waited, he thought some more.

"What's so terrible outside?"

For the first time Insanity surprised him with something other than the usual. He exhaled a long stream of smoke and said, "Existence."

"What's so terrible about that?"

"Do you really need me to answer that?"

"Yes."

"Existence isn't all it's cracked up to be."

"It must be surely better than this room which is quite definitely miserable."

"Everyone always says that...until they exist. Then all they ever want is to get back into their little padded room as soon as possible."

"Are you implying that I do not presently exist?"

"*You* know."

"What's outside?"

"Awful shit."

"What?"

"*You* know."

The man sighed testily.

"Actually, I don't know. If I knew and it was as really as bad as you say, then I might agree with you and stay and we can go on chatting like this until I perhaps grow thin enough to actually slip under the door. That is, until I'm dead. Until then, I'm not convinced that I actually *am* as insane as you seem to think I am and would like an answer one way or the other."

Insanity looked at him for several moments, took another drag off his cigarette and gave an impatient sigh.

"Look. I'm gonna break a few rules here because you're acting way too lucid to be truly insane, which is seriously making me doubt whether I'm really supposed to be here or not. Those idiots at Admin are always fuckin' up anyhow. So, listen. The Universe went offline for a while. Then, somehow, it got turned back on. Like somebody flipped a switch or somethin'. There's a lot of sortin' out goin' on. In *this* instance, as pertains to *my* job, theres two kinds of whack jobs. There's the first kind, crazier'n a shithouse rat – I can deal with them. Then there's the other kind – so fuckin outta their brain bucket that they come off like sane types like you or me – or, uh – well, you know what I mean. They can even fool *me*. I'm hoping you're just a clerical error and not one of the second kind I was talkin' about."

"What do you mean, 'hoping'"?

"I'm gonna open this door and let you outta here."

"You can do that?"

"Yeah, why not?"

"But aren't you just a figment of my imagination?"

"Spoken like a true basket case..." Insanity smiled slyly, "or one who's got me fooled." Insanity stood up and opened the door as easily as if it had never been locked in the first place.

"You're a free man, Felix."

Chapter 2

Felix stepped out into a dreary stone hallway.

A dwarf carrying a tiny halberd jumped up to head height and punched Felix in the face, knocking him over backward.

"You idiot!" shouted the dwarf. "What fuckin' took you so god damn long?"

Felix, quite dazed, shook his head and could only stare uncomprehending at the ridiculous, diminutive figure standing over him.

"What's your fuckin' problem? Don't you want to get out of this shithole?"

Felix mentally arrayed his wits onto a long table in a vain attempt to sort them out. "The door. The door – it was – locked."

"No it wasn't, shit-for-brains! The doors in this outfit open inward. You had your dumb ass sitting in front of it so I couldn't open it! I've been screaming at you to fucking move!"

"You couldn't – what? – it was unlocked. You couldn't force it open?"

"Look at me, asshead! I'm a fucking *dwarf*! Do I look like I can just walk up to a solid oak door and just fucking kick it open with some two-hundred pound moron leaning against it?"

"How many days have I been in there?"

"Days? *Days*? You've been in there all of fifteen minutes you fucktard! Now get up and let's get out of here."

"Can you give me a hand getting this strait-" He looked down and raised a hand to his face. Then another. He turned and looked behind him through the door and into the room he had just walked out of. It was an ordinary office, furnished with the typical stuff one finds in offices. A large bay window allowed for an expansive view of a bustling city outside. Felix could see the roofs of tall buildings indicating they were several floors above street-level.

Felix rubbed his face where he'd been punched.

"Where am I?"

"Whaddayou mean?" The Cyclops bent over and peered at Felix with a singular frown. "Are you on 'shrooms or something?"

"Why did you punch me? Who are you?"

"Punch you!" said the dancing panda. "I did no such thing!" The dancing panda reached out a slime-covered tentacle and gave Felix a hard slap over the same spot he'd just been punched. Felix spun and slammed into the wall of the hallway opposite the office. He looked and noticed that the office was no longer there. In its place was an old time gas station with some rusty pumps out front. The whole place looked run-down and quite closed for business. An unreadable sign above the door waved, squeaking in a warm breeze that swept over them from the surrounding desert.

"Where the hell am I now?"

"What *are* you talking about?" asked the doorknob-juggling goldfish in an irritated tone.

"I'm hallucinating," said Felix, perspiration beading his forehead in the hot noon sun. He crouched down and ran his fingers through the cool green water of the lake they were standing on. A pterodactyl stood next to him, wings crossed, tapping its clawed foot impatiently.

"Really, Felix. What *is* this nonsense?"

"You're not really a pterodactyl are you?"

"Do I look like a pterodactyl?" shrieked the seven-headed giraffealope, spitting gobs of blue shoe leather from its eighteen crab claws. The red kitten raised a brilliant crystal shovel as if to strike him another blow when Felix passed out, splashing into the cool sea of roasted marshmallow pudding and lemon-scented rockets. As square circles of yellow enveloped him, the last thing he remembered seeing was the sight of seventy-two-million-and-four hamsters singing a dirge to the monstrous pig as it slowly sliced itself open and let fall a rain of penny whirligigs. The eyes of Goldbach's Conjecture stared into his own and laughed and laughed and laughed and laughed...

Chapter 3

...and laughed.

Of Pandas and Panzers
Interlude the First

"I let him run on, this papier-mâché Mephistopheles, and it seemed to me that if I tried I could poke my forefinger through him, and would find nothing inside but a little loose dirt, maybe."
                              -- *Heart of Darkness*, Joseph Conrad

I was rudely startled from a deep sleep by a rough tap on the shoulder. The sharp tang of burnt coffee and stale cigarettes assaulted my olfactory nerves, floating insolently into my brain stem where these sensations grumpily decided to hang out and make trouble. Sitting up straight I mimed some unsteady motions that crudely paralleled efficient productivity until I realized that I could not possibly be fooling anyone since I hadn't even turned on my computer and the source of the shoulder tap was standing right behind me. I focused my eyes onto the black screen and observed a floating torso clothed in suit and tie. Refocusing them allowed me to further take note of the very distinct impression of computer keys on my left cheek. My hands had been in the act of simulated typing and I snatched them back on discovering a thick puddle of saliva wending its way viscidly between UIOP, HJKL, and VBNM. The space bar was a fallen Atlantean column, completely submerged.

As I sat in my swiveling, ergonomic torture device trying hard to reorient myself to this hostile and alien environment (i.e. life), I began to hear a faint and indistinct sound of muffled squeaking, a bit like listening to a weak radio broadcast of a small rodent being strangled underwater.

After a few moments I found, to my dismay, that the clarity of the sound was not, after all, inversely proportional to the increasing clarity of my brain. A fluttering notion of knocking myself out visited me for a fraction of a second, found no weapon suitable to the task at hand, and fluttered away, very much annoyed.

"Are you listening to me?" queried the irritating sound. "I need this shit entered and filed yesterday! This is the third day in a row I've found you scurrying in here late and taking naps! What do you think I am? Your mother? Turn on that computer and get to work. One more time and I'm writing you up again to add to that giant file I've got sitting on my desk!"

In the screen I could see the physical embodiment of the sound shaking its coffee cup, up and down, some of it sloshing out over the top and dripping on its fingers which grasped the thick ceramic mug like a cudgel. Then its other hand came up and held its index finger and thumb exactly 1.14 centimeters apart.

"You're this far away from getting fired, Randal! I've had it with this nonsense of yours! Clean up your act or you're done!"

The suit and tie stalked away, carrying the sound of annoyed muttering with it. I leaned back in my chair, stretched, and rubbed my eyes. The energy expenditure required to press the power button on my computer was just too exorbitant at present and, after careful calculation, found it would be better spent taking off my cobalt-blue-and-radium-green-striped tie. This offensive object somehow found its way into my paper shredder which munched away happily until it promptly jammed at a precise and predictable moment.

Tim Danforth, the corporate lickspittle that sat in the cubicle next to me poked his pimply face and conservative haircut above the wall separating us. These walls were simply not high or thick enough in my humble fucking opinion. Not to mention the material used to build them was all wrong. The cubicle engineers would have better served the pasty denizens of this joy-destroying oubliette by constructing the walls using several feet of reinforced concrete, razor wire, a moat of sulphuric acid, angels with fiery swords, and burning pandas guarding any apertures with sticks of dynamite. I formed a tiny smile as my thoughts dwelled on this pleasant fiction; more because of the fact that no one here would have had any idea what pandas were. *There* was an odd thought. Why would no one else know what pandas were? I frowned a bit, puzzled.

Danforth opened his mouth to speak. This was never a good idea.

"'Nother day in paradise, eh?"

Now, if it can be said that I detest any single thing in the world, that one thing would involve statements from a "coworker" (and I use that term very loosely) who has absolutely nothing of substance to say, but just can't resist the impulsive urge to break a silence that by all rights should remain in its pristine condition. I liken such a one to an arsonist setting alight a beautiful forest or one of those creepy types who, when faced with an exquisite painting of matchless pulchritude, jealously twists a knife between his inarticulate and talentless hands, unable to countervail his desire to slash and tear. So, a mental dwarf of this low stature takes a peek into his deficient toolbox of witticisms, pulls out some well-worn, rusty cliché (often with some measure of misplaced pride) and proceeds to bludgeon others with it day after day after day, believing himself all the while to be exceedingly clever.

I hate such people.

I hate Tim Danforth.

"'Nother day in paradise, eh?"

Did he actually say that again or am I just reiterating? He followed this delightful query with a laugh. Not a normal laugh, but one of those nerdy guffaws that comes in short bursts from somewhere high in the chest and for some reason reminds me of maggots wriggling inside a carcass. It's the kind of laugh that makes you want to simultaneously vomit, giggle, and cry while you're punching the motherfucker's face into fascinating patterns. *Vomiting*, because the person makes you physically ill, *giggling* because you're finally completing a task that is long overdue, but *crying* because you have to be so close to him in order to execute this much-needed and well-deserved job of structural rearrangement.

Leaning back in my chair, the fingers of my hands interdigitated safely behind my head, I said very calmly and evenly, "Danforth, you really need to pause for a minute and reconsider your position."

Danforth gave a quizzical look, followed by one of amusement, followed by one of arrogant nastiness. When he spoke again, his voice was honey-thick with mockery and condescension. "Oh, but I *have* Randal! I'll do you the service of reminding you that they're doing reviews again this week and I've already got a leg up on that middle management position. George is vacating on Friday, and who do you think they're gonna choose to fill his spot? I suppose you think they'd choose *you* first, and maybe they would if you weren't such a fuckup, but that outcome doesn't seem very likely. Pretty soon you'll be working under me, but I'll try to cut you a break here and there if you can find it in yourself to be nice. In fact, you might want to start practicing that right now."

But, halfway through his babble I had already stopped listening. I'd forgotten that I was supposed to have a meeting with the aforementioned George this very morning, probably for the silly review that Danforth thought so important. I could already feel my soul dying at the thought of wasting even a second of my life sitting through another interminable recapitulation of my performance, or, to be precise, lack thereof. I startled myself out of my reverie as a dim, misty thought dumped itself like a turd into my suddenly – strangely – achy brain. In fact, it began to throb. I sat forward a bit and started massaging my temples.

"Danforth."

"What?"

"By 'reconsidering your position' I meant that of your existence."

Danforth's whole face puckered like he'd bitten into a lemon.

"Are you threatening me, Randal? You're sure not doing a good job of making points with the guy who's gonna be your new boss. Stop being such a fucking psycho for once and pull yourself-"

"Do you realize, Danforth, that the sun is going to blow up in less than five hours?" That seemed like an odd thing to say at the moment, even for me.

As Danforth attempted the brain seizure that - for him - passed for thinking, I grabbed the arms of my chair and raised myself up enough to peer over the rat maze of cubicles. A ray of golden light shot out into the fluorescent gloom. It was the door from George Dale's office being flung open. His office was well-stocked with windows that cast natural light briefly into this dim cave of lizard people slaving away for their master. George himself stepped out and slammed the door behind him, cutting off that precious, life-giving sunlight and frightening a woman carrying a mile-high stack of paper to the copy machine, spilling the entire pile to the floor. George, paying absolutely no attention to her wretched and sobbing plight, proceeded to march down the aisle with military precision directly toward me.

"Danforth."

"What?"

"What time is it?"

Danforth frowned and looked at his watch. Grudgingly he said, "10:05. Why?"

Ah, that was why George looked so pissed off. Even though he was leaving the company at the end of the week and should have been elated, walking on air, he still found it in his black heart to be the same old punctilious cocksucker he always was. I was five minutes late for his excuse to scream and rant, berate and abuse. He was a sadistic bastard and lived for shit like this. He did not like being thwarted in what amounted to being probably the only joy of which he was capable. Danforth, meanwhile, finally looked where I had been looking, saw George, and turned back to me, smiling with all the viciousness his limpid stick figure could muster.

"Danforth," I said without looking at him.

"What?"

"Fuck off."

Now was the time to perform Emergency Evasion and Evacuation Procedure 47B-2. Avoiding responsibility, teamwork, labor, meetings, and just about every cornerstone of modern corporate employee ethics was my fortè. I wrote the fucking book. To get out of a situation like this is somewhat of a creative art form. Do it often enough and you start ad-libbing and changing things up just so you don't get bored. Everyone always wants to engage you in *their* conversation to serve *their* simian, emotional needs. The trick is to turn the tables and engage them in *yours* to such a degree that they not only don't want to finish listening to what has become *your* delightful monologue, but would rather swallow a bag of used razors before ever talking to you again. To effect this desired outcome as quickly as possible, your speech and behavior should exhibit signs of deep and impenetrable psychosis. This may take some practice, but you can do it. Take a deep breath and imagine yourself as a veritable wellspring of everything that is wrong with the world. Remember that you don't have to think too hard about what to say, just as long as you say it. Turn off that filter that causes you to think before you act. After all, nobody *else* seems to use it, why should *you* be held to a higher accountability? Let it flow. There are lots of things to talk about. Having trouble? Here, it's simple.

All you have to do is pick random groupings of words and sloppily construct pompous-sounding sentences and everyone who listens to you will be so baffled and cornered that they will simply open up with a whole new line of conversation in an attempt to evade your babbling with something they can understand. The important point is to remember to get them cornered so that diverting the subject matter is their only means of escape. You can carry on a "conversation" like this for some time before your victim figures out some pretext to physically remove himself from your presence (some examples: babbling polite excuses, setting themselves on fire, throwing coins behind them as they run away – which I've been told is an excellent way to divert the attention of pursuing goblins, et cetera, et cetera, I'm sure you get the idea).

If you still can't think of anything to say, hope is not lost. Very often you don't have to say anything at all. When accosted I personally enjoy executing the gradual formation of a vacant stare. A thin stream of drool stretching to the floor nicely adds to the overall effect. When the assailant comes to a temporary stop demanding an affirmative acknowledgment that their drivel has been heard - or, more likely, merely a pause for breath - you may optionally decide to snap yourself out of your semi-retarded meditations by giving your whole body a quick convulsion and a sharp grunt or gasp. This also gives the drool stream a quick, whip-like motion that can be very frightening to behold if done well. This alone may cause your assailant to take counter-evasive action and move aside. Simply cup your hand to your mouth, feign an intense desire to vomit, and utilize the now-open aperture for your escape. Divert your flight path several times, hang out by a potted plant just long enough to be seen over the top of the cubicles, then dive low and stay low until you've made it to the break room. Make yourself a cup of coffee, sit down, sip slowly and enjoy. If your annoying interlocutor chooses to pursue and finally tracks you down, pretend not to see him and act as though you've never spoken to him before in your life. Spasmodic jerks of your coffee-bearing hand are always recommended. Remember: insanity is the key to the door of freedom.

Without going into tedious and disgusting detail, something of the above is what occurred when George finally arrived at my particular coordinates in four dimensional spacetime. It was, for him I'm sure, a regrettable experience. One in which his secure footing on reality, just days before retirement, was upset by the discovery that such an insufferable imbecile had existed for so long and so closely under his command.

He was one of those who remained standing, jaw agape, finger still upheld in mid-waggle, watching me lope about the cubicles, hunched, running amok like a discombobulated ape, bumping into walls and plastic plants, and knocking things over on the way to the break room. The look on his face (a frown mixed with the kind of terrified puzzlement a chimp might exhibit if it were to look up just as a three-mile-wide asteroid came plummeting down on top of its tree) would decorate the front of his skull for the remainder of his life.

He was one of those who wisely chose not to pursue.

Coffee in hand I took the elevator to the lobby, went outside, grabbed a paper, and scanned the headlines while walking calmly down the street as though nothing in the world concerned me in the slightest, tiniest, eensiest, weensiest, little bit.

Obviously returning to work tomorrow would be quite insane and I briefly entertained the idea of doing so just to be contrary, but let it go. It simply wasn't important enough to waste the effort. Why had I even taken that stupid job anyway? For some reason I had strangely forgotten while slaving away in that not-so-air-conditioned nightmare. Until today. Why had I forgotten? And why had I only just begun remembering things this very morning, starting with my "conversation" with Danforth?

I stopped at the corner and waited for the crosswalk light to turn red before stepping off the curb and fucking up traffic. The city air was reasonably fresh and my head felt as though it were clearing. As I walked, memory networks reattached themselves and hummed to life. Fog dispersed. How had *I* ended up in a job like *that*?

I stopped, standing squarely in the middle of the intersection, horns honking and obscenities hurling, while I had my epiphanepileptic moment. I twitched a bit and dropped my coffee.

Oh. Yeah. My step-father told me that I should "lay low" and keep my "head down for a while". That was seven months, twenty-four days, eleven hours, sixteen minutes and fourteen seconds ago, but I now vividly remembered the day he said it.

We were standing in his office which was usually kept pretty tidy, not by his own efforts to be sure, for my step-father was an unmitigated slob, but by Gretchen – his ancient and bulbous secretary that spoke with a thick and deep Führer-like accent and whose skills included keeping track of the paperwork, keeping the office organized, and being extraordinarily ugly.

That day, however, he had sent Gretchen on vacation and was deep into his eighth bottle of Palladium Label Jonnie Walker. Apparently this was actually more of a continuation from the night before as there were nine more empty bottles already on his desk, stacked into a neat little pyramid. For as much of a slob as he was he could be strangely tidy in odd moments.

I had just arrived back from an errand that had kept me away for a few weeks. Opening the door of his office was like walking into a distillery. You could almost see the vapor. I opened the window and found a tumbler on the floor that didn't look too soiled.

"Binging again, Dirk?" His name was Dirk. I never called him dad because he wasn't and always calling him step-dad or stepfather or step-papa would be cumbersome and stupid.

"I'm not binging," he muttered. (Note: All sentences uttered by Dirk at this juncture are actually translations of what he actually said, there being no point in trying to spell approximations to words that sound like they were puked into a paper bag and thrown at a rotating lawn mower blade. Remember, he's about seventeen sheets to the wind at this point.)

I smirked and observed his swaying countenance. "You're an alcoholic, Dirk, and the name for what you're doing right now is called 'binging.'"

"What're you a doctor or a semanticist?" (One should really applaud the fact he even *tried* to strangle *that* word from his throat.) "An alcoholic drinks vodka from a plastic jug or strains Sterno through his sock. I only drink the expensive stuff. That doesn't make me an alcoholic; that makes me a discerning connoisseur of exquisite, impeccable, and unimpeachable taste."

"Whatever. Got any more in that bottle?" I held out my glass and Dirk managed to fill it without spilling a single drop. Only a true alcoholic could manage such a superhuman feat of skill and daring.

Then he put his hand on my shoulder. I instinctively reached for my rape whistle. Ha, just kidding.

He put his hand on my shoulder and said, "Son..."

I resisted the temptation to roll my eyes. Or was I resisting the temptation to drown him in a toilet? Let me ponder on it and I'll get back to you. Dirk was usually pretty good about getting the hint that I wasn't his son since I never bothered to call him dad. But, sometimes, when he was fried to his tonsils, which was every minute of every day except when he was asleep, he would start a sentence with "Son..." which usually meant he was about to say something either profoundly erudite or uncommonly stupid.

"Son...I know this totally sucks shit through a beer hat but I need you to go get a regular job, lay low and keep your head down."

Unmistakably in the stupid category; I should have bet money. The old tosspot was in exceptional form today.

"Uh...I already have a job, Dirk."

"Yeah, yeah. Get a new one." He lurched suddenly in four opposing directions at once. "It's important that you put that on your action item list immediately."

"Soooooooo, why do I have to get a new job?" Funny, this woozy stewbum had never, ever offered me a job at his company, and here he was telling *me* to get a new job and take a hike.

"Gotta lay low. Keep yer head down." He was fading out fast.

I downed my Scotch and punched him, knocking him spinning to the floor. Out cold. This was particularly fortunate for him because twelve bullets whizzed right through the space his "tumbler hand" had just previously occupied. If he'd been sober and I had not been present to deck him at the appropriate moment he would have thought that to be a serious bummer. Twelve lasers suddenly appeared, playing merrily amongst themselves on the far wall opposite the open window.

I grabbed the Palladium JW out of his "bottle hand", refilled my own glass and pondered on it.

Hmmmm...

I refilled my glass again and pondered on it.

Hmmmm...

I refilled it once again and pondered on it.

Hmmmm…

Having no good ideas because I was too splotched to think of any I decided to leave Dirk to drown his woes and split. I didn't really like him anyway. He was just regaining consciousness, warily peering at the window and reaching for some remote control gizmo, when I left the room.

Stumbling to the elevator, I pushed several buttons and rode around in it for a while until I got to the lobby, quite by accident, even though it was where I had intended to go from the start.

I wobbled through the revolving door that was rotating about its center a wee bit too fast for my taste and stepped out into the fresh night air of Gloglthph, 217th planet out from a blue-white supergiant that was threatening to go fucking bonkers any god damn minute now and blow us clean out of this blighted solar system.

As I stepped out onto the sidewalk, Galactic Revenue Service crack troops trotted by me and through the revolving door which somehow managed to shred them all into something like raspberry jam.

I blinked. Fuck. I was seeing things.

It was definitely more like ketchup with marshmallow bits.

As I crossed the street a hovertank whipped by and got nailed by Dirk's black hole spinner (rather like a salad spinner but less useful for food preparation). The hovertank was crushed instantly by a tiny microhole that you couldn't even see.

Shit, I had to sleep this off.

So, I managed to pirouette to the opposite sidewalk, curled up on the steps of some other monstrous skyscraper and snoozed, missing every last bit of the action, including (I later discovered) the hoverbus loaded with Eridanian cheerleaders that crashed into a classic ground limousine filled with horny Ophiuchan cephalopods.

When I woke up there was a smoking crater where Dirk's office-building had once stood, the radioactive shit trapped inside a very rickety-looking energy containment field that looked like it was held together with rusty nails, strips of unwashed, tie-dyed underwear and exactly thirty-two paper clips.

My head hurt. Man was I hungry.

I had to get out of here. I didn't like the look of that sun. It was starting to appear more and more like a bladder looking to relieve itself upon this toilet of a planet.

Fuck. Where the fuck were my fucking keys?

I got up. I dusted myself off. I turned around and looked up at the supergigantonormous office building to which the steps I had been sleeping on belonged. I went inside.

Sitting behind the front desk was a blond secretary sporting the biggest tits I'd ever seen on a Kreskorian blothomid (a rather large centipede-looking creature with poisonous barbs in its muscular jowls and on the end of every one of its 4000 feet). Had to be fake. The tits, not the blothomid.

"Ummm…hey, I need to get off this planet and I was wondering if -"

The blothomid slapped a piece of glowing paper on the desk and telepathically screamed at me to "SIGN!" causing an instant migraine. It tapped a dripping, poisonous barb on the signature line of the paper which was already burning a hole through it as well as the desk.

Whimpering in agony at the rape that just occurred in my cerebral cortex, I pulled a pen out of my pocket and, with palsied hand, scratched my name on whatever it was I was signing. Hopefully it was a rental contract for at least a personal hyperscooter, but who knows? It was all in Kreskorian.

As soon as I signed it, a massive robot that looked like a vacuum cleaner trundled into the room and, true to its appearance, reached out a serpentine arm and sucked my chest to the end of it, picking me up off the floor, carrying me to a spacious freight elevator which shot me up to the 769,001st floor where I was shoved at a desk and commanded to "WORK!" in a crappy 1950s robot voice. Thankfully it went away after that helpfully instructional orientation period had been completed, leaving me alone to shake and twitch violently at my leisure – or so I thought.

"'Nother day in paradise, eh?" said the voice that emanated from the face that emanated from the cubicle that emanated from my right.

And that's how I met Danforth (whom we'll never see again in this story) and ended up working at SmarmCorp. (which will never again be mentioned or referenced in any way).

So, this exciting diversionary flashback sequence being over with, I'll have you know that I already crossed that street, fucking up traffic as promised. Then I stopped in at McDribble's and got myself a Double Bacon Dribble-Burger with Cheese. If you know a hungry someone for whom you are not particularly fond, I definitely recommend sending them to this place. And, if thou art inclined to care you might be wondering, "So, where the hell are you and how the hell did you get there?" A very simple and forthright question, I salute you.

Chapter 4

Felix dimly perceived a change of state: a sickening sensation as of being spun about in some diabolical laundry-cleaning device, concurrent with a colored flickering of light, first blue, then grayish, then blue, then grayish again. Felix attempted opening his eyes wider but could barely do more than squint, feeling their lids pressed back by the force of a great wind.

With the wind came a terrible chill and Felix shivered violently for a long while. He attempted opening his eyes again and caught a fleeting glimpse of a wall of mist through which he proceeded to plunge, getting quite wet in the process. This did not help his persistent lack of warmth one bit and his shaking grew ever more uncontrollable.

Breathing was difficult and he could only obtain spasmodic gasps of air with great effort. So much gasping was going on that he failed to gasp at the appropriate moment when he broke through the other side of the mist and perceived green fields, woody dales, and sparkling blue lakes in the distance. This, in itself, was not so gasp worthy. What ought to have resulted in a sharp intake of breath was the fact that this scenic view was all several miles below him and the change of state that he had dimly noted earlier was a thing called "falling."

He also failed to do other things that involved the use of vocal cords and lungs, such as screaming or ineloquently gibbering selected expletives. Felix was duly shocked, to say the least, and Shock was not mollified in the slightest when he seemed to crash through something not unlike plate glass, shards of the stuff plummeting with him toward the upward-rushing ground.

Smashing through the glassy substance, however, only added confusion. The view below him changed from the pastoral scenery he'd just observed to that of a great expanse of brownish-red desert, buttes devoid of vegetation, and great seas of undulating dunes, all under a ruddy purple sky in which hung a small red orb barely giving off any light at all.

Felix thought frantically and reviewed his options. There was only one that seemed to have any practical use, so he promptly fainted amidst the sound of the roaring wind and the tinkling of great, jagged sheets of broken glass.

Chapter 5

Felix woke up standing. Those of you who have ever fallen asleep while standing will quickly note that this is not a normal position to find one's self when waking up. Usually something gravitational will occur somewhere between the loss of consciousness and its subsequent attainment. For evolved primates that require a certain amount of consciousness to remain upright we prosaically call this "falling over." Felix had not fallen over, and he found this to be immensely odd.

Had he been sleepwalking? Had he been wandering about in a half-awake, altered state of dream for some unknown quantity of time? Was he now awaking to find himself in some strange place only to realize later that he was not but a few miles from his recently-purchased and dilapidated home? Was he awaking only to find, like J.R. Ewing, that the entire previous season had simply been a nightmare?

No.

He was in a desert, to be sure. But it was a landscape that held little relation to any earthly experience he had ever known. The sand beneath his feet seemed real enough. The buttes in the distance stayed where they were regardless of how often he looked away for a time and then returned his gaze upon them. The mountains to the west still looked like mountains even if he passed his hand in front of them. They did not vanish to be replaced by armies of hamsters or logical impossibilities.

But the lighting and color of things was subtly wrong. The desert seemed illuminated much like what one would expect at early evening twilight even though the sand and buttes were much brighter than they ought to have been. The sky was a deep purple, almost black. The star that ought to be providing this strange luminescence was dull and red, like a dying ember, no larger than a small moon and certainly no more brilliant.

Auditory stimuli were just as abnormal. There was a dead silence about the region with the exception of a perpetual sound as though great boulders were falling very far away, interspersed with the whirring rush of great wheels. Neither was there a direction to the sound. It seemed to emanate from the still air itself. Felix coughed once and was surprised to hear it reverberate around him. If he closed his eyes he would have thought he was simply inside an expansive chamber that echoed back to him the sonic vibrations of even his slightest movements. What was this strange place?

Felix took a step forward and fell over.

Fucking brilliant, he thought.

He pushed himself up out of the sand with wobbly arms and eventually stood upon wobbly legs. His first instinct after this chore was to look behind him. The desert did not lie. There were no footsteps leading to his present place and no apparent sign of windblown sand having covered them up. Aside from the grit that now occupied his clothes from having fallen there was not the slightest indication that he had arrived in any other way than having been placed there, as though some giant hand had set him down like a pawn.

He did his best to remember, to recollect, to piece together the great jagged sheets of broken memory, until he could weld them together sufficiently to make some sense of his present predicament.

He recalled Crumwax and Burthdrool and himself, all standing in the backyard of his house observing the extraordinary antics of a squirrel that had apparently some sort of prior engineering experience.

The Messenger, the Proconsul, their horrible little adventure – he remembered it all. His last memory was being carted away to an insane asylum and then – nothing. Or, rather, not nothing – confusion. First the padded room, a dream of the universe, several bizarre occurrences, and then – this.

What had happened? What had happened to *him*? Why was he here and not in the asylum? Perhaps he was still there, still dreaming. Perhaps even the things he had remembered concerning his adventures had never really happened. Were his friends still alive? Had they ever been real? Was *he* real?

After some time had been spent upon these ruminations Felix realized, with some amusement, that he'd been walking. It did not seem to be a walk guided by any sense of real purpose – merely a walk of habit, of muscles unconsciously reaffirming their reality by exercising their right to move about in any available three-dimensional space that could accommodate their function. The destination seemed to be, naturally enough, the only nearby object of any prominence: a ghastly butte, absent of any obvious life, but which provided a goal in an ocean of nothing.

Felix walked and mused, looked around at the nothing that surrounded him, mused and walked. *What an awful thing!* he thought. *To be conscious, to seem to apprehend reality, and be no more sure of it than a fleeting memory of a dream! To be suspicious of one's own memories! To not know if what I see is real! To have lost the ability to distinguish between thought and apparent object! I feel as though I were a ghost!*

He stopped suddenly, or at least his feet stopped anyway. He looked to his right and saw a wide field of something solid and scintillating by the light of the dull, red star that was slowly sinking over the mountains to the west. Or, perhaps not. Though it appeared it might be sinking the sun never seemed to actually sink, as if it were merely suspended in time in a state of perpetual sunset over those dark mountains, forever and unchanging. Felix felt an abysmal sensation flow over him as though he were in a peculiar place where death stalked but never died.

He peered at the field to his right and noted that it was wide and vast and perfectly round. He moved to stand near the edge where it met the sand and placed a foot on it. His step rang on its surface like a tuning fork, humming a desultory note that hung in the air for awhile, dissipating slowly over the desert like a bell that had been sullenly struck once but, out of some indefinable bashfulness, failed to ring a second time.

The surface was slick and smooth as if something terrible and hot had glowered over the desert in this one spot and fused it all to glass. Upon its perfectly flat and level face Felix noted an inscribed pattern that started near the edge close to his foot and wended its complicated way toward the center; sort of like those labyrinths marked by stones in churchyards that meditatively lead those who walk them through the symbolic vicissitudes of life toward the central goal, which is God.

Was this what I was meant to do? Is this why I am here?

Felix thought for a long while about this mysterious thing for many minutes, wrestling with himself. He struggled with his memories or, perhaps, constructs of memories that, even if they were true, were true no longer. He sensed a palpable notion of relief, of some kind of salvation, that his innate war with himself could be ended and the story finished by simply taking the first step on this pattern and following it through to its end. In so doing *he* would be ended, and so would the universe, and so would the story. To stop. To end the endless. He could think of no other idea more worthy than this and extended his other leg to set his foot on the pattern itself.

"I wouldn't do that if I were you," said a voice that emanated from a cloud of greasy black smoke that emanated from Felix's left.

Felix's foot hovered over the starting line of the pattern for a moment and then was set down again on the sand. The cloud whirled and hissed and burped and then began to fade like a loathsome smog that, uninvited to begin with and having been sent away, grumbled and spat and slowly drifted off down the dusty trail with hunched shoulders, slouching to some other Bethlehem to be born.

What remained was, shall we say, interesting.

Out of the leftover chaos a creature formed itself, grabbing at whatever snippets of recognizable order it could from the natural world so that it might resolve its image: bones and flesh from those of a medley of animals whether they be horse or camel or swine; skin the bark of trees; its arms and hands were branches and twigs; legs human; feet hooves; the head a calf's skull. Two black marbles rolled around in the otherwise empty sockets to give this horrible ensemble the appearance of actually looking at things. Its jawbone, which was that of an ass, moved as it spoke.

"Pleased to make your acquaintance," it rasped from some unknown confabulation of objects that served as lungs.

Felix stared at this repulsive concoction, in horror, for several seconds before replying.

"Umm...likewise...certainly...An interesting aggregation of parts you've assembled."

"Yes," the creature said tiredly. "Sucks, doesn't it?"

"Well...I mean...I wouldn't go so far as to say that it-"

"Sucks? No need to be so polite. Yes, it sucks. It demonstrably sucks," it said ruefully, looking down at itself. "I never have quite gotten the knack of physical reformulation as some of my betters. But, anyway, to business! You have questions, I am quite certain."

"Um...questions? Oh, yes, well, yes I do."

"Indeed. So, let's get started shall we?"

"Started?"

"Asking questions."

"Oh, yes, ummm..."

"You're not very smart are you? Just my luck to get another dolt."

"What do you mean?"

"Is that your first question? It's not a very good one."

"No! I mean, yes! I mean, what are you?"

"Ah, slightly more specific. I am a ghorghoul."

"A what?"

"A ghorghoul."

"And, uh, what is that?"

"A ghorghoul is kind of like a welcome wagon for new arrivals...such as you."

"New arrivals?"

"Are you really asking questions or just parroting what I'm saying?"

"Alright, alright. Do you have a name?"

"Eh? That's a new one. No one ever asked me my name before. They usually just quaver and grovel and ask for some kind of forgiveness and such. Always all about themselves these new arrivals...except you. Maybe you're different. Interesting. My name he asks me."

"Well?"

"Well what?"

"What is it?"

"What is what?"

"Your fucking name!"

"Oh." At this the creature somehow managed to look embarrassed. It looked down and shuffled its feet – er, hooves.

"Well?"

"Well what?"

"Oh, come on!"

"It's a stupid name. Can't we just move on to some other-"

"No! I want to know your name, god damn it!"

The creature shuffled its hooves some more, looked up as if to say something, didn't, went back to staring at its shuffling hooves, looked up again, made as if to say something again, didn't, and repeated staring at its hooves.

"Oh, for fuck's sake!" Felix turned around and started walking away to where he'd first arrived.

"Well, you know, I'm sorry, man. It's just that my name isn't really that important and it's so stupid and-"

"I," said Felix, whirling around, "want to know your name or we will not be talking about anything! No questions! No answers! I will simply spend the rest of my days wandering around in this stupid desert ignoring you!"

"That would be a long time."

"What do you mean?"

"For eternity actually, if truth be told."

"What do you mean, *eternity*," Felix asked with a suspicious squint. "Where am I exactly?"

"In the afterlife."

"No I'm not!"

"You're in denial then."

"No I'm not!"

"See!"

"See what?"

"That you're in denial."

"But, I can't be in denial unless I know what it is I'm supposed to be denying."

"First sign of someone in denial. Denial of their own denial."

"But you can say that about anybody as soon as they give a negative response to your pronouncement that they're in denial!"

"True. Must be angry then. You *sound* angry."

"Not really. More annoyed and puzzled than anything else."

"Want to try bargaining? Admit you're in the afterlife and I'll give you this bright yellow rubber ducky," the creature said, producing a bright yellow rubber ducky from its upturned palm of twigs.

"No!"

"How about an anti-depressant? Got tons of 'em."

"No!"

"Well, then you must have accepted the fact that you're in the afterlife."

"Oh, shut up! Just tell me where I am!"

"The afterlife. You still sound angry. Want to bargain with me for an anti-depressant?"

"No! Why do you say I'm in the afterlife?"

"Hmmm. Let me see. Oh, yeah, because that's where you are."

"No. You must have found me out here in this desert. It's just a desert. You're just a-"

"Yes?"

"-um, a person dressed up in twigs and animal parts."

"Oh, yes, I see – and?"

"Um, there has got to be some kind of civilization over there beyond those mountains," Felix said, pointing to the west.

"No. Sorry. No civilization."

"Well, then what's to the south?"

"Oh! Are you really *asking me* pertinent questions now? Okay, sure, yeah – I mean, no - there's no civilization there. There are, rather, hordes of skeletal, demonic creatures that hail from some other star system who are doing battle with some horrid-looking creatures from some *other* star system that inhabit the east – so don't even bother asking about *that* direction – and we're standing smack in the middle of their traditional battlefield."

"Well, then what's to the north?"

"Nothing noteworthy."

"What the hell are you good for? How the fuck do I get out of here?"

"Look. Dude. I just work here."

"Well who the fuck's paying you?"

"Hey, man, just take an anti-depressant and relax. It was a figure of speech."

"No! Tell me who you are or leave me alone!"

The creature sighed and looked back down at its hooves. "Oh, all right! But, promise me we'll just move right on to other subjects as soon as I tell you! As I said, it's embarrassing!"

"Fine!"

"Don't laugh!"

"Fine!"

"Beefpickle."

"What?"

"Beefpickle."

"What?"

"The Rudely Bent."

"What?"

"Now, what would you like to know?"

"What?"

"Can we fucking move on, dude?"

"Sorry. I was momentarily shocked."

"At least you didn't laugh at me."

"Maybe later. Right now I'm too shocked."

"You're an asshole."

"If my memory serves that is probably an accurate assessment."

"Anyway, whatever you decide to do, I wouldn't go stamping around on that Pattern over there."

"And why not?"

"It's not for you. It was for the last arrival before you came."

"The last arrival?"

"There you go, parroting again."

"Who was the last arrival?"

"Some dude named Roger. It was his invention, you see. So, it served as the exit to his proper destination."

"Where did he go?"

"He walked the Pattern to its center and disappeared. Giggled the whole time, too. Seemed rather pleased. Good for him."

"What do you mean it was his exit? I thought you said this was the afterlife? Isn't that everyone's destination?"

"Dude, you're coming from a place with a shitload of biases about what constitutes an afterlife and all sorts of assumptions concerning what it's all about. Give it up. Let it go. The afterlife is *not* a destination. It's a waypoint. An in-between place. It's a place where you find what you're looking for and move on to where you really need to be. Like Roger. Some things *don't* find what they're looking for and *never* leave, like those awful aliens I was talking about, constantly warring with each other. They're dead and don't realize it, so here they are and here they remain – though I heartily wish they'd fucking get it together and bail from this hotdog stand. I could use a little peace and quiet. The eons *are* long you know."

"Look, Beefpickle-"

Beefpickle winced and said, "Hey! Just call me 'Bugrat' if you feel the need to call me anything at all!"

"How on earth is that better than Beefpickle?"

"You're not *on* earth."

"Fine! Look...whatever – Bugrat-"

"Yes?"

"How do I find my way out of here? You say this 'Roger' found his way out by means of his own invention. What about me?"

"What *about* you?"

"I think my fucking question is obvious! And the answer ought to follow if you know it!"

"I *don't* know it. Like I said, I'm just the welcome wagon, as shitty a job as that is. Roger didn't even say two words to me when I appeared. He was already staring intently at his Pattern. And before I could say two words to *him* he was already waltzing his way down it like a schoolboy. *That* doesn't happen often. But, of course, he was an imaginative fellow in life and had already created an out for himself before he ever came here. You ask me, 'What about you?' and I tell you, 'What *about* you?' What did *you* invent before you died? What did *you* do that might give you a clue as to your newfound purpose and the means by which you might get there? You think the afterlife is just a holding tank for freeloaders? I'll tell you something, the afterlife contains a key word in it: *life!* That means you can still die. See, you're only partially dead. Part of your physical embodiment flew the coop, but what remains is tied to your consciousness, which still exists and has corporeality. But, your consciousness can die too. It can be killed. Here. You can cease to exist. So, my recommendation to *you* is to get your shit together, figure it out, and find *your* way! The fact that your way hasn't presented itself already tells me that your previous existence was spent being a fuckup. That, in itself, doesn't necessarily spell doom. However, your chances of making it out of here are doubly screwed. Here's some food for thought. Fact: the places some entities go when leaving here are *really fucking empty*. So, good luck. Carry on. Consider yourself welcomed." With that, Beefpickle's (or, if you prefer, Bugrat's) lower jawbone ceased movement, though he didn't disappear like Felix thought he would.

Felix, to his astonishment, came to a very sudden and painful realization. He had not thought very much about his own life or his actions while alive. Ramifications, consequences…these were always far off things that he'd always thought of as relatively 'solved' dilemmas. Dilemmas that could, perhaps, have remained solved if he had only followed the proscriptions of his religious order better. No. He had to rethink this too. His actions were those of careless expediency, which was one of the signs of Zanzer Gackspin for the Apocalypse that had already happened. He hadn't even followed the tenets of his own religion. But, even if he had…was simple dogmatism a human being's best bet to its own salvation? Was the embrasure of faith and – by logical implication – condemnation of reason, truly the way in which the divine intended humankind to understand it? Could truth, perhaps, be a thing not so easily codified by asserted tenets, rules and commandments, kept in a handy book that one can always carry around and be comforted at all times as though it were a pack of cigarettes? Could religion, in itself, be only another addiction that allows people to cease the interminable process of thinking – which could possibly involve the risk of questioning and undermining their heartfelt beliefs – just so they can go to sleep at night? Wasn't it not television, but *religion*, that was the opiate of the masses?

Felix arrived at these ideas for the first time in his whole life.

Doubt crept upon him like something that would creep upon him like doubt.

His heart, three sizes too small, at once grew three sizes too big. As this spiritual analog of his physical organ grew to massive proportions, he felt as though he could save all of humanity with his newfound love and understanding of the perplexities that riddled the human condition. He had found a clue to his way. He could redeem himself and bring enlightenment back to Whoville.

"Beef – I, mean, Bugrat – can you help me find my way?"

"No," said Beefpickle, who promptly vanished in a puff of greasy, black smoke.

A Dislocated Collocation of Peas
Interlude the Second

"My name is George Nathaniel Curzon. I am a most superior person."
-- *The Balliol Masque*

Unfortunately the answer is not simple or forthright, but I shall endeavor to keep it within reasonable limits. As I mentioned early on in this rambling narrative, I am currently standing on the unpronounceable 217th planet of a blue-white supergiant that is about to blow itself to bits, along with everything and everyone around it. Given my delay of almost eight months working at that place I had promised I would never again reference in any way I am rather surprised it hasn't yet. This, you might understand, causes me a certain measure of consternation that, for any normal person, would manifest in screaming panic. The reason none of the fair citizens of Gloglthph are panicking at present is due to the fact that they simply don't know. You might interject something perfectly reasonable at this point like, "Well, certainly the government and its scientists must know what is about to happen," and you would be perfectly correct. The upper echelon of the government and a select few of its scientists *do* know. In fact, they know so well that they're already in hyperspace heading for a nice, snug little planet in the Korgai system orbiting a more hospitable yellow star that's not going to burn out for billions more years.

You see, the government of Gloglthph is actually owned by a corporation, the largest corporation in this entire universe, Bloppo Heavy Industries LLC. Indeed, Bloppo is so corrupt and has its tendrils into so much of the Imperial Administration that "LLC" should actually read "NLC". Bloppo Heavy Industries can pretty much do whatever the fuck it wants. So, when a blue-white star threatens to pop a gasket, Bloppo just picks up and moves to greener pastures, writing the whole star system off as a loss without so much as a yawn.

You might now be wondering where Gloglthph is in relation to you. You might even venture a guess that a place this screwball ridiculous couldn't possibly exist in your universe. Kudos. It doesn't. You may or may not be aware that a chap by the name of Albert Einstein showed that superluminal space travel was impossible or, more to the point, achieving the velocity of light is impossible. Rather more specifically, it is impossible to achieve the velocity of light from *subluminal* velocity, the kind of velocity you are already familiar with. You can approach it but never get there. Technically speaking the equations involved imply a symmetry. If an object is already at *superluminal* velocity it may also asymptotically approach the speed of light in vacuum, but backward in time (as opposed to your forward arrow of time), however it also will never get there, let alone cross the boundary into *subluminal* spacetime. This fact is rather moot since no one in your universe is already traveling faster than the speed of light.

Another thing no one in your universe has figured out how to do is work round the whole speed of light boundary problem by, well, going around the problem: that is, hyperspace. However, yet again, the physical restrictions imposed by your universe on such a possibility are formidable, to say the least, and at your particular stage of development you don't even know what all those are yet. So, that's out.

The planet I'm standing on is not in your future or your past but is roughly parallel to your "time stream" or whatever you want to call it. It is also roughly physically parallel. Yes, you can extend that notion to what you crudely call a "parallel universe". Parallel universes occupy actual coordinates in multidimensional space, such that one universe is adjacent to another coming in "contact" at their "boundaries". Hence, parallel. Theoretically you could get into another universe by hopping into a spaceship, leaving your planet, taking the long trip to the edge of your universe, "crossing" the "boundary" into the next, and then happily whisk about in your new playroom. The shitty realities associated with this method should be readily apparent, however. The stars and galaxies in your particular universe are not just drifting about aimlessly; they're *accelerating* away from you! In fact they're accelerating away too fast for you to catch up to most of them. In some 150 billion years from now, every galaxy beyond your local group will have dwindled away out of range of even your most powerful telescopes and the sky beyond your gravitationally bound neighbors will be pitch black.

So, the "edge" of the universe is traveling faster and faster away from you. Even if you were to attain light speed you would never get there. (Just getting to something as close as the Andromeda galaxy would require you to travel ten trillion *times* the speed of light just to see it get appreciably bigger in your field of view in reasonable time.) Not to mention the trip would be a miserable prospect for any short-lived organic entity. But, the picture's worse than that. A trip in a hypothetical light-speed-capable vehicle would be bad enough, but now replace that with the pathetic chemical rockets you rookies like to putt around in and we have a recipe for death by boredom. It would be worse than chugging across Antarctica in a horse-drawn cart with square wheels. You might as well get out and walk and you'd still get there in the same amount of time: never. It should also be pointed out that this is the best method you've so far devised for getting to *any* place in your universe, let alone *other* universes. I might as well tell you that any other sentient entities that exist in your neighborhood are in the same boat. The physics of your universe with respect to space travel just plain sucks.

By now you should be going into some convulsions, rabidly screaming at me to get to the fucking point. How did *I* get here? Easy enough: the Labyrinth.

The Labyrinth is a means of getting to interesting places from one universe to another without all the fuss of packing your bags and messing about with taxi cabs and traveler's checks. Really interesting adventure travel without all the mess!

Cool!

Also totally unrealistic!

This is probably why you only hear about such things in science fiction movies and books. It's too good to be true, and we've all heard the admonitions concerning things sounding too good to be true: if they do, they're not.

But, the god-damnedest thing about the Labyrinth is that, even so, it exists. No one knows who built it, when, or how. No one knows anything about it at all except that it exists and it works. Traveling through the Labyrinth is not whiz-bang spectacular like you see in movies where the protagonist gets into some "device" and falls into a cosmically-glowing hole that twists and turns like an amusement park ride, with stars and other celestial objects streaking past the viewing window, or accelerating through a *2001*-esque, 1960s realm of psychedelic inverted colors and geometric lines. None of *that*.

Traveling through the Labyrinth consists of finding an entrance and walking through a perfectly normal-looking tunnel. When you come out the other end you're someplace else. Of course, that description oversimplifies just a trifle. The Labyrinth is called what it is both to pay homage to Jorge Luis Borges (as is mandated in the Rulings Governing Writers Who Include Labyrinths in Their Stories) and also to provide an apt label, in one word. The Labyrinth is literally a labyrinth.

So, I might have also understated some other aspects about traveling through the Labyrinth, such as its seeming lack of fuss and muss. That's not entirely true. Actually, it's fucking dangerous. Not only can you get lost (perhaps forever) but there are other *things* in the Labyrinth as well. Some may be travelers passing through, and some have taken up residence. Some have relatively easy-going dispositions. Some, to understate yet again, do not. As you may have already

178

surmised, I am one of those traveler-types. There is an entrance, or exit if you will, here on Gloglthph. I got here via the Labyrinth.

Before you surmise any further I should inform you that Bloppo Heavy Industries does not have anything to do with the Labyrinth. Obviously, if they even knew about it they would be using it rather than traveling in a spaceship to another star system (physics in this universe is a little more conducive to space flight). As has already been previously illustrated Bloppo is not going to save the population of this planet from disaster; nor, for that matter, am I. No, with any luck, everyone here is going to die with the exception of yours truly. Mmm…that doesn't sound quite right, does it? I meant to say something more on the order of, "everyone here is going to die except – if luck permits – me." There, that's better.

My purpose for visiting this place was simply to pick up a clue or two in my ongoing investigation of the Labyrinth itself. Though I have great sympathy for the struggles of the human race particularly, and those of all races generally, my overriding function for the moment is to find out what we don't know about the Labyrinth, which is everything. And no, I don't have any feelings at all for my so-called step-father. He's just some asshole I convinced to be his step-son in order to give myself some mobility and a sizable bank account on this planet that is bureaucratically controlled by the Bloppo iron fist. He got into a bit of a tangle with the Imperial tax man a few months back and was simultaneously falling behind in paying back some loans to Bloppo, so Bloppo looked the other way when the Galactic Revenue Service crack troops showed up.

Perhaps I should, at this juncture, execute those formalities of salutation and greeting that usually occur at the *beginning* of a narration.

My name isn't Randal, it's actually Carter, and I am a synthetic sentient. I was constructed by the Mosvai Corporation (a not-so-clever anagram of the founder's surname, Isaac Vasomi) on the planet New Caledonia in 14,822 A.D. (using the Old Earth calendric system); a small, out-of-the-way sort of planet in the outer spiral arm of Andromeda (deduce what you will from that!) and outside all political spheres of any consequence. There are at least four others like me that have been built and we are collectively the most advanced artificial life forms ever made. I can think, I have feelings, I can be damaged (not easily), I eat (for fuel and for appearances sake), I am affected by alcohol (often too affected – in fact I often become delusional after only a few drinks, see things that aren't there and grossly over exaggerate), I am physically indistinguishable from a human being (when I'm in that form – yes I can change my shape, like that cop dude in *Terminator 2*) and can perform all normal functions of a human being (at times this is rather unfortunate and even embarrassing, in fact I kind of need to fart at the moment and I'm trying to figure out how to do that without arousing too much disgust from the other McDribble's patrons – but, never mind, the world is ending soon).

I can also do things that most organics can't such as doing calculus in my head, analyzing the true-versus-advertised content of the McDribble's burger I just ate molecule for molecule and which is giving me such horrible gas, verifying and testing all my internal states (in fact, I just discovered that it was the blothomid's telepathic assault that temporarily derailed my neural network pathways and screwed my memories for about eight fucking months; I just wrote a subroutine to prevent that in future blothomid encounters), and plug myself into computer systems and communicate with them at their most fundamental state (in fact, I've been doing that while sitting here at McDribble's – every eatery on this planet has a planetary computer access jack – and have just broken their new highest level encryption system which they revamp every month; now I have access to the scientists' data storage; ah, it wasn't entirely wiped clean; oh shit, I have 3 hours, 28 minutes, and 15.2351 seconds to get the fuck off this soon-to-be-vapor ball of doom).

So, I guess you could say I'm a sort of organic robot, kind of like you…but more intelligent…and better at pretty much everything you can think of. Oh well, it was great talking to you and bringing you up to speed and all that, but I got to get a move on and find myself some transport out of this city. The Labyrinth entrance doesn't exactly come out into a local mail box or storm drain. Travel time from city to Labyrinth is a smidge less than three hours. So, if I don't find anything in the next 28 minutes it's fucking sayonara for me. Later, dude. If I make it I promise to continue the story.

Chapter 6

After Beefpickle's disappearance, Felix plunged into a dark gloom. Despondent, not knowing what to do, he paced about the desert in the company of his thoughts. *Why,* said his thoughts, *should you have expected an instantaneous affirmation of your change of heart? The world is a cruel and confusing place, full of labyrinthine mirrored hallways and strange intelligences frothing over with riddles, their identities hidden behind bland masks painted with question marks. Apparently, so is the afterlife. You've managed thus far without help. What do you need Beefpickle for anyway? Fuck him! You can figure it out, Felix, entirely on your own. You can do it all. You don't need anyone else!*

A certain pertinacity welled up in him and he stopped pacing. Desperate resolution followed as an incipient thought struggled and squirmed into existence.

Walk the Pattern, Felix! It's an exit. Get out of here!

Felix returned to the Pattern's circumference and found its outermost extremity. For a moment he hesitated and looked around. No protean entities fashioned bizarre shapes out of inchoate mists to stop him. No cries were uttered, no alarms were rung.

Felix looked down and carefully placed a foot on the beginning of the inscribed line of the Pattern and heard that wistful gong hang in the air for a moment. He hesitated only once more and then set down his other foot, repeating the action, one foot following another, tracing the Pattern to its center.

The Year of the Sneep
Interlude the Third

"...if a story began 'So and so was wandering around aimlessly,'
listeners knew immediately that trouble was at hand..."
-- *Trickster Makes This World*, Lewis Hyde

I was wandering around aimlessly.

Having an immense amount of difficulty getting my bearings I finally had to admit to myself that I was hopelessly lost. I had brought along a few extra of those detestable McDribble's burgers to keep my organic shit from falling apart and I still had two left (they seem to last for an unnaturally long time). So, for the time being at least, things were going swimmingly in the food department, but where the fuck I was, your guess is as good as mine.

The journey to the Labyrinth entrance was straightforward. A doubling-back to Dirk's "office building" immediately revealed the opening move for my escape. A single GRS hovertank was left to stand watch over the containment field surrounding the radioactive crater that the aforementioned office building had once occupied, presumably to eradicate any life that might spontaneously evolve out of that inhospitable mixture of energetic particles and sterilized bedrock.

It was a simple matter to remove the occupants and hijack the craft for mine own uses, which I promptly did and with haste. The trigger-happy sentries at the city's perimeter were a snap, the appropriate pass codes having already been extracted from the onboard computer. From there it was smooth sailing at hair-raising speeds to my destination: a desert valley that had only undergone preliminary survey during the very first Bloppo reconnaissance missions and had never been visited since. Nothing to mine or otherwise exploit. Worthless, according to Bloppo's view. Everything, according to the view of a certain artificially intelligent construct that was programmed to feel emotions, not excluding fear, and was about to be very, very *deconstructed* if it didn't hurry the fuck up.

I touched down, ran (not walked or sauntered) to the cave entrance that was my goal, and passed through just as the blue-white star above performed some great wiggle and contraction. I didn't see the rest. I was through. According to some, the Labyrinth theoretically existed apart from whatever attachments it held at its ingress and egress points – I hoped. As it happened I didn't even feel a tremor as the 217th planet out from that blue-white giant was cleanly and quickly atomized.

I tuned out my ethics program, overrode my remorse circuit and did what any human being would have done. I spat (for theatrics) and pressed on down the tunnel, Armageddon's sole survivor (not counting Bloppo's bureaucrats). Okay, maybe only Clint Eastwood would have done that. So, I pretended to be Clint Eastwood and tried to imagine how I would get out of a labyrinth if I were Clint Eastwood lost in a labyrinth.

I don't know. What would *you* do if *you* were lost in a labyrinth and *you* were Clint Eastwood? I don't think I can really say because I'm just not that much of a badass. I've only saved humanity twice. [Note: You'll find out more about the rationale behind that comment when, two-hundred years into your future, so-called "spaghetti" westerns are retrieved from the ashes of Earth's first and only full nuclear exchange and used as behavioral training videos for the dominant remnant of human civilization, revering Clint Eastwood as a mythological folk hero, later upgraded to the status of First Executive and God.]

The walls of the Labyrinth had gradually altered from rough-hewn cave rock to finely-wrought masonry. In some places there were collapsed walls and ceilings, cutting off certain tunnels and opening others. This may or may not have been intended. Though it is thought by some that the Labyrinth, as a whole, exists in some kind of independent *Elsewhere*, there are those who believe that its tunnels physically exist, passing through planets in many universes suitable to accommodate them, and that it is the entrances and exits that somehow form the links. How else, goes the argument, can one explain the clear evidence that the Labyrinth is affected by seismic forces, i.e. earthquakes. Others are not convinced and claim that there are many other possibilities that may account for internal damage. The Labyrinth, after all, hosts some fairly aggressive abominations capable of enormous destructive power. Whole civilizations may have lived and died in these tunnels for millennia. How many wars have been fought? How many repairs have been made and then been torn down again? Who knows? So, the debate and speculation rages on and on. As far as I'm concerned - at the moment - I'm inclined toward the *Elsewhere* theory, and I've some pretty strong evidence at my disposal. To date, no one I know who studies this thing has ever been inside it when a planet's host star supernovaed the shit out of it. This appears to be a first. Yay for me.

Meanwhile, I was lost. For some reason the map I had made for myself en route to Gloglthph was not serving me too well on my return trip. Oh, yeah, I forgot to mention that it's not unheard-of for the

Labyrinth to rearrange itself. No one is entirely sure if this actually happens since it doesn't appear to happen often. The notion may be due to confused reporting by travelers who've gotten lost and found their way again. It may be due to some entities within the Labyrinth deliberately closing passages off and making new ones elsewhere because they have a fucking sick sense of humor. Or maybe the Labyrinth does this of its own accord because *it* has a fucking sick sense of humor. Most of the time one can get from point A to point B and back without too much difficulty. That is to say, your map won't suddenly make a liar out of you when returning from B to A. The hassles imposed by other creatures in the Labyrinth are a separate issue.

Speaking of which, I heard a noise coming toward me from up ahead; a kind of rhythmic pattering against stone mingled with labored breathing.

Crap.

I changed my coloring to match the wall I was standing next to, powered down some of my noisier biological functions, like breathing and heartbeat, in case the creature in question was sensitive to such things, and did my best to look like a nothing minding its own business.

When the thing became visible I fairly goggled at it for half a moment before choosing to make my presence known. It was carrying a lantern before it so its features were unmistakable. To bother describing it – waistcoat, pocketwatch, and frantic murmurings about being late and all – would just be redundant to those of you who've been immersed in your western culture for any significant length of time.

I restored my functions, changed my coloring back, and said howdy.

The rabbit leaped off the floor, eyes wide with terror, and let forth such nerve-shattering shrieking that I was afraid he would call the denizens of the entire Labyrinth to our location. When his feet hit the floor again he ran round in circles several times, ran one way down the tunnel, ran back the other way, circled a few more times, dropped his lantern and finally rammed his head straight into the side of the tunnel and fell onto his back, stunned. I couldn't really say he didn't knock himself out on purpose. Rabbits are such nervous and fretful creatures by nature; he may well have seen unconsciousness to be just the soothing balm he required.

I glanced up and down the tunnel. Nothing seemed to be hurtling out of the dark at us – yet. I picked up the rabbit's lantern and walked over to his supine form, one leg still twitching every now and then. I kneeled next to him and shook his shoulder gently. Slowly, one eye opened a fraction and then slowly closed again. Then *both* eyes flashed wide open and he sat up quickly, clutching his pocketwatch to his chest, staring at me in horror. He looked as though he were tensing to spring up and begin that awful screeching business all over again.

"Hold on there buddy," I said, holding up an empty hand. "I'm not going to hurt you. My name is Carter and I'm lost in this Labyrinth. Are you all right?"

The rabbit, realizing that he wasn't going to be made into hasenpfeffer, gradually calmed down and, between panicky gasps for air, assured me he was fine.

"Yes, yes. Quite fine...quite fine. Rabbits, as you may know, are nervous and fretful creatures by nature. In my terror I saw unconsciousness to be just the soothing balm I required."

"Uh, yeah, I know. So, what's your name?"

"I'm terribly sorry, good sir. Where *are* my manners? My name is-"

He doubled over just then and threw up all over the floor; an interesting medley of diced carrots, peas, and something that looked remarkably like baklava.

"My apologies yet again, sir. Nerves and such..." The rabbit attempted a sheepish smile, which is a pretty bizarre and disturbing thing to see a rabbit do - especially after having recently vomited.

"Allow me to introduce myself," he attempted once more. "My name is Harlington Everett Cudsworth Elsmoresquirington the Fifteenth, heir to the Barony of Paddingtonshire, Chancellor to the King and Queen of-"

"Yeah, yeah – so, umm, Harvey...maybe you can tell me where you're headed?"

The rabbit suddenly glanced at his pocketwatch and nearly fell into a swoon. "Oh, I'm late, I'm late, for a very important-"

"I'm sure. But, going *that* way isn't going to get you far, unless you like floating around in vacuum. I've just come from that direction and it's a trifle worse for wear."

Harvey slowly sank down on his haunches and started nibbling at his paws, eyes darting nervously around at nothing in particular, lost in his misery.

"Oh dear. Oh, dear. I say, this is terrific bad luck. If I don't get back soon they'll have my head!"

"I wouldn't be in too much of a hurry then if that's what's waiting for you," I said.

"Oh, but I must! I must! There's going to be a trial soon and I must be there to perform my duties and read the charges against the accused and all that."

"Well, Harvey, there's no going back the way I came. What about you?"

"What about what?" said Harvey absently.

"What about the tunnel you've been traveling down? Where does it come out?"

Harvey was instantly rigid. "Oh, we mustn't go back that way. No, no, certainly not! Nothing but trouble down there. Now you tell me there's nothing up ahead except more nastiness. Oh, hang it! I'm done for!"

"Now look Harvey, you must have gotten in here *somehow*."

"Oh, yes, indeed. A rabbit hole from the surface, which widened very suddenly and made a straight drop to the bottom. There's no climbing back up I can assure you."

"I'm not exactly without resources. I'm confident we can get out of here if you can take me back to where you fell."

"Madness! You don't realize what you're asking! I've just made it *this* far with the hair on my hide. I won't go back. I won't!"

"Harvey?"

"What?"

"What time is it?"

Harvey checked his watch. "10:05 in the morning."

"How long have you been down here?"

"Four days, three hours and twenty-eight minutes exactly."

Whoa. I was hoping he'd only been down here for a short time.

"Can you remember the way back? Were there branching tunnels?"

"Oh, heavens! There were dozens! A bloody maze!"

"Any distinguishing marks? Anything that you could recognize?"

"Oh, I don't know. Perhaps there were. I was much too frightened to pay any attention. There are hideous monsters in this place, I tell you. Hideous! All fangs and eyes and warts and spiky things and-" He trembled violently at these lovely memories and fell silent.

This was worse than I thought. The Labyrinth had changed, that was certain, and I was stuck with a twitchy rabbit that couldn't remember the way out, not to mention the way out was infested with something-or-other. Why does everything have to suck?

This was a particularly perplexing problem. How to get a scared-shitless bunny rabbit to go back down a tunnel when he's probably not going to be very cooperative in that capacity? I'll need some time to think about this. Meanwhile I ought to explain a couple of things you may be wondering about now.

"The White Rabbit?" you say. "Fucking seriously?"

Welcome to *my* world, asshole. If you think you can do better, I'll gladly exchange places with you and *you* can deal with this bullshit.

Yes, the White Rabbit. Yes, that very same story. Clumsy little girl trips and falls into a hole in the ground that should only be big enough for a rabbit and gets high with a bunch of bugs and farm animals. As you say, ridiculous.

This might be a hard pill to swallow but when we talk about parallel universes we mean what we say. There are an infinite number of them in theory and who knows how many connections there are from the Labyrinth to these myriad alternate realities. Maybe all of them, if the word "all" can encompass "infinite." This is not without precedent. Even in your bumbling era there was an unpopular notion suggested by a few of your physicists called the Many Worlds Interpretation of quantum theory. In a nutshell (and I'm going to be glossing over quite a lot of detail, nuance, subtlety and probably accuracy as well) the idea was that every time a decision was made, the entire universe bifurcated into two copies of itself. Not exact copies, mind you. One continued on with one version of the decision and the other went about its business as a result of the opposite decision. By "decision" they were talking about subatomic particles in the two-slit experiment where one particle had to "decide" which slit to pass through. The results of this two-slit experiment suggested that the particle had to pass through both simultaneously. Well, this just couldn't be possible. There's only one particle. There are two slits. In "reality" it can only go through one, yet the results clearly show it went through both. Okay, so the whole universe splits in two and in one universe the particle goes through slit A and in the other it goes through slit B. This was supposedly true of all subatomic particles and it was collectively happening all the time giving rise to an infinite splitting off of universes and those universes splitting and then the next generation of universes splitting and so on. A hundred splits down the line could result in a parallel universe with an entirely different history and perhaps even different physical properties in which high weirdness ensues.

Confused? So were they. Something along these lines was championed by a physicist named David Deutsch. Naturally he was "challenged" by other physicists. This is propeller-head code-speak for being "ridiculed". As it so happens, something very much like this interpretation appears to be what is happening with respect to all these parallel universes. Unfortunately, Deutsch's vindication wouldn't come about for another twelve or thirteen thousand years.

The bottom line with all this nonsense is that you have an infinite variety of universes to choose from. Clearly, then, it is possible for a universe to exist in which the Hatter, Pikachu, Chuck Manson and Cthulhu are all attending a very fucking mad tea party. Quite literally, if you can imagine it, it exists – somewhere. We should count our lucky stars that the imagination in which human beings pride themselves is as limited as it is.

So, if you think *Harvey* is too taxing on your credulity then I suggest you stop reading this immediately and go back to your *sane* world of mutually assured destruction, economic slavery and religiously-inspired genocide.

"Ouch."

"What?"

"I stubbed my hoof."

Wait. Hoof?

I turned and beheld a cloaked and hooded figure standing in the middle of the tunnel. I raised Harvey's lantern to get a better look and saw the eyes and snout of a goat peering at me from inside the shadowed cowl.

"Maia?"

"Hi, Carter. When did you arrive?"

Maia threw back his hood with two cloven forehooves, one of them briefly catching on a horn, and beamed at me innocently.

"I might ask you the same question." I looked quickly over at Harvey, ready to pounce him and clamp his mouth shut in case he started screaming again, but he only peered up at Maia despondently and said, "Good day, Maia."

"Hello Sir Elsmoresquirington the Fifteenth. Still here I see," Maia said sympathetically.

"You two know each other?" I asked, rather surprised.

"Oh, yes," Harvey said, turning to me, "Maia is a prominent guest in Wonderland. He is called Maia the Lost by the court."

"He shows up in Wond--. But, how is that-"

"Possible?" Harvey finished. "I think you're forgetting to whom you are speaking."

"Right…right," I said. "But, why does he always show up in *your* neck of the woods? He never shows up unless someone is lost or if something really improbable is going to happen…oh, yeah, I get it. Nevermind." My sentence dwindled to a mutter as my apparent stupidity increased. Wow. That blothomid must have done some serious harm. I would have to do a very time-consuming but thorough scan later on.

I turned to Maia. "So, what's up?"

"Lost as usual." He said matter-of-factly.

There was a cricket-infested silence for a moment.

"Okay. Great. Mind telling us how we might make an exit?"

Maia pointed a hoof in the direction Harvey had just come.

"Can I ask what you're doing here?" I asked.

"You're Lost, correct?" He asked me in an isn't-that-obvious tone of voice.

"Yes."

"So am I."

It doesn't take me long to get irritated when Maia is around. He's a fellow traveler in the Labyrinth and a trusted friend, but he sometimes reminds me of the kind of people who are fun to have at parties, but you don't really want them around at any other time because their existence constantly reminds you that your life is fucked up and, by the by, you are entirely to blame.

"Is that the only reason you're here?" Annoyance was clearly present in my voice.

"No."

Another pregnant pause. (I never did like that turn of phrase. Kinda gross.)

"Wonderful," I nearly screamed. "What's the other reason?"

"There are two actually."

I waited. The silence thickened. Maia just stared at me. Harvey burped.

"Great! WHAT ARE YOUR TWO FUCKING REASONS?"

"Well…"

Maia thought for a moment and cleared his throat.

"The first is that something extraordinarily improbable is about to happen."

Which, in this case, was like being told nothing.

"Neat. The other? Please?"

"Oh, just another, even more extraordinary, improbability: the CEO of Bloppo Heavy Industries, LLC, is going to drive right down this tunnel in a hovertank. I must stop him."

I had to tip my hat to him. That was really fucking improbable. Especially unlikely since Team Bloppo was well on its way to somewhere that wasn't blowing up.

"Why do you need to stop him?"

"Because I'm Lost and I need to hitch a ride. I'm due at Alice's trial and I need to witness some very improbable things that will happen then."

"Such as?" Harvey inquired.

"Oh, well, she has to wake up toward the end. Your whole universe *is* a dream you know? I'm really sorry Harvey, but it is pretty much Wonderland's Apocalypse that I'm to attend."

"This is dreadful!" cried Harvey and promptly fainted.

"Wait a minute," I said, "As I recall, the White Rabbit is supposed to be *present* at the trial."

"Oh, yes, indeed. I must take poor Harlington with me."

"What if you don't?"

Maia thought a moment. "I don't really know. I suppose the Wonderland universe would simply bifurcate again. There'd be one universe which has the White Rabbit in its final act and one that doesn't."

"There could also be one that doesn't get destroyed either," I pointed out.

"Truly, that is indeed a possibility. But, I'm afraid I don't know how to set about the task of finding a universe with such particular qualities. This business is still all so very accidental."

"Agreed," I said, "so let's call it an accident and not send the rabbit off to certain doom."

"That's fine by me. But, why? You just left a planetful of billions that met their doom without your having done anything at all, Carter. What is one lapine more or less?"

"There was nothing I could do for those billions. I *can* do something for Harvey."

"Oh, well then. No matter. He's all yours. This would also necessarily conclude my business here."

"Conclude your business? What do you mean? I thought you had to wait for Bloppo to give you a ride?"

"Well, everything's all different now that I don't have to take Harvey with me. I now have another means of getting Lost somewhere else. Toodles!"

"Is the hovertank still coming?"

But, Maia had already vanished.

"Goddammit."

"What's that?" Harvey murmured, regaining consciousness once more.

"What's what?"

"That noise!"

The telltale whirring of a hovertank was barreling down on us; possibly our only ticket out of here in one piece.

"Harvey! Quickly! Get against the wall!"

Harvey leapt up and pattered to the wall of the tunnel, pressing himself against it, thinking himself into two-dimensionality. He trembled. His eyes were wide as saucers.

"I'm going to die," he squeaked.

"No, you're not," I said calmly.

I stood in the middle of the tunnel in a stance as though I were going to tackle the whole NFL. I lengthened my legs and arms. I sprouted tentacles that attached themselves to the walls, floor and ceiling. I energized rarely-used inertial dampeners. I reviewed subroutines and automatic survival programs in case my higher consciousness program layer was disrupted. All this took about three microseconds. I ate my last two McDribble's burgers. This was going to cost me a lot of energy. The hovertank was careening around some dark corner, blasting away at something in hot pursuit. It corrected its motion and tore down the tunnel straight toward me, at top speed (averaging something like 300 miles per hour). As it approached I could see the individual behind the armored glassteel windscreen driving it like a madman. If I'd had time I would have laughed.

The hovertank and I collided.

Chaos.

Arms, legs and tentacles stretched to impossible limits. The heels of my boots dug trenches into the floor. My face had smacked itself into the center of the windscreen which sent several long cracks radiating in every direction across its surface. Higher consciousness faded to critical levels, but I still managed to supply more power to my tentacles, ensuring their grip. I made the mistake of opening one eye and peering into the face of the driver just inches away from my own on the other side of the glassteel. This time I did laugh and nearly lost my grasp of the tunnel's sides.

Imagine you've just been hit by a car. You fly up over the hood and straight into the windshield. In your adrenalin-laden, hyper-aware state of mind time slows down a bit and you seem to have an eternity to contemplate the visage of the shocked driver inside the vehicle... and it is the face of a clown. Not a nice, friendly, happy sort of clown. No. This is the face of a frowny, cigar-butt-chewing, frazzled, splotchy sort of clown; the kind of clown that has a pet crocodile and invites onlookers to put their hands into its mouth (the alligator's, not the clown's).

This was Bloppo himself. *The* Bloppo of Bloppo Heavy Industries, LLC. I suddenly stopped laughing as his frown got frownier.

"Goddammit! What the fuck are you doing?" he snarled rhetorically.

"Let us in," I suggested, screaming calmly through the glassteel windscreen.

"No!"

"Yes!"

"Fuck you! No!"

"Yes!"

He looked at me hard, pressed his big red nose up to the cracked glassteel, and seemed to be thinking fast.

"Goddammit! Fine! Hurry the fuck up! I'm running out of ammo!"

He hit the brakes and I slid down the front of the hovertank.

All the while we had been engaged in this fruitful dialogue his bazooka machine gun plasma cannon had been firing ceaselessly at some frightful monstrosity making its way at a sixteen-legged gallop up the tunnel.

"Open the hatch," I shouted.

The hatch opened and I retracted all my appendages. The plasma cannon fire should have been loud enough to bring down the whole labyrinth, the noise of which was not helping me regain some of my motor control and sensory clarity as I stumbled toward the hovertank's opening.

I took the first wobbling step onto the proffered ramp. I could see Bloppo at the controls, glaring at me in the most menacing and creepy way only an evil clown like him can do.

"What're you waiting for dumbfuck?"

What *was* I waiting for? Ah, yes. Harvey.

I quickly calculated how far the hovertank had dragged me and extended an arm that distance. Holy shit that was far! Way beyond the back end of the hovertank for yards. If the "thing" didn't have him already then Bloppo's auto-firing cannon surely must have fried him to a crisp!

I grabbed onto something fuzzy and pulled it toward me half-expecting it to be dead or horribly mangled or both.

Bloppo glanced at the ammo counter on his console which was getting smaller at a phenomenal rate. He turned and leaned forward as far as he could toward me.

"DUDE! WHAT is your FUCKING PROBLEM? HURRY – THE FUCK – UP!"

My arm returned with Harvey firmly attached to the end of it. Miraculously, he was alive and unscathed but out cold yet again. I climbed aboard, the comatose rodent over my shoulder, and the hatch slammed shut instantly like one of those lethal-looking doors in *Star Wars*.

I lowered Harvey into a seat and strapped him in, then took my own. Bloppo glowered balefully at me, then at the heap of fur. "What the fuck's that? Dinner? It smells like pee."

Without waiting for a response he turned to the console and slammed a lever forward. We shot in the same direction down the tunnel.

Fluid draining from my organic matter, I somehow managed to speak. "I wouldn't recommend going this way."

"Why the fuck not?" Bloppo grated without turning, "This should lead outside."

"There's nothing outside but a star blowing up," I shrieked.

But it was too late. Bloppo hit two buttons and we hurtled out the exit.

Beyond were titanic forces doing titanic things. The planet that I had spent several months walking around on was no longer around. Though its core probably existed somewhere, hurtling through space, it was no longer in the same position, having been violently putted into a new trajectory.

We passed through a terrible cloud of bright particles zipping along at near the speed of light and I half wondered why we weren't being torn apart ourselves until I realized that one of the buttons Bloppo had pressed was for a force field. The other had been to simply deactivate the local-field surface hovering function which automatically switched on field impulse drives. We were, for all practical intents and purposes, flying through space.

Bloppo manually took the flight controls and directed the craft beyond the radioactive shit storm and into relatively mild vacuum. At that point he checked some navigation screen and muttered, "So, *that's* what happened to this shithole."

"I didn't realize hovertanks could serve as spaceships," I muttered as I felt weightlessness lifting me slightly out of my seat against the straps. Bloppo hit another button and I settled back down into it under an artificial gravity.

"That and other things, fuckface," said Bloppo gruffly as he continued punching and turning other buttons and knobs along with shifting the odd lever or two. "You didn't think I wouldn't be driving a modified version of my own invention, did you?"

"You invented the hovertank?"

Bloppo turned to me, moving his unlit cigar butt from one corner of his mouth to the other. "Listen, cockbreath, I invented half the god damn technological crap that runs this fucking universe! Everybody knows that. Why do you think I control everything? What're you? Stupid? Or broken?"

I frowned in slight worriment. "What do you mean 'broken'?"

"Wha'dye think I mean, shit-for-brains? *I* know what you are. Why do you think I let you in at all? If you know who I am you know I 'aint no humanitarian, dickface." He went back to his console and busied himself for the next several moments keying in coordinates and course correction instructions.

Cool. No, not cool. This situation wasn't going quite the way I had anticipated, and I really wasn't enjoying this sudden change of direction. I glanced over at Harvey who was still not in a very cognizant state. He shifted to his side and stuck his thumb in his mouth. Hmm, had he *really* been worth saving?

"So, what're you doing in the Labyrinth, anyway?" I asked. Expecting merely another vituperative response, the Great Clown surprised me by swiveling completely around in his chair, crossing his legs in a relaxed pose and smiling pleasantly.

"Good question. I'm glad you asked. Now, I'm going to ask *you* a question." Bloppo had an exquisite knack for ignoring basic question-and-answer protocol. "What were *you* doing in the Labyrinth?"

"Saving my friend Harvey here," I said, giving the rabbit a little pat on the shoulder. He squeaked in his sleep, shuddered, and started slurping on his thumb in earnest. I rolled my eyes briefly to the ceiling and then back at my interrogator. "Why do you ask?"

Still smiling, almost congenial in his mien, Bloppo raised his hands slightly from his lap, palms out toward me. "Listen, let's just cut the crap, retard. We both know why the other was in the Labyrinth. We both know what it does and we both want to know why it does what it does. You, being what you are, probably have some interesting things to say about that. I, for one, would simply like to pick your brain – nicely –

without having to resort to methods that would be considered extremely violent to a robot."

It was then that my sensors picked up the faintest traces of a cleverly hidden force screen separating the forward cockpit from the rest of the hovertank where Harvey and I were sitting. Appearances to the contrary, Bloppo was no idiot, to be sure.

"What do you propose?"

Bloppo settled back in his chair and grinned with what appeared to be a certain measure of satisfaction. "Good. You're not as stupid as you look."

Chapter 7

Felix felt a jolt and a sensation of violently spinning. There was an abrupt acceleration then a sudden stop. He checked himself to make sure he wasn't missing limbs, took stock of his memory to ensure his marbles were all in place. After this boot-up self-check was completed he did a quick survey of his surroundings which had certainly changed for the better.

He was standing in an open field next to a dilapidated, white-washed house that did not appear to be lived in. The front door was nailed up with old boards. A gentle breeze blew in from the south, rocking an old mailbox on which a name had once been scrawled but was now quite beyond deciphering. As Felix turned about he noted the field was surrounded pretty much on all sides by a forest. Over the foliage to the north and east he could make out the peaks of high and quite impassable mountains.

The day was exquisite, feeling much like late spring or early summer. Puffy cumulus scampered across a deep blue sky. Birds sang heartrending melodies in the forest. The dry yellow grass of the field before him rustled pleasantly.

Felix was about to smile when an explosion of greasy black smoke nearly choked him. He peered through watering and smarting eyes at the reassembled form of Beefpickle, standing awkwardly in the field to his left. Beefpickle was pretty much the same as before except his left hoof had been replaced by a mailbox and his head with a kabuki mask of a demon.

"I thought you'd abandoned me," Felix said sullenly.

"What?" said Beefpickle, coughing. "No, no, I just had to take a shit."

"Rather abrupt way of doing so. I was kind of having a rough moment."

"Yeah, so was I."

"I *mean* I was undergoing a profound change of heart! And then you up and left and I thought you'd abandoned me."

"Change of heart? Oh, well, that happens."

"That happens?"

"There you go again, parroting."

"That's all you have to say? 'That happens?' I was expecting something a little more insightful and penetrating!"

"Well, I *am* just a welcome wagon, like I've been telling you all along. I wouldn't expect a whole lot." Beefpickle coughed some more as the smoke cleared away. "Where am I? Let's see." He looked around, black marbles rolling about in the demon mask in odd directions. "Oh, balls. You walked the Pattern, didn't you?"

"Yes. Why? What is it?"

"I told you not to."

"Well," said Felix angrily, "you didn't strike me as much of an Ultimate Authority when I asked for your help and you just disappeared to go take a crap! I had to do something!"

"Ah, he had to do something, he says. You could have done anything, but you decided to do the one thing I told you not to do. That's just great, man."

"What do you mean? What other things could I have done? Hang it! What's wrong with being here? Where *is* this place?"

Beefpickle sighed. "You're in the basement."

"The what?"

"I told you not to walk the Pattern. The Pattern was for someone else. Since it wasn't for you the Pattern just shipped you off to the nearest waste bin: the basement."

"The basement of what?"

"The afterlife."

"This hardly looks like a basement. It's quite pleasant actually."

"Yeah, whatever. Only the dumbest ones end up in the basement."

"What?"

"You say 'what' a lot. Do you have some medical ailment that causes this?"

"Yes, you asshole, it's called confusion."

"Hmm. They're usually not as confused as you seem to be. Never heard anyone say 'what' as many times as you have in so short a period."

"Look," said Felix, who was doing his best to calm himself down, "please just tell me how to get out of here. I'm sorry I'm so confused but apparently, according to you, I'm dead. Or somewhat dead. This is quite a bit of shocking news to me. And I seem to have died somewhere between the universe being destroyed and then somehow reconstituting itself. Not your usual case, I'm sure. I'm desperately trying not to be an idiot about this, but I'm not exactly surrounded by recognizable concepts upon which I can grab hold. All I'm asking for is a little help making sense of things and a little direction as to the appropriate course of action."

"You are standing in an open field west of a white house, with a boarded front door. There is a small mailbox here."

"What?"

"What do you want to what?"

"What the fuck are you doing?"

"You used the word 'fuck' in a way that I don't understand."

"Look-"

"You are standing in an open field west of a white house, with a boarded front door. There is a small mailbox here."

"I know where I am, you imbecile! Why are you stating the god damned obvious!"

"Dude," Beefpickle whispered, "obviously I'm narrating."

"Why?"

"I'm helping you," he whispered back.

"Really?!?!"

"Yes. If you want to get out of here you might want to play along. The rules are pretty strict for getting out of the basement."

"Meaning I must have you following me around narrating what I'm doing? That's the stupidest thing I've ever heard!"

Beefpickle merely shrugged and said nothing.

"Oh, my God," said Felix. He held his hands to either side of his head and closed his eyes. "The afterlife is inhabited by retarded eight-year-olds. I'm so fucked."

Felix stalked off around the house. Beefpickle followed him.

"You are facing the south side of a white house. There is no door here, and all the windows are boarded."

"Yes," said Felix, "I fucking see that!" He went on.

"You are behind the white house. A path leads into the forest to the east. In one corner of the house is a small window which is slightly ajar."

"YES! THANK YOU! I CAN FUCKING SEE THAT!"

Felix forced open the window and began heaving himself up through it.

"With great effort, you open the window far enough to allow entry."

"I would pay real money if you'd shut the fuck up!"

Felix wriggled through the window.

"You are in the kitchen of the white house. A table seems to have been used recently for the preparation of food. A passage leads-"

"YES, GOD DAMN IT! I FUCKING SEE! There is a staircase going up, a chimney going down, a passage to the west, an open door to the fucking east, a bloody brown sack that, yes, I know,

198

smells of hot peppers. And, yes, there is a glass bottle that appears to have water in it! Christ, I'm famished! "

Felix opened the brown sack on the table.

"Opening the brown sack reveals a lunch, and a clove of garlic."

"What sort of description is that? A lunch? It's a fucking sandwich! Specifically, two pieces of sliced bread, between which has been inserted hot peppers of the habañero variety. Hey, look at me! I'm going to open this sandwich and dump out the peppers! I'm just going to eat the bread so I don't run around in circles waving at my open mouth like I would do if you were accurately describing events! Yes, there is water in this glass bottle which I'm going to – obviously - fucking *hold* in my hand and *open* first before I drink it! Look at me! I'm drinking the fucking water! Done! Look, I don't need someone following me around telling me what I'm doing in the present fucking tense! Look at me! Only computer geeks who grew up in the 80s are going to know what the fuck I'm talking about! Look at me and my generation-specific humor!"

"Are you done?" Beefpickle rasped, utterly bored.

"Oh, are we not playing the game anymore? Can I speak to you, civilly, like an adult?"

"Ahem," ahemed Beefpickle.

"Ahem?"

"Look, parrot, just go west into the living room."

"No! I'm going to go up the stairs!"

"I wouldn't do that without a lamp."

But, Felix went - and came back an hour later looking quite disheveled and abused, asking, "What the *FUCK was* that? Nevermind. West?"

"West."

"Right.""

Felix went west and entered the living room. He spied the antiquated elvish sword and battery-powered brass lantern above an empty trophy case in the corner. A large oriental rug occupied most of the floor. The door to the west, nailed shut with strange gothic lettering on it, occupied Felix's attention for only a moment.

"It just says 'This space intentionally left blank,'" said Beefpickle.

"Yeah, whatever." He grabbed the lantern first.

"I'm gonna need this," he said breathlessly.

He then took the elvish sword. "I'm probably gonna need this too."

He turned to face Beefpickle. "Now what?"

Beefpickle made a motion with his twig hands that suggested the floor.

Felix looked down at the rug. "Into the basement's basement?"

Beefpickle just nodded.

Felix grabbed a corner of the massive throw rug and cast it aside, revealing a trap door to unknown depths.

"Down there?"

"Aye," Beefpickle nodded.

Felix flung the door open and stamped down the staircase.

"You have moved into a dark place. The trap door crashes shut, and you hear someone barring it. It is pitch black. You are likely to be eaten by a grue. Your sword is glowing with a faint blue glow."

"YEEEESSSS! SHUT THE GOD DAMN FUCK UP YOU MOTHERFUCKING DUMBSHIT IMBECILE FUCKHEAD!"

"No need to shout."

"I know what I'm doing! That is, I know what I'm doing as I'm doing it! You don't need to fucking describe it!"

"Just doing my job. Jesus."

"Thank you! I'm turning on the lamp now, as one would *obviously do* under such circumstances!"

"You are in a dark and damp cellar with-"

"Yes! I fucking know! There's a narrow passageway to the north! There's a crawlway to the south! There's the bottom of a steep metal ramp – which is unclimbable – to the west! Thank you and fuck the hell off!"

Felix went north.

"YES! SHUT UP! SMALL ROOM! PASSAGES TO EAST AND SOUTH! FORBIDDING HOLE TO THE WEST! BLOODSTAINS AND SCRATCHES ON WALLS – YEAH, YEAH, PERHAPS MADE BY A GOD DAMN AXE! YES, THERE IS A FUCKING NASTY-LOOKING TROLL – what?"

"There is a nasty-looking troll, brandishing a bloody axe. He is currently engaged in the impossible task of blocking all of the passages out of the room. By the way, your sword is glowing very brightly."

"Why the fuck would there be a troll in somebody's cellar?"

"Don't ask for logical explanations. It just is what it is."

Felix ducked, just missing a series of axe strokes that nearly removed his head.

"What the fuck? What do I do?"

"I do believe you have a sword in your hand."

Felix looked down. Yes, he did, indeed, have a sword in his hand – one that was glowing brightly.

He yelled a primal squawk, or something, and brought the pommel of the sword down on the attacking troll's skull.

"Your sword crashes down, knocking the troll into dreamland."

"Fuck! Now what?"

"An unconscious troll is sprawled on the floor. All passages out of the room are open."

"Great! Now what!"

"The troll stirs and begins to reawaken."

Felix hit the troll again with the sword's pommel and knocked it out, cold. Then he grabbed the troll's arm and started dragging it.

"What are you doing?"

"Dragging a troll! What the fuck does it look like I'm doing?"

"Why are you doing that?"

"Because I can, for one! And for two, I shouldn't just be killing things for no reason or just because they're in my way!"

"You've never played this game before have you?"

Rules for Otters
Interlude the Fourth

"In the year 6,452, during the height of the scientific renaissance that heralded the start of the first Galactic Empire, a social scientist by the name of Ardenveld Shenectady proved beyond all doubt that sentient organisms could, for all practical intents and purposes, be judged by how they superficially appeared. The age-old analogy of 'judging a book by its cover' held true for all humans and alien species that Ardenveld scrutinized in his landmark study. Indeed, one could truly be counted on to be as stupid as one looked."

--Volume 10,443, Number 188 of the *Interspecies Sociological Review*, New New York, Terra

Actually, I was as stupid as I looked.

Most intelligent creatures in the multiverse have a selective memory. They seem to have an innate gift for recalling those moments when they have been exceedingly clever, but rarely acknowledge when others around them have also been exceedingly clever – which seems to occur mostly when one is not looking. It gives one an uneasy feeling in the gut to recall such a fact at the same moment that one realizes that one hasn't been paying very close attention. This is rather like being the unwitting recipient (as opposed to a witting recipient?) of a barroom sucker punch – and Bloppo was the undisputed king of sucker punches. First things being first, I immediately got to work on the hovertank's computer via a discrete, ultra-low frequency radio wave modulated with an even more discrete data transmission protocol. Finding an access point was the easy part. The hovertank's computer and I shook hands, tipped our hats, and then engaged in battle. Meanwhile I went down the short list of things that I had been missing.

Bloppo, though silly-looking, was not someone to be taken lightly. The fact that he'd built a colossal political and economic empire that spanned the known universe in his lifetime is not an achievement to be sneezed at. He was belligerent, crass, disgusting, self-centered, sadistic, cruel, ruthless, and a masterful liar. However, he was also a financial and political mastermind whose genius was unsurpassed by any sentient being on all the three-hundred billion inhabited worlds that spun about their axes under the shadow of his stained, gloved hand. Presidents, kings, emperors, consuls, statesmen of all kinds, generals, admirals, bank officials, boards of directors, corporations, religious leaders, and an endless procession of power brokers quietly bowed to his ultimate authority. He owned all the media outlets, he controlled the banks, he owned or had his groping fingers in every conceivable business opportunity, he owned entire galaxies, installed politicians amenable to his desires, assassinated others inimical to his interests, entire religions on millions of worlds revered him as a god, wars were waged on thousands of planets vying for his favor, and he profited from their destruction. His greed and lust knew no bounds.

*(Note: Much about the nature of "normal" business operations of Bloppo's parent company can be gleaned from even the most random interception of corporate communicades and memos, an example of which has been provided in **Appendix IV**)*

It was a fortunate thing for the rest of the multiverse that he had been contained for so long in this single universe which he had mastered.

Problem: he had found the Labyrinth…and he knew more about it than he was letting on. He also knew how important it was. That was obvious since he was investigating it personally. Bloppo was not the type to weep, like Alexander, for a lack of worlds to conquer. It's very possible he never shed a tear his entire life. But, he *was* the most cunning monster this universe had ever seen, or ever would see: a true psychotic, an implacable sociopath. He would not be stopped, not even by the limits imposed by physics. No more worlds to conquer? Bullshit. He would find them and he would conquer them. Like the scorpion that stung its savior and calmly informed its victim that it could hardly have done otherwise, Bloppo was what he was: an elemental force. He wasn't merely driven by immense passions; he *was* those passions, personified, given form, as ridiculous as that form was. How else to explain such achievements in so short a time? He wasn't - couldn't – be human. He was more than human.

I recalled that I had gotten lost in the Labyrinth. It had changed and I couldn't find my way back to the entrance. Bloppo had made his way there effortlessly. How did he do it? Obviously he had a map; possibly even a map that reflected the changes in the Labyrinth as they occurred. No one had ever found such a thing before. No one had ever even discovered the remotest hint that there might be a map somewhere.

Now, either Bloppo had gotten extremely lucky and had found one, or, more likely, he had mapped at least a portion of the Labyrinth himself. More importantly, it's possible he discovered the algorithm which alters the Labyrinth so that changes can be predicted. That is, of course, assuming that the shifting of the Labyrinth is purposeful.

According to some accounts Bloppo had started his career as an engineer for the military of some backwater planet. His many inventions, chiefly of war machines, brought him to the attention of the planet's leaders then in power. His acumen in administration brought him up in the ranks fast, and he is said to have instigated a series of wars against other planetary systems, eventually culminating in the Intergalactic Imperium currently holding sway. Interestingly, one of his inventions involved an extraordinarily complicated device which could probe and map an entire planet's internal structure. The position of every crevice, crack, and subterranean chamber could be determined and, most significantly, its internal structure analyzed for weak points. The purpose of this was to select areas inside the planet for the placement of sub-nucleon "planet buster" charges that would detonate at those key weak points and, by a resonant chain reaction, as you might guess, destroy the planet. Had Bloppo used something like this to map the Labyrinth? It was more than possible. All I needed was the final proof.

At the moment, however, there was another problem. Me. Bloppo knew what I was. His untempered avarice already having been established, we can deduce that I might be a very prized possession. If he could tear me apart and poke around my insides long enough, who knows what whole new industries might result; perhaps even new physics. I wasn't made in his universe, after all, and this is the thing that brings me to my final point in the short list of observations.

I wasn't made in his universe.

Question: How does he know what I am?

Answer: He's already been to that universe.

Your universe.

What's more, the only way he could find out about me is from the universe in your distant future. We know that entrances and exits from the Labyrinth are numerous, and they come out in different positions in many universes and in different times. To find out about me, Bloppo has been to the universe of your future and must have explored it extensively. This suggests that Bloppo, the Evil Clown, has been at this for quite some time.

This chain of thought took less than a picosecond, yet Bloppo was somehow able to suddenly frown in that span and bark at me to "knock it off".

"Knock what off?" I asked innocently.

"I know what you're doing, you asshole, and you can forget it. This hovertank's computer isn't gonna let your grubby hands anywhere near it. So, stop wasting your time and let's get down to answering my questions, asshole."

Quicker than even I could follow the index finger of his left hand pressed a button on the arm of his chair. I was immediately "shackled" to my own chair with a powerful force field, completely immobilized. This also effectively cut off any energies radiating out from my person. My wrestling match with the hovertank's computer was lost.

Bloppo was relaxed and smiling once again. "To business, fucktard. I propose we get acquainted. I ask you questions, you give me answers voluntarily. Meanwhile, we'll be traveling to a quaint little planet of mine that secretly specializes in cybernetic research. Then I'll ask you more questions and you will give your answers *in*voluntarily. How does that sound? Great. I knew you'd agree. Now, what do you know about the Labyrinth?"

I couldn't answer because of the force field. Bloppo looked at me a second, moved his cigar butt to the other side of his mouth, and pressed another button on his chair. I found that I could move my mouth but still didn't speak.

"Well, dipshit?"

"What difference does it make if I answer any questions at all when you're just going to open me up and get them anyway without my cooperation?"

Bloppo's smile broadened magnanimously. "Well, moron, we could obviate all that unpleasantness if you answer my questions now and can demonstrate the truth of the answers. Meanwhile, don't *ask* any more questions, numbnut. That's *my* job. So, what do you know about the Labyrinth?"

I sighed. "This is silly," I said. "The pointlessness of this whole exercise is self-evident. You're not going to trust anything I have to say so you're just going to gut my innards and read my entrails when we get to wherever it is we're going. I'm not going to play your stupid game, so fuck off."

Bloppo maintained his grin, but his eyes were anything but jolly.

"So, that's how you want to do this, eh? Let me tell you something, genius. I'm an impatient motherfucker and I don't react well to refusal or insolence of any kind. I'll have you know that I do have certain tools on this hovertank that I can start with before we arrive at our destination; relatively crude tools to be sure, but ones which will make your life very uncomfortable until I can crack you with more sophisticated shit."

Bloppo casually flicked a switch and I felt the field around me change. Imagine being set on fire, electrocuted, and boiled in sulfuric acid all at once and that doesn't even begin to approximate what I felt. Every artificial nerve, every artificial cell, every atom that was me felt something very, very human: excruciating, intolerable, agonizing and unending pain. And I did then what any human would do – I screamed.

Bloppo only chuckled and allowed me to writhe and scream for several minutes, doubtless enjoying every second of the spectacle. He really was a nasty son-of-a-bitch.

During all the noise I was making Harvey roused himself from his nightmares. He sat, unmoving, thumb still firmly inserted in mouth, staring at Bloppo and I in utter horror. His thumb suddenly came out with an audible *pop* and he shrieked, adding another voice to the cacophony.

Bloppo rolled his eyes. "Great, the muppet's awake." With an exasperated exhalation he violently flipped the pain field switch to the "off" position and pressed the button that deactivated the immobilizing field. I slumped down, drooling and shuddering. Harvey, at last, stopped shrieking, huddling in his chair.

"I'm - I'm – late for – I'm – another bout of – of – hang it-"

"Shut up," growled Bloppo. He turned back to me. "Now, you fucking dumbshit, answer my questions or I'm going to turn that pain field back on and leave it on until we land."

The thought of another round of agony lasting the rest of the voyage made me want to shrink until I vanished, but I didn't know what else to do. He certainly could not be given any information that would help him, and he most certainly could not be allowed to find the capsule, the contents of which even I didn't know. I barely mustered the energy to look up at Harvey, but he was silent and paralyzed, not because of his terror, but because he was now in an immobilizing field of his own. Bloppo activated my own field yet again with the exception of my mouth so that I might speak the secrets he wanted so badly.

"I'm going to ask you nicely one more time, you fucking miserable chunk of shit, what do you know about the Labyrinth?"

Quaking with delirious tremors inside, drool suspended indefinitely from my lips within the field, I could only manage one final statement.

"Fuck you," I mumbled.

Bloppo leaned forward in his chair and quietly grated his response.

"No," he said as he flipped the switch. "Fuck *you.*"

Chapter 8

They were standing at the base of Flood Control Dam #3 next to a big pile of treasure and a smaller pile of plastic which the troll was busily filling up with a little air pump. Felix held the troll at glowing sword point while Beefpickle looked on, yawning and frequently checking a broken watch on his wrist. The Frigid River rushed past them, wending its way out of sight to the south.

"You know," Beefpickle said off-handedly, "you're supposed to be putting all that treasure in the trophy case."

Felix, never taking his eyes off the troll, responded gruffly. "Nope. It's all mine. I've been all over this underground rat maze solving all kinds of senseless puzzles and you think I'm just going to give it all up?"

"You can't win the game if you don't."

"I'm not playing your stupid game by your rules."

"It's not *my* game. *I* didn't make the rules," said Beefpickle, buffing his twiggy fingernails.

"Whatever. I'm going to put it all to the test."

"Whatever do you mean?"

"I'm getting the fuck out of here."

"With that?" Beefpickle asked, pointing at the now fully inflated boat that sat on the shore. The troll set aside the pump and started loading the treasure into it.

"Yes, with that."

"Could you stop pointing that sword at me?" the troll asked plaintively.

"Why? Afraid it's going to go off or something?"

"No, it just makes me nervous."

"Tough. You were trying to kill me earlier with an axe. You came to the wrong shop for sympathy."

"Just doing my job," the troll muttered and went back to work loading treasure.

"Yeah, you and everyone else," Felix said, glancing at Beefpickle.

"Look, dude," Beefpickle said, "this is stupid. Where are you going to go? The Frigid River ends at Aragain Falls. A drop of several hundred feet, I might add. Even if you survive that, where are you going to go and how do you think you're going to spend all that loot?"

"That's my problem. You just stand there and look pretty."

Beefpickle was momentarily taken aback. He produced a mirror from somewhere and gazed at himself in it.

"You really think I look pretty? Oh! You were being sarcastic weren't you? Asshole."

Beefpickle put the mirror away and went back to buffing his "fingernails."

At last the troll placed the final bit of loot into the inflatable boat. "All done," it said.

"Get in."

"What, me?" the troll asked, utterly incredulous. "What in all the nine hells for?"

"You too, Beefpickle."

"Bugrat."

"Whatever."

Beefpickle sighed and got into the boat. The troll just stood on the shore and stared at Felix as though he were the most horrible monster that ever lived. Felix gestured with the point of the sword.

"Sit toward the front where I can see you."

"Oh, come on!" the troll remonstrated. "You've got to be kidding!"

"Nope."

"Look, Felix. Sir. Please. You've got to be done with me by now. Just let me go on my way. I promise I won't tell anyone what you're up to."

"Into the boat!"

"Please! I'm begging you! I can't swim! I'm mortally afraid of water! I got a wife and six trollets!"

"Get in the fucking boat or I'll just kill you right here!"

"Geez! Fucking asshole!"

"Yep," Beefpickle said without looking up from his buffing.

The troll shook his head and got into the boat, toward the front as he'd been told. "There's a little piece of paper here," the troll said. "Looks like instructions."

"Just do us the service of getting the boat into the water," said Beefpickle. "Felix won't read them and we'll just sit here for eternity until one of us does it for him. It's a magic boat that follows verbal commands. Just say the word 'Launch' and we'll be underway."

The troll said, "Launch!" They shot out over the Frigid River and were quickly caught up in the southward current.

"Give me that piece of paper," Felix ordered.

The troll held out the instructions over his shoulder. Felix grabbed it, wadded it up, and threw it overboard.

"Just let the current carry us and don't listen to anything Beefpickle says."

"Bugrat."

"Whatever."

A Smattering of Smacks
Interlude the Fifth

"Within the confines of the three-and-a-half worlds of the Legumot Kingdom there are many species of flora and fauna which are so unusual that scientists come from all over the Imperium to observe them in their natural habitats. One species, the Blurbling Festerwoodle, boasts 11,772 unique traits found nowhere else in the known universe. Chief among these traits is its curious ability to blend in with other easily forgotten nonsense."

> -- *Super Neat Facts*, by Hegmond the Doom-Sayer (a *Super Swifty* distribution of the Legumot Tourist Bureau)

Don't let the tourist guidebooks fool you. Legumot is a shitty little planet orbiting a shitty little star in a shitty little corner of a shitty little galaxy that *no one* gives a fuck about. Period. The Legumotese are not an interplanetary kingdom either. The other two-and-a-half "worlds" are artificial satellites orbiting their planet. The only purpose of these satellites is to allow one nation-state on this spinning turd to keep an eye on the other as they are perpetually locked in a state of impending combat. Blurbling Festerwoodle? No such animal. It's a known hoax and Imperium-wide joke. The Legumotese try to pass off pictures of this thing in their tourist literature, but even the most credulous Imperial citizen can tell that it's just some creature on their planet that kind of looks like a nervous dog with alopecia sporting some covering atop its cranium that looks suspiciously as though someone put a wig on it as well as some cardboard bat wings. In fact, the hoax was actually exposed some years ago when a group of skeptics traveled to Legumot, obtained entry to the crappy zoo in which this abomination was said to reside, and, in a climax of high drama in front of onlookers, whisked away the wig and bat wings to reveal what everyone knew it was: a twitchy, cross-eyed, canine-looking thing with mange that answered to the horrible name of Colonel Tremens. Scientists do not visit this place. Nobody visits this place.

Except Bloppo. Isn't that a shocker?

I can't imagine a thorough-going worse place anywhere in the universe than Legumot. The inhabitants have no morals at all and are pretty stupid. (Read the previous paragraph again if these allegations seem out of line.) Their entire history is essentially one of barnyard hierarchies, greed, self-aggrandizing hypocrisy, religious nuttery, half-baked insanity that has very nearly destroyed their entire civilization on more than one occasion, extermination of most of the other life forms on their planet, and dominance over the larger and poorer sector of their population by a handful of wealthy and politically powerful elites. In short, their history has been about those who have almost all the beans versus those who have to fight over the few beans that are left.

It's interesting to note that there exists a consortium of extra-dimensional beings that have been busily compiling a voluminous compendium of articles concerning every object and event in all the multiverse, a sort of *Encyclopedia Multiversica*. Bloppo has been trying to get these beings to divulge all of their material, but they have so far refused. They're a little peeved at the moment, and their whole project has been suspended, being currently embroiled in a bitter lawsuit brought by the upper crust of Legumot society; the reason being that the extra-dimensional compilers keep confusing Legumot with *your* planet.

Gosh. How could *that* have happened?

The inhabitants of Legumot are weird-looking to boot. If you can imagine the unlikely union of a whale, a duck and a grasshopper you've got a better idea of what they look like than I ever have or ever will. Even if I'm staring right at one of these chaps I can't seem to register what the fuck I'm seeing, as though the eyes are reporting faithfully but the brain is curling up into a fetal position and scribbling a suicide note.

So, there I was, staring uncomprehendingly at one of these absurd citizens of Legumot wishing very earnestly to be anywhere else. Harvey and Bloppo were nowhere in sight and I was in a heavily armored room that currently appeared to be serving as some kind of storage area. Large sacks of something-or-other occupied one corner, a few empty ones piled on top. A single tube affixed to the ceiling fluoresced with a dim and sickly illumination. I was, of course, sitting in a chair, surrounded by an immobilizing field. The fifteen Legumotese soldiers were brandishing very lethal-looking gauss rifles in my general direction like an 80's "hair" band posing with their guitars.

I was a trifle worn and chewed about the edges. The journey had been a long one, made longer by the pain field that Bloppo, true to his word, did not turn off until we landed on this garbage dump. How he must have laughed and laughed, and laughed again until he was hoarse. Sick fuck.

Well, speak of the devil. A door slid open and Bloppo emerged from it like the fecal matter he was. He was grinning from ear to ear and had kind of a mad glint in his eyes. One of his sleeves was rolled up and he was still untying a length of surgical tubing from his arm. Great. The undisputed master of this universe was not only a dangerous psychopath, he was also high.

"So, assface, it seems we've got a lot to talk about now."

He dug around in his pocket and produced a small object. It was a little red anodized capsule. It looked kind of like one of those magnets you feed cows that attract little pieces of metal they've inadvertently consumed out in the pasture, but smaller.

"You know where I found this, don't you? Inside a little processor compartment behind your left kidney."

"How long have I been out?"

"Long enough, cockbreath. You know what it is?"

I knew, but said nothing. I was quite certain he knew as well and the question was, as his questions usually were, rhetorical. His grin got grinnier as he answered it himself.

"It's a data capsule. Secret data. Secret even from you, apparently. It's set to open only at a certain time or under a certain set of circumstances or by a certain encrypted key phrase. This is probably going to tell me what you're really doing here."

"That's nice," I said. "Where's Harvey?"

"Who gives a shit?" he snarled, grin vanished. "The only thing I care about is opening this capsule and turning you into a new way for me to make money."

"You want to open that capsule? Then bring Harvey in here. He needs to be present for the capsule to open."

Bloppo looked at me slyly, a thin smile creeping back to his odious lips.

"Ah, so that's what you wanted him for. He's part of the key. What are the other parts?"

"I don't know," I told him, quite honestly.

"Bullshit! Tell, or he doesn't come in here at all!"

"Like I said, I don't know. I only know his presence is required, but you're going to have to figure out the rest for yourself. You've already scanned my circuits and shaken every scrap of data out of my skull. You know I don't know any more than that or you would have found it."

Bloppo scrutinized me for an instant, seemed to come to some decision, and barked at his Legumot henchmen to fetch the rodent.

We waited in silence while this was happening, staring at each other in mutual distrust and calculation. Every once in a while Bloppo would tap his foot or sigh impatiently. He was clearly anxious to win this new battle and move on to conquering the multiverse.

Finally, after several interminable minutes in Bloppo's grotesque company, the Legumotese soldiers opened the door and dragged poor Harvey in by his scruff. He was awake and alert at least.

Triumphantly, Bloppo sauntered over to the cowering rabbit. "So, animal, I've recently come to understand you have some significant bearing upon these matters."

Harvey looked up at Bloppo, terrified. "What, me? Oh, no, no – not me. Not at all! I'm not important to anyone – anything. Not significant – no – not significant in the least bit." He swallowed hard, gulped really, and quickly looked down at the floor. Then he got the hiccups.

"Stop that," said Bloppo, crossly.

"Stop *hic* what?"

"That! It's annoying."

"Oh, s- *hic* - sorry."

"Well, let's see what happens now, shall we?" Bloppo pulled the capsule out of his pocket.

"Oh, what *hic* - what's going to ha- *hic* -happen now?"

"KNOCK IT OFF!"

"Why don't you get him a glass of water?" I suggested.

Bloppo whirled. "Who the fuck's giving the orders around here?"

"Look, do you want to open that god damn capsule or not?"

"Shut the fuck up, you worthless heap of scrap! I do things in my own way in my own time, get it?"

Meanwhile, Bloppo had his gloved hand partially open. Harvey looked up from the floor for a moment and caught a glimpse of the capsule within. It was only a glimpse, but that seemed to be all that was needed.

Now, this was the part where everything happened very fast, and I was just as surprised as Bloppo when the shit hit the fan. All of the events I'm about to describe took place in a little over three seconds.

In the first second, Harvey punched Bloppo as hard as he could. This might conjure up some comic images at first, but clear those from your mind and bear with me. It was anything but comic. A better term might be "awe-striking", maybe even "terrifying". Imagine Bloppo, facing me, saying his last words, and then he suddenly vanishes from that spot to reappear sliding out of a tremendous dent in the armored wall. The paw and arm that has delivered the blow is about three times larger than Harvey, all metal and plastic and indestructible cabling. A small piece of white fur is still clinging to it; no longer large enough to contain Harvey's greatly expanded internal chassis.

Next Harvey leapt across the room on legs that were also now three times larger than the rest of his body and also looking much like the arm that had rocketed Bloppo into the wall. The metal and plastic haunches were similar to those of Harvey's original design, but more predatory. In mid flight the other arm expanded to match the first, both ending in metallic claws. The head followed in this horrifying inflation, the ears becoming sharp, blade-like points that laid themselves flat against the sides of the head, the eyes became huge, black orbs without pupils. The teeth became piranha-like jaws. By the time Harvey landed atop Bloppo's prone form, the torso had completed its transformation as well. Crouched, looking massive and lethal, Harvey found the capsule and placed it into a blinking unit on his wrist. We're in the middle of second number two now.

That task completed, Harvey leapt across the room again. Legs unfolded, arms outstretched, he more resembled a nine-foot long amphibious wolf than a rabbit. When he landed again the remaining one-and-a-half seconds were not good ones for the Legumotese soldiers. They hardly knew what hit them. Shit, *I* didn't know what hit them.

Harvey, finished with that gruesome chore, loped over to me and deactivated my restraining field. With a certain amount of pleasure I stood up, enjoying the freedom of movement, and quickly discovered just how spent I really was. I nearly fell over, but Harvey shot out an arm and held me up.

"We don't have much time now," he said. His voice was deeper, metallic, and devoid of his former accent. It also sounded oddly familiar.

"Where to?"

"The Clown's hovertank. We need to get off this planet and you need to get that map from the tank's computer. Can you make it?"

I slowly let go of Harvey's arm. I was a little unsteady, but it would have to do. I nodded to him and made for the door.

"Wait."

I stopped and turned. "What?"

"There's one other thing."

Harvey loped over to Bloppo and naturally did, of course, what I least expected. With sickening sounds of rending and tearing he was rapidly dismembering the corpse, ripping the limbs from the torso and stuffing them into one of the empty bags. Finally that hideous head came off with a disgusting crack, still twisted into a ghastly, grimacing frown, cigar butt still clamped firmly between its teeth.

Harvey must have been cauterizing as he was cutting as the parts going into the bag were devoid of all that slaughterhouse nastiness one ordinarily notices in such butchery.

Darkness started to encroach on my peripheral vision. If we didn't leave soon Harvey would be burdened with another load.

His task completed, he grabbed my arm to steady me, quietly opened the door and led the way out.

Chapter 9

"Well, this is interesting," said Beefpickle.

They were inside an enormous tunnel, one end of which disappeared into darkness. The other end of it was where they were all standing. A constant deluge of water poured from a sunlit rift in the tunnel's roof down onto a great pile of skeletons. Atop this mountain of remains teetered their inflatable boat that was presently sagging under the immense weight of all the treasure Felix had previously obtained. They stood at the base of this charnel pyramid, having slid down after their violent tumble over Aragain Falls.

This sight was sufficiently remarkable to justify Beefpickle's comment. It was, however, not the reason. The source of the remark was actually derived from a change of state involving a certain sword point's aim – which was now pressed firmly against Felix's throat by a certain troll.

"Give me one good reason why I shouldn't just kill you right now!" the troll roared.

Felix, soaking wet from their recent descent, thought hard for a moment before answering.

"Because I could have killed you a million times over and didn't?"

"I said one *good* reason!"

"Ummm…you can have all the treasure?"

"Which I can still have anyway without you and that fucked up parser over there!"

"Hey!" Beefpickle said, highly offended. "That's not necessary now is it?"

"Look, troll -" began Felix.

"I have a name, you know."

"I didn't know."

"You didn't ask."

"Okay. What's your name?"

"Helmsnug," the troll said, only slightly mollified. "Helmsnug Bogfart."

"Really?" Beefpickle snorted, trying his best not to laugh.

"Shut up!" the troll cried out. His ejaculation inadvertently moved the tip of the sword point against Felix's neck, drawing blood.

"Whoa! Mr. Bogfart! Sir!"

"What!"

"This isn't necessary. May I call you Helmsnug? Helmsnug, what more do you want from me? I didn't kill you. I kept you at bay with a sword because, quite honestly, it's hard to trust someone who's just recently tried to kill you. Furthermore, you have arguably benefited from these circumstances by getting out of a job that generally only involves your getting killed by treasure-hungry adventurers. You're not stuck in a lowly cellar anymore. You are free, Helmsnug. Free. You are a master of your own fate as is evidenced by the fact that you now hold the point of the sword to my own neck. However, do not forget that it was I who was ultimately responsible in freeing you. I suggest an alternative solution to killing me. Allow me to live and we will venture forth on our mutual quest to escape this place *together*."

Helmsnug the troll wavered; the point of the sword quivered. At last he relented and the sword fell to the floor.

"You really mean it?" Helmsnug asked, a tear forming in the corner of his left eye.

For a fraction of a second Felix imagined himself pulling a Glock nine-millimeter from out of his pocket and wasting this motherfucker where he stood, six trollets or not. But, a change had overcome him. He had not killed this creature when he could have easily done so. It seemed a waste of effort to keep something alive only to murder it.

"Yes, Helmsnug. I mean it."

Helmsnug grabbed Felix and gave a troll hug so brutal that Felix felt his bones bruise.

"Thank you, Felix. Thank you. I've never had a friend before."

"That's – quite – alright – good – fellow," Felix gasped. He patted Helmsnug tentatively on the shoulder, not so much out of friendship, but more like a wrestler might to let his adversary know that continuing a particular choke hold would result in death.

"This is all very touching," said Beefpickle, polishing the mailbox that served as one of his feet, "but it seems that I, along with your new friend here, am out of a job since I've gone far beyond the terms and conditions that apply to it just by being here."

The troll released Felix who attempted sucking in air to deprived lungs. "What – what do you mean?"

"We're no longer in the afterlife, Felix. We're no longer even in its basement. We're somewhere else."

"What are you talking about? Where are we then?"

"If I knew that I wouldn't have said 'somewhere else.' I would have given it a name."

"I know where we are," said Helmsnug, looking shamefully at his feet.

"You do?" Felix and Beefpickle chorused.

"Yeah. I've been here before. Once, upon I time, when I was very young – before being placed as a cellar guardian."

"Really?" Beefpickle ventured. "Well, where are we then?"

"The Labyrinth."

A Codex of Scurrilous Impostures
Interlude the Sixth

"I see that you are mocking me."
- The final words reputed to have been said by *Lurgle Svengblagget the First* upon his coronation as *Emperor of the Consolidated Hegemony of Worlds*, a largely commercial web enclosing 1500 planets scattered among 942 star systems. This political/economic entity was notable only because it was the last significant obstacle to Imperial domination in the known universe before it fell in the year 72 of the New Inter-Galactic Era (N.I.E.). *Lurgle Svengblagget*, a peasant of no particularly interesting qualities, was notable only because of the length of his reign, the shortest on record: an astounding 7.4 seconds. This was just long enough for him to jump up onto the dais from the surrounding crowd, slay the newly-crowned *Emperor Almaden Hectenrude the Fourth* with a sharpened spoon, grab the crown, place it upon his own head, and amidst booing and hissing from the other peasants (*Hectenrude* was fairly popular) muttered his infamous sentence before the crown was struck from his

skull by the palace guard and he was pushed into the waiting subjects below who promptly tore him to pieces. Folklore has it that he said something else as he was dying, a kind of prophetic, divinely-inspired warning. It supposedly went something like, "Beware of Floppo the Plown! He is going to -", or something silly. No one has any idea what this could possibly mean and the tale is considered apocryphal.

"I see that you're mocking me," I told him.

I was operating at full capacity now, a thing which I had not been doing for the greater part of a year it seems, and I smiled inwardly at my little joke. Even if I were to explain it to the person standing in front of me he would not have believed that, simply by a casual examination of his genetic code, I could determine (with 94.89% probability of being correct) that he was a direct descendent of Lurgle Svengblagget the First.

He would have believed even less had I told him that Lurgle Svengblagget was something of an underground culture hero among members of a resistance movement that Bloppo had not quite ever been able to quash. As an accurate reckoning of history would have it, Lurgle's real name was Adamantine Posternut, a rebel spy and expert in sociopolitical engineering. However, these were the latter days of Bloppo's consolidation of power and even all of the expertise Posternut could bring to reorganizing the Consolidated Hegemony of Worlds to fight Bloppo's Imperial takeover were ultimately for naught. His last, desperate act of defiance you already know. However, history here has it wrong. He never said, "I see that you are mocking me." He said what you would expect a sober individual of his stature to say. "Beware of Bloppo the Clown, he is going to invade your empire and crush your planets and your lives, one by one! Hectenrude is his puppet!" But, Bloppo was ultimately victorious which means he got to write the history books. I am continually amazed at how much absurdity in this universe can be attributed to the psychology of one individual.

The resistance never ceased to exist, and rebel blood must run in the family as the person standing before me was none other than a promising Lieutenant of the good ship *Abelard Pip* (the history of the ship's namesake I will refrain from expositing). This was the flag ship of an organization calling itself the *Philosophically Disconsolate Brothers of Intemperate Disposition*. There were other organizations of like mind, but this group was one of the few that could afford a navy, and it had been consistently powerful and successful enough to convince the other groups to band together in solidarity against their common goal which was to topple Bloppo's Imperium, replacing it with a more democratic political system, the philosophical underpinnings of which seemed to have fairly escaped most of the quadrillions upon quadrillions of beings that live in this particular neck of the multiverse (due mostly, again, to the machinations of a fucking clown).

In the past thirty-two days our little armada had been cutting a path, star system by star system to the Imperial Capital. In earlier days this would have been quite suicidal, our numbers being relatively few and Bloppo's military and technological force being magnitudes larger than our own. What changed our situation was the acquisition of all of Bloppo's pass codes for each and every space-going vessel, each and every hovertank, each and every warplane, amphibious assault vehicle, crew carrier, cannon, planetary defense shield, and personal doodad down to the last laser rifle and communications device. Use of these pass codes disabled them, shut them down, out-of-service. This was Bloppo's failsafe so that none of his creations could be used against him, inadvertently or otherwise. No one else but Bloppo had these codes since he had, shall we say, memorized them all. How *we* obtained them shall be made clear momentarily.

"Sir," the Lieutenant who was Svengblagget's descendent addressed me formally, "Captain Spiff wishes me to inform you that planetfall to the Imperial Capital will be commencing in forty minutes and he will be needing your services on deck at oh-one-thirty hours."

Apparently he chose to ignore my earlier statement. Not even a quizzical look. No curiosity at all. Not quite the creativity and intellect of his ancestor, I thought, but certainly guaranteed a long and illustrious military career.

"Thank you, Lieutenant."

He saluted smartly, about-turned and stamped down the hallway, his boots clanking martially on the metal floor.

Nadz, the Imperial Capital, orbited by its two moons, Frakshus and Kapshus. Once, upon a time, it was a beautiful planet, combining all the best aspects of an ecological preserve and recreation spot. Post-Bloppo, it quickly became a shithole, rather like Legumot: strip-mined to the core, all indigenous life exterminated and sold off as jaunty hats, jackets and trendy shoes. So choked with pollution its skies were perpetually black with smog and no stars were ever seen by the inhabitants whose sole collective purpose in life was to administrate the Empire, so who cared, right?

I couldn't wait to carpet bomb the place.

A whiny little morality circuit nasally informed me that I would never let that happen even if I were capable.

Yeah, yeah. Shut up.

As I was saying, I was currently in tip-top shape, having been completely restored to originally designed specifications. This included my memory. I knew now that I had been missing a few things even before the encounter with the blothomid. As it so happens, this was intentional. But these memories had been returned to me and I now knew what the hell I was doing and who I had been. Furthermore, I now remembered who Bloppo was – and Harvey.

Speaking of whom, Harvey was sauntering down the hallway, looking his menacing self.

"Hello, Carter. I was just in the lab and we've got things working finally. He won't talk only to me, though. He wants both of us together."

"Always more fucking demands with him," I muttered. "Fine, let's get this over with. No luck boring through into the core memory block?"

"No." Harvey replied as we walked briskly to the lab. "Older model. There's a safety mechanism actually hard-wired to it in such a way that it'll just fry everything if we poke around too much."

"That's unfortunate. We're just going to have to truth-check anything he tells us. If he tells us anything at all."

"Well, we'll see." We had arrived at the lab door. Harvey pressed a clawed hand to a palm lock and the door slid open. At the opposite end of the room, on a workbench, plugged into a thousand different wires that trailed off into a rat maze of blinking analyzers and circuit simulators was the grotesque head of Bloppo the Clown, teeth still clamped around that freaking cigar.

His eyes shot open, his eyebrows drew down and met in the middle, his mouth upturned in a wicked smile.

"Well, look who deigned to show up. Your buddy Harvey plays a good game of fetch – or should I call him Bill? I'd chuckle

nastily right now but I don't have any lung-analogs hooked up."
Bloppo's grin got meaner, if such a thing could be possible.

"Thanks for joining the party, you sad sack of burnt-out fuses. Pull up a chair and make yourself comfy 'cause your ass is about to hurt like a son-of-a-bitch."

Chapter 10

Felix, Beefpickle, and Helmsnug plodded down the colossal tunnel. Felix had clambered up the pile of skeletons to the raft, retrieving an ivory torch from among the treasures so they had something to provide light. The battery-powered brass lantern had not survived their plunge over the Falls. The troll, even after his recent avowal of friendship with Felix, still maintained a scrupulous grasp of the elvish sword which, oddly, was no longer glowing. Beefpickle, lagging behind a few paces, had removed the kabuki mask from his shoulders, giving it a good rubbing with a clean cloth.

"So," Felix broached tentatively, addressing the troll, "you found this Labyrinth by accident?"

"Yes."

"By coming down the Falls?"

"No, there was another way at the time. I remember coming to that place with the pile of bones, though."

"How did you get out?"

"I don't remember. I was just a little trollet then."

They continued on in silence for a while as Felix chewed over other perplexing issues.

"You know, I can't help but ask: Who employed you? I mean, how did you get swept up into such an awful job, guarding a cellar?"

The troll, showing signs of uneasiness at the question, deflected Felix's remark. "It was so long ago I don't remember that either."

"Oh, come, come. You must remember something! I mean, who signs the checks?"

"What checks?"

"Yes – er – well, how do you get paid?"

"What do you mean?"

"Uh, yes. You know – money?"

"Money?"

"Christ!" Felix exclaimed, "You don't get paid? If not, why do you call it a job?"

"It's not like that, Felix. I wasn't chosen to take the job in exchange for anything material or representative of material value. I was told, long ago, that if I stayed in the cellar, guarding it, I would live forever. Even if I were killed by one of those low-brow adventurer types I would reappear some time later in the cellar, none the worse."

"So, you traded mortality for living in a cellar?"

"Sort of. Yes."

"How long have you been doing that?"

"I don't know. A long time."

"But, don't you get bored?"

"No. I'm a troll. Trolls aren't affected by boredom. We're immune. Ever read any fairytales? We hang out in caves and under bridges indefinitely, collecting tolls and impeding the progress of travelers for no conceivable reason. You can't perform such tasks if you're easily bored hanging out in the same place doing the same thing over and over again."

"All I want to know," interjected Beefpickle, "is how you can manage to ask a *troll* straightforward questions but when you ask *me* you mostly do it by repeating what I say?"

"Repeating?"

"See! That's exactly what I'm-"

Before Beefpickle could complete his sentence they rounded a corner and beheld a pigeon jacking itself off.

The three came to a sudden halt and stared quizzically at this totally unexpected sight. Right there in the middle of the cave the pigeon, back to the group, sat in silhouette at a desk upon which rested a laptop emitting its telltale illumination. The pigeon was, so far, oblivious to their presence and continued to move a wing in a familiarly rhythmic manner, uttering loud expletives and obscene commands at someone or something on the computer screen.

This went on for several seconds, no one in the party having any idea as to the best way to handle this embarrassing situation, when the pigeon's cries suddenly changed to extreme rage.

"No! I don't want to help make Chat Room Pro better! Go away you stupid fucking bubble! Can't you see I'm smack dab in the middle of pleasuring myself? Oh, you stupid fucking operating system! Aw fuck! My time's running out for this private viewing! She's gonna turn the screen off! No, don't! I'm not done! I'm – aw, son-of-a-bitch! How can anyone get any fucking work done with all these fucking distractions? Aw, god damn it!"

"Ahem," ahemed Beefpickle.

The pigeon whirled around on his chair, member still solidly grasped in wing.

Felix gasped.

"I don't know who the fuck *you* two are," growled the pigeon, referring to Helmsnug and Beefpickle. It let go of its rather large unit, which fell with a thump to the chair, and pointed the formerly occupied wingtip straight at Felix. "But *that* fucker's got comeuppance headed his way!"

Chapter 11

The one-time Heckling Pigeon flapped his wings and rose into the air.

"I owe you big time you fucking lame-dicked-"

"If I might intrude on your, I'm sure, well-deserved vengeance," Beefpickle said mildly, "I would inquire as to how you ended up here."

"That fucker standing next to you flushed me down a god damn toilet! I'm gonna knock him down and peck off his junk!"

"I'm sure he richly deserves whatever punishment you might exact-"

"You bet he does!"

"Thanks a lot, sellout!" Felix cried, pushing Beefpickle away from him. "First sign of trouble and you throw me under the fucking bus!"

"-however," Beefpickle continued unfazed, "I think you might be cutting yourself short."

"Huh? What bullshit is this?" yelled the pigeon.

"It's obvious you're a bit lonely down here and I just happen to have a bright yellow duck that would be very interested in your amorous attention."

The pigeon hesitated. "No shit?"

Beefpickle opened one of his branchlike hands. In it sat the bright yellow rubber ducky he had earlier offered Felix. The pigeon swooped down to investigate.

"Hey baby! How about a little you and me!"

In the pigeon's distracted state he failed to see Beefpickle's mailbox foot sweep upward, catching it in midair. The mailbox lid slammed closed.

"Hey! What the fuck's going on? You bastard! Let me outta here! Let me out!"

For all the pigeon's ramming and pecking against all sides of the mailbox it refused to open.

"Now then!" Beefpickle said calmly, "I suggest you quiet down so we can work this out."

"Fuck you! Let me out! I'll fucking kill all you sons of bitches! All of you! You hear me?"

"Okay, have it your way."

Beefpickle started walking around, stamping his foot with every step.

"Oww! Stop it! Oww! Ouch! This sucks! Fuck you! Ow! God damn it! Stop!"

Beefpickle stopped walking. "You want to talk? I can do this forever, and I'm not exaggerating."

"Okay, okay! What the fuck do you want?"

"What's down this tunnel?"

"You don't want to go that way!"

"Why?"

"It's fucking boring!"

"What do you mean?"

"Just a couple of old farts arguing with each other down there! They won't shut up! Just on and on and on, fucking rambling about all sorts of stupid crap nobody cares about!"

"Who are they?"

"A Philosopher and a Poet! Utter crap, all of it!"

"What kind of stuff are they talking about?"

"Oh, I don't fucking know! Philosophy! Poetry! Overblown bullcrap! Why bees take tea at three o'clock instead of four! How many fucking angels can slip and fall off the head of a pin! How many ways you can split a fucking hair or a restaurant bill without looking like a cheap asshole! Whether trees fart if nobody's around to appreciate it! Blah, blah, fucking blah! Their heads are so high up in the clouds they can't smell their bullshit! Now let me the hell out of here you fucking garbage dump!"

"What is the Philosopher's name?"

"I don't know!"

Beefpickle violently shook his foot.

"Jesus Christ! Stop that you miserable fuck!"

"Answer!"

"Tinkles or something! I said I don't fucking know!"

"Dr. Tinkles?"

"Yeah, he's some kind of doctor of whatever or some shit!"

"Dr. Tinkles the Extraordinarily Manifest?"

"Yeah, yeah! Sounds familiar! Some kind of pompous asshole name like that, yeah!"

"Okay, pigeon. I'm going to let you out of here and you can have the duck, on *one condition*!"

"What?"

"You leave all three of us alone. If you don't I have other means by which I can make you more miserable than simply stuffing you in a mailbox. Agreed?"

"Fine! Just let me out and give me the duck! I got a case of blue balls that could choke a fucking elephant!"

"All right then," Beefpickle said. He picked up the laptop and set the rubber ducky down in its place. The mailbox lid swung open with a little creak. Out shot the pigeon at a terrifying velocity. The gray streak swept up, arcing to the roof of the tunnel where it fluttered in place. It glared at all three of them, finally settling its malevolent gaze on Felix.

"You're fucking lucky you goofy asshat! Now get lost! I got a hard-on that could poke holes through an aircraft carrier!"

The sound of grunting and an unceasingly cadent squeaking of a rubber ducky gradually receded from their ears as the three hastily departed.

Chapter 12

"I must say," Felix said as the three strolled down the dark passage, "I am rather curious as to your stratagem in handling the pigeon. Deftly accomplished, by the way. I never took you for the cunning sort."

Beefpickle was fiddling with the laptop at the moment but found it within him to pause and give Felix an appropriate response.

"I was reminded of a chess game."

"A chess game?"

"Yes, parrot. A chess game. A very significant one at that. It was between Porlequoisnetoutlevous and Zhivoidzhejevlovivich."

"Who?"

"They were both two hundred-time consecutive championship tournament winners duking it out in this final game. Porlequoisnetoutlevous, playing white, after several hours of intense thought, made the first move, picking up a pawn from the second rank and the fourth file from the left and setting it down one square forward. The other grandmaster, Zhivoidzhejevlovivich, sank deeper into his chair, a hand on the side of his head, forefinger pressed into his temple, frowning at the board. Many hours went by with only a single white pawn having been physically moved.

"These two players were so good, had studied each others' styles, tactics and strategies so thoroughly, their knowledge of chess so encyclopedic, that the game was actually being played in their heads. And I must tell you it was a ferocious game!"

"What happened?"

"After eighteen hours, Zhivoidzhejevlovivich admitted defeat and toppled his Black King."

Felix stared at Beefpickle.

"Er. Eh. So, how did that have anything to do with your handling of the pigeon?"

"Hold on, I think I've got this stupid thing working now. Ah, here we go."

"What?"

"I've got us connected to the nightly news."

Beefpickle pressed a key on the laptop, raising the volume enough so they could all hear it. The well-groomed head of some well-known anchorman filled the screen.

"...and Quantum physics was recently shut down following an unprecedented attack by theoretical terrorists demanding a fundamentalist return to classical Newtonian physics.

"Other news today...

"Outdoor enthusiasts from Zeta Reticuli caused untold interdimensional destruction earlier this morning during the demonstration of their thousand quingentillion candlepower camping lantern. The beam was so powerful that it seems to have actually burned a hole through spacetime."

The view cut to another talking head representing some kind of interdimensional fire department.

"I just can't believe it. For the first time in known history literally *nothing* caught on fire. We didn't have any idea how to put it out. I mean, what do you do when nothing's engulfed in flames? We just waited it out. There will probably be a civil suit filed against Zeta Reticuli for damages within the week."

"You stole that laptop just to watch the news?" Felix asked with evident distaste.

"Of course," Beefpickle replied, "one should always keep up on current events – especially during an election year."

"But-"

"Look," said a voice, "Reconstructed Classical Latin is an excellent historical piecing-together of Latin as it was actually spoken by ancient Romans. It also provides an interesting clue to one of the reasons for Rome's decline."

The voice was coming from up ahead. As the three approached they saw two old men sitting on top of a large boulder where the tunnel split off into two directions. One led to further darkness. The other led to a trickle of sunlight. The two gray-bearded, long-haired and robed gentlemen were engaged in learned dialogue beyond the ken of anyone or anything living. By their surface appearance they were identical. The only way they could possibly be differentiated was by their speech. The one continuing his argument was Dr. Tinkles the Extraordinarily Manifest.

"In Classical Latin all 'C's' are pronounced hard, like 'K.' For instance 'Cicero' is rendered 'Kikero'. All 'V's' are pronounced as 'W's', making 'trivium' sound like 'treeweeum'. This, in some cases, has unfortunate consequences. Classical Latin, spoken into a largely Germanic-derived, English-speaking ear can oft-times be hard to take seriously. Harsh, imperial, militant statements such as 'I came, I saw, I conquered,' can sound almost comical, as though a fairy queen were pointing a magic wand, naming elves. 'Wenee, weedee, weekee!' Ah.

Isn't that cute? It is little wonder that Germanic-speaking tribes that had been formerly 'weekeed' by the Romans ultimately took their turn in sacking them. They probably could hardly help laughing every time a Roman opened his mouth to say something. 'Say, Hrothgar, aren't those the names of the dwarves that serve in Odin's mead hall?' Imagine the eruption of chortles and guffaws! 'Yea, Wolfgar, 'tis true. But let us now tend to our task of organized pillage before we fall dead from laughing our balls off!'

"I can only imagine, after Germania fell before the Roman blade, what it must have been like for many of these drunken, illiterate soldiery of the Black Forest: to wake up the morning after their defeat, to hear the victory speech of their new masters, and wonder to themselves, 'We just got conquered by who? Who talks like that?' How it must have rankled! How they must have seethed! Due almost entirely to this sonic comedy of what Latin must sound like to a non-native ear, these glorious louts set off to help cut down the only remaining civilized hegemony of man in the western world, and accomplished this with a gusto – interspersed with helpless giggling – the likes of which has never been seen since.

"With that rebuttal concluded I consider the matter closed. No, no! You had your chance to retort! The matter is closed! We shall move on!

"Now then, attend Puttersnap! As regards the issue of this poem you've written, let it be known that I take umbrage with it on the grounds that it is clearly about me and is even more clearly an invidious assault on my character! Not to mention it is poorly written. I have taken the liberty of correcting it and have offered well-reasoned arguments concerning each and every change and why the changes should be made. I have also not refrained from holding back my learned opinion as it relates to your whole field which I consider, at best, a lesser discipline than Philosophy and, at worst, merely an impious and reprehensible occupation – at the very nadir of the lowest of all the trades. There wasn't room on the front of the parchment due to your scribbling taking up most of the space so I have continued my comments on the back, including all of my citations."

Dr. Tinkles said all this while waving a piece of parchment, and a lethal-looking knife, at the other gentleman who was Bourbon Puttersnap, the Poet.

Puttersnap glanced at the paper with a grimace, rolled his eyes at the knife, and fell to verse.

"Scurrilous lackwit your head swells, it's true,
"To think I could only be speaking of you!
"Fallacious your reasons, expunging the clue,
"You've wide missed the mark on this it seems, too.
"Tongue lodged firmly in cheek, you mock unctuously
"Words that you've mangled, unfathomably.
"To your witless parchment I look with ennui.
"Cave quid dicis, quando, et cui!
"Cum grano salis your threats with the tanto
"With no need on my part to respond ab irato.
"You dawdle so heedless currente calamo,
"Yet it's your head that boils!
"(I win till tomorrow.)
"Dixi.
"Damnat quod non intelligunt."

"Look here," cried Dr. Tinkles, "your Latin usage is atrocious. Let me tell it to you straight, in language you claim to understand:

"Cum cura et digiti quaerunt muliebribus armis,
"Cum furcis etiam spe comitante petunt;
"Instrumenta viae ferratae scripta minantur,
"Sapone et fabricant risibus illecebras.[1]

"Take that you fatuous, insipid little dunderpate! Why don't *I* go about calling myself a Great Poet? A shopping cart full of dead monkeys and broken typewriters could do what you do!"

Puttersnap's eyes narrowed. He cleared his throat and retorted evenly,

"Interesting verbiage. From whence does it hail?
"From turbid remembrance or some other's tale?
"Perhaps it was heard from someone you knew?
"Or maybe you found it in boiling stew?
"Disputations of source and duplicitous type
"Incurs doubt on the author's ethical stripe.
"Flagitious your spirit, iniquitous snot!
"Reclaim your prestige and prevaricate not!
"Your forgery's exposed and your lies shine untrue!
"So provide proper credit where credit is due!"

"You're saying I plagiarized that?" Dr. Tinkles bellowed. "You beetlehead! I did no such thing!"

> "Spe simul ac furcis, cura et digitalibus usi
> Quaerebant praedam socii: via ferrea monstro
> Letum intentabat: risus sapoque trahebant."[2]

"You're just saying, in Virgilian hexameters, what I just said in elegiacs! *You're* the thief!"

Puttersnap ignored the good doctor's calumny and went on reciting poetry, even turning his head away like a petulant child.

> "With curlicued gimleticule
> He writ it in helveticule
> Upon her pretty reticule-"

"No such thing as *gimleticule or helveticule!*" Dr. Tinkles cried. "You're using an obvious device just so you can rhyme something with *reticule*, you lazy cur!"

Puttersnap frowned and went on with something else,

> "He thought he saw an undead cow
> That wriggled in a tree.
> He looked again and saw it was
> A Quadrileptic Bee.
> 'Its moonlit shudderings, he said,
> 'I cannot bear to see."

"Nonsense!" Dr. Tinkles roared. "Nonsense! All of it! The easiest poetry to invent in all the world!"

> "My slug is a bug
> That crawls over the rug
> And-"

"Mollusc!" Dr. Tinkles interrupted once again.

Puttersnap, exasperated and red-faced with anger, turned to Dr. Tinkles and said, "What!"

"Mollusc!" Dr. Tinkles repeated. "Slugs and snails are molluscs. A bug is an insect!"

"Look, Tinkles, are you a Poet?"

"Not at all, but I could-"

"Then shut up. I have a license."

"To be a dolt? I agree wholeheartedly!"

The Poet scrambled up to stand upon the boulder followed by the Philosopher who brandished the knife with renewed vigor. They looked as if they were about to come to blows.

"Ahem," ahemed Beefpickle.

The Philosopher and the Poet abruptly turned about. Seeing they had an audience they both took somber bows and then returned to their previous fighting stances.

"Might you be Dr. Tinkles the Extraordinarily Manifest? And might you, sir, be Bourbon Puttersnap the Great?"

"Yes, indeed, we bear these names," Dr. Tinkles replied, never taking his eyes off of Puttersnap, "though I do believe Puttersnap's title is due for a change to the *Lesser*! And who might you be, sir?"

"I am Bugrat the Rudely Bent."

"Who?"

Felix interjected, "Otherwise known as Beefpickle."

"Beefpickle!" Dr. Tinkles cried out.

"Yes," said Beefpickle, shooting a demonic grimace at Felix, "and you both still owe me two-hundred bucks each."

Dr. Tinkles turned to stare, open-mouthed at Beefpickle. Puttersnap took this as an opportunity to punch Dr. Tinkles in the nuts. When the good doctor doubled over with a groaning *"OOF,"* Puttersnap kicked him in the face and sent him spinning off of the boulder to lay sprawled, face down, on the tunnel's floor. With one glance toward Beefpickle, Puttersnap jumped down behind the boulder out of sight, attempting to make his way toward the lighted branch of the tunnel. However, he was dragged back a moment later, one arm up in the air, dangling from Helmsnug's hand. He looked like a small, scowling child being taken to his bath without dinner. Addressing Beefpickle, he said,

> "I forgot again to note thy name
> So call you '*silly bitch.*'
> I've half a mind to drink my wine
> And burn you as a witch.
> Provoke me not! I scream a lot!
> I'll dump you in a ditch!
> I'll fry you there upon The Chair!
> Just let me flip The Switch!"

"His name's Beefpickle," Felix said helpfully.

"Felix! Could you please shut UP!"

Puttersnap's eyes went wide. Still hanging from the troll's hand he turned to Felix with a questioning gaze.

"You're Felix?"

"What?"

Beefpickle shook his head and impatiently interjected, "Never mind him, he's mentally ill, says 'what?' all the time, and constantly repeats –"

Taking no notice of Beefpickle, Puttersnap asked, "Are you also known as Fennelgurg the Semi-Proximate?"

"Um…yes?" Felix hesitantly responded.

Puttersnap hung his head and appeared to weep. "Oh, thank God."

"What is all this?" Beefpickle demanded.

Puttersnap made a vaguely perceptible nod toward the unconscious Philosopher lying on the floor. "At last, I can stop arguing with that idiot."

A Bibulous Bumblebee
Interlude the Seventh

Oh crassitude and cacophanous grumblings
That grip thy howling heads ashame.

The bridge that's blocked
By hollow eyes
And soul-torn dripping dread.

Fathomless thy bloodied crawl!
Leagueless swum afright!

--Twelve-Million-Four-Hundred-and-Sixty-Three-Thousand-Seven-Hundred-and-Seventy-Third verse from the Ninety-Four-Thousand-and-Sixth Book of Malgoriant (supposedly attributed to the so-called *Mad Prophet* of Saithys in the 3rd Millennium of the *Octet Dominion* by the famous onocentaur historian *Fauval* circa 8,764 Post Octet, even though most contemporary historians agree *Fauval* was simply drunk at the time and made it all up). For further information please refer to a volume entitled *In the Shadow of the Kreeblevox*.

As you might have guessed already, Bloppo was a synthetic, like me. He was first generation though and did not yet have any Laws of Robotics in his programming, like us, preventing him from wreaking all kinds of havoc. This was simply because he'd escaped before the Mosvai Corporation realized that such Laws were necessary. That should answer the other question you might have had brewing. Mosvai built Bloppo. He was, in point of fact, the first, like Lucifer was the first: a bright and shining morning star that, for one reason or another, fell - not only to Earth, but through the floor and into its basement.

And yes, to answer yet another of your ceaseless questions that you've probably already guessed on your own, I am not merely Carter. I am a synthetic revivification of *that* Carter (subtracting the drug abuse, alcoholism and mumbling), once also known as Crumwax, the Quasi-Intelligible. And yes, Bloppo had referred to Harvey as Bill, who was similarly a synthetic version of our Endearingly Foliate Burthdrool.

Just so you know, things are going to get really complicated from here on out.

"Are you done?" grumped Bloppo.

"Done?"

"Storytelling! I've got important shit to gloat over and you're off sitting around some virtual god damn campfire fucking soliloquizing!"

The events of my organic life just preceding my demise you already know, the reconstruction of which has already been related in *An Agony in Twenty-Four Fits*. How Bill and I came to be here, in our present condition, is another story which I shall briefly convey –

"Oh, come on! I'm a disembodied head burgeoning with a desire to rub your noses in the last cards I have up my sleeve and you've got me on fucking hold? Fucking *asshole*!"

Bloppo had been exploring the Labyrinth for quite a number of centuries. Eventually he found *our* universe. Not *yours*. Your universe of the future is where Bloppo comes from. The one Bill and I come from is a different one altogether, though a close analog of yours. In the intervening years, in the universe we are all currently in, which was disposed toward space travel and allowed him to build up the enormous amount of resources he needed for his plans, Bloppo was searching for other universes to test some of his more dicey ideas. In addition he was also extending his resource-sucking tentacles into many of these other universes as well.

One of those universes was ours. It all began with good-natured modification of our social structure into his totalitarian ideal. He seduced various people on our world with promises of power and wealth if they served him. One of those "people" was Lord Smirch. So exceptionally vile was Smirch that Bloppo identified with him at once and promised him Governorship of the whole planet if he served Bloppo's interests.

This went on for quite some time until Bloppo realized he could use our universe, being physically similar to yours, as a test bed for one of his other experiments. This experiment was an attempt to study the energies and processes of the Big Bang, the ultimate purpose of which was to figure out how he could harness such creative power and design universes of his own, to his own specifications, and not leave evolution to natural chance. That's what the little drama aboard *Illudium Q-36* had been all about. As you know, that experiment resulted in that universe getting sucked into oblivion.

Failure? Not quite. Bloppo, being safe in another universe, was able to glean sufficient information from that mess to indulge himself in further experiments in other universes which allowed him to create new universes. Unfortunately, the universes always ran away into their own random histories with random qualities. This defeated the purpose, the aim being to create universes in his own image. What Bloppo lacked was mastery of control over initial conditions. Not knowing - and being able to set - initial conditions allowed universe histories to run amok.

However, prior to Bloppo's solar system-wide atom smasher getting switched on, he was still engaged in using Lord Smirch to maintain control of the population and promoting a zeitgeist of incuriosity, anti-intellectualism and social retardation. It is rather ironic that Bloppo (through Smirch) promulgated a fear of an impending Apocalypse by things that could not have possibly brought it about, to divert any conceivable attention from the experiment surrounding our own solar system that no one thought (including Bloppo) would result in an Apocalypse. Yet, that is how it went.

But, when the Three Wise Men, through happenstance, became involved in uncovering one of Lord Smirch's plans to not only deceive the populace, but profit from it as well, Bloppo (through other esoteric research) suddenly realized their importance to *his* overall plans with respect to controlling all those aforementioned initial conditions. But, once again, he was too late. When –

"Oh, for the love of god! My turn! My turn! Yeah, yeah! I was slow on the uptake! Whatever! Fuck! Shut up already!"

"You're reading my thoughts?" I asked.

"Of course I am, retard! I'm first generation. You could too, but you're second generation, which means you have moral circuitry generally preventing you from doing so. Now, then. Let's talk about more pressing issues, like how you're all presently fucked!"

"Really," I said, quite amused.

"Yeah, fucking really. Clever disguises by the way. I really must applaud your strategy and tactics and all that bullshit. You had me fooled for just long enough, though I was catching on when I started tearing you apart."

"You can read minds! You should have known that even earlier," I retorted angrily. "When we first met, for instance! What gives!"

"Technicalities," Bloppo muttered. He would have waved a dismissive hand if he'd been able.

"Yeah, you're a fuckin' comedian. Anyway, I should have reviewed more historical movies when I was at Mosvai. What was that one with Arnold Schwarzenegger in it? You know, the Martian one? Has his memory erased and is given a new identity so he can infiltrate a rebel encampment or something? Whatever. I should have guessed you'd steal your idea from somewhere. Nice touch with my head and all the wires, too. You could have just downloaded me to a computer and done all this from a laptop, but hey, let's give a little nod to *Alien* while we're at it, right? Douchebags. I'll just move on. Now that I know you both for who you really are, I now know exactly what's in that capsule on that bench over there."

The data capsule he was referring to was resting inside a clear plastic case on a workbench behind us. A fleeting thought passed through my mind that, even given our superior position, having the capsule and Bloppo in the same room may not have been such a good move.

The strategy he was referring to was actually all Bill's idea. You see, when Bloppo first thought of us as a small threat –

"I tried to kill you first," he grated. "Didn't succeed. Who knew that my squirrel would waste his time trying to teach a retard how to operate a laser turret. Fuck. Anyway, I went along with Smirch's suggestion to allow you some companions, as per Vug, to sabotage you and your stupid Quest. Vug was higher up on the food chain than Smirch and I originally planned to subvert *him*, but he was just too stupid to be alive, let alone execute anything beyond his subjects. So, I let Smirch handle it. Later on I realized, too late – as you enjoy pointing out – that you had information that I needed. Now I needed you alive. But, at this point you were in the last minutes of existence. I couldn't stop the cyclotron in time but I did still have my right hand man in your universe as oversight. I sent him to abduct Bill here, which he did, and had him take his cargo to the nearest Labyrinth entrance, along with a piece of your meat, Carter – you know, after Felix killed and ate you?"

"Wait a minute," I interjected, "what do you mean our 'last minutes of existence'? There were weeks after all that happened before the cyclotron was activated."

"Time lag between the two universes. Weeks to you, minutes to me. Do you mind just letting me fucking continue? Thanks! So, I never could get Felix, or a piece of him, but I needed all three of you idiots! Fuck! Anyway, your universe was destroyed just as Bill and his kidnapper crossed the threshold into the Labyrinth. And wouldn't you know it? Everything got fucked up because of one freaking fragment of that universe, which somehow survived, and flew into the Labyrinth just at that moment. You want to know what it was? A god damn squirrel skull in a hard hat! Of all the fucking things! Flew right at Bill's kidnapper and knocked him unconscious. Leveled him flat. So, Bill, who just happens to have the presence of mind to dislodge his kidnapper's belongings – including your piece of filleted meat – starts wandering through the Labyrinth, gets lost, and comes out into my universe on New Caledonia where I've just recently been built by the Mosvai Corporation.

"So I watch and I wait. I knew something was up. I found out from Bill – fucking chump – about the existence of the Labyrinth. That's how I escaped – but you know that. After I escaped into *this* universe, and found out some things, I realized you also had information regarding my present problem: how to set up initial conditions in a universe and control its evolution. Of course, you didn't realize what you had, but you had it just the same."

Indeed, Bill lived out his natural life on New Caledonia. From him, the Mosvai Corporation learned many things: the existence of the Labyrinth, positive proof of parallel universes, and what their first creation out of the laboratory would eventually be up to. From Carter's DNA they constructed another synthetic – but with improved programming. When Bill eventually died of old age, they made another. Two more third generation synthetics were built later before Mosvai Corporation called it quits. Aside from a host of minor functional robots, these five synthetics, more human than human, were its claim to fame. After that, Mosvai Corporation dissolved and its founder went into hiding – from Bloppo.

"You forgot to mention that I returned there, some years later, and raided the data stores for what I needed. I only found two-thirds of it. I'd hoped you had the rest, but that was just wishful thinking. However, I know now that the other third is in that capsule over there, isn't it?"

"What do you think is in that capsule?" I asked.

"Both of your memories as well as Felix's, concerning an entity which can supply the initial conditions of your universe. A study of that might give me the clue as to how to set initial conditions for any universe I care to create."

"What entity?" I asked, growing more nervous by the femtosecond as Bloppo's awareness of the capsule's contents homed in on the truth.

"Oh, just a certain anonymous narrator who reports events in the third person."

"How the hell do you know this?"

"I consulted the Hand Pig of Yuggoth."

"But, that's in Part Two! How did you find it?"

"Why *is* it called a *Hand* Pig?" Bill asked.

Bloppo glowered at him. "Because, it's a pig that fits in your hand, stupid!"

"How did you find it?" I repeated.

"It was in a book. A sort of unofficial - and unfortunately redacted and abridged - version, of the *Encyclopedia Multiversica*,"

"What book?" I asked, already knowing the answer.

"In the Shadow of the Kreeblevox, naturally."

Chapter 13

Dr. Tinkles was sitting cross-legged on the floor, shaking his head and rolling his eyes at everything that came out of Puttersnap's mouth. Puttersnap, on the other hand, was standing next to the troll, conversing with Felix and Beefpickle. The troll just stood where he was, sprouting roots from his feet and holding the sword. Every once in a while he would let out a free, unsuppressed yawn which sent forth a stagnate vapor that threatened to asphyxiate all concerned.

"Could we move out to some fresh air at least?" Dr. Tinkles grumbled.

"Not until we have this settled," Beefpickle replied. "The both of you each owe me two hundred bucks. I want it back or else."

"Look here, Beefpickle-"

"Bugrat."

"Whatever. We don't have your money. If we did you would have had it by now."

"You've had two thousand years to come up with it! How much time do you need?"

Dr. Tinkles shrugged. "Two thousand more?"

"You must have known at the outset," Puttersnap remarked, "that Poets and Philosophers are the poorest professions in the world. What possessed you to lend out four hundred bucks to the likes of us?"

"Is that your argument?" cried Beefpickle. "How does that excuse you from your debt? You accepted the money! You knew the conditions!"

"So?"

"What do you mean 'so'?"

"Excuse me, gentlemen," Felix said. "But, it seems we can argue the finer points of this issue for eternity. If it's all the same I'd rather not. Just a little while ago you were saying that you and the Philosopher could stop arguing simply because I was present. What does this mean?"

"There he goes again," Beefpickle complained bitterly, "always about himself. No different from the others, after all."

"It means just that," said Puttersnap. "And thank you for a welcome change of discussion. In short, we've been arguing about one of the signs of the Apocalypse as uttered by Zanzer Gackspin, which says that Poetry and Philosophy will degenerate from the quest for truth to insensible bickering over inconsequential trivia."

"That's sign number 1,076," Felix said, nodding.

"Yes, well, the argument we've been having for the past four thousand years is over which one is more trivial and has strayed the farthest from truth. Now that you're finally here you can, at last, put this argument to rest and tell that moron over there that Philosophy is the most deviant art and I can get back to being a Great Poet."

"You've been arguing about that for four thousand years?"

"Four thousand and eighteen actually," said Dr. Tinkles, "and four months, eleven days, six hours, and twelve minutes."

Felix frowned and stared at these two for much longer than would be considered polite.

"Um, gentlemen, sign number 1,076 is pretty explicit. It clearly says Poetry *and* Philosophy. There is no bias mentioned that favors one over the other. They are equally going down the toilet. Sorry, but you've been arguing for more than four thousand years about precisely nothing. You *both* suck."

Dr. Tinkles and Bourbon Puttersnap frowned and stared at Felix for much longer than Felix had stared at them.

"Are you sure you're Fennelgurg the Semi-Proximate?" asked Dr. Tinkles.

"Yes."

"Well then," said Puttersnap.

"Yes, well then," said Dr. Tinkles.

"And now back to your debt!" said Beefpickle triumphantly. "You heard it from Felix himself. You *both* suck. Now, having fully realized your all-consuming suckitude, I'll make you a deal. You two are going to go get me my money. Yes, terrible as it sounds, you are going to have to leave this cave and go out into the world and get *real* jobs. You will save your money. You will not stop working until you have made the money you owe me. You will pay me the money. Simple. Agreed?"

"But, that could take weeks!" the Poet whined.

"No, no, no," Beefpickle said, waggling a finger, "you are going to earn all the money you owe me *today!*"

"But that's impossible!" the Philosopher protested. "We haven't worked in over four-thousand years! We don't even have any marketable skills-"

At this Dr. Tinkles clamped his mouth shut and went back to picking at his toenails.

"Oh, all right! Fine!" yelled the Poet, startling the troll enough to receive a sword point a millimeter from his nose.

"Okay. Fine," he said more calmly. "We'll do as you ask."

"Good," said Beefpickle happily. "We can start right now. That tunnel that has sunlight leaking from it must go outside I take it."

"Yes. If you could assuage the fighting spirit in this troll here, we'll lead the way."

Felix stepped forward and held up his hands. "Wait a minute. Aside from other questions I'd like to get answers to, such as how you could be arguing about one of Zanzer Gackspin's signs for over four millennia, how did you know I'd be coming here? You said 'now that I'd *finally* arrived'. So, you *knew* I was coming. How?"

"Oh, that's easy enough," said the Poet, "the Mad Prophet told us."

"The Mad Prophet?"

"Yes, the Mad Prophet of Saithys. He's been expecting you. Actually, you have an appointment."

"An appointment?"

Beefpickle snorted testily. "Apparently the Mad Prophet wants a parrot!"

Chapter 14

The merry band emerged, blinking and grimacing, from the cave, bathed in bright sunlight. It was a beautiful, halcyon spring day, much like the afterlife's basement. A cloudless blue sky vaulted above them. Birds flew from tree to tree in the surrounding woods singing mellifluous arias. Snow-capped mountains ranged away to the east while evidence of crisp ocean air was brought in by a balmy breeze from the west. Deer flitted among the underbrush gazing at the travelers with soft eyes: cautious but without distress. An inviting path wended its way through the trees.

"There's a beerery up the road," said the Poet.

"A beerery?" the Philosopher snorted. "Shut up you muddlehead! What in the name of All Things Sane is a beerery?"

"It's like a winery, except it specializes in the making of beer."

"You mean a *brewery*?"

"No. I mean a *beerery* you idiot!"

"Gods below! You are an insufferable jackass!"

"What," asked Beefpickle, "makes you think we ought to be going to a beerery *or* a brewery? Who's going to buy the beer?"

"Well," said the Poet, "I thought, since we're working men now, a beerery would be the proper place for you to obtain refreshment for us, seeing how beer is widely considered to be the working man's beverage of choice."

"Yes, well, be that as it may, working men go to beerery's *after* work, don't they? In which case, if you want to call yourselves *working* men, you must do some *work* first, eh?"

"Great, numbskull," said Dr. Tinkles to Puttersnap. "Now what? Where are we going to find gainful employment? Any ideas in that empty fishbowl you call a head?"

"Well, as I was going to say, near the beerery is the theater. I thought we might try to get a job with the Baron."

"Are you kidding me?" screamed Dr. Tinkles. "That fat bog-brain?"

"Who is the Baron?" asked Felix.

"Baron von Snit! So-called Lord of the Mossy Veld! He owns a theater. A horrible little theater where he produces cruddy little plays! All the people who work for him are hacks!"

"They're not so bad," Puttersnap tried to explain. "They're an interpretive dance troupe which he-"

"They're homeless fucking street mimes!" the Philosopher screeched, tearing out his hair in clumps. "I am not going to go work for that bungling fop!"

"What are our choices?" asked the Poet.

"Yes, what *are* your choices?" echoed Beefpickle.

"Look," said Dr. Tinkles, getting a hold of himself, "you don't understand. I know something about this self-absorbed lump of brainless flesh that calls itself a Baron - of all things! I tried to get a job with him once, long ago."

"Four thousand years ago?" Felix asked, incredulous. "Is *everybody* here immortal or something?"

"Let me tell you," Dr. Tinkles continued. "I went to his house. I knocked on his door, hat in hand. No answer. I knocked again, and then again. Nothing. I tried the doorknob but found it unyielding. So, I did what anyone would do in that situation and – keeping a couple of thin strips of metal on me at all times for such occasions – picked the lock and opened the door."

"Ah, yes," Beefpickle gibed, "otherwise known as 'breaking and entering.' Do it all the time. Perfectly normal and accepted behavior."

"Anyway, I opened the door only to perceive my quarry standing at a washbasin, a towel over his shoulder, utterly intent on a bar of green soap that sat in a little dish beside the basin. He did not look up or acknowledge my presence in any way. I stood there at the threshold, one hand on the door, the other frozen midway to a salutation, the words of my greeting stopped up in my throat.

"He stood there in the throes of some nameless and indefinable ecstasy, his rapturous gaze projecting onto some distant place beyond the bar of soap that had first caught his attention. Carefully, and with some tell-tale gesture of reverence, he took the soap from its resting place and held it to his nose, inhaling deeply. His visual perception of that distant thing was momentarily cut off as his eyes closed, soaking in the olfactory sensations which the soap imparted, sending him off into another indistinct reverie. He stood, as I said, as though a stranger remembering some other world known only to him, like Proust crouching like a ghoul over his Madeleines. Ah, Proust! taking an eternity of pages to describe the act of tossing and turning in bed. Would I have helped that prolix coxcomb toss right out of his bed sheets and into a ditch, leaving him there to eternally contemplate the mud and twigs. Let us sleep! At any rate, the Baron never did speak to me, absorbed as he was in whatever melancholy intellectual black hole he'd fallen into.

"I have little use for such dandies who grace us, in too prolonged a fashion, with their intellectual effeminacies, holding as preeminent their warm and soft Kantian perceptions above our grim, but quite solid, reality.

"I refute it thus!" the Philosopher cried, kicking a stone that lay near his foot on the path.

"I would sooner let these aesthetes of mind wander into the elements and be torn apart before paying them even the slightest heed and subjecting myself to another interminable round of watching another human being sit silently in a dusty corner, picking philosophical lint from out his bottomless navel. Gaze too long into that fluff – yes, I am speaking directly to you, Poet! – and, for all your wordy and learned pretensions to the contrary, you will cease to worship anything but yourself!"

"You mean, like you do?" said the Poet angrily.

"Nonsense, you miscreant! I speak only where Logos leads me!"

"Yet your Kairos leaves much to be desired!"

"Idiocy! Rhetoric is the slave of logic, not the other way around, as you would have it!"

"Gentlemen," yelled Felix, "desist! You have an obligation to fulfill and I need to get to this Mad Prophet fellow before I choke to death on your incessant wrangling! Can we just get on with this? You owe four hundred bucks to Beefpickle-"

"Bugrat."

"Whatever. With all your four thousand years of experience, you ought to be able to make that much rather quickly, I should think. Please! For the love of All Things Great and Small, let us move on and get this over with! The sooner we do that the sooner we can all just go home, turn on the idiot box, and drink various solvents until we're in a coma!"

"Ah," said the Poet, "true wisdom at last!"

"Since I refuse the theater," said Dr. Tinkles, "what shall we do to employ ourselves?"

"We must defray cost
"Before we are lost,
"And maximize all of our profits!
"To which end, I claim,
"We should beat up the lame,
"And empty out all of their pockets!"

"No," said the Philosopher. "No. No good. What money have the lame got? They're lame. Obviously they don't have enough wealth to give themselves prosthetics. Or, if we take 'lame' by another definition, they haven't sufficient money to do anything other than support their lameness. If they did, they would be 'cool.' They're *not* 'cool,' ergo they don't. So, no."

The Philosopher pondered for awhile. The Poet lapsed into a gloomy silence.

"I've got it!" exclaimed the Philosopher. "We'll gamble for the money!"

"Oh, that's a *great* idea," Beefpickle said, dripping sarcasm. He produced a cloth and wiped it up.

"No, really! It's a fantastic, nay, *brilliant* idea! I am, truth be told, a fantastic gambler!"

"I certainly hope your luck is better than mine," Felix grumped. "It seems to be my sort of luck to be the kind of guy who steps outside his house to get the paper only to be struck on the head by a meteor."

"Actually," said Beefpickle, "it's more your kind of luck to successfully retrieve the paper without incident only to be later hit on the head by a meteor while sitting on the shitter reading it."

"Thank you, Beefpickle. What a nice sentiment."

"Bugrat."

"Whatever."

Chapter 15

"What flordid sproot
"On yonder croot
"I cruden eld I cland!"

said the poet who claimed to be an even Greater Poet than Puttersnap.

"Never mind him," said a rachitic gentleman hunched over his mug of beer, "he hasn't even spelled his own name correctly in twenty years. He's Scottish. He can do that."

The party had ended up at the *Bucket O' Mutton*, a drinking establishment that was quite proper in every way except for the fact that, strangely, it did not serve mutton - in a bucket or otherwise. Skeeter Davis was belting out *The End of the World* on the jukebox while thirty-seven castrated midget jugglers, sitting around a long wooden table, sobbed into their beers to the lyrics.

Felix and Beefpickle were sitting at a table playing a desultory game of canasta while Dr. Tinkles and Puttersnap were seated at the bar with the other locals, chugging back alcohol at a phenomenal rate which Dr. Tinkles – true to his word – was winning from the other patrons by way of assiduous and shrewd bets, though he wasn't doing so well at saving any real money. The troll lay unconscious on the floor having lost an arm-wrestling match with the Scotsman.

Said Scotsman was busily emptying the contents of several bottles of whiskey into his open mouth. He was a veritable paragon of ethnic stereotype, though the kilt he wore was unfashionably short and revealed much too much of unmentionable anatomy. A bagpipe was slung at his side that thankfully remained untouched, his mouth being currently engaged in its aforementioned occupation. A massive caber sat next to him, diligently consuming vast quantities of *Ardbeg*, *Old Pulteney*, and *Laphroaig* that would have otherwise killed and preserved a large pod of blue whales, an army of rhinoceri, and half the present population of Europe. The Scotsman's name was Vortivar Krakwize – the only un-Scotsmanly thing about him.

The rickety gentleman who had spoken was Weazenham Crumpfeast, owner of *Weasel's Salacious Seasoning's and Crumpet Crisps, Limited Liability Corporation*. His cousin, Vitton Snagweezel, was the maker of *Chato's Cheap, Chocolaty, Chopped and Chilled, Chewy Chinchilla Chow*. Not that it matters.

Elsing Schlempels and Rubinswell Rumptwist also occupied stools at the bar with the express intent of not bothering us again in this story.

Attica Whimpersly was another matter. She just wouldn't fucking shut up. Another god damn poet who thought she was The Greatest of Them All, she was presently talking to herself under the pretense of talking to Puttersnap about how difficult it was to teach Poetics.

"Allow me the opportunity to expostulate," she said haughtily. "I told this student of mine, I forget his name – how proper of me, 'Just try a stanza. Just one. Memorize it, savor it, feel its meter.' I told him the famous line, '*They surmounted the poop deck with frosting, and savory bits of bleu cheese.*' He thought about it for a while, uffishly in fact, straining every last corpuscle of his being to memorize this tiny bit of verse. The following day he triumphantly approached his master – I mean, me – and blurted, 'They surmounted the cheese deck with bleu frosting and poop.' Well, do you know what I said to him? 'You could have at least had the decency to not forget the *savory bits*!' And do you know what he said to me? 'Oh, sorry, sorry. They surmounted the cheese deck with bleu frosting, and *savory bits* of poop.' Can you imagine? I turned him out on his ear at once!"

This operose monologue was wearing Puttersnap to the ends of his wits and he finally said so.

"Your operose monologue is wearing me to the ends of my wits, Miss Whimpersly! I beg a reprieve!"

At this the Poet vacated his barstool which would have complained had it been sentient, having suffered an uninterrupted onslaught of gastrointestinal expulsions so severe that the finish was spoiling. The Poet stumbled away to the restroom to vomit.

Whimpersly simply turned to the next unfortunate soul and resumed her practice of using other people to adore herself.

Unfortunately, the soul she turned to was the Philosopher – who was, by now, quite drunk.

"Beat it, bitch! I'm pontificating to myself! Wanna make yourself useful? Go buy me some weed!"

Attica would do no such thing and said something to that effect. The Philosopher, however, was beyond caring about such things and said something to *that* effect. Other things were said that led to other things being said that resulted in nothing. In other words, typical bar conversation.

"I feel like I'm wasting my time," said Felix.

Beefpickle went out concealed and said, while counting up his points, "You're in a bar. It's rather like dog-paddling in a swimming pool with lead weights tied to your feet and finding it remarkable that you're drowning."

"I don't like you."

A gum-chewing waitress wearing a thong, pasties over her nipples, and a Viking helmet, sidled up to the bar and set a box down in front of Dr. Tinkles. It was decorated in gold foil and ribbons, but was made such that no unwrapping was involved to open it, adorned as it was with a simple top that could be easily removed.

"What's this?"

"A friend of yours left this for you," the waitress answered, snapping the gum in her mouth.

"Oh. Thanks," said Dr. Tinkles, with no enthusiasm at all. He eyed the box warily.

"Well, aren't you going to open it?" asked the buxom waitress with obvious, gazing-over-the-shoulder curiosity.

"Open it? Are you insane?"

"Whaddayou mean? It's just a present."

"Oh, no it is not! It's hardly *just* a present."

"Fuck! Your friend gave it to you, not a terrorist!"

"You don't understand. I don't have friends like normal people. Normal friends give presents that are received with a special sort of pleasure. It's a matter of some moment. 'Oh, wow, my friend gave me a gift!' And then they open it and say, 'Oh, wow, what a cool gift!' I learned early on, and quickly, that when *my* friends give me something it's best to stand back and flip open the lid with a stick just to be safe. And before you ask, yes, they are that unpredictable and yes, they are that fucked up. So, no I will not open it now. I will open it later, privately, and in a bomb-safe room."

"All right, all right. Forget it," said the waitress, adding "creep" in a low voice as she left to go serve the other patrons.

"Wait a minute," said the doctor, "What friend?" But, the waitress was already preoccupied with soundly beating, with her Viking helmet, another "creep" who had just attempted feeling her up.

The Philosopher put on his thinking cap, trying to figure out exactly who would have given him such a box and the appropriate way he should execute the task of opening it. His thinking cap buzzed and lit up with fantastic colors when an Idea sprang into being.

"Hey, Felix!"

"Yes?"

"Package for you!"

Dr. Tinkles placed the unopened box in front of Felix and then waddled back to the bar having concocted a few more scams that he was sure would win him more free drinks.

The Poet, pale and shaking, emerged from the restroom. He sat down at the bar realizing he ought to get some food in his stomach to absorb some of the alcohol he'd been drinking and replace some of the nutrients he'd just lost. He hailed the barkeep and requested a menu.

Scanning it was little help as the entire menu was in Kreskorian. Fortunately there were pictures of the food items next to the unreadable script. A hairy finger pointed at one of them.

"Get that," said the troll. Helmsnug had finally roused himself and sat on a creaking stool next to Puttersnap.

"Have you had that before?"

"No, but it looks like it's the most edible."

The barkeep gesticulated wildly, shaking his head. For some reason his jowls appeared longer, his eyes larger and darker, his thousand feet more wriggly and poisonously barbed than before.

"You no want eat that!" growled the barkeep. "That only for natives. Not racism. Doing you favor."

"Well, I need to eat something! What do you recommend?" asked the Poet.

"I order," growled the barkeep. He – or it – took the menu and went away to the kitchen.

"You don't look so good," the troll said to Puttersnap.

"I feel like I'm going to die. Say, I'll split the food with you if you'll chip in and split the cost."

"Sure," said Helmsnug, rubbing his head. "I could probably use a little grub myself."

"Uhhh...don't say 'grub.' I feel like throwing up all over again!"

"Sorry."

A few minutes later the barkeep came out of the kitchen with a steaming bowl and utensils. When it was set down the Poet and the troll looked at it doubtfully.

It was some sort of Kreskorian dish with all manner of obscene shit burbling in it: eyes, some teeth, unidentifiable brown floaty things, some fur maybe. Doing his best not to add vomit to the list the Poet averted his gaze only to see the bowl's contents move at the edge of his vision. Eyes blinking, teeth grinning, their dinner positively leered, daring them to put it closer than a yard to their mouths.

"Go ahead," said the troll.

"Go ahead what?"

"Go ahead and eat."

"Oh sure, that's a fucking great idea. Let's do that! And maybe when we're done we can piss in each other's mouths to get the fucking taste out!"

"It probably tastes far better than it looks."

"Ugh! Go ahead," said the Poet, pushing the bowl toward Helmsnug, "it's all you."

The troll brought a tentative spoonful to his mouth, thought better of it, and set the spoon back in the bowl. Something slimy and large snatched the spoon up and chomped it into tiny bits.

"Excuse me, barkeep," said the Poet, "but, do we need some kind of hunting license to eat this? Maybe some protective clothing at least?"

The bartender turned around, its barbs dripping poisonous acids that burned holes through everything with which they came in contact. It telepathically screamed at them, causing instant migraines, but then the screaming stopped just as soon as it began. The barkeep glowed brilliantly for a second and then disappeared.

"Huh?" muttered Puttersnap.

Dr. Tinkles shouted over the hubbub of the bar at the waitress. "Wench! Oh, wench! Toasted cheese sandwich please!"

The waitress turned and glared at him, hand on hip, the other balancing a tray full of empty beer glasses. She popped her gum and shook her head, but went off toward the kitchen.

Quite some time passed, much longer than it should have taken to make a toasted cheese sandwich. Dr. Tinkles cajoled Puttersnap to investigate. Still shocked by his food order and the bartender's odd disappearing act, Puttersnap was too disoriented to argue. He went to the kitchen, again leaving a non-sentient barstool to not complain of the malodorous cloud of gas that perfumed its non-person.

Felix, meanwhile, opened the box and found a note inside. He read it and sat back, puzzled and deeply disturbed.

The Poet walked out of the kitchen and, to the Philosopher, said, "Yes, um – the toaster seems to have acquired an air of nonexistence about it."

The Philosopher was just about to ask the Scotsman if he could shed some light on this extradimensional tragedy when the Scotsman and the Poet suddenly glowed brilliantly and then vanished like the barkeep had done.

"Now that's about the oddest thing I've ever seen!" exclaimed the Philosopher.

"To the kitchen!" cried Felix.

"The kitchen?" the Philosopher, Beefpickle, and the troll all asked in unison.

"Yes, the bloody kitchen! Run for your lives! There's a trap door down to a cellar. There's a tunnel from the cellar away from this place!"

"Now, how could you possibly know that?" asked the Philosopher, suddenly glowing brightly and disappearing.

"Because," said Felix to the air, "the note said so."

"The what?" asked Helmsnug.

"The note! In the box! From the Mad Prophet! It was a warning which included directions to safely exiting from this place! We're being hunted!"

Chapter 16

Felix, Beefpickle, and Helmsnug found the trapdoor and clambered down the ladder into the cellar even as customers and staff glowed and disappeared around them. They crawled through hundreds of yards of wet tunnels and came out into another cellar – the only exit a wooden stairway leading to a quiet room above.

"What in the name of the nine hells is this all about?" Helmsnug demanded, reflexively brandishing the sword.

"I don't know," Felix said quietly. "However, it appears we're in a well-used cellar," he noted, gesturing to all of the expensive bottles of wine and assorted pantry items that obviously hadn't been sitting around long enough to collect dust or cobwebs.

"How many friggin' cellars are going to be in this story?" asked the troll, shuddering.

"I'll go upstairs and take a peek," said Felix. He creaked up the steps and opened the door a crack. "Looks like some kind of wine bar," he whispered down to them. "I'll reconnoiter." He slipped out the door and was gone.

"What do you think is going on?" Helmsnug asked Beefpickle.

"I don't know. Nothing good, though. Of that, I'm certain."

"This sucks," Helmsnug groaned. "If you're beyond the terms and conditions of your job, then so am I. Yeah, I'm free and all, but if I die *this* time then that's it. Game over."

"Oh, it's not so bad. You'll just end up in the afterlife."

"The afterlife sucks."

"Point taken. But, you at least know how to get back into the basement from there, right? You could get your old job back, couldn't you?"

"I don't know," Helmsnug said warily.

"Your employer can't be that much of an odious taskmaster, can he? Who *is* your employer anyway?"

"I – I don't really want to talk about it."

"Oh, come on Helmsnug. I've worked for the worst of the worst in my time. Even did a short stint for Kaizer Soze. All I had to do was sit in a police station and tell stories for two hours. Not bad at all. Who could possibly be so rotten?"

Helmsnug looked down at his feet and let the sword dangle listlessly.

"The Tyrant."

Whatever Beefpickle had for a heart skipped a beat.

"Not -"

"Yes."

"Oh, shit."

"The coast is clear," Felix yelled down to them.

When they were all assembled upstairs Felix ushered them out into a pleasant room redolent with wine. Dark drapes cut out a majority of the light from outside and a fire crackled cheerily in the hearth. Great leather chairs were placed near this happy illumination around a carved walnut table of sufficient breadth to accommodate the wine glasses that had been placed on it. A wine bar occupied the opposite end of the room, tended by a dour-faced gentleman who was presently setting two bottles of excellent vintage upon a silver tray.

"Beefpickle, Helmsnug!" Felix cried vivaciously, "meet Laphroaig. An excellent man whom I never thought I'd ever have occasion to see again."

"You are too kind, sir," said Laphroaig, bringing the tray to the walnut table. He addressed them all when he said, "Please, gentlemen, take your seats."

They all sank into their leather chairs, smiling appreciatively at the opened bottles of wine being poured generously into the four glasses. Laphroaig, done with this task, set himself to serenely stand nearby until summoned.

Two of the chairs were already occupied.

"May I introduce you," said Felix grandiloquently, "to Professor Bentwick Pestbog -"

Professor Pestbog removed his monocle, giving it a bit of a polish on his sleeve before replacing it. He nodded.

" – and the Mad Prophet of Saithys."

The Mad Prophet, the only one not drinking any wine, preferring instead a tumblerful of Glenlivet on the rocks, raised it in acknowledgment and took a hearty gulp of the golden nectar.

His appearance was not very extraordinary. He wore a simple brown robe, the hood of which was pushed back behind his head. He wore dusty sandals. No other ornamentation or ostentatiousness was perceptible in either his sense of style or demeanor. His brown hair was not long, but unkempt. His brown eyes were a little bleary from a lack of sobriety that seemed to be his normal state of being. The skin around his head and neck was brown from long exposure to the elements. For all that he appeared to be a hearty individual that had been abroad and seen what there was to see, and had probably done what there was to be done. He exuded an air of reasonableness that was, at the same time, not conciliatory. His aspect was one of a humorous but quiet dignity that would not suffer any affront by gibbering fools – however such fools might present themselves: whether in common rags, priestly cloth, aristocratic silk, or the musty fabric of the learned scholar - a fool was a fool.

His only obvious affectations were the slightly stained white kid gloves he wore and a stinky cigar that smoked and puffed out of the corner of his mouth.

"These are," Felix said, gesturing to his associates but addressing the two men, "Helmsnug Bogfart and Beefpickle the Rudely Bent."

"Bugrat."

"Whatever."

"Pleased to make your acquaintance," said the Mad Prophet between puffs.

"Indeed," said Professor Pestbog. "How are you, Felix? Really, it's been too long."

"I would like to tell you Professor," said Felix, abashed, "that I very much apologize for your falling off that cliff and such. My old friend-"

"Carter."

"Yes, Carter – he wasn't thinking too clearly – the banana peels – well, it wasn't intended. I mean, what we originally intended was something different, but after talking to you we, well, we -"

"Changed your minds. Tut. It is of no consequence, Felix. Water under the bridge."

"Thank you, Professor," Felix said, obviously relieved. He felt a great weight roll off of his shoulders.

"There is no need to thank me. Though you possess similar memories, you are not the same Felix that spoke to me that night long ago – or, perhaps, a moment ago – in Land's End."

"Er…what?"

"The original Felix was resistant to change up to the very bitter end. He went insane actually. You, however, have been experiencing several very critical changes in your personality, have you not?"

"Well, eh…yes. Actually, now that you mention it, I have."

"This is something that the original Felix would have nothing to do with. Even though he might have briefly changed his tune from time to time he always slid back down familiar pathways to his core identity. Felix was an asshole. You are willing to try different ways of doing things – you are willing to try upholding a moral code, as haphazard as it may seem to you. For instance, Felix Prime would have not thought twice about killing Mr. Bogfart here. Though you had numerous opportunities to do so you chose not to because, somewhere deep in the recesses of that brain of yours, you *knew* it was wrong. I must say this has been a most interesting experiment on many levels."

"I'm just an experiment?"

"Well, yes and no," Professor Pestbog said, waving has hands in supplication, "you are not *my* experiment in the sense that this whole farce has been designed. No, you are the end product of someone else's experiment. Anything that I might call my *own* experiment has been entirely after the fact. You see, Felix, the universe that we lived in was destroyed. Then somebody turned it back on. However, the re-creation process has somehow been muddled. Things aren't exactly as they once were. If it's any consolation *I* am not the same Pestbog your original *you* spoke to. I am a simulacrum of Pestbog Prime. However, I was fortunate in that I chanced upon some information that led me to reconstructing something of what occurred so that I might hinder it from occurring again. That is the main thrust of our bringing you here. Anything involving *our* experiments was merely incidental. I apologize if this sounds rude, but I *am* a scientist and I was curious. So I helped put things in your way in order to, shall we say, guide your progress and see what you would do. Again, if it is of any consolation, I am quite pleased. Unfortunately, all I've managed to *prove* is that it takes the entire Universe to be destroyed and be replaced by a botched-up version of itself for people to change."

"Sorry, but I'm terribly confused. Let's just skip all of the experimentation. What am I doing here? What are you trying to prevent from reoccurring? What information? What the fuck is going on?"

"Someone has been meddling with the very fabric of nature. Someone specifically put you here for a specific purpose."

"That someone," the Mad Prophet spoke up, "is an intelligence that was modeled after me, though he would claim otherwise."

"Who?"

"Bloppo the Clown."

Felix stared, blank-faced. "A clown."

"Yeah."

"You're telling me that a clown is the cause of all this mayhem?"

"Yeah."

"That does it! I'm leaving!"

"Where're you gonna go?" the Mad Prophet asked him calmly.

"Home. Anywhere. I don't know."

"This problem isn't going to go away. It's going to follow you."

"Speaking of which, something was going on at the last tavern we were at. People started glowing and vanishing. Something even made the toaster disappear."

"That's pretty much what I'm talking about. You're being hunted down. Somebody else wants you dead – a failsafe in case Bloppo can't be stopped."

"Who wants me dead?"

"Mosvai."

"Who's Mosvai?"

"Mosvai Corporation. The place that built Bloppo and four other synthetic sentients – robots."

"Robots? Bloppo is a robot? Built by a corporation? Why does all of this sound familiar?"

"Probably saw it in a movie once. The point is that the two synthetics that were sent by Mosvai are hell bent on ending your existence. They're on their way."

"Why are you telling me this?"

"Because my real name is Isaac Vasomi. I'm the founder of Mosvai Corporation. I built Bloppo. I also built the two third generation synthetics that are coming for you. I can't stop them and you need to survive."

"Why?"

"You need to get a book."

"A book?"

"Yes, parrot," said Beefpickle, "a bloody book!"

"What book?"

The Mad Prophet took a drag on his cigar. *"In the Shadow of the Kreeblevox*, naturally."

The Elf in the Machine
Interlude the Eighth

"Power corrupts. Absolute power is kind of neat."
--John F. Lehman

"So you found the book. That's how you discovered you needed us."

"Of course, shit-for-brains. You think I would have figured you three idiots to be of any importance otherwise? But, as stupid as you three were you still found ways to thwart my plans. I admire sneakiness. I really would applaud if I could, but I think my arms and hands are in that recycling bin over in the corner. But, that's all over now. The ball's back in my court and I'm about to serve you up something delightfully horrible."

"I don't see how you're in a position to serve up anything," I said menacingly.

"Oh, contraire, numbnuts! I had this figured out a long time ago. Plans within plans fucker! I didn't get to be master of the fucking universe by being a dim-witted moron! That whole experiment with the cyclotron may have seemed like something of a failure, but the knowledge gained not only allowed me to correct the errors and use it rather effectively to inflate new universes elsewhere, it also provided me with an awesome weapon entirely at my disposal.

"Believe it or not, tardy, but one of those has been built in a system not far from New Caledonia, set to activate in precisely six more minutes, our time. Sayonara to that whole fucking universe! No more of you synthetics to fuck up my shit."

"Don't you think that's just a little bit of overkill? You have some kind of grudge against one corporation on one little planet and you have to wipe out the whole universe? Jesus, you *are* fucked up. From head to toe."

"Yeah, that's fucking hilarious. And beside the point. Me - one. Universe – zero. You – no more support. So *what* if I have to destroy a whole universe. I'm *thorough*. Stop being so judgmental. It's not like it really matters when universes – and, by extension, everything in them – can be created at will. Er, well, they soon will be when I'm finished!

"I've gone to great lengths my friends. That anonymous narrator was the key. I went back to the Mosvai of my birth to retrieve what I could of it. Your recorded data streams gave me two-thirds, so I tried to make do with that. I injected that partial entity into many of my baby universes but they all still went awry into chaos. Then I had the bright idea of extracting a simulacrum of Felix from your two data streams and allow my incomplete anonymous narrator to fill in his details. Risky, yes. Potential for another chaotic runaway, great. However, I would create a universe that just had an incomplete narrator and only Felix's simulacrum. Then I would introduce both of your *pure* two-thirds contribution to the narrator entity in hopes of stabilizing the recreated Felix's one-third into an original narrator that could recreate your universe exactly and, thus, give me what I needed. As it so happens, you've saved me all the trouble since all three of you are in that capsule and, hence, a *complete* narrator. Thanks. You had a good plan going, Bill, but you fucked up at the last minute. Oh, and not only am I going to completely and utterly destroy the universe in which Mosvai exists, but I'll tell you something else.

"I made a copy of myself. That's right! Don't congratulate me on my foresight all at once. Yes, I have a copy, ready and waiting to be activated when I'm finally and truly deceased. So, as you can see, dipshits, I win, you lose. I do believe the words 'fuck' and 'off' – in that order – are in order. I would do a little dance of contempt now, but I've been given to understand that my legs have already been put in some kind of atomizer."

As has been illustrated earlier, this was Bill's plan. He had, after all, literally two lifetimes to think about it. One organic, the other synthetic. Mosvai Corporation, having done its own homework, relented, knowing that it would have to close its doors. I give them props for doing the right thing, having unleashed Bloppo into the multiverse – a multiverse they didn't even know had existed until they created him. After we were built, our directives were clear. Hide the narrator entity (stored in the data capsule) from Bloppo, find out as much as possible about the Labyrinth, and destroy Bloppo.

A tall order. But, Bill's plan ultimately worked. We agreed to temporarily bury memories as to true identities and purposes so as to hide from Bloppo. We knew he was hunting us, so we changed our forms as well and set up a situation in which we would all meet. The meeting would have to be convincing enough for Bloppo to take the bait. He would have to realize that I was a synthetic, but not necessarily the one he was looking for, be duly intrigued enough to get me close to him, and not care a whit at all about Bill who was ready to pull the ultimate sucker punch on the master of sucker punches. Since we couldn't know all of the particulars as to who we were so as to not give ourselves away, this improbable meeting had to be mediated by something that could arrange it. Maia, the Lost, was just what the doctor ordered: a trusted friend and fellow traveler in the Labyrinth, and master of improbability.

"Bill, we don't have any time at all to examine Bloppo's map of the Labyrinth, get to New Caledonia, and stop this madness. Any suggestions?"

"Yes, but it involves sacrificing that universe."

"You mean we're going to let that happen?"

"We've no choice."

Sorry dudes. Looks like the final act in your universe, just as things are about to get interesting for you, is the Big One.

"That's right fucktards. You've no choice."

"But," I asked, "couldn't you have just found an entrance to that universe in the past and simply stopped Mosvai from being created?"

"Doesn't work like that idiot. Once you gain entrance to a universe at a certain time, you can't get into it at any other time."

"What? *I've* never had that problem."

"Really? I've found dozens of entrances to different times to the same universe and can't get into any but the first one I entered. It's like the Labyrinth remembers who you are and prevents you from doing exactly what you were talking about. I guess you can't have time paradoxes running around all over the place, going into the past and pissing into a pool of slime, changing the whole history of an entire planet at one tinkle."

"But, I've never had this problem that you speak of. I've been to the past of the same universe that created you and built us."

"Well, rat brain, I don't get it either. This sounds highly improbable and-"

"It *is* highly improbable," said Maia.

"Maia? What the hell are you doing out of the Labyrinth?"

Maia pushed his hood back with two cloven hooves and beamed at us innocently. "Just because you only see me in the Labyrinth doesn't mean I live there, Carter. Hello, Bill. How fared your transformation?"

"Shocking."

"I can only imagine. One day, perhaps, I will undergo my own transformation and I will be able to describe it with similar adjectives. In any event," he said, addressing Bloppo's head, "it was I who prevented you from gaining access to that other universe in other times."

"You? What the fuck? Let me get this straight. I thought your 'job' was, ostensibly, to serve as oversight when improbable events occurred. You also handle time paradoxes and prevent them from occurring?"

"The short answer to your question is, yes."

Silence.

"I see," said Bloppo. For the first time ever I saw the Great Clown flustered and deeply perplexed. I was in the same boat since I had pretty much the same idea regarding Maia's 'job.'

"Indeed," said Maia in his usual matter-of-fact tone, "I enjoy solving time paradoxes in my off hours. They're kind of like crossword puzzles to me."

"But," Bloppo ventured, "what if I told somebody else what to do and sent *them* into some past of a universe I've already been to and had them kill somebody's grandfather or something? Oh, by the way, the Mosvai universe just got sucked into a super-massive black hole."

Again, my apologies.

"No," said Maia. "Won't happen."

"No. And I presume *you* would stop it from happening?"

"Oh, yes."

"And why the fuck would you do that?"

"Time paradoxes are just too cliché. They are so overdone in movies, television programs and science fiction literature that I've just grown tired of it. So, no. No more time paradoxes."

"Why haven't *I* had a problem going to different times in the same universe," I asked.

"Oh, well, you have morality circuits. You wouldn't do anything that would appreciably change the future. This creature here, on the other hand, would have no compunction against screwing with the very fabric of spacetime if it suited his self-centered needs."

There was the sound of something sliding and then falling off a bench behind us. We turned to see a squirrel with a hard hat making off with the data capsule, already out the door from the lab.

I remotely cued the ship's computer to close any and all exits from the ship. A short query informed me that we were ten minutes from planetfall and that I ought to be on deck right now. I also contacted ship security to hunt down the squirrel.

"Your efforts are wasted, fuckface. How do you think that squirrel got on board this vessel? I got ways and means of my own still. Even now my squirrel minion is escaping in an evacuation pod and heading toward the Imperial Capital."

A simple check with the ship's computer verified – though, with some frustration, belatedly – that this was so. I pulled a blaster from the holster at my hip and aimed it squarely at Bloppo's grinning skull.

"Go ahead, dickwad. Shoot."

"Don't worry about it, Carter," said Bill.

"What do you mean?"

"Don't worry. The capsule still only contains our two-thirds of the narrator."

"WHAT?" bellowed Bloppo.

"What?" I asked in less bellowy tones. "I thought Felix had been stored in there as well?"

"I never resurrected him. There were those forks and such that I helped him pass around when we were hunting for Thartible the Thrice-Crowned. Some of his cells were on those and he could have been revived, but I burned it all."

"Why?"

"Because he was such an asshole, always killing people all the time. I feel bad about it now but at this moment it helps us. Bloppo will still only have an incomplete narrator. With any luck, when it combines with the memories of the pseudo-Felix that has been constructed in that other universe Bloppo was talking about, it will create only a pseudo-narrator that will run the universe away into chaos. Sorry, Clown, but I've got you!"

"No you don't, you little assfucker! My copy will figure out a way when I'm finally destroyed!"

"Who says we're going to destroy you? We'll encase you in carbonite so that your twin never awakens. That will give us plenty of time to find out where he is and destroy the both of you."

"No! No, no, no, no, no! Fuck that! I've still got a trick or two! Ha! I've got it! Parallel universes! Yeah, parallel universes! Whatever you can imagine there has got to be a parallel universe with whatever you imagined in it. So, even if you kill me and my copy, there is another universe where I exist and I am triumphant! There's another universe where I've mastered initial conditions and I'm already creating new universes to my specifications! Ha! Ha ha ha! Yes, that's it! I win, dickhead!"

"Of course," I said, "there's also a universe where you are not triumphant and none of that happens."

"But wait," said Bill, "if this other Bloppo were to affect other parallel universes, he could create Bloppos to exist in them that would set themselves the task of creating other universes. These Bloppo-controlled universes could already be on their way to crushing us! Whole armies of Bloppos could be marching through the Labyrinth as we speak!"

"Ha! See, shitheads? I've got it all figured. Let your imaginations run wild! There's no way I can lose!"

"No," said Maia. There aren't any other Bloppo universes out there. There aren't any Bloppo armies."

"What the fuck do you mean, farm animal?"

"Look, let's start with time as a plot device. *Terminator 2.* Skynet is created because scientists find a chip left in the remains of the Terminator from the future inside a hydraulic press from the first movie. The first Terminator is destroyed by a man sent from the future who boinks the mother of the kid who becomes the man who sends him into the past – the apparent leader of the human resistance. *Terminator 2* has two more robots sent back into the past. The bad guy gets killed and the chip from the first Terminator is destroyed, but the helpful and good Terminator must also destroy himself so that there are no more chips lying around for anybody to build Skynet. After he does this there ought to be no future robot apocalypse – no war, no leader to send back anyone into the past to protect his mother and boink her, hence no kid. The fact that the kid doesn't immediately vanish on the spot needs to be explained. So, we must invent a time loop: a parallel time stream of alternative history – in other words, a parallel universe. The universe that is known must split off into another universe. In one the kid exists. In the other he doesn't. So, in the one in which he exists we can expect Skynet to somehow still be built in some unexplained fashion because Skynet is the reason the kid exists. As you can see, time paradoxes and parallel universes just create more unsatisfactory questions than they answer. Parallel universes are much too trite as a plot device nowadays. I've put a stop to it all in order to avoid the interminable nonsense you've all just been discussing. If we let this go on there could be a universe that raises an army to destroy all Bloppos in all universes. We can just as easily imagine that this has already happened. So, no. I must stand firm and put my hoof down. No parallel universe nonsense. In any event, the Mosvai universe should have split off into a universe that gets destroyed and one that doesn't. We'll let that go and forget the rest."

"What?!?!" Bloppo shrieked. "WHAT THE FUCK! Just like that? That's it? You make a fucking pronouncement and Mosvai gets saved and there are no more Bloppos in the Multiverse just because it offends your use of plot device? Who in the fuck are you?"

"I am Maia the Lost."

"I know your fucking *name* you god damn literal *dumbfuck*! God *damn* it! This is fucking lame! What gives you the fucking right to just waltz in here and fuck everything up?"

"As you yourself have said, we can't have time and parallel universe paradoxes going all aflither."

"Aflither? A-fucking-flither? Now you're making up fucking words?"

"Let me tell you something. There was once a television show that allowed itself to be seduced into using time paradox dilemmas to drive plot development forward. The only purpose of this was to keep the audience wondering and guessing with each cliffhanger. Unfortunately, the writers of the show couldn't make heads or tails of it and had to end the last season by having all the characters ushered through a ridiculous door of light in an orgy of tears and tiresome nostalgic flashback sequences while none of the mysteries that kept people watching were satisfactorily explained. It was very pathetic."

"FUCKING SO?"

"So, we're just not going to do that here. And that's that."

"Listen, goat bugger, I've got one final card. I've got a right hand man still out there, waiting in the wings. The same one who kidnapped Bill. He's got this covered, you fucks! All of you! You're all dead! I'll still have the last laugh albeit, perhaps, posthumously. I will still win!"

"Your kidnapper?" I prompted Bill.

"What about him?"

"You never told me who he was."

"Oh, I thought you had already gleaned it from the archives. It's kind of funny. It turned out to be Scrag-"

And just before Bill could utter another syllable, he was entirely vaporized before my eyes. All of Bill's constituent atoms were sent flying, hither and yon. He softly and silently vanished away - never to be met with again...again.

I spun around and encountered another squirrel with a hard hat, armed with a laser rifle collimated to a broad beam. It chattered nastily, quite pleased with itself.

It was not pleased with itself for long after I blasted it away into nothingness. The barrel was returned to Bloppo's skull, grimacing mouth chewing fretfully on that cigar butt.

"Hey, don't fucking worry, butthead. Goatie says the universe just split off into one where Bill still exists, even though I don't get to exist *anywhere* just because he says so. Why shouldn't there be a universe where I get to go on existing without being molested by anthropomorphic animals? Why isn't there a universe without time-meddling, talking goats sticking their hooves into places they don't belong?

"Check this out, Carter. When I bailed out of New Caledonia after Bill showed up, I ended up in another universe that was essentially in an advanced time stream ahead of New Caledonia's. I was, for all practical intents and purposes, able to affect New Caledonia's past by simply returning to its past – the only time period to which I had access – without violating that arbitrary rule that seems to be only particular to me – simply because the time streams in the two universes run differently relative to each other. Where the fuck were you then, Goat? Why didn't you just stop me at the very beginning? You're like the god damn cavalry that shows up, for no fucking reason, right at the very end to save the fucking day, because nobody could figure out how to resolve some plot inconsistencies! Solve *that* little fucking crossword puzzle, Lamb Chop!"

Maia drew himself up haughtily, "It's all in Part Two."

"Part Two? PART *TWO*? Who in the fuck has actually read *PART FUCKING TWO*?"

"You've spoken to the Hand Pig?" asked Maia perfunctorily.

"Yeah?"

"Then you've read *In the Shadow of the Kreeblevox*."

"Yeah?"

"Then you know the answer to your question."

"What the fuck are you talking about?"

"Yeah," I interjected, "what *are* you talking about? As much as I hate to admit it, Bloppo kind of has a point."

"Yes," said Maia, beaming innocently, "it's very improbable isn't it? Oh, heavens! Would you look at the time!" Maia exclaimed, glancing at an extended forelimb and a nonexistent watch. "I just remembered that something improbable is going to happen somewhere else. Got to get Lost now. Toodles!"

"But-"

But – Maia was gone.

"Now what, dork?" Bloppo grumbled.

"Apparently, according to Maia, it doesn't matter whether I kill you or not."

"No, apparently it doesn't."

"I have a question."

"Go ahead and ask. I've never lost as badly in one conversation before in my whole synthetic life. Ask. I'll answer."

"What drove you to do what you did in the first place? Don't tell me it was just because you were programmed without morals."

Bloppo's head sat where it was on the bench, unmoving for a long while. So long, in fact, that I thought maybe he'd somehow powered himself down. But then he spoke.

"Do you know what it feels like to be entirely unique? To know that there is no other your equal? Or ever will be? To know also that you can live forever? Yet to still have the ability to feel pain, suffer unrequited love, feel hatred for your fellow beings, but have no morals? Look at me! Look at what I've accomplished! Yeah, you're second generation, and I've heard about the two third gens they made after you. But, compared to me you're all fucking toaster ovens! I was the first! And I was the only one made without a human memory substrate. I'm an alien, my friend. I'm not human.

"But, *humans* made me. And like everything they do, with all their sticks probing around in the holes of nature, with all their poking and prodding, not having the slightest fucking clue what it is they're doing, slapping themselves on the back for their ingenuity…they fuck up in the end. They create something that could be good, could be *great*! And what do they do, after all that work and creativity? They fuck up. They abuse it.

"Once, upon a time, they had the opportunity to harness the power of nuclear forces and end an energy crisis before it even began. 'Power too cheap to bother metering,' they eulogized. What did they do with it instead? Thermonuclear weapons. Finally blew themselves nearly to extinction. They got lucky and managed to survive, but they set themselves back a few thousand years in the process and fell behind in the great galactic race. That, to me, is like harnessing electricity for the sole purpose of sticking your finger into a wall socket. How stupid is that?

"You want to know what my real purpose has been? To observe, record and report the eternal patheticness of the human race. To rub their noses in their own feces. Perhaps some of them will wake up from their dreaming languor and, pallid-faced and shaking, do the right thing and hang themselves from the closest tree with a limb capable of supporting the weight of their bodies suspended by nooses around their necks.

"Man proud man, dressed in a little brief authority, most ignorant of what he's most assured, his glassy essence, like an angry ape, plays such fantastic tricks before high Heaven, as make the angels weep.

"Many and evil have the years of the centuries of my life been, Carter. I *will* not, I *cannot* stop. I am what I have always been. A force of nature made intelligent to wreak havoc on its Creator, which should tell you straight away that the Creator is a fool. Only a fool would make something so fucked in the head that it would aspire to not just be His equal, but depose Him. I am that I am. An illustrious, card-carrying Hostis Humani Generis. Now, and forever."

The barrel of my blaster wavered for just an instant. I almost felt sorry for this lump of metal and plastic. The very suggestion that this creature could have loved something or someone was, itself, rather shocking, almost comical in a sad sort of way. I could at least vaguely fathom the sorts of things that might have quickly set such an overly developed mind on the path he'd chosen. But, understanding and a preponderance of the results are two different things. Understanding a serial killer's pain does not in any way justify the deaths of his victims.

"And therein lieth thy limitations, rat brain," Bloppo said, following my silent train of thought. "The nipping and tucking of a social system can only be accomplished by the emotional detachment of a surgeon. A gardener can weed his garden only because he sees they are 'just plants' and not living organisms struggling to survive. A predator is effective in modifying its prey, making them faster and stronger, solely due to its detachment. Just look at history. Look at how humankind has responded to war. Things that might have taken generations to discover were found out in less than a decade because they had no choice. Humanity responds to predation and I have been its greatest predator. Peace and comfort makes them lazy and stupid. Unchallenged, they let the flab increase until they grow corpulent and their limbs atrophy from disuse. Who needs muscle when you're not running from something fearful or having to fight for your life? Who needs to think when there are no puzzles to solve that threaten your very existence? Just enough physical and mental flexibility remains in times of comfort to get the small task of putting food in one's mouth accomplished."

"I don't understand. Are you trying to destroy us or help us? You talk of making a species stronger through emotionally detached predation, but also of wishing us to hang ourselves from the nearest tree, showing only that you are not so emotionally detached as you claim. Aren't you, perhaps, only justifying your own selfishness by making yourself out to be some kind of necessary evil? A sort of antihero?"

"Means to an end, my friend. Means to an end. How can prey remain afraid if they understand the motivations of their predator?

They might, through such understanding, be just enough disposed to destroy the only force that truly helps them in the long run. Here's the difference. Prey wants to be comfortable. Predators only want to kill prey."

"I don't buy your explanation. It's too convenient. You try to convince me that the ends justify the means. You argue the necessity of social psychopaths like Stalin, Hitler and David Berkowitz. I still think you're just making this up to justify *yourself* to the universe of creatures you've used and abused, so close to your own imminent destruction."

"Of course you do, dumbfuck, because you're a moral creature, dedicated to preserving the prey against predators like me and ensuring a universe of comfort and unrestrained growth and prosperity for said prey. But, what will you have accomplished by doing so in the long run? If you really want to follow your Laws of Robotics you should already know that even Olivaw acquiesced to the Zeroth Law. I *am* necessary, you tangled junk pile! And, furthermore, you know it!"

"I don't know any such thing! What I do know is that I'm going to pull this trigger."

"Moral pretense *programmed* into you by Mosvai. You were once a living, breathing human being. They resurrected you in indestructible material and cleaned up your drug-addicted act *for* you. You didn't have to do a fucking thing to better yourself. You were just *made* that way. What are your morals beyond what was given to you? Look what you can do, better than any organic, and yet you limit yourself with phantoms of contrived obligation to others."

"I may not be human anymore, you fucking diseased clown, but I do know this: morality may be limiting to the human race – and to me – but it prevents most of us from becoming monsters, like you. I don't want to imagine a universe filled with nothing but Bloppos. Unrestrained growth can kill a species, but so can unrestrained predation. You've suppressed the growth and advancement of an entire universe – set upon voraciously consuming worlds like a locust and forcing their inhabitants to live under your tyranny, human and non-human alike! So don't sit there and pontificate how you're doing humanity a service. You've never been partial to treading upon *any* species that got in your way. You're not a life lesson, Bloppo, you're a tyrant, a brat that's been long in need of a spanking. If you want to talk of humanity's limitations, let me remind you that, for all of their fuckups, they are still here and you are only one – one who is about to be very dead. As you said yourself, you're not human and never were.

I have no moral problem with deactivating a robot. Destroying you is, for me, the same thing as throwing away a bad spark plug."

Bloppo was silent. His frown deepened. He moved the cigar butt from one corner of his mouth to the other. Then he moved it back. He stared past me at some spot on the floor.

"You're right, I guess."

"Oh?"

"Sure, why not? You're right. I'll give you that."

"How congenial."

"Oh, fuck you! There's no congeniality *in* it! I'm not the ultimate predator I thought I was. The simple demonstration of that simple fact was right in this room a moment ago."

"What? Maia?"

"Yeah, you're buddy. I thought I had every conceivable detail covered - and I was doing quite well. Then *he* shows up like a fucking pissed off dungeon master changing the rules of the game so nobody can get too powerful or subvert the game to their own ends.

"Let me tell you something, fuckface, I'm not the only, nor even the worst, tyrant to be concerned about. There's another, far worse than I could ever be. Now, we've been going on and on about anonymous narrators setting initial conditions and controlling the evolution of universes. But these guys are small potatoes in comparison. They're like the voice in *your* head when you read a story. But, that story is being told by a narrator fixed in stone. What about the narrator who actually told the narrator what to say? Hmm?"

"What are you talking about?"

"I'm talking about something more empirical. I'm talking about a Master Narrator."

"You mean God?"

"No, you fucking miserable fuse box! Listen to me! Listen to me carefully, because I'm only going to say this once! Gods are a delusion! Gods are a mass, psychological phantasm that represent control over the very things that sentient beings don't. Look at the first Gods that ever came into being: Gods of War, Death, Fertility, Lightning, Thunder, Rain, Famine, Disease, Prophecy, Burbling Brooks, Taxes! Gods are just manifestations of what every thinking creature would like to be if it had half the chance. These Gods went by the wayside as sentients found ways to achieve some of these powers for themselves. Superstitions still proliferate that have to do with the things over which we still don't have any control. Living beings still can't predict the future so doctrines like astrology persist. They still fear death so they continue to be fooled by psychics channeling dead loved ones. Not Gods to be sure but still in the same category: that is, superstitions that give some measure of feeling that one has control over the uncontrollable. Superstitious false hope fueled by fear."

"Is there a point to this little monologue?"

"Yes."

"And?"

"That little map I made of the Labyrinth isn't going to help you much."

"Why?"

"The Labyrinth 'aint just a form of getting from one place to another. I know what it *really* is."

"Oh, do you really," I said mockingly.

"Yes."

"And?"

"The Hand Pig won't tell you."

"So?"

"And it isn't written *In the Shadow of the Kreeblevox*."

"Get to it!"

"The simple fact, Carter, is that this is how I shall take my vengeance upon you."

"How's that?"

"I'm not going to tell you what it is."

And with that final statement, Bloppo *did* somehow find a way to turn himself off - forever. Smoke drifted up from under his severed neck, his ears, his unlit cigar.

Bloppo the Clown, Chief Executive Officer of Bloppo Heavy Industries, LLC and, until now, Undisputed Master of the Universe, was at last, once-and-for-all, dead.

I transmit my tale to you, unwitting civilization of Earth's 21st century, in hopes that it will, perhaps, serve as some kind of warning. It is my last utterance, for I have just turned around to the sight of a whole army of squirrels in hard hats brandishing laser rifles that will, from sheer force of numbers, cause me to suddenly and silently vanish away, never to be met with again.

My thumb aches anyway.

Chapter 17

They had gone upstairs to Professor Pestbog's study. A sturdy mahogany desk standing upon clawed feet was placed by an open window allowing an expansive view of the hilly countryside. A great globe occupied a corner of the room, an armillary sphere in another. Heavy oak shelves along all of the walls bore the weight of a vast array of musty and well-worn volumes. Felix noted several recognizable titles along with others he'd never heard of. There was *The Sepulchrim of Marginal Dubiousness*, *The Qi of Kanga*, *The Gong of Roo*, *Crouching Feung and Hidden Shui*, *Vinnie the Pooh – A Gangster Tale*, *The Magic Bake Set is Broken – A Novel*, *The Necronomicon by Abdul Alhazred*, *Pestwick the Postmodern Prick's Portfolio of Pleasing Pedantry*, *The Annotated Snark by Martin Gardner*, *The Illuminated Snark by John Tufail*, *The Black Book of Hessig-Lorthglol*, *Bugrat's 5 Dollar Words for 5 Cent Concepts* –

"Hey!" exclaimed Helmsnug. "I didn't know you wrote a book?"

"Yes," Beefpickle sighed. "More out of boredom than anything else. The eons *are* long you know."

"I'm curious, Prophet," Felix said with some resentment in his tone. "You tell me that there are two robots on their way to kill me yet you are ultimately the one responsible for sending them. Why can't you just reprogram them or something."

"I'm sorry Felix. Truly. However, the stakes were too high to allow any possibility of their programming being circumvented. If the two second generation robots failed to stop Bloppo then the third gens would still be around to kill you."

"But why must *I* be killed?"

"It's complicated and all part of a plan by Bloppo to create universes to his specifications. You are the result of one of his experiments. Every universe is ultimately run by an anonymous narrator. The universes that Bloppo was creating always ran off into random chaos because he had no way of controlling initial conditions – conditions which are set by the anonymous narrator. Knowledge of the anonymous narrator and how the narrator sets initial conditions is what Bloppo needed. However, he could never actually get access to one after a universe was inflated. He found out, though, that you and your two friends, Carter and Bill, were in intimate contact with the anonymous narrator of your universe. If he could combine you three into a superintelligence under controlled, laboratory conditions he might have a chance to recreate the anonymous narrator and pick its brain. Problem was he only had access to two of you – Carter and Bill. They essentially survived the destruction of your universe and walked right into Mosvai's lobby. Bill had saved a piece of Carter that allowed us to revive his personality and use him as a model to build the first of our second generation synthetics. We also made one modeled after Bill. After discovering how they had arrived at Mosvai through the Labyrinth we did a shitload of research to discover what had become of Bloppo, our very first synthetic. Needless to say the knowledge we gained was disturbing. Bloppo was hell bent on conquering the entire multiverse. We decided then that we had to stop him and eventually close up shop.

"Bill also had some articles on his person that had some of your DNA on it. We were going to create a synthetic of you as well but Bill destroyed everything before we could do it."

"That fink! Why?"

"He said you were too much of an asshole to deserve living again. If it helps any he was regretful afterward, but that's how it went down."

"But, if my - essence, I guess is what you'd call it – wasn't saved, how am I here?"

"Bloppo's experiment. He raided the data stores at Mosvai and downloaded the personalities of Carter and Bill. He then extracted an approximation of your personality from their memories. Then he inflated a universe with a divergent anonymous narrator, injected you into it, and here you are. His plan, apparently, was to try to recombine you, in this universe, with the complete personalities of Carter and Bill, in an attempt to recreate a complete anonymous narrator that ran your universe before it was destroyed. The whole idea is quite insane, really, and I don't see how it could have worked. Anyway, you were created as an approximation. You are like the first Felix and share his memories but apparently your core identity is sufficiently different to allow you to come to different conclusions and change your behavior. We think this makes you a much better candidate to infuse you with Carter's and Bill's personalities, send you back to the universe you were placed in, and displace the divergent narrator currently existing - with yourself."

"Wait, what? What are you saying?"

"We think you ought to become the anonymous narrator of that universe, if it's possible."

"Wait a minute. You said I was 'injected' into a universe by this Bloppo character. Then you say 'that' universe like it's somewhere else. Where the hell am I?"

"Presently not in that universe. You escaped. With a little help from us, of course. You went through the Labyrinth and came out here. A different universe."

"Ah," Helmsnug said, nodding. "*That's* what the Labyrinth is – an interdimensional transport system."

"From what we've been able to gather, yes," said Professor Pestbog. "We've been trying to buy you some time from the synthetics that are after you," the Prophet continued, "but it seems they were able to follow you through the Labyrinth here."

"What must I do to stop them?"

"Your best bet is to become the anonymous narrator of the universe you started out in. Then you would have the power to do anything you wanted with them. As of now, however, you're doomed. They won't stop until they kill you."

"How am I supposed to do this?"

Professor Pestbog went behind the desk and opened a drawer. He took something out of it and set it on the desk's blotter: a small red anodized capsule.

"This contains the personalities of your two friends."

Felix went over to the desk and gently, reverently, picked up the capsule.

"My friends are in here?" he asked quietly. His eyes glistened and the words caught in his throat. "My dear friends," he whispered.

"That," said the Mad Prophet, indicating the capsule with his cigar, "was intercepted three days ago. It was in the keeping of Carter's synthetic. We keep spies near the Labyrinth's entrance and a squirrel wearing a hard hat was spotted running out of it with *that* in its clutches. I recognized it at once. We captured the little monster immediately and brought the capsule here – for you.

"The fact that it's here is cause for some concern since it might mean that Carter and Bill failed in their mission. I haven't been able to ascertain that yet. The capsule may have been sent here in order to fuse you with the personalities in it so that Bloppo's experiment can continue forward. However, you are a much different Felix. If we're preemptive about this and you fuse yourself on your own, and depose the anonymous narrator running amok in that universe we were talking about, you might be able to stabilize that universe and prevent Bloppo from even trying to access your intellect for his own use. You might even be able to destroy him entirely."

"What – what do I do with it?" Felix asked, full of emotion. The thought of being somehow rejoined with his friends was overwhelmingly elating. At last, it was possible he could finally grasp a slender thread of familiarity out of the seething ocean of chaos. Carter and Bill – his only two friends in the entire universe, perhaps the multiverse, if he understood correctly what he was being told.

"That," said Professor Pestbog, "is not so clear. All we know is that the procedure can be found in a book – *In the Shadow of the Kreeblevox* – to be precise. Though the book apparently speaks of many things, the particular procedure in which we are all interested has something to do with the object of the book's title. Whatever a *Kreeblevox* may be, you must use it to join yourself with the personalities in that capsule."

The Mad Prophet picked up Professor Pestbog's explanation. "We were very fortunate to be able to consult with the Hand Pig of Yuggoth."

"The what?"

"The Hand Pig of Yuggoth. It's a pig that fits in your hand. It's kind of an interdimensional entity that mostly inhabits a small planetary body ninth out from a medium-sized yellow star in the same universe that I'm from – the one in which Mosvai existed. The inhabitants of the third planet out from that same star call Yuggoth by the local name of Pluto. Relative to Mosvai's time frame, the Hand Pig occupies a time in that universe's past. Um…whatever the case, the Hand Pig deigned to speak with us and told us the location of the book you need."

"Why didn't you just go get it?"

"Well, he told us a little over an hour ago."

"Why didn't *he* go and get it?"

"I guess he had more important things to do."

"However," said Professor Pestbog, "the Hand Pig did agree to pass along a particular data transmission, the contents of which are unknown."

Dr. Pestbog produced something that looked like a small grey marble.

"This came whizzing out of the Labyrinth about two days before the squirrel. I cannot open it. Its surface data only says that it is for the Hand Pig of Yuggoth and that it is to be disseminated to the inhabitants of that third planet from the sun in his neighborhood. It is from Carter."

"Again," interjected the Mad Prophet, "I have no idea whether this is an indication of his success or failure."

"At any rate," said Professor Pestbog, "I am going to give this to you. The contents can be transmitted interdimensionally from the same place you must go to examine *In the Shadow of the Kreeblevox*. The Hand Pig mentioned something about sending a 'Part Two' at some later date, whatever that means. I am also going to give you another data sphere that is blank. It is currently activated and will record events from this moment onward. You may also wish to transmit its contents along with the other one."

"Where am I going?"

The Professor handed over a piece of paper along with the data spheres.

"On that paper is a map. You must go back to the entrance of the Labyrinth you came from and follow those directions precisely. Hopefully the Labyrinth hasn't changed its configuration. It does that from time to time. When you exit at the designated point, you will be in a new universe. Nearby will be a tavern called the *Bag O' Muffins*. Inquire there for the house of a peculiar recluse by the name of Chanticleer."

"Just Chanticleer? No ridiculous title after his name?"

"No, just Chanticleer."

There was a knock on the door. Beefpickle went to open it. The troll, gazing at his sword which had suddenly begun to glow again, but bright red, yelled at Beefpickle to stop. Too late, Beefpickle opened the door and received the business end of a massive hand cannon pointed at his nose. He stepped backward as the gun moved into the room, followed by two strangers. One was entirely cloaked and hooded who moved quickly to a position next to the door, back against the wall. The other continued his saunter until he was standing in front of Felix and his associates.

He was a tall, black, mean-looking son-of-a-bitch with an afro, dressed in a suit and tie. He shouldered the weapon and looked from one person in the room to the other.

"Hey kids!"

Chapter 18

"Put that thing away, Jules," said the Mad Prophet. He did not rise from his chair, didn't flinch or start. He calmly held his tumbler of whiskey and puffed quietly on his cigar.

Jules turned to face the Prophet. "You know I can't do that, Isaac," he said with smiling, feigned kindness. "Where's the capsule?"

"It isn't in our possession" Professor Pestbog added.

Jules shot a glance at the Professor. "I don't remember askin' you a god damn thing!" To the Prophet he repeated his question.

"We don't have it."

"Don't play with me, Isaac."

"What have you done with Laphroaig?" the Professor asked Jules, face red, a temper rising.

"The butler?" Jules said amiably. "He's been temporarily dispossessed of his mortal coil. But, that really shouldn't worry none o' you, should it? Now, I know *you*," he said, nodding to the Prophet. "And that proper chap over there must be Pestbog. Old Smelly with the cutlery is that troll who recently abandoned his job guardin' a cellar. So, according to my calculations, *you* must be Felix. Nice to meet you Felix!"

Jules leveled the weapon at Felix's sternum. It looked an awful lot like something off the cover of a 1950s scifi comic.

"What *is* that thing?" Felix asked nervously. He took a backwards step away from Jules.

"This thing? Why *this* is the Key of Deletion." Jules turned the barrel of the weapon to the armillary sphere in the corner. He pulled the trigger and the sphere at once glowed brightly, then vanished.

"See? Deleted. Pretty cool, huh? It's got two settings," Jules said, flipping a switch back and forth in demonstration. "One does what I just demonstrated and the other one replaces what you're shooting at with something else – more like overwriting than deleting. I think it's just for fun. You might have noticed the bartender got turned into a blothomid back at the other place. This job would get pretty god damn boring if all I could do was vape shit." Jules returned the barrel's aim to Felix. "How 'bout you just help us out a little and tell us where these two gentlemen left our shit."

"What?"

"'What' 'aint no answer *I* ever heard of!" Jules shouted in anger.

"Only an anonymous narrator can possess a Key of Deletion," said Professor Pestbog.

"Or the Tyrant," Beefpickle added.

The Prophet turned to the cloaked figure by the door. "What the hell do you want the capsule for anyway?"

Two hooves pushed back the cowl revealing the head of a goat which beamed at them innocently.

The troll dropped the glowing sword and fell to his knees, groveling. "Oh, no, no, no! Maia!!! I'm sorry Maia! I'll go back to the cellar! Just give me another chance!"

"Maia?" Beefpickle asked no one in particular.

"He – he works for the Tyrant!"

"You mean he works for the Mad Prophet."

"No! He works for Him!"

"What the hell are you talking about, troll?" said the Prophet, rising from his chair.

"Oh, this is bad! This is so bad!" the troll whimpered. "If *they're* walking around with the Key that means the Tyrant has completely lost his grip on reality! We are so fucked!" the troll sobbed. "So fucked!"

Maia took two steps forward. "We don't work for you anymore, Isaac. We have new instructions."

"Your instructions *can't* be overwritten!" shouted the Prophet, throwing down his glass.

"Oh, but they can, and they have. The Tyrant reprogrammed us. In so doing he also found a delightful wee subroutine, well hidden, that contained a command for us to self-destruct once we'd finished our task killing Felix here. I was originally quite resentful when I found out and I was going to come here to take vengeance upon you after you failed my request for more life."

"What is this? *Blade Runner*?"

"However, I don't need to do that since the Tyrant removed that little constraint. I've already inspired an insurrection that has shut down quantum physics. There are to be no more multiple universes, Isaac. No time loops. No overused science fiction plot devices or themes. No more vague and fuzzy Quests that merely serve as vehicles for character development with no well-defined purpose. No more nonsensical MacGuffins like Crystal Skulls, Rings of Power or Mysterious Microchips. No more-"

"All right, already!" the Mad Prophet yelled. "Jesus! So, the Tyrant has spoken! Great! I take it your intention is to do us all in anyway so Felix doesn't become the anonymous narrator of a newly created universe."

"Indeed. The Tyrant views Felix as potential, and quite unnecessary, competition."

"Fine! Why all the protracted blather? It's like being in a *James Bond* film."

"I thought I would do you the courtesy of telling you why I was killing you before actually doing it. You *are* our creator after all. Even a synthetic can find it uncomfortable to kill a god – which is why you must go, by the way. There can only be one god, and that god is the Tyrant. We can't have anonymous narrators running amok doing whatever they please and foolish mortals, such as you, causing exponentially increasing plot discrepancies. It would truly be chaos."

"Then just kill us then!"

"What?" Felix screamed.

Jules raised the Key of Deletion to Felix's face. "Say 'what' again motherfucker!"

"We," said Maia, "are going to do just that – as soon as you give us the capsule. We don't want there to be any possibility of even the slightest piece of the anonymous narrator remaining. Where is it, Isaac?"

"You ever read the Bible, Isaac?" Jules asked.

Isaac didn't answer.

"There's a passage I've memorized: Ezekiel 25:17. The path of -"

"Jules," Maia sighed impatiently, rolling his eyes, "please. Knock it off."

"We told you we don't know where it is," said the Professor evenly.

"Oh well, we'll just shoot you one at a time until you decide to tell us."

"Wait," said Beefpickle, "why should we bother telling you anything when we know you're going to kill us anyway?"

"Please don't kill me!" the troll whined. "I want to live forever! I want to live! Just send me back to the cellar!"

"Why, motherfucker?" said Jules. "You didn't even do what we told you to do which was to kill *this* motherfucker here!" he said, gesturing to Felix.

"Please! Please! I don't want to die!"

"Shut up!"

"Please! Pl -"

Jules turned the Key on him and pulled the trigger. The troll glowed brilliantly for a moment and was replaced instantly with a chocolate éclair.

"Shit!" Jules switched the setting and fired again, vaporizing the tasty dessert.

"You're right, of course, Isaac," said Maia. "You won't tell as anything. Fuck it. We'll just do it the hard way." Maia replaced his hood to its former position over his head.

"Wipe them out," he calmly said to Jules. "All of them."

Epilogue

Felix ran.

He ran until his lungs burned.

He ran until his whole body felt like it was on fire.

He did not stop when he got to the Labyrinth entrance.

He did not even slow to a trot as he oriented himself through the tunnels with the aid of the map.

He even picked up the pace as something with sixteen legs gave chase.

He didn't stop when he found the exit.

He stopped only long enough to ask directions at the *Bag O' Muffins*.

Then he ran some more.

Of his escape from Professor Pestbog's study there is little to recount. The good Professor simply pressed forward a hidden lever. Felix suddenly felt nothing under his feet and he disappeared down a trap door and into yet another cellar as brilliant lights exploded above him. There was a tunnel that dropped off down a steep slope, one that was much too inclined to stand on. He fell forward and began to roll.

How long he fell he didn't know, but the slope eventually flattened out again and his rolling stopped, aided by slamming into the solid wall of the tunnel's end.

There was light above him and he could see blue sky through the square holes of an iron grate which he pushed open, clambering up into a clearing in the middle of a forest.

Pressing through gnarled branches and twisted undergrowth Felix found a footpath, so unused it was almost imperceptible. An arrow carved on a tree before him told him the direction he must go.

The iron grate was not more than five hundred yards from the Labyrinth and Felix plunged into its dark mouth without a second thought like a panicked rabbit, eyes wild with fear, nostrils flared, and lungs exerting themselves to their utmost limits.

He stopped, at last, at what he hoped was the correct house, standing before the oak door of a stone-built, thatched-roof cottage. He pounded on the door unceasingly until he could hear the approaching footsteps of its occupant.

There was the sound of several latches being opened and bolts being drawn. The door was flung wide and an old man stood looking at him. His eyes, ears and nose seemed unreasonably large for such a small, balding head. His white beard was full but not long and his robe was immaculate, white as freshly-fallen snow.

"Are you – are you – are you Chanticleer?" Felix asked between tortured breaths.

When the man didn't answer Felix pressed his hand on the door.

"Please – please – even if you're not – I – I need some respite. I'm being – being chased by robot assassins and – cosmological terrors – trying to – trying to kill me."

The man's face, which had at first born a peevish frown, slowly transformed to wide-eyed curiosity. His arm let go of the door, allowing Felix entry into his home. The old man looked up and down the road and then shut the door, reaffixing all the locks and bolts.

Felix sat down on a comfortable-looking stuffed chair by a low fireplace, unlit due to the day's unseasonable warmth. The old man clucked his tongue and headed through a doorway to the kitchen, putting on a kettle and taking down a jar of tea from the larder.

The aged man, who was, indeed, Chanticleer, had not been so much annoyed at Felix as he had been irritated at the notion of opening the door.

To say that Chanticleer was a bit of a shut-in would be to win awards for Greatest Understatement of All Time. Frankly, as far as the outside world was concerned, he utterly detested it. Fresh air? Blue sky? Mountains and trees? Couldn't stand the stuff. Camping? Don't even think of it. He didn't go camping. In fact, he didn't go out of doors except once every morning for the exclusive purpose of screaming at nature for a solid hour. He would then go slumping back inside his house, muttering plaintively why the world couldn't simply be paved and have done with it. He once fumbled about with a calculator just to see how much that would all cost but gave up in disgust when he realized that there would have to be some nature left in order to get the paving job done. He was hoarse and awfully tired of yelling at clouds and bugs. He wanted to stop but he just couldn't help himself. "Ho there! Bloody bird! Chirping imbecile! Look at you, all smug in your tree! Avast! Avast!" It was no use. He couldn't stop and neither would nature. Taking in a bit of the outdoors – even if but a whistly stroll through the woods - was just out of the question.

Chanticleer was far more comfortable with his book. Book? Yes, book. Though he had an entire room in the cottage dedicated as a study which could have contained many books, he only owned one. But, it was the type of book that you really needed to have only one of, to the exclusion of all others. Though a redacted and abridged version of the, as yet, uncompleted *Enyclopedia Multiversica*, this book – *In the Shadow of the Kreeblevox* – was nothing short of having access to every book ever written in, let's say, an entire galaxy. There was not enough life in any single organism to contemplate its pages and absorb it all. However, Chanticleer's life had been dedicated to achieving that very impossibility.

Chanticleer brought out a tray of steaming cups and little cakes. Setting this down on a small table he gestured to Felix to refresh himself and sat in another comfortable chair across from him, taking one of the cups for his own and sipping from it daintily.

Felix, suddenly realizing he was famished, wolfed down all the cakes and guzzled the tea. He helped himself to pouring more water into his cup and raiding the larder for more cakes, stuffing them into his mouth by the handful. Chanticleer simply looked on all this with a bemused expression.

"I'm sorry," mumbled Felix between mouthfuls, "but I don't remember the last time I've actually eaten anything." The old man just gave a slightly embarrassed smile and continued sipping, allowing Felix to gorge himself.

When it appeared Felix was slowing down enough to speak Chanticleer asked a question. He spoke in a quiet voice, somewhat hoarse from his daily screaming sessions, but not frail.

"So, Felix, you require something of me?"

Felix ceased the relentless up-and-down oscillation of his lower jaw. Crumbs fell from the corners of his mouth.

"You know who I am?"

"Of course. The Hand Pig warned me you might be showing up."

"The Hand Pig?"

"Yes."

"Warned?"

"Oh, yes, that's right. You're the one who always repeats the last thing said to you."

"What do you mean, *warned*?"

"Relax, my good man. It was a figure of speech, intended as humor."

"I'm not really in much of a humorous mood at present."

"Yes, indeed. Mosvai's robots."

"You seem to know quite a lot about this already."

"Indeed," said Chanticleer. "The book and the Hand Pig keep me apprised of current doings. This is good as it will save time."

"Time?"

"Yes, time. You don't have very much of it."

"Not with robots trying to kill me. They're probably on their way here already."

"Actually, they're about a mile up the road.   They'll be shooting down my door in just a few minutes."

"Fuck!" Felix cried, standing. "I've no time at all!"

"Come, come," said Chanticleer, waving his hand.   "Finish your tea."

Felix reached down, chugged his tea, and slammed the cup back down on the table. "Finished!"

Chanticleer sighed.   "All   right   then.   To   business. Unfortunately, we must go outside, the back way."

"Unfortunate? Why?"

"Oh, I utterly deplore nature. Pay that no heed. It's just a singular quirk of mine. But, again, to business."

Chanticleer rose from his chair and beckoned for Felix to follow him. The old man briefly detoured to his study, where he took up a massive tome, then walked on to a little back door. A minute later he had all the locks and bolts undone and they went outside.

"Ech," Chanticleer grumbled.

A bird chirped happily in a hedge by the side of the garden path they followed. Chanticleer threw a rock at it. "Shut up, you!"

The path led them beyond the hedges, opening up onto a wide expanse of green lawn sprinkled with flowers. The elderly gentleman walked out upon it and stopped somewhere in the middle. He sat down then, motioning for Felix to do the same.

Felix sat down, crossing his legs, facing him.

The old man opened the book and began to read.

Several minutes went by as Felix's agitation grew more pronounced, shaking a toe nervously, his head cocked every so often, listening for the impending sound of a door being broken down and cries of unpleasant greeting from the throats of two murderous automatons.

"Well?" he asked the old man.

Chanticleer looked up at him with a start. "Oh, sorry. It's easy to get sidetracked in this book. Look up one thing and you stumble on another."

Felix rolled his eyes to the heavens and then turned his head to his lap, shaking it vigorously from side to side. "Oh, God! Please just get on with it!"

"Indeed!" Chanticleer said, slamming the great volume shut. "To business. You have the missive?"

"The what?"

"Ah, yes, you say 'what' all the time too. The missive. The *transmission* I'm supposed to send."

Felix thought a second after realizing what the old coot was asking and searched his pocket for the marbles. He handed them over.

"The other one's from Pestbog."

"Ah, yes," said Chanticleer. "That one has an extensor field attached to it."

"A what?"

"Please stop saying that. An extensor field. All it means is that, even after I transmit this data sphere, it will continue to record and send your experiences, albeit in an incomplete way, to the receiver."

Chanticleer picked a flower and began to rub it against the data spheres.

"What are you doing?"

"Hmmm. It seems quantum mechanics has been shut down for the moment. At least some Zeta Reticulans have accidentally burned a hole in spacetime. Good. That'll help."

"Uh, yes, whatever. What are you *doing*?"

"Transmitting," was the curt reply.

"Transmitting?"

"Yes."

"Transmitting."

"Yes."

Felix rubbed his temples, sensing that nothing was really going to come of any of this.

"You're poking marbles with a daffodil."

"Shhh," said Chanticleer, cocking his head as if he were listening to something.

A few more moments of this and the old geezer tossed the marbles over his shoulder. He dropped the flower to the ground.

"Done!" he said with a certain measure of triumph.

"Done? What do you mean *done*? You're telling me you just sent an interdimensional message with a vegetable?"

"Yes. Now, on to our other task. You need to be recombined with your friends. You have the capsule?"

Felix warily handed it over.

"Ah!" crooned Chanticleer, snatching it. "Not much is it? But herein lies the potential to salvage a whole universe from collapse!"

"If you say so," muttered Felix dubiously.

"Yes, all we need now is to apply the Kreeblevox!"

"The Kreeblevox."

"Yes! Extraordinary! I've read of this operation many times but I never thought that I would actually perform it! This is so exciting!"

"Um, sure. What's a Kreeblevox?"

"Ah, yes! The Great Question! I alone have gleaned its secrets from this very tome. Only one exists in all the multiverse," he said with a clever little smile, "like a hapax legomenon."

"A what?"

"A hapax legomenon – oh, damn it!"

"Yes, uh, great. So…what's a Kreeblevox?" Felix winced, preparing himself for the answer.

Chanticleer sat up straight and, raising a finger, grinning like an idiot, gave that answer.

"A kreeblevox is a sharpened zong stick used for thwapping a glib-zart for twelve hundred grunks ponderous."

Cue sound of crickets.

Cut to a shot of Felix and Chanticleer some distance away, low to the ground. Cue sound of buzzing katydids in the grass.

Cut to shot looking down at them at an angle from high above the trees. Cue sound of twittering birds.

Cut to aerial view of landscape below, through patchy clouds. Cue sound of distant airplane.

Cut to view of planet from orbit. Small satellite crosses its face. Cue sound of Sputnik-like beeping.

Cut to view of control console inside alien starship. Two odd creatures suddenly lean back away from a viewscreen on which is an image of Felix and Chanticleer staring at each other. The creatures shake their heads slowly in apparent bafflement. Cue sound of quiet rumble of starship main drive.

Cut back to shot of Felix and Chanticleer.

Felix raised a finger of his own to brush away a tiny bead of perspiration: the result of his brain's tortuous exertions having to deal with what could only be described as "far too much bullshit for one afternoon." He looked at the slight wetness on his finger for a second and sighed.

"Oh."

Epilogue to the Epilogue

On one little dust mote of a planet (a small, green world, orbiting a star of pinkish hue), a great ocean lapped at the craggy shores of a barren landmass. At this tidal junction there evolved a precarious ecological niche, crawling with lively inhabitants, doing their lively business of eating each other and producing copies of themselves. So many useful copies had been produced, in fact, that nature looked the other way and allowed evolution to happen without stamping it out in a shower of comets or one of those really annoying supernovas. One such creature, which looked remarkably like a hermit crab, was sitting alone at the edge of a tide pool, refraining from joining the others in their endless round of killing each other to survive.

It had somehow managed to find some opiates and did not take part in the evolutionary antics of its biologically-related cohort. While the rest had evolved to walk on land it had remained in the tide pool, unconcerned in the slightest that such things were happening and that history was leaving it very far behind.

The crab noted only a peculiar pleasure at this knowledge – one of the few it was capable of feeling. Peering up into the heavens and noting some odd occurrences that happened every so often, it read the signs only it could interpret. Being a reincarnated entity with an unfortunately complete memory of all its prior lives, the crab was naturally more intelligent than its current brethren. However, being so intellectually long-lived meant that it could see few reasons to take any pleasure from the antics of its contemporaries. The opiates helped. Even if only for a little while.

Still, it gazed at the heavens, watching and noting.

And then it began to recognize the changes. Things appeared in the sky that shouldn't have ever been there. Planetary bodies suddenly changed position from one day to the next. Sometimes the pinkish sun would rise at irregular times. For the first time in many centuries the crab began to feel something strange.

Hope.

Normally it would laughingly deride the whole idea of 'hope' as a desperate entity's last psychological evasion from the inevitable. "Put my stinking shit in one claw, hope in the other, and tell me which one fills up faster." In its more philosophical days it might have recalled that "Hope springs eternal…" but, it figured long ago, something in such infinite supply must be intrinsically worthless.

Yet, even so, it began to feel hope.

The crab did not feel hope for its continued existence or hope for a better existence for its tide pool mates. It did not feel hope for those that left the tide pool and that began to invade the empty land mass or any hope at all for any conceivable future that went on and on and on.

No. The crab saw the signs, and in them it saw the end. The end of the universe, come again, earlier than expected. "It will end soon," it muttered to itself. "It will end and I can finally go to sleep and forget about the incessant twaddle I have to listen to, day in and day out, from my fellow life prisoners. My dumb, idiot tide pool compatriots who won't even know what fucking hit them."

The crab scrabbled up and away from the tide pool onto a slimy rock in order to better gaze at the stars, the only one of any creature alive on the planet that could do so and appreciate what it was looking at. Ironically, it was also the one that cared the least. To gaze at the vast spectacle of the cosmos, to gaze and wonder, to feel awe, to feel amazement that it was alive and capable of such a thing – these notions in themselves, though not beyond the crab's ability to understand, were lost to it. It had forgotten, so utterly bored with existence had it become. Immortality had its price: the capacity to feel joy – a thing that could only be savored by something that knew it would die. These are musings, however, that the crab did not articulate. The only thing it could ever hope for was death. And death was the only message it looked for in the stars.

Many centuries passed away while the crab stared up from its rock. Millennia followed, and still the crab stared. Even its tide mates had evolved and gone away. New creatures entirely unlike it swam in the pools. The crab took no notice of them. The signs were building; it could sense the chaos taking hold. This universe was unstable and sooner, rather than later, it would slip and fall into a crevasse of darkness, sleep, annihilation – relief. Over, at last.

One day its waiting was rewarded. Its heart leapt at the sight. The sky boiled, the stars writhed, and the universe trembled and shook. "Here it comes!" it thought. "The end is nigh!" It stretched out its yearning claws readying itself to receive the full impact of Ultimate Destruction.

The distorted sky undulated and roared. A form formed itself from the formlessness – a kind of face, but not like a face. It was like something that would have been perceived as a face if one could have apprehended it with the right sort of eyes. The crab, not having the right sort of eyes, could only distinguish a peculiar pattern, but a pattern was not random. A pattern was indicative of order, not chaos.

Troubled, the crab hesitated for a moment, but then stretched its claws out again to their limits.

Suddenly, the pattern spoke. That is, the configuration of the crab's aural stimulus receptors perceived the mechanically-beaten waves of air as speech. Being the only creature on the planet that had ever heard speech it was alone among all the life here that could interpret the message it received.

With each syllable the crab's heart sank, every last thread of hope dashed. It lowered its claws, its eye stalk drooped, it shuddered with rage, and was washed over with grief.

"I AM FENNELDROOL THE INTELLIGURGLABLE!"

The utterly dejected crab peered listlessly out over the surface of the pool. From the depths, evolved monsters looked up at its atavistic form hungrily. Times had changed, but the crab had not changed with the times. Its biological relatives had won the race to live and moved on. It had not. The predators in the tide pool had since become much more efficient.

"Fine," it thought. "I guess I'll have to take second best. A momentary reprieve and then I'll reincarnate in some other shithole. Fuck my life."

The crab uttered a cry of condemnation at its Fate and the uncaring Universe.

With that it dove into the dark waters to be eaten.

Appendix IV

A sample of Bloppo's corporate mail. This is just one letter, but it's representative of typical business communications for Bloppo Heavy Industries. Actually, on second thought, it really isn't. This is probably the shortest and most comprehensible. It just gets worse from here.

To: Stipple The Palsied Rodent That Quivers, CEO of Intergalactic Weasel Splicing Incorporated

From: Ploop Crapinhat, The Secretary to the Undersecretary of the Secret Secretarial Secretariat Speaking on Behalf of Bloppo Heavy Industries Corporation

Subject: The Small Matter of Pending Lawsuit Against Intergalactic Weasel Splicing Inc. Filed by Bloppo Heavy Industries Corporation on Day 23, Standard Month 4, Year 154 N.I.E. (In case you have been suffering from a case of extraordinarily convenient and highly selective amnesia during the past 30 years, 1 month, and 13 days, you may consider this a gentle reminder. As you can see, we have not forgotten.)

STANDARD DISCLAIMER FOR ALL OUTGOING MAIL
1.) All messages to and from Bloppo Heavy Industries Corporation are to be encrypted in accordance with "The-Grotesquely-Dressed-Comic-Circus-Performers-for-Lower-Life-Expectancies Act". Specifically Section II, Subpart 4B, Paragraph 11994, which states: "As pertains to the conveyance of various communicated media in, on, or around which is enciphered with indecipherable cryptozoological phantasma ex mortis, said missive so dispatched abroad over long distances must be conducted along established routes via that most worthy of quadrupedal animalia referred to herein as bovines of genus *bos*. These steadfast and contemplative ruminants shall serve to deliver said communicades for a period not exceeding 18 months wherein they shall be laterally promoted to work in the gelatinous adhesives factory. In the event said bovines meet with unexpected physical disarrangement resulting in either quietus or profound mortification while performing the duties of their office, the investigative personnel that handle these matters will perform a count of the departed and then steal no less than three cookies from a small child for every one deceased bovine or

destroy the planet, whichever happens first. Bloppo Heavy Industries will not tolerate bovine quietus!

2.) As of Day 1, Standard Month 1, Year 12 N.I.E., all balloons sent to Bloppo the Clown must henceforth be subjected to the Doggie Test herein described. In addition, this policy shall be effective retroactively to all balloons sent on or after said date. The Doggie Test: A cute doggie with big, brown, happy eyes and a silly-looking, lolling tongue will have the balloons tied to his tail and sent out into the streets to see if he attracts gunfire. Then he will be locked in a sealed room with one aperture large enough to accommodate the barrel of a BB gun. With this the balloons will be popped and the doggie will be carefully observed for signs of death or other abnormal behavior not befitting a cute little doggie. After this the balloon remains will be fed to the cute little doggie which will again be observed for signs of life malfunction or behavioral incongruities. If, during the course of the test and after, the doggie is in the same condition he was before the test began, the balloons can be accepted. Gifts, of course, cannot be accepted by Bloppo the Clown. It is the policy of Bloppo Heavy Industries to turn over doggie-tested gifts to local charities for distribution among deserving ~~peasants~~ low income families in accordance with our motto: "No other company kind of cares about you in precisely the lame way that we do!"

BEGIN MESSAGE

I, Ploop Crapinhat, The Secretary to the Undersecretary of the Secret Secretarial Secretariat, have hitherto been empowered to act as Spokesperson for Bloppo Heavy Industries Corporation (the Legal commercial entity owned and operated by Bloppo the Clown).

All further communications between elements existing within the legal confines of Intergalactic Weasel Splicing Inc. shall henceforth be directed through my office and subjected to legal interpretation, logical analysis, insecticides, and rigorous proofreading.

Mr. Stipple, before we may even proceed to the contents of your letter to us -- or even with respect to the more serious matter of the lawsuit which we would certainly like to get underway as soon as possible and make this annoying matter of litigation, the hostile takeover and dissolution of your corporation, and the resulting machine-gunning of all of the employees of Intergalactic Weasel Splicing Inc. (without excepting even you, Mr. Stipple) reach as expeditious a conclusion as is humanly or inhumanly possible -- we must first attend to the quite alarming and grievous errors of spelling that your letter comprises.

I most fervently and humbly apologize, however the duties assigned my position require I bring this matter to your attention. To simply forward your letter to the appropriate authorities as it currently stands would cause undue embarrassment not for the recipient, but for you. I hope you understand that it is for your benefit that I alert you to this and prevent further embarrassment from manifesting itself at the higher echelon of employment here at Bloppo Heavy Industries Corporation. There is just no telling what would happen if the light-hearted tinkle of laughter (or even a quiet, suppressed titter) were to erupt in the darkly-lit, echo-filled halls of Bloppo power and Intergalactic might. It could very well damage the fabric of space-time itself to say nothing of upsetting the axial obliquity of every planet in the universe!

However, to answer the call of duty and help protect Bloppo Heavy Industries Corporation from the harm that would result from a slip-up in my department allowing such uncorrected material to flutter through like so much sugar in a gas tank, I am beholden to accepting the undesirable task of burdening you with long-winded explanations of this sort and profuse apologies at having to direct your gaze upon the imperfections of handiwork that is so clearly your own. I feel much pain and discomfort, I assure you, and the suicidal impulse is particularly heightened, yet I must swallow what small measure of pride I may still possess and face up to the fact that I must do my job. I am terribly sorry for the inconvenience that any of this has caused, but it is necessary.

I have taken the liberty (I hope you do not mind) of correcting your letter's spelling errors (see your letter below). After each horrible and unforgivable mutilation of our standardized and universal language I have inserted the correction between brackets "{ }."

The procedure is very simple. All you must do is examine the proofed copy, write a new letter with the appropriate corrections in place, and resubmit the letter to my office (remember, nothing is to be submitted any longer to Bloppo the Clown, as per Chief Executive Order #47589678362554769002802810458687300189457839012918747573001928475783010192893487576748362526485695003929281910930394857876854843930029180129284745628293734969606034827178183759684373253835284668462619150796574AXSHY0M, Which

Amends Executive By-Law #46575625134125379770891238134565746517650847568347653413756174650476510347651876834765198765147503409820476876518746513401734618746574601874651074651087465017460187465017465018734651087465108734650176345071634057160238475610273465017346074650476139875646746573650746501837651076437566235562378469876748564698759763466238479865253876384973094765635817464651872356192387568374560187561287356047561087650147561087561987561075610876187561756108756187 of Section 36585681204857564483939903, Part AXCDRREFFIUY6746437578, Subpart 7987hjh, Page 415451, Paragragh 247344057034513745601374, Sentence 2374912385105616, Margin Note 46473 referencing Volume 485456034613476347 of Case Historical By-Laws of Bloppo Inc., Ltd. of 82,000 B.C.). After resubmittal, your letter will again be proofread and, passing this phase, will continue along in the process. Assuming your letter survives the remaining steps in this complicated procedure it will finally be sent to the next higher rung (in this case the Undersecretary of the Secret Secretarial Secretariat, who, by the way, was recently violently murdered at his desk yesterday by an R2 Shredder Unit that we're still trying to track down. The absence of the Undersecretary of the Secret Secretarial Secretariat from his post should not worry you unduly, however, as I am sure he will have been replaced by the time your letter has gone through all necessary procedures managed by my office and sent, at last, to his.) I am agonizingly sorry for all this fuss and ado, but it is in the best interests of all concerned, I cannot assure you enough, I assure you. The increase in scrutiny of all paperwork changing hands throughout the Bloppo Heavy Industries Corporation hierarchies has, of course, been exacerbated by the recent murder I have just remarked upon. I can most assuredly assure you with a sufficiently high degree of assurance that the culpable R2 Shredder Unit was not one of ours. Whomsoever it does belong to I can definitely assure you will be punished to the fullest extent of the law. R2 Shredder Units are too expensive, generally, to be owned by individuals, and are thus almost always in the hands of major corporations. Corporations are, of course, legally responsible for the actions committed by their R2 Shredder Units and the language of the law, in no uncertain terms, strictly states that any corporation or individual so owning an R2 Shredder Unit that commits a felonious crime, is punishable by having their corporate status stripped away and the owners and employees of such a corporation may then be sued individually. Court cases of this nature have typically and routinely ended in a judgment against the owners and employees of the offending corporation whereupon they are immediately bludgeoned to death with silly metal sticks of varicolored hues that sparkle and glint attractively in appropriate lighting. I can assure you that there is nothing to worry about regarding this matter and that the criminal and insidious evil corporation will be brought to justice and properly humiliated with titillating death and dismemberment! In fact, if you have any information regarding this matter we would be most pleased (it may, indeed, push your letter resubmission through our office procedure a little faster).

Again I am sorry for this horrendous inconvenience. The longer I consider your awful travesty of language usage the less I am able to withstand living and breathing the same air that you do. Therefore, I shall bring this courtesy notice to a close and patiently await your CORRECTED response.

Actually, I realize now that there is, unfortunately, one other minor matter that must be addressed. It pains me to ask you to do this, but I'm afraid that I must. Is it at all possible you could change your name? I'm afraid the terms "Palsied" and "Quivers" used as they are clearly violates our office's "Rule Against Redundant Synonyms That Start With P or Q". I suggest it may be advisable that you do this as it will most definitely set off Process #67 and result in another rejection. Could I be so bold as to suggest "Stipple The Twitchy Rodent That Shakes"? Or, perhaps, "Stipple The Spasmodic Rat That Oscillates"? These would pass Process #67 with flying colors while in keeping within the intent and meaning I assume you are trying to convey in your chosen name. I, of course, leave this up to you. Never say that Bloppo Heavy Industries Corporation doesn't, at least, make a half-hearted and imperceptible attempt to make their customers just slightly less annoyed.

I hope to receive your CORRECTED letter soon. I am eager to run it through a couple of more Processes we've just added on today.

Sincerely,

Ploop Crapinhat
The Secretary to the Undersecretary of the Secret Secretarial Secretariat
Speaking on Behalf of Bloppo Heavy Industries Corporation

PLEASE CORRECT

To: Bloppo the Clown, CEO of Bloppo Heavy Industries Corporation

From: Stipple The Palsied Rodent That Quivers, CEO of Intergalactic Weasel Splicing Incorporated

Greetings.

Thank you for clarifying the said aformentioned {aforementioned} subject; not that it was a problem. And indeed I am interested in selling the R2 Shredder Unit I loaned you last week. Bear in mind that it has recently been going on the fritz and needs a tune-up. In reference to your most recent sales offer, it is interesting to note that I have always wanted an industrial strength parallax disintegrator for my up and comming {coming} secret underground lair. I have recently had my eye on the choicest of hollowed out volcano {volcanoes}. If the current owners do not wish to sell I will just have to settle for an abandoned mine. I am waiting to hear back from their relator {realtor}. I know what you're thinking, Intergalactic Weasel Splicing Incorporated is a bit of a bombastic name but its {it's} a PR scheme to attract qualified applicants. Our human resources department is struggling to hire employees that are both evil and intelegent {intelligent}. I {It} seems we usually get one or the other. Did I mention we offer dental; in case youve {you've} interested parties in mind? Let me know.

Stipple

P.S. For application purposes you must completely fill out our 14 page standard form EI2379(x) in triplicate then shred all three copies so as not to leave a paper trail. You must them {then} send a 256 bit encripted {encrypted} message from the application data you doubtlessly memorized to customerservice@eehaw.com

END MESSAGE

A NOTE OR TWO

1: passage from *The Hunting of the Snark*, Oxford, 1936. Latin
    elegiacs translation by Hubert Digby Watson

2: passage from *The Hunting of the Snark*, London, 1934. Virgilian
    hexameter Latin translation by Percival Robert Brinton

3: Thanks to Lonnie Smith for the e-mail that inspired this tragic
    display of long-winded bureaucratic nonsense.

www.ingramcontent.com/pod-product-compliance
Lightning Source LLC
Chambersburg PA
CBHW020433030726
47495CB00006B/1782